MW01503972

TRANCE

TRANCE

Richard Kessler

This first world edition published in Great Britain 1993 by
SEVERN HOUSE PUBLISHERS LTD of
9–15 High Street, Sutton, Surrey SM1 1DF
First published in the U.S.A. 1993 by
SEVERN HOUSE PUBLISHERS INC of
475 Fifth Avenue, New York, NY 10017.

British Library Cataloguing in Publication Data
Kessler, Richard
  Trance
  I. Title
  813.54 [F]

  ISBN 0-7278-4426-1

Typeset by Hewer Text Composition Services, Edinburgh.
Printed and bound in Great Britain by
Dotesios Ltd, Trowbridge, Wiltshire.

For Linda
And My Family
With Love

With special thanks to
Police Officer S. Mount
Los Angeles Police Department
West Los Angeles Area
for his courtesy and help

Chapter One

The girl on the couch gave a gasp and a whispered "Oh!" that expressed a plethora of emotion: wonderment, excitement, but mostly disbelief.

Her gasp triggered in Drummond a rush of adrenalin that coursed through his body, accelerating his heartbeat. Not for the first time, the similarity of his role to that of a voyeur disturbed him.

Drummond leaned closer to the girl. He needed to maintain the momentum of these long-buried emotions now welling to the surface. He had to drive them on and out, to bring her to that long- and hard-fought release that might change her life forever.

His voice whispered hoarsely, compellingly, "Go on. Tell me what you see."

Her pretty features were contorted into a mask of ugly repulsion as she rolled her head from side to side, desperate to escape the nightmare. Though her eyes were tight-closed, she was not asleep; yet the vision of her hypnotic trance was no less real or frightening than if she had been.

"Oh, God," she gasped, "I don't believe this."

"What? Tell me what's happening."

"It's . . . it's like a movie. Like I'm watching a movie."

Her slender body, clad in white T-shirt and blue jeans, tensed, went rigid. Her fingers became claws. Her hands rose, as though preparing to defend herself. She rolled

1

her head again and whispered, appalled, "It can't be me. It can't be happening to me. But it is."

"What? Tell me what you see."

She gave a shudder. Her hands fell upon her ample breasts. She pulled at the thin material of her T-shirt, as though in detestation of her clothing, or of some iniquitous thing that soiled it.

Her voice broke. "I'm . . . in the orchard. The orchard . . ."

"I remember the orchard," prompted Drummond. "The orchard behind your house – when you were seven. Go on. What's happening there?"

Again, the evasive roll of her head, dismissive, denying, desperate, yet no longer able to escape a memory so long repressed. "I'm playing – by myself. And there's man – in the trees."

"Do you know him?"

A nod, almost child-like. "He's Ben . . . works on the next farm."

"What is he doing?"

"Watching me. Now he's – coming towards me through the trees." A sob broke from her. A tear squeezed from the corner of her eye. "Oh, God, now I remember!" It was an exclamation that embodied both relief and horror. "He's opening his pants. I try to run away but he grabs me . . . throws me on the ground. Now he's over me – straddling me, up on his knees. And he's – oh, Jesus . . ." Again the head shake, more vigorous, desperate this time, impelled by loathing, her face screwed tight with abhorrence. "He's come all over me. I remember now – all over my face and my new sweater. It's in my hair – everywhere. I *hate* it . . . hate it."

"Does he do anything else to you?"

A negative headshake. "Just grins. He has rotten teeth. He just kneels up there grinning."

"And then what?"

2

"He – gets off me, goes away."

"And what do you do?"

"I'm – trying to clean myself. There's a rain barrel behind the house. I'm trying to wash off the stuff when . . ."

"When what? What happens then?"

"My mom – comes out of the kitchen door. She sees what I'm doing and yells at me, says I've spoiled my new sweater. She spanked me and sent me to bed."

Her switch from present tense to past tense was an indication to Drummond that her story was done.

"Dianna, you know now, don't you, that what happened to you so long ago was that man's crime, not yours?" She gave a barely perceptible nod. "Unfortunately, in such circumstances, children assume guilt because they feel grown-ups can do no wrong, so what happened must be their own fault. All right, I want you to return to the present now – and I'm going to count you up from one to five. When I reach the count of five, you'll be wide awake, feeling calm, confident, really fine. One, two, three . . . eyes beginning to open . . . four . . . all systems returning to normal . . . five . . . wide awake . . . now."

She rolled her head and looked at him, seated beside and slightly behind her, gave a disbelieving shake of her head and sat up, lowered her face into her hands and wiped away her tears.

"*How*," she muttered through her fingers, "can you possibly forget something as awful as that?"

"A child can forget it simply because it is so awful. But it isn't really forgotten. It's repressed, denied by the conscious mind, but stored away in the subconscious. It lies buried there, unbalancing the psyche."

"And producing my phobia," she said in a tone of disbelief.

"And producing your phobia," nodded Drummond.

"But why – "

3

He smiled. "I know – 'But why don't I have – correction, *didn't* I have a phobia about semen or sex or apples or rain water? Why was my phobia about horses?' – which, incidentally, is known as 'Hippophobia' in the trade. Well, there are literally hundreds of phobias, Dianna, ranging through the alphabet from 'Air' to 'Young girls' – but they're really all the same thing – an outward, symbolic expression of an internal anxiety. Curious thing is, the mind usually hits you where it hurts the most. The opera singer will likely develop 'Halophobia', and lose his voice. As an actress, you might have suffered the same thing. As it is, you've passed up two good roles because you were required to ride. But that's all over with now. Now you've exorcised your particular demon. Horses will hold no terrors for you from now on."

She was nodding, awed. "Hey, that's right. Before, all I had to do was *think* of getting on one and my heart would start banging. Now . . ." She gave a shrug and a smile. "You really did it."

"No, you really did it. I helped." Drummond checked his watch and stood.

"Do I need to see you again?" she asked, getting up.

"Alas, no," he smiled, teasing. "The Dianna Hart file is closed. I shall miss you. Your beauty hath lighted up these poor consulting rooms."

She stepped to him, placed a hand on his arm and kissed him lightly on the cheek. "Thank you, Paul, sincerely. You've been so patient, so sweet all these weeks. I feel as though a huge, black weight has been lifted from my soul."

He patted her hand. "Go make some marvellous movies."

He accompanied her to the outer door of the office suite, then walked with her along a corridor onto an open verandah that overlooked a car park at the rear of the two-storey building.

"Thank you again," she said, and went down a staircase to the ground floor.

Drummond watched her emerge from beneath the verandah and cross the car park with an unconsciously sensual, leggy stride, blonde hair bouncing; a gorgeous, vibrant woman hungrily devouring life, and this reminder of his own brutal loss dealt him a blow to the heart and tightened the muscles at the back of his throat. Two years. Would he ever stop missing Viv?

Leaning on the iron rail, squinting into the dying sun as it dropped behind the San Jacinto Mountains, he followed the actress as she headed for a stunning yellow Rolls convertible, waving cheerily to its occupant, her husband, a handsome young actor whose most recent picture had projected him into world-wide fame and considerable fortune.

Drummond smiled as, with histrionic dash, the young man leapt up from the driver's seat and struck a swashbuckling pose, one hand on his heart, welcoming his beloved and pledging his undying love. Picking up her cue, Dianne Hart responded, climbed into the car and fell into his arms. Now Drummond laughed and waved as they turned to him, indicating that the performance was for him.

They waved again as the car swirled flamboyantly around the near-empty lot and disappeared from view onto El Paseo.

Drummond remained motionless for a while, savouring the fading warmth of the early-October sun, but thinking of Vivian, of their own young and mad-cap love.

Grief was a trauma that he frequently treated. Why couldn't he treat his own?

Closing his eyes, he mentally repeated for the – millionth? – time the admonition: "Gone is gone . . . life must go on" and felt absolutely no better for it. Time alone, if anything, would heal. Perhaps in two or three hundred years . . .

With a sigh he pushed himself away from the rail and headed down the corridor towards his rooms. The building was a modern block, tastefully done in Spanish style, its ground floor divided into four segments by cooling breezeways, its upper floor by corridors. Each segment contained three suites of offices. Drummond's close neighbours were a lawyer and an internist. Elsewhere in the building were realtors, other lawyers, an interior decorator and a beauty parlor. Drummond had been there eighteen months and liked it. Its quietness, even though it fronted onto the busy, prestigious shopping boulevard of El Paseo, suited the needs of hypnosis. His own suite of rooms occupied the rear, quieter side of the building.

Pushing through glass doors at the end of the corridor he entered a small waiting area, partitioned to provide privacy for clients who were waiting or leaving. Drummond had never employed a receptionist, or any other office staff. Experience had taught him that in the world of neuroses his clients, perhaps especially his rich and famous clients, valued confidentiality very highly. The prospect of their darkest secrets being revealed to some loose-lipped receptionist or secretary did not appeal to them at all. And so he had structured a staffless operation, well supported by computer and electronic technology, which worked well for everyone.

There was also another reason for his preference for this one-man structure. Three days out of seven – Monday through Wednesday – he returned to his still-existent practice in Los Angeles, and being staffless obviated human complication, afforded him the freedom he needed to switch, as circumstances dictated, between the Valley and the city.

Of late, he had questioned his motive for continuing the LA practice. At first, after Viv's murder and his escape to Palm Desert, there had been the legitimate necessity of seeing his existing LA clients through to the conclusion

6

of their therapy. But that no longer pertained. Also, he could offer that in Los Angeles he was ministering to the needs of the less affluent, often *pro-bono*, and that was true. But it wasn't the whole truth.

Deep inside, he knew he was holding onto the practice because it had been his first, it had been his and Viv's, and in holding onto it he was holding onto the past. One day, as with the house in Malibu, he would have to let it go.

One day.

Right now, the arrival of that day constituted a major portion of the nightmare he had lived with for two years, and seemed an impossibility. For now, he would drive that one hundred miles each Monday morning, and gladly.

Turning right from the waiting area, he passed along a short corridor, containing a bathroom, and entered his consulting room, a spacious, air-conditioned room with a view of the mountains. The San Jacinto range, which ran like a granite vertebra down the western edge of the Coachella Valley, looming close, but never threateningly so to the mini-city of Palm Desert, were purpling now, haloed with brilliance by the invisible setting sun, the sky above dashed with streaks of blinding gold and crimson and yellow that faded, at their fingertips, into the cobalt blue of approaching night.

It was a sight that always stirred Drummond, a wondrous yet treacherous time of the day, evoking memories of other, shared sunsets, of . . .

He shook the thought away.

The "incoming call" light on his answering machine, rigged for silent operation, was flashing. Grateful for the distraction, he pressed the replay button. The apparatus clicked and clacked and then a familiar voice, in a pseudo-gay performance, was chiding him, "Oh, Doctor, is that really you? Can I *really* be speaking to *the* Doctor Paul Drummond, late of Los Angeles, now Thuper-Thhrink to the Thtars in Palm Thprings, Palm Desert and all points Thouth?"

Drummond laughed out loud. Dick Gage was a born actor, did a terrific impersonation of the 'thufferin' thuccotash' cat in the Tweety Pie cartoons.

"Well, Doc," Gage continued as Bogart, "if yuh could quit countin' all that money for a minute an' call an old chum . . . waal," now Jimmy Stewart, "you just might, ah, ah, hell, I've just plumb forgot what I was gonna shay. But call anyway." Chuckling, Drummond picked up the phone and dialled a number branded on his memory, the number of the West Los Angeles bureau of the Los Angeles Police Department. It was Dick Gage who had headed the investigation into Vivian's murder, and Dick Gage who had who had been a supportive friend ever since.

"Robbery Homicide."

"Lieutenant Gage, please . . . Paul Drummond."

Jimmy Cagney came on. "Well, you doity rat, 'bout time, too."

"Swear to God, Dick, that's the best Sonny Bono I've ever heard."

"That was Edward G., you prick." Gage's normal voice was a rich Harrison Ford growl, quiet but authoritative. Gage didn't usually have to ask twice to get things done. In appearance, however, he more closely resembled Peter Falk, and dressed about as snappily as Columbo. "How's it hangin', Drum?"

"It's been so long since I looked."

"Yeh, well," said Gage, and left it at that.

He and Drummond had had long discussions about grief – Gage having suffered more than his share – and he shared Drummond's view that time was really the only effective healer. Recently, Gage had tried in a subtle way to re-awaken Drummond's libido with invitations to make up a foursome – Gage and his attractive wife, Anne, plus an available girl – but he hadn't pushed it. If nothing else, Dick Gage was an accomplished psychologist.

"You planning on slumming next week?" Gage asked, meaning was Drummond planning on coming into Los Angeles as usual.

"Sure. Monday morning. Why?"

"Got something might interest you. Fella named Keegan, innocent bystander, got caught up in that Mar Vista Savings and Loans heist last week – literally bumped into the two punks as they were leaving the place."

"I heard about it. They killed a guard?"

"The bastards put twenty-four bullets in him. We want them real bad."

"Aren't the FBI in on it?"

"Not yet. The punks shot up the street in the getaway, wounded a senior citizen. He died in hospital three days ago, so it's our jurisdiction for now."

"What about this Keegan?"

"Damnedest thing. They bundled him into their car, took off their masks – we got an eye-witness saw that much but can't describe them, car was going too fast. But Keegan must have got a good look at them."

"So?"

"So they drove him around a bit then threw him out of the car, tried to run over him, for laughs. An eye-witness saw that, too."

"And?"

"They clipped him once, sent him through a store window, then must've heard a siren and blew."

"Jesus. I always said you had a better class of punk in West LA."

"You think so? You oughta see what they've got in Hollenbeck and Newton."

"So – how is Keegan?"

Gage gave a sigh. "I dunno. Weird. Physically, he's okay, some cuts but superficial. But his memory's gone.

9

Couldn't even remember where he lived. He was carrying ID so we found his address – a dump off Pico in South Hollywood. But nobody around there knows him. We checked his place but found nothing – except he might be ex-army. We're checking that out now."

"What d'you want me to do, Dick?"

"Try hypnosis, old bean. We need a description of those pus-buckets, and Keegan's our only possible source."

Drummond said, "Let me check my LA service, see if anything's come in. So far I'm clear Monday afternoon. Would that suit?"

"You name it, I'll have Keegan here."

"I'll get back to you."

Drummond rang off, dialled his answering service, something he did every evening before leaving his Palm Desert office. While he waited for them to respond, he ran an eye over his appointments book for the coming Monday through Wednesday, confirming what he had told Dick Gage: that Monday afternoon was free. He had two clients Monday morning, three on Tuesday and two on Wednesday. Staring at the pages, it suddenly came home to him how rundown his LA practice had become. Time was, with Viv, when they would each have had seven clients every day, and would be turning business away.

The reason for the decline was, of course, easy to understand. Many of his former clients had been referrals from MDs, doctors who knew of Viv's death and his own removal to Palm Desert. They would now be referring their patients elsewhere. Also, he and Viv had advertised their joint practice quite extensively, and he no longer did. His few clients now came from the odd referral and word-of-mouth recommendation, occasionally from the LAPD or an insurance company, but not often.

Once again, that pestilential voice of reason demanded, "Let it go, Drummond. Let *her* go. Wrap it up." And, as with the Malibu house, he knew he would.

One day.

His service came on the line, "Hi, Doctor Drummond," and he recognised the voice of the girl on the early evening shift.

"Hello, Tina, how're things in LA?"

"Smog-*gee*," she groaned. "How I envy you out there in the Valley. It's like a different planet – right?"

"Right. How's business today?"

"Five calls, Doc. You got a pencil?"

"Go ahead, I'm recording this."

She reeled off the names and phone numbers. Drummond thanked her and rang off, replayed the details, jotting them on a pad. He then dialled the number at his Malibu home and called up the recorded messages on the answering machine there with a coder, adding those to the pad.

A total of ten calls. Instinct and experience told him seven were junk calls – sales pitches, charity pitches, time-wasters and frustraters, major contributors to the psychopathology of American life. He phoned them and proved himself right.

The other three were genuine enquiries about hypnotherapy – two anxiety cases and a hundred-a-day smoker. Drummond fitted them into his schedule and called Lieutenant Gage.

"Okay, Dick, all clear for Monday afternoon. I'll get my equipment over there and set up by – what? Three?"

"Three'll be fine, Drum. Thanks a bundle. We'll have a brew or two after the show."

"Done. Love to Anne."

Drummond terminated the connection – and with it his working week. As always, he fought the wash of emptiness that accompanied the realisation. In his childhood there'd been a song, a track on a family LP – Sinatra, if he remembered correctly – "Saturday night is the loneliest night of the week". Lately, it had been running obsessively through his mind. Though in his case it was Friday.

Since his arrival in the valley there'd been an abundance of invitations. There were eighty golf courses and a thousand tennis courts in this desert playground, and it was virtually impossible to meet anyone who did not play one or both games, who did not press him to share their enthusiasm.

But, risking offending their good hearts, he always refused, made excuses (he had a hundred of them), lied. It wasn't the game he was rejecting; it was the ever-attendant complications. For a thirty-four-year-old, presentable, professional widower, the valley was a sexy, mischievous place that abhorred such waste. And he was simply not ready to be salvaged.

It was not an easy game to play. Part of him yearned to recapture even a semblance of what he had had with Viv. To cruise Palm Canyon Drive on a Saturday night and see the Valley's "beautiful people" enjoying each other, living each other, tore at his heart. Twice, only, he had succumbed, each occasion a disaster. Drummond was simply not ready.

Mechanically, he filed the computer disks and audio tapes from the day's sessions, locked the steel cabinet, checked around the office, and prepared to depart. The cleaning would be done the following day by a professional, bonded company.

As he locked the external glass door, his internist neighbour emerged into the corridor, locking his own door. Kieron Connor was a contemporary, a five-foot-four energised butter-ball with an aggravated, self-confessed Casanova complex. Once, over a friendly beer, Drummond had voiced his suspicion of Connor's motives in allowing himself unlimited professional access to the naked female body, and Connor had laughed, "Trouble is, I can never get rich enough to be age-selective."

12

Connor now greeted him. "Hey, Paul! Another week, another ten thousand dollars. My, how they fly."

"The weeks or the dollars?"

"Both, my man, both."

He accompanied Drummond along the corridor and down the rear stairs to the parking lot, a head shorter, almost running to keep up with Drummond's long, easy stride.

"You fixed for the week-end?" he panted.

"What're you offering?" Drummond asked, just to hear it.

Connor rolled his eyes. "Catalina. This babe . . . got a hundred million dollars . . . and a yacht the size of the *Lusitania* . . . crewed by fifty nymphets in see-through bikinis . . . and it never leaves port. How's that grab yuh?"

Drummond grinned. "Right where it does the most good, but no thanks, I'm fixed. Have fun, Kieron."

Drummond walked away to his car, a sage-green Daimler Sovereign, climbed in and started the engine. For a moment, as he sat there, the thought passed through his mind that maybe an outrageous week-end in Catalina with a covey of nubile airheads was exactly what he needed; an experience so awful and degrading it would shock his psychic system like a massive abreaction.

But as he drove the mile of winding road to his home in the San Jacinto foothills, another thought was in his mind. The bank robbery victim.

Keegan.

The man and his circumstances went on tugging at his mind all weekend. Yet Drummond did not question the persistence of these thoughts.

During his study of the psychosciences, he had lingered on the matter of prescience, precognition, the foreknowledge of future events claimed by so many people, and had formed his own theories about its reality. What struck him

13

most was not that so many people experienced foreknowledge, but that they paid so little heed to the information at the time. There appeared to be a gap between receipt of the information and its acknowledgement by the conscious mind, so that, for instance, precognition of a family death became meaningful only after the real news had been received. People did not sufficiently trust their intuition.

With hindsight, Drummond would later recall his own failing to acknowledge and appreciate the full force of his week-end obsession with Keegan – and to fore-arm himself against the ocean of troubles that their association would bring.

Chapter Two

Monday.

Drummond was up at dawn, his usual awakening time in the desert. From the front deck of the house, sipping coffee, he watched the sun rise over the San Bernadino Mountains, which formed the eastern boundary of the valley.

The house was spacious, two-bedroomed, single-storeyed, built almost entirely of glass to capture the views on all sides. There was a staff bedroom, unoccupied, at the rear of the attached double garage.

Eighteen months ago, Drummond had chosen the house for its comparative isolation. But gradually he had grown to appreciate not only its location but the house itself and the views it offered, and never more so than at this time of day.

Situated at the end of a minor, steeply-rising road, the house commanded a one-hundred-and-eighty-degree panorama that encompassed almost the entire valley. To Drummond's right, the view extended above and beyond the lush tree-tops of the Ironwood Country Club and the granite hills of the Living Desert Reserve to the distant reaches of the San Bernadino range. Ahead, Drummond looked down upon tree-lined avenues of Palm Desert; and to his left, he could follow the main artery, Highway One-Eleven, out of the valley, to Rancho Mirage, Cathedral City and Palm Springs.

Even though most desert-dwellers were early risers,

and he could see traffic movement along the distant One-Eleven, at this time of day Drummond felt he had the world to himself. At this modest altitude the air was cool and clear and clean, and, after the fog of Los Angeles, a joy to inhale.

Watching the blazing sun emerge from behind the San Bernadino peaks, savouring the air, Drummond was suffused with a heady awareness of the advent of a brand new day in these moments, and felt the stir of faith that on one such day he, too, would feel reborn, renewed, able to start again. It was a feeling he could never have experienced in Los Angeles, or in any city. The desert was magical.

At six o'clock he joined the modest traffic on the One-Eleven, also known as Palm Canyon Drive, and ran easily through elegant Rancho Mirage with its pristine country clubs and its cross-streets named to honour famous local residents – Bob Hope Drive; Frank Sinatra Drive; through less-exalted Cathedral City; then into the jewel itself, Palm Springs, and on into the desert, the immediate transition from emerald oasis to barren scrub never failing to astound Drummond.

Born in mountainous, fertile, arborial Northern California, where the physiognomy of the land remained fairly constant, he had, since his first visit, remained amazed at the miraculous transformations that perpetually took place in the Valley.

Sumptuous housing developments, set in verdant, exotically landscaped golf courses, shot up overnight like mushrooms out of the raw, stone desert. It was possible to drive along a road and see a prestigious development of homes on one side, desert on the other, then to drive that road again a few weeks later and find the desert gone, replaced by a golfer's paradise.

For Drummond, the Valley seemed vibrant with creative energy, yet it was not the frenzied, neurotic power that

16

drove Los Angeles or New York. Here, perhaps because of the heat, activity seemed slower, yet things still got done. The Valley had a soul, and, gradually, Drummond was growing to feel part of it.

A few miles north of Palm Springs, the One-Eleven joined the Interstate Ten, the highway that stretched east across the continent to Florida, and would take Drummond west, almost to his front door in Malibu.

At this junction of the highways, the San Bernadino range pressed close to the San Jacinto Mountains, forming a gap that Drummond regarded as a psychological gateway to and from his California Shangri-la.

From this point on, all things were different. Here, suddenly, was the dirty, noisy, frenzied outside world. Traffic boomed along the I-10 with a manic urgency unheard of in the Valley, and Drummond had to quickly shift into mental high gear, accelerate hard, as a giant tractor-trailer bore down on him from the rear, air-horns blaring.

He smiled wryly to himself. How many times had he, on precisely this stretch of highway, questioned his sanity – and his motives – in returning to the city? But what transpired was always the same schizoid condition – half his mind telling him the sane thing to do was about-turn at the next exit and fly back to Shangri-la, the other half compelling him towards Malibu.

His inability to decide and take action annoyed him, and yet he knew, professionally, that the dilemma was a common human condition. He recalled treating a teenage girl, the only child of divorced parents, who, torn between living either with her mother in San Francisco or her father in LA, was so stressed with indecision that she attempted suicide.

The facile solution was: share; but that, as he now knew from personal experience, was no answer at all. The girl, in a chronic state of stress, had told him, "When I'm there, I want to be here; and when I'm here, I want to be there. I just want to die."

There were certain decisions in life that seemed impossible to make. His treatment for the girl was concentrated suggestion therapy for mental relaxation, and the advice: "Wait. Circumstances change. Life is constant change." In the girl's case, she did not have to wait long. Her mother re-united with her father and moved back to Los Angeles. But the kicker was, within six months the girl fell in love and moved to Duluth with her boyfriend.

"Wait. Circumstances change" was advice Drummond had given himself many times in the past eighteen months, and he did so again now. Accelerating into the fast lane, he turned on the radio, found quiet, uninterrupted music, applied suggestion therapy for his own mental relaxation, and settled into the journey.

Moments later, into his reverie, passed a shadow of prescience that on this return to Los Angeles his circumstances would change. Wishful thinking? With a mental shrug, the shadow was gone.

Cruising, relaxed, cocooned by the music and the flow of traffic, Drummond glanced reflexively at the dashboard dials and saw he was low on gas. The Daimler was equipped with dual tanks. He pressed the switching mechanism, waited for the needle to rise, and groaned. The second tank was empty. Since moving to the Valley, where his mileage was minimal, he'd lost his LA habit of always ensuring the spare tank was full.

Moving to the inside lane, he took the exit ramp for Upland, turned right into the town and found an Exxon station almost immediately. He had filled the empty tank and was topping up the second when a voice behind him asked, "Sir . . . you heading for LA?"

Drummond turned, gave the young man a slow, thorough appraisal. The threat of hitchhiker robbery notwithstanding, Drummond liked to talk to these young people, usually found their histories interesting, invariably learned something from them, occasionally could offer help. This one, medium height, blonde curly hair, wearing glasses, clean jeans and a good black leather jacket, looked studious and okay. He met Drummond's gaze with an understanding, whimsical grin and said, "I haven't mugged anyone all day, honest."

Drummond returned the grin. "Okay, you pay for the gas, I'll take you in."

The kid winced at the pump tab. "Sir, if I had eighteen bucks, I'd have been on the bus yesterday."

Drummond sighed. "Why is it I never pick up rich hitch-hikers?" He crossed to the office, paid the bill, motioned the young man to get in as he returned.

"Paul Drummond," he said, firing the engine.

"Alan Forrest. Thanks a million, I was getting desperate. Boy, would you listen to that engine. This is the first time I've been in a Jag."

"Daimler, but close. Why desperate, Alan?"

"I'm heading back to UCLA. My aunt died in Phoenix, she brought me up. I've taken a week off for the funeral and sorting things out, and I'm missing lectures. Also I work nights off campus, in a hamburger joint, and should've been back last night. I hope I've still got the job."

"UCLA was my alma mater."

"No kidding! What was your major?"

"Psychology. What's yours?"

"Law – with Politics a close second."

"What's your ambition?"

Forrest gave his amiable grin and a shrug. "To be president."

Drummond nodded. "Why not?"

19

There was silence while Drummond negotiated their entrance back onto the I-10, slipping skilfully into the stream of thundering trucks and out into the fast lane with a burst of acceleration that brought a gasp of admiration from Forrest.

"No doubt you're studying the current dogfight very intently?"

"The campaign? Yes, *sir*."

They were referring to the presidential election, to the increasingly vociferous contest that was developing between the candidates – Democrat Senator Milton Byrne and Republican Jack Crane, Governor of California.

With only four weeks to go before the general election, the race was building into a knock-down, drag-out battle, the tactics of which were becoming increasingly questionable, and were even beginning to capture the attention of the politically indifferent public.

"Yes, sir," Forrest repeated, thoughtfully. "That guy Crane – he's something else. It'll be a sad day for the USA when he gets in."

"'When'? Not 'if'?" smiled Drummond.

Forrest shook his blonde locks. "He'll get in. Milton Byrne is a nice guy, but he's a wimp, an innocent. Crane will eat him alive."

"Crane comes highly recommended," said Drummond, not argumentatively, just to draw Forrest out, hear his views. "War hero . . . effective state senator and governor. And he has a popular platform – anti-crime, anti-drugs . . ."

"But have you heard his *rhetoric*?" protested Forrest, and gave a rueful laugh. "He comes on like General Midwinter in *The Billion Dollar Brain*. 'I love my country with a deep and abiding passion – and will fight to the death those who wish to destroy her!' Jesus."

"And you don't approve of such patriotism? Don't you

think it's time somebody *did* wage war on crime and drugs in this country?"

"Oh, hell, yes. Of course it is. But – " Forrest sought the words. "It's the guy. It's Crane. There's something about him." He looked sideways at Drummond. "Are you something in Psych now?"

Drummond dipped into the breast pocket of his dark blue suit and produced a business card.

Forrest grinned. "Yeh, you're something in Psych. Well, you ought to be able to get inside Jack Crane's head."

"To be honest, I haven't given him or the election much thought. I hear the issues, but tend to ignore the games. There is a theory that a man can become presidential material only after he's elected president. It all depends on how he responds to the greatness thrust upon him. We've seen weak men become strong in office, and vice versa. There's no way of knowing what kind of president Jack Crane will make if – " he smiled, gave a deferential nod, "*when* he gets into the White House. Anyway, what makes you so sure? Come on, now, I want some profound and learned argument."

Forrest nodded, enjoying the challenge. "Okay – point one, Jack Crane is one *tough* sonofabitch. He was a Vietnam war hero, and a shoo-in into state politics *as* a war hero, he didn't have to try. During his terms in the state capitol he made a lot of powerful friends in very high places, and when it came to the gubernatorial race, there was no contest. The sub-points here are – (a) the guy doesn't know what it means to lose, so he's coming over now as super-confident, and (b) he's still got all those powerful pals behind him – and all the money in the world.

"Point two – *because* he's got all the money in the world behind him – and Milton Byrne hasn't – Crane is going to lay down an advertising campaign like a napalm strike. He'll incinerate Byrne over the next four weeks with a campaign of 'negative attacks' – what Crane's political consultants euphemistically call 'contrast' or 'comparative' campaigning, but which means Crane's cronies are going to dig up as much dirt about Byrne as they can find – and probably plenty they can't find – and splash it across the nation's screens nightly.

"Point three – " Forrest held up three fingers. "Crane has, by virtue of his financial backing, by far the superior management team. Hell, he's got an army – and they're the best in the business. And with his army he's going to wage an air war like you wouldn't believe."

"You mean the ad. campaign?" said Drummond, slowing as he encountered a traffic build-up, harbinger of the inevitable rush-hour crawl. "No, that's something else. I mean the manipulation of TV time by Crane's professionals. You'll see, they'll produce an agenda for him that will dominate the networks' newscasts. He'll be on every major newscast – Crane-crowing and Byrne-bashing to fifty million Americans – every night."

Drummond laughed. "'Crane-crowing and Byrne-bashing'. I like that. But what will poor old Byrne be doing in the meantime? Surely he'll be doing his share of 'Crane-clobbering and Byrne-boosting'?"

"*Touché*," grinned Forrest. "But no, he won't. Byrne hasn't got it in him. He's a scholar, an idealist. He just isn't capable of dirty tricks. He's going to pin his hopes on the television debates with Crane – which no doubt Byrne will win hands down – but they'll have nowhere near the effect of Crane's fire-storm attacks. Any day now, Crane will go on the offensive, Byrne will be slammed back on the defensive, and he'll never recover. Bet good money on it, Doc – come next January, Jack Crane will be taking the presidential oath – and God help us all."

Drummond looked at him, frowning. "Why are you so frightened of him, Alan?"

Forrest gave a pensive sigh. "I've met Jack Crane. I've

been around him during his gubernatorial campaigns, a bunch of us kids did gopher work for him. The guy's a pig, Doc. He's got a mouth like a Brooklyn hood. In public he comes on like the Messiah, the saviour of America, the guy who's steeped in the old-fashioned virtues of truth, honesty, and respect for the law, and who's going to restore those virtues to America. In private, I believe he's an opportunist and a thug. I really don't think we can afford Jack Crane as our president."

Drummond raised his brows. "That's pretty scathing stuff."

"I mean it. You had to be there, see him in action. They used to say Tricky Dick was a cold fish, but Crane . . . boy, when the cameras aren't turning, that's one ice-cold sonofabitch."

"What d'you expect he might do that could hurt the country?"

Forrest shrugged. "I dunno. Look what Tricky Dicky did. I can't imagine anything specific. It's more a feeling that the . . . the *mood* of the country will change. Y'know, things are pretty good for us right now – we're getting on better with the Communists than we ever did. And the rest of the world, even the Arabs, thinks we're okay. I think Crane could change all that."

"Why should he want to?"

Forrest thought about it. "Because everything's too damned slow and quiet. No new president can shine when things are so peaceful. Jack Crane hates the status quo. He's a military animal, a bloody war hero. He needs conflict, confrontation – and where there isn't any, he'll create it, in order to shine when he puts it down."

"Well, he's got plenty to be going on with, right here in LA – the crime, the gang wars, drugs."

Forrest grinned, acknowledging that Drummond was proving his point. "Exactly. Hence his campaign platform."

"But it's what the voters want!" Drummond laughingly protested. "Presumably, it's why Crane was elected Republican candidate – the delegates *want* a strong man in the White House."

"Strong, yes. We all want a strong president. But it's a question of degree . . . and how that strength is used. In many respects, Nixon was a strong president – and we got Watergate. Kennedy was strong – and we got the Cuban missile confrontation and the Bay of Pigs fiasco. And let's not forget that other little head-to-head . . . what was it called? . . . oh, yeah, Vietnam."

Drummond capitulated with a grin. "I was going to say we've got Congress to keep an eye on any potential abuse, but I guess you just shot me down. Well, if Crane is, as you believe, an opportunist and a thug – and, as you predict, a certainty for the White House, all we can do is hope that elevation to the presidency will elevate his morality. I'll tell you one thing, though . . . no, two things. From now on I'll be watching and listening to Jack Crane with more interest than I would have if I hadn't met you."

"Good. He sure needs watching. And the second thing?"

"You ought to skip law and go straight into politics. Your country needs you."

By now they were in the thick of morning traffic, and well into the centre of the vast, formless sprawl that was Los Angeles. The I-10 had by now assumed an additional title – the Santa Monica Freeway – which cleaved the city in a virtually straight east-west line, running south of Hollywood, Beverly Hills and Westwood Village, the latter accommodating the huge campus of UCLA – the University of California at Los Angeles.

Approaching Mar Vista, and the junction with the north-bound I-405, the San Diego Freeway, Drummond checked the time and made a decision.

Even though, from this point, UCLA was less than

24

three miles distant, such was the structure of the city that, without a car, his young passenger might take half a day to get there.

"I'll take you in," he said, running off the I-10 onto the 405.

"To campus? Wow, thanks, Doc, I really appreciate it."

"My pleasure. I appreciated the political thesis."

Forrest grinned. "Hope I didn't run off at the mouth too much. Where Jack Crane is concerned, I tend to get pretty opinionated."

"Oh, really?"

They both laughed.

"It's been terrific meeting you," said Forrest, as Drummond left the 405 and joined Sunset Boulevard for the short run into the campus grounds. "If I ever need analysis, I'll be sure to call you."

With the time at just after eight o'clock, Drummond reached out and switched on the radio. And with uncanny coincidence, as he brought the Daimler to a halt and Forrest opened his door, a familiar voice, steel-hard and righteously acerbic, crackled from the multi-speaker system.

". . . there are elements in this great country of ours that would bring this country down . . . *Godless* elements who thrive on crime . . . on drugs . . . on violence . . . who bring terror into the lives of decent, God-fearing citizens . . . and would turn the United States of America – *my* United States of America – into a vile, drug-ridden cesspool for their own despicable ends. Well, I'm here to tell you folks – JACK CRANE AIN'T ABOUT TO LET IT HAPPEN!" Thunderous applause, cheering, whistling. Over it, quelling it, "Jack Crane spent four hard years of his life fighting the *Godless* in someone else's country . . ." more cheers, whistles, shouts of approbation, ". . . but that fight was *nothing* to what

25

you're going to see around *here* when I get to the White House!"

Tumultuous applause, and as it subsided, "I hear there's another guy in this contest. I haven't actually *seen* him, myself, because he's such a nonentity he tends to disappear into the wallpaper!" Roar of laughter. "But I hear things about him. I hear he's hot on education – which is just dandy, provided we've got any schools and students *left* after the muggers and the pushers and the arsonists have finished with them. And I hear he's hot on rehabilitating criminals . . . and on disarming the people, so they can't *defend* themselves against the criminals, who are going to be the only ones who *do* carry weapons! My, my! What a glorious day for this great country if, God forbid, *he* should get into the White House. Well, folks, I'm here tonight to tell you . . . JACK CRANE AIN'T ABOUT TO LET IT HAPPEN! . . . JACK CRANE AIN'T ABOUT TO LET IT HAPPEN! . . . JACK CRANE AIN'T ABOUT TO LET IT HAPPEN! . . ."

As the audience took up the chant, filling the car with deafening, hysterical fervor, Drummond switched off the radio and raised his brows to Alan Forrest.

Forrest grinned. "There's just *nothin'* like the smell of napalm in the morning. *Apocalypse Now*." He held out his hand. "Thanks a billion, Doc."

"Good luck, Alan. Listen, if you need help – call. I don't mean therapy. Any help at all."

"Thank you."

He watched Forrest walk away, turn and wave, and disappear into the trees.

Driving out onto Sunset Boulevard, Drummond again switched on the radio, catching a political commentator in mid-sentence. ". . . tone of his entire campaign since the Republican convention. Crane rode to state power on his war record and he's doing it again now. He's a warrior –

26

and he's selling war . . . war against crime, poverty, drugs, violence . . ."

A female voice cut in. "Yes, fine, but these are mostly urban matters. What does Jack Crane know – or care – about the broader issues? How knowledgeable is he about Foreign Affairs? Where does he stand on national defence? All I seem to have heard from this guy throughout his entire time on the stump has been a kind of jingoistic jackboot march back to a Nineteen-thirties' isolationism."

"Well," said the male voice, "time and the television debates will tell. Milton Byrne is bound to hammer this very point."

The woman laughed scornfully. "'Hammer' is not a word one uses in association with 'Milton Byrne', Cy. And certainly never in Jack Crane's presence. Byrne is already reeling from Crane's attacks. I really can't see much changing in the debates."

"Well, as I said, time will tell. That's all from the campaign trail for now . . . back to the newsroom for . . ."

Drummond turned off the radio. "Jingoistic jackboot march" he mused aloud. "Nice ringing phrase."

As he passed beneath the 405, heading for Malibu, he added mentally: nice . . . and deadly.

Chapter Three

Drummond turned off the coast road, parked on a gravelled frontage, and used a key to open the street door. He entered a paved courtyard, shaded by citrus trees and landscaped with numerous flowering shrubs – bushes and climbers – set in wooden and earthernware pots, tubs, urns and barrels. Against the right wall blazed a colorful rockery. The yard had been Vivian's creation, her pride and joy.

Near the house, the yard descended steeply in crazy-paved steps. Drummond felt the spectral presence of ennui as he unlocked the solid oak front door and entered.

At once, the past was upon him. It was as though the shutting of the door activated a time warp. He could smell her perfume. The voice of commonsense said: floor polish . . . sensory delusion. But his heart wouldn't wear it; he could smell her perfume.

Doors to two bedrooms, a cloakroom and a guest bathroom led off the stuccoed, white-tiled hall. At its end, wide stone steps descended into a glorious oak-floored living room, its furnishings light and colorful, desert tones of sand and green and turquoise predominating. An open, fieldstone fireplace occupied the right wall; to the left, an archway led to the kitchen.

The house was immaculate, cleaned every Thursday and aired every Sunday by a diminutive Filipino lady, Mrs Foy, who also replenished Drummond's refrigerator with his modest needs.

He crossed the room and drew heavy, sun-proofed, bleached-cotton drapes. A wall of glass with sliding doors revealed an elevated wooden deck and a view of Surfrider Beach and a gentle Pacific Ocean.

Drummond unlocked and slid back the doors, stepped out, leaned on the wooden rail and sniffed the air. In this second week of October the weather was still good, temperature in the high seventies, the air pollution bearable. Still, it smelled tainted, and nothing like the desert.

There were a few kids out with their boards, making the most of an indifferent swell, and on the beach walkers and joggers abounded. On the deck of the house to his lower right, a nubile, blonde, topless airstew, one of three who rented the place, sat cross-legged in perfect yoga composure; on the deck to his lower left, a young male actor, a current soap-star, reclined on his lounger, reading a script. Everything Malibu-normal. It was as though he'd never been away.

Returning to the living room, he switched his mind to business, ignoring the house. With practice he had learned to live within it, without being a part of it. To help, he had removed all intimate reminders of Viv, all photographs, all personal possessions.

Immediately after the murder, when instinct urged him to get as far away from the house as was geographically possible, he had consulted a Psych colleague, needing help, intellectually aware that, in grief, abandonment of the home was a bad move, yet emotionally unable to practice what he professionally preached. Gradually, however, he had been able to fashion an attitude which comprised a degree of denial, the exact nature of which he never did dare stop and analyse.

Now, he simply used the house, dwelt there, without mentally touching its walls or artifacts, shutting things out, like the long-time occupant of a haunted house who *knows* things are happening on the edges of his vision, but never turns his head to verify.

He checked his answerphone. Three calls had come in since the previous evening. He played back the tape. Two, he sensed, were pitches. The third made him smile.

He called the first two, rejected offers of help to manage his financial affairs and cleanse his water supply, then played the third tape again.

A breathy, overtly sensuous Monroe voice whispered, "Doctor, I keep having this *terrible* nightmare. I'm sunbathing on my deck in the absolute nude . . . and suddenly I just *know* there's someone ogling me. I turn my head – and there he is, on the deck of the house next door. And he's *gorgeous*. I fancy him so much my teeth ache. And now comes the awful part. I wave to him, invite him over . . . and he can't see me! Does this mean I'm transparent or what?"

Now another female voice, jokingly terse, "Gimme that damn phone. Hi, Paul, this is Grace, that was Tilly. What Feather-head was trying to say is – all *three* of us have this *terrible* nightmare . . . no, sorry, I mean, we're having a tiny farewell bash on Friday night for Lou who is marrying some zillionaire creep who owns Venezuela, and we'd be absolutely knocked out of our socks if you could join us. Do try."

For a fleeting moment he felt the stir at the image of the lovely Tilly, meditating half-naked on the deck next door, and of the equally beautiful Grace, either of whom, he knew, would be sexually available to him should he give the sign. A tempting, impossible image.

Dispelling it, he dialled their number, got a machine, expressed his congratulations to Lou and regret that he'd be out of town.

Then he occupied himself loading and checking the video and recording equipment he would need for the forensic hypnosis session.

The West Los Angeles Police Station is a modern, two-storey structure of pale mauve stucco panels in white cement frames; it has a startling entrance faced in fire-engine-red ceramic tiles. The building occupies a corner site on Butler Avenue, close to the junction of the I-10 and and the I-405 which Drummond had used that morning.

Facing the station, on the east side of Butler Avenue, is a parking lot, with service bays, for the patrol and unmarked cars of the bureau. At ten minutes to three, Drummond drove the Daimler onto the lot and unloaded his equipment from the trunk.

"Hey, Doc, need a hand with that stuff?"

It was Carl Younger, a Homicide detective, coming out of a service bay.

"Hello, Carl, yes, I'd be obliged."

Younger picked up a tripod and a case of lights, Drummond the video camera case and the audio equipment.

"Hope you can get something out of this Keegan guy. We're in a bind on the Mar Vista thing."

"So I hear."

They crossed Butler Avenue and entered the red-tiled maw, its architectural style described by Dick Gage as "early Deep-throat".

From the reception hall they turned right down a corridor, through a door, passing the holding cells, and up a staircase into a huge room of desks and computers.

Dick Gage, in conference in a small adjoining office, spotted Drummond's arrival and came out. Gage was thirty-six, five-feet ten, with a strong, handsome face and a mop of dark brown wavy hair. Characteristically,

31

his grey slacks and white shirt looked rumpled, his tie loosened to mid-chest.

He hit Drummond with a broad grin of genuine pleasure at seeing him, ran a teasing eye over his friend's appearance and shook his head. "Paradise is sure agreeing with you, chum. You make me feel like a tank testing ground."

Drummond, returning the inspection and the grin, said, "Funny you should say that . . ."

Turning to business, Gage gestured towards the stairs, relieving Younger of the equipment.

Drummond said, "Thanks, Carl, see you later, maybe."

"In Duke's? I'll be there."

"Oh, do you drink, Detective Younger?" cracked Gage.

The Lieutenant led the way down the stairs, saying over his shoulder, "I'm bringing Keegan in at four-thirty – okay? An hour and a half to set up?"

"That's fine. Where are you putting us?"

"Same place as last time."

"Good."

A meandering route took them to a small office at the rear of the building. The usual furniture had been cleared from the room and replaced with a comfortable, fabric-covered recliner chair for Keegan, and a typist's chair and small table for Drummond.

"We'll be through there," said Gage, indicating a second door to an adjoining office.

"'We'? Who else will be observing, Dick?"

Gage gave a headshake that indicated vagueness and some puzzlement. "I don't know. I've had word that the Parker Centre will be sending people down . . . maybe the FBI, too. I don't yet know names or how many."

"Well, that's okay as long as they all understand the rules of forensic hypnosis – absolutely no interference

32

or interruption, and any questions must be handwritten, initialled and passed through the door. You know the drill. Anything less than absolute professionalism will never stand up in court."

"I'll make sure they toe the line. You need a hand with anything here?"

Drummond opened the door to the adjoining office, looked inside, saw that a TV monitor was already in place. "No, I'll manage, Dick."

"Anything more you want to know about Tom Keegan? – not that we have much."

Drummond shook his head. "Only the usual – name, address and case number. I already know too much from the papers and I'm trying to forget that as it is. If this ever gets to court, one leading question from me could negate this entire session. And as it's pretty well the only thing you've got . . ."

Gage rolled his eyes entreatingly. "Per-*lease*, no leading questions."

Drummond grinned. "Okay, get outta here, let a pro get to work."

When Gage had gone, Drummond set up the video camera and lights, framing to encompass both chairs, and ran cable beneath the interconnecting door to the TV monitor next door.

Satisfied with the arrangement, he took his seat, switched on the camera, which had its own sound system, and a back-up tape recorder, and did a test run.

Into camera he said, "This is a test of my video and cassette recording equipment. My name is Doctor Paul Drummond, Forensic Investigator. I am at the West Los Angeles Police Station." He added the date and time, which was also being generated on tape by the camera.

He allowed a few more frames to run, then stopped the camera by remote control, rewound both the video and audio tapes, and replayed them, opening the door to the adjoining office to check the quality of replay on the monitor.

Satisfied, he stopped the tapes at the end of the test and kept them in place. If the tapes were ever shown in court, the test would help his credibility. In matters of law, it paid to do everything absolutely by the book.

Promptly at four thirty, hearing the murmur of approaching voices, Drummond switched on all the recording equipment. Dick Gage, now wearing a suit jacket, his tie straightened, entered. He handed Drummond a slip of paper bearing Keegan's details, and held the door open as Keegan came in.

Although Drummond was concentrating on Keegan, he was aware of four other men out in the corridor. They passed quickly out of his view and entered the adjoining office through its own corridor door. Drummond raised his brows questioningly to Gage, not expecting a verbal response, but getting an eloquent shrug that said Gage was in the dark about the identity of the men.

The Lieutenant said, "Tom, this is Doctor Paul Drummond. Paul – Tom Keegan."

As the men shook hands, Gage said, "I'll leave you to it, Paul," and went into the corridor, closing the door.

Drummond's first priority was to put Keegan at ease. Behind an easy smile and manner, he regarded the man intently. Keegan was six feet tall, muscular, with close-cropped greying hair, wearing a dark-blue pinstripe suit of poor quality and two decades out of style. Drummond noted the nervous washing of the man's corded hands, the tension in the prematurely-lined face, the darting of his pale green eyes. Drummond, reminded of a hunted animal, felt a rush of sympathy for the man.

He said gently, "Now, Tom, I want you to try and relax. We've got a nice comfortable chair here for you. Would you like to take your jacket off?"

Keegan gave a nod, removed the coat, handed it to

34

Drummond who slipped it over the back of his own chair. Keegan's movements, as he settled into the recliner chair, seemed poorly coordinated, though whether from nervousness or something pathological, Drummond couldn't determine. There was certainly something odd and pathetic about the man's manner and bearing.

Sitting, Drummond said, "Tom, I'd like to draw your attention to this video camera and tape recorder, both of which are now recording this conversation. Is that okay with you?"

Keegan nodded and mouthed, "Sure," but no sound came out.

Drummond turned to camera and repeated the ident he had recorded for the test, adding, "With me today is Mister Tom Keegan of – " he consulted the slip of paper Gage had handed him, "four-five-nine Lomita Street, Los Angeles, and we will be discussing the events of September twenty-four of this year."

He addressed Keegan, "Tom, did anyone force or coerce you to come here today?" A headshake. "Will you please tell me why you are here today?"

Now, for the first time, Keegan spoke, and surprised Drummond. From long experience Drummond knew better than to judge a person by their appearance, yet with Keegan he'd fallen into the trap. To accompany the clothes, the lined and weatherbeaten face, the gnarled hands, Drummond had expected the voice of an ill-educated man. What he heard was halting, overtly anxious, bemused, but undeniably polished.

"I'm here . . . to undergo . . . hypnosis . . . in the hope that it will . . . help me . . . recall what happened on September twenty-four. I know . . . I received a head injury . . . and have been in hospital since that . . . day."

Drummond said, "Would you please tell me, in your own words, what you do remember – only what you remember or recall of that day, nothing else."

35

Chin lowered, Keegan stared at the carpeted floor in front of him, his features fixed in concentration, his mouth a compressed line, eyes glaring as though trying to penetrate a veil that denied him access to life-vital information. When finally he spoke, the word came, with a shake of his head, as a breath of despair and desperation.

"Nothing."

In the years Drummond had been practicing, and among the hundreds of anxiety cases he had treated, he had never encountered anyone who looked so lost, so totally out of control as Tom Keegan did at that moment.

"All right, Tom, now I want you to be entirely comfortable. Do you need the bathroom?"

"No."

"Do you wear contact lenses?"

"No."

"Prior to September twenty-four, had you been treated, or were you being treated, for any physical or emotional problem?"

The same effort of recall distorted Keegan's features. "I don't remember."

"Do you have any fears or phobias?" It was patently obvious that the man was riven with fears, but Drummond wanted to hear his response.

"I can't remember."

"You can't remember what?"

"Anything!" Keegan's hands balled into fists. "I can't remember anything."

"All right, Tom, just try to relax – and tell me what you know about hypnosis."

"Not much."

"What do you think hypnosis is?"

Keegan gave a shrug. "It's – like going to sleep?"

"No. That's a popular misconception. Hypnosis is a state of relaxation. The deeper the hypnosis, the more relaxed you are. But you can always open your eyes and end the session any time you wish. You will not be asleep, nor will you be under my control. Please be reassured on that point."

Keegan nodded.

"Now, I'll be asking you questions and we'll be discussing events that are relevant to September twenty-four only. I will not knowingly ask you anything that will be embarrassing or distasteful. Should it prove to be embarrassing or distasteful to you, please tell me or simply refuse to answer the question, is that clear?"

"Yes."

"I'm going to use a hypnotic induction called Progressive Relaxation. It's very simple and will be very pleasant. When you are properly relaxed, you'll be able to speak quite easily, and don't be afraid to move and shift position if you become uncomfortable. Is that all clear?"

"Yes."

"Any questions before we start?"

"No."

"All right, let's tip that recliner back and get you really comfortable."

Drummond left his chair and settled Keegan into the reclined position. Close to him, touching him, Drummond could feel an intense heat radiating from his body. He patted Keegan on the shoulder. "Just take it easy."

Returning to his chair, Drummond paused for a moment, fixing his concentration, then said in a soothing, monotonal voice, "I'd like you to roll your eyes right up, as though you were trying to see the inside of your forehead, while I count one . . . two . . . three. Now just allow your eyes to close . . . just close your eyes . . ."

Drummond continued with the induction, fixing Keegan's attention on areas of his body, urging him to relax that part completely, then progressing to another, from the top of his head down to his toes. By the time Drummond had reached the toes, Keegan seemed to be in hypnosis, with a significant flush in his cheeks.

Drummond continued with a deepening process, counting Keegan slowly down through the numbers, elaborating at each number with suggestions of heaviness, drowsiness, tiredness. Reaching zero, Drummond was assured that Keegan had responded perfectly to hypnosis, was deeply in trance.

"All right, Tom, I'll remind you that we will be discussing the events that took place on September twenty-fourth, and nothing else. I'd like you to go back now . . ."

It was as though Keegan had suddenly been given a massive electric shock.

He shot bolt upright in the chair, levering it into the erect position. His body was rigid, quiveringly stiff, every joint and muscle locked in a rigor of shock. His eyes, staring straight ahead at a blank wall, were wide with terror, his features contorted with dread. Sweat poured from his face, ran down into his collar. White-knuckled fingers clawed the arms of the chair as though he was holding on to his very life.

Aghast, Drummond could only stare. In the thousands of hypnotic regressions he had induced, he had never experienced a reaction like this. Then, prompted more by intuition than training, he said with authority, "Return to the present, Tom – now!"

Again, there was a startling reaction, this time in reverse. Keegan relaxed with equal suddenness, slumped back into the chair, which remained upright, and keeled sideways, head lolling, eyes closed.

Drummond was faced with a dilemma. His only brief here was to attempt to refresh Keegan's memory about a past event. If, for whatever reason, Keegan was allergic to regression, the session would have to be aborted. And yet he was aware of how vital Keegan's recollection could be to the police investigation.

The question was – in view of Keegan's terrified reaction, did he, Drummond, have the ethical right to try again, to experiment with other approaches, different wording, and risk a repetition of the reaction? A convulsion of such severity might easily trigger a heart attack or snap bones, to say nothing of inducing severe mental trauma.

Deep in concentration, he became aware of the inter-communicating door opening, and of Dick Gage's arm proffering a note.

Drummond took it and read it. "What happened?" The writing was not in Gage's hand; the author's initial was an illegible scrawl.

Drummond moved from his chair, saying, "Tom, I'm going to touch you, just to make you more comfortable. Just relax exactly as you are, remain in hypnosis, and ignore what I shall be saying for the next few moments."

He eased the chair back into the reclined position, settled Keegan, returned to his own chair and spoke to camera. "What you saw was an extreme allergic reaction to regression. There could be numerous reasons for it, and finding the cause might take extensive investigation. I'm loath to attempt further regression. Another convulsive reaction might cause Mister Keegan great harm. I suggest this session be terminated."

In the silence that followed, Drummond heard an angry, "Shit!" from next door. It was not Dick Gage's voice.

The door opened slightly, Gage's head appeared and gave a nod.

Drummond said, "Tom, you can hear me now. Is there anything you would like to say to me or tell me . . . about anything at all?"

Keegan took a while to answer. His voice cracked and he had to clear his throat. "I can't remember. Help me remember."

For a moment Drummond hesitated, then made a

decision. "Yes, I'll help you. But not here, not now. We'll talk about it later. I'm going to count you up from one to five now . . . and when I reach five you will open your eyes, be wide awake, feeling very relaxed and comfortable . . ."

As Keegan roused himself, Drummond said to camera, "This session is now ended," but, as always, left the camera running until the subject had left the room.

He helped Keegan to his feet. "You feeling okay?"

"Yeh, fine." He looked anything but fine.

"What d'you remember of the session, Tom?"

Keegan frowned. "I felt good . . . nice and relaxed. I don't remember any questions, though. Did you ask me any questions?"

"Did you feel nice and relaxed all through the session?"

"Sure."

"You didn't feel . . . disturbed by anything I said?"

"Nope." But suddenly the mask of anxiety that had previously distorted his features was in place again. "Could you help me remember, Doc?"

"I'm going to try, Tom. I'm going to arrange something."

The door opened and Lieutenant Gage came in, his expression an amalgam of disappointment and sympathy. "He okay?"

Drummond nodded. "Tom's asked me for help. I'm going to take him on as a private patient. Maybe all is not lost."

Gage's face brightened. "Great."

Then, as though the thought had just occurred to him, Keegan said dolefully, "But I've got no money, Doc. How much will it cost?"

Drummond winked at Gage. "Don't worry about money. LAPD will pick up the tab." He handed Keegan a business card. "I'm in town every Monday through

40

Wednesday." To Gage, he said, "What's happening to Tom now? Is he going back to hospital?"

"No, he's been discharged. He'll be taken home."

To Keegan, Drummond said, "I'll see you next Monday at ten o'clock, at the address on the card, Wilshire Boulevard. If you need me in the meantime, call any of those numbers, leave a message – okay?"

"Thanks, Doc. Thanks a lot."

"Just try and relax, Tom. Once you're back home, in familiar surroundings, your memory might well start to return. At the moment you're very stressed, and you're trying too hard to remember things. Give your mind a chance to heal itself."

Gage ushered Keegan out into the corridor, but returned to say to Drummond, "I'll be back in fifteen, give you a hand with the equipment."

Drummond frowned in Keegan's direction. "Will he be alone at the apartment?"

Gage nodded. "I know what you're thinking – his name's been in the papers and he may be in danger. To be honest, Drum, except for his address, we don't know anything about the guy. Up till now his background hasn't been important. But I'll send someone with him, maybe come up with a relative who can keep an eye on him."

Gage made a move out of the door.

"Dick . . ."

"Yeah?"

"Who were all those guys in there with you?"

"I don't know, buddy." Gage's eyes signalled something more than puzzlement. "They didn't bother to introduce themselves."

Chapter Four

Duke's Bar and Grill on Pico Boulevard was pretty much a cops' hangout, frequented not only by members of the LAPD and the Santa Monica PD, on whose boundaries it was located, but also of the Beverly Hills PD, and by sundry others who, though not actually police officers, were professionally associated with law enforcement.

The place, dim and comfortable with few fancy frills and incessant TV coverage of news and sport, was owned by Ralph Duke, a twenty-year ex-LAPD sergeant, who had discovered this way of taking retirement while retaining a close connection with the Force.

Not surprisingly, Duke's was one of the few bars in town that had never been robbed.

Just before six o'clock the place was filling, as Dick Gage and Drummond slid into the only vacant booth of the eight that lined the right-hand wall. There were vacant tables, small, round, four-seater, in dark wood with hammered brass tops, dotted around the room, and some space at the bar, but the booths offered privacy and were always in demand. It was an unwritten house-rule of Duke's that, since much arcane information was traded therein, the booths should be regarded as off-limits, their occupants free from interruption, unless and until an invitation to approach was extended.

"Cheers," said Gage, hoisting a draft beer.

"Here's to crime . . . detection."

Gage took a long swallow. "So – what the hell happened?"

"Several possibilities. The regression – just those few words, 'I'd like you to go back now' – triggered a recall of his experience at the hands of those punks that was so vivid and horrific that he was virtually reliving it. In which case, the experience must have been pretty damned bad. God knows what they did or said to him, even before they sent him through a plate-glass window."

Gage nodded. "Well, I reckon that alone would do it. What else?"

"The regression may have triggered a recall of some entirely different, perhaps even more horrendous, experience. I mean, his reaction was unbelievable – it was stark terror. I've done a lot of hypnoanalysis and I've witnessed a few awesome abreactions – copious tears, wracking sobs, even fear and violent anger – but I've never seen anything like Keegan's performance. The guy actually convulsed – as though he'd been given a massive ECT."

Drummond shook his head, drank some beer. "Keegan puzzles and interests me, Dick. I'm intrigued by his background. Also, I'd like to help him. No one should have to live with that kind of terror, repressed or otherwise. I'll take him on, *pro bono*." He grinned. "Salve my conscience about the fat fees I'm earning in the Valley – there, I got it in before you did."

Gage mugged in mock protest. "Was I going to say that?"

"Damn right." Drummond signalled the waitress for two more beers.

Gage waved to someone at the bar. Drummond glanced in that direction, did a double-take. The girl was stunning.

Drummond jerked a look at Gage, who ignored him, pulling something here, Drummond suddenly sensed. Over the past year, his perception of Gage's attempts at matchmaking had been honed razor-sharp. This one was as subtle as a kick in the groin.

"I must go," said Drummond, making a half-hearted move to rise, for she was indeed stunning.

"You park your ass," hissed Gage, still grinning at the girl, waving her over. "This is business."

"Sure – monkey business. Gage, you're a terrible actor."

"Trust me."

"Ha!"

And then she was there – tall, slender, elegant in a grey wool suit, sun-streaked blonde hair framing a lovely face, confident green eyes smiling at Gage and studiously ignoring Drummond. If he hadn't been entirely certain before that this was a Gage set-up, he was now.

"Well, Lieutenant," she greeted him.

"Well, Karen," he pretended, half-rising and shaking her hand. "How good to see you again. And how utterly, utterly you look."

From the two words she had uttered, Drummond had detected an English accent, which explained Gage's attempt at one.

"Why, thank you, Lieutenant. You're looking very . . . spruce yourself."

Gage, regarding his crumpled suit and shirt, his disarrayed tie, exploded a laugh. "Yeh, that's me all over – spruce. Karen, say hello to Paul Drummond and join us for a drink."

The engaging smile and humorous green eyes turned on Drummond, who found himself not caring too much that he was being set up.

He half-rose, took her hand, experiencing pleasure at the touch of her skin.

"Karen Beal," she said.

"Paul Drummond."

"I know." Her eyes teased him. "Dick just told me."

"Oh, yes."

Drummond was aware of Gage's triumphant, idiotic grin on the edge of his vision.

Gage slid out of the booth, ushered her in, as though ensuring she would stay awhile. "Karen," he said, resuming his seat and signalling the waitress, "is with the *LA Times* – Metro section. She covers crime."

"Ah," said Drummond.

"And Paul," Gage said to her, "is Doctor Paul Drummond, Ph.D. Hypnotherapist, Hypnoanalyst, Psychotherapist, Psychoanalyst, Forensic Hypnosis Investigator, and all-round good egg – and what, lovely lady, would you care to drink?"

The waitress had arrived with their beers.

"A vodka gimlet, please."

Gage sighed. "So polite, the English. I'll bet your criminals doff their hats and apologise while they mug you." He ordered the drink and the waitress departed.

Karen said to Drummond, "You should know that Dick has already told me about you."

"Who – me?" said Gage, mock-shocked.

"I'm interested in doing a piece on Forensic Hypnosis. Dick says you're very experienced in the field, that you've worked with him successfully on several cases, and I wondered if you'd like to give me some background. You'd get full credit. Better still, I'd write the article around you. It would be terrific publicity for you."

Her voice was soft and warm and persuasive, naturally so, Drummond felt, not affectedly. She was asking for help, not pitching a deal.

He glanced at Gage, who was pretending to study the bubbles in his beer, his lips pursed as though whistling soundlessly.

"I'm . . . only in town two more days. How much time would you need?"

"I don't know. I know nothing at all about Forensic

Hypnosis, so I can't make a guess. Two . . . three hours, maybe."

"When would you like to start?"

She gave a shrug. "Anytime. I'd like to get the piece in this week – Wednesday. So, any time you can spare in the next twenty-four hours . . ."

Drummond laughed. "Oh, I see." He narrowed his eyes accusingly at Gage who reacted with a guileless, questioning arching of his brows.

"Is that a problem for you?" Karen asked, her expression equally innocent.

Drummond was confused. Either his friend had master-planned the set-up to perfection, in collusion with Karen Beal, squeezing him into a date situation with her that very night . . . or the situation *was* innocent and was simply unfolding this way.

But then, he asked himself, did he care one way or the other? He liked the look of her, and the grounds for their being together for several hours met the requirements of his conscience. This was business. She needed help. If she had come to his consulting room for help, he wouldn't have hesitated to spend time alone with her. It was strictly business.

"Is it a problem?" she prompted gently.

"No. I can manage a couple of hours."

"Could you say when?"

As though on cue, Lieutenant Gage's pocket pager began beeping. "Damn. Gotta phone. You guys do your best to talk to each other until I return."

When he had gone, Karen smiled and shook his head. "He is so sweet."

"Dick? Whatever gave you that idea?"

"He's very fond of you."

"What exactly did he tell you about me?"

"Not much. I was talking to him last week about the Mar Vista bank job, and he said he was thinking about trying Forensic Hypnosis on Tom Keegan because he was the only potential lead they had. And it suddenly occurred to me that hypnosis was an aspect of crime investigation that hasn't been written about much, but which the readers might find interesting. When I told him, he said if he brought you in, he'd get us together. He called me Friday night to say be here."

"So how, from that, do you deduce that he's fond of me?"

She tilted her head quizzically. "Why the third degree? You've looked and sounded suspicious of me since I arrived."

"You answer my question, I'll answer yours."

"All right. He told me how you two met, that your wife was killed and he was on the case, and you've become good friends. That's it. Paul, Dick *is* a friend, he's not a gossip."

Drummond smiled. "He may not be a gossip, but he's one helluva matchmaker."

Enlightenment dawned in her eyes. "Oh. And you think he's arranged this little tête-à-tête . . ."

Drummond was nodding. "It is not without the bounds of possibility, I promise you. Dick and Anne – you know his wife? – should be running a wedding chapel in Vegas."

She gave an exaggerated nod. "Gotcha. Well, that may have been an ulterior motive of his *after* the hypnosis thing came up, but I promise you that's how it started out, and it's still a very serious interest on my part."

"Okay. That's fine. Forgive my suspicion. And let's start again, now that I can concentrate on helping you instead of . . ."

"Instead of?"

"It'll sound rude."

"Instead of worrying how best and soonest you can dump me."

He shook his head. "What man in his right mind would want to dump you? It's just that – a couple of Dick's machinations went spectacularly wrong. I have to work things out in my own way and time."

"Of course you do."

A roar of laughter went up over at the bar. A small crowd was reacting to something on TV. Looking across, Drummond could see a familiar face filling the screen.

"Crane," Karen Beal observed scornfully. "What's he up to now? A little more Milton Byrne character assassination? Or maybe he's revealed a new plank in his platform – a plan to napalm Moscow at Thanksgiving."

Drummond smiled. "Funny you should say that."

"You support the idea?"

"I picked up a student on the freeway this morning. Nice kid, real politics hot-shot. He uttered dire warnings about Jack Crane all the way from Upland to UCLA, and his parting shot was Robert Duvall's line in *Apocalypse Now* about the smell of napalm in the morning. You follow American politics, Karen?"

"There's no avoiding it at the paper. But I love American politics. They're so much more colorful than ours. Your politicians say the most delightfully dreadful things about each other. Their negative TV commercials are really outrageous. Our bunch are – or at least appear to be – so terribly civilized. Your fellas still have the whiff of frontier huckster about them. This campaign is going to be a dirty contest. I only hope Jack Crane isn't as totally hard as he looks and sounds. I think he could be an international disaster."

Before Drummond could speak, Dick Gage returned, his face crumpled with apology. "Guys, I'm sorry, gotta blow, another stiff just turned up in a supermarket dumpster. Jesus, these gang wars. Drum, thanks for trying, let me know if you get anything out of Keegan."

"Of course."

"Lovely lady, adieu, parting is such sweet sorrow. Give this guy a good write-up, he needs the money."

With a wave he was gone.

Karen said, "You had no luck with Keegan?"

"None. Listen, are you busy tonight?"

"Nope."

"Care to have dinner, talk hypnosis?"

"Adore to."

"Let's go."

He took her to Casa Renata in Santa Monica, two blocks from the pier. It was a small, unostentatious, genuine Italian place that catered mainly for office lunch trade, and was quiet at early dinner time.

Settled, they ordered drinks and veal.

Inspecting the room, Karen said, "Lovely. For an awful moment I thought we were heading for one of those swish joints on the front."

Drummond grinned. "I can't stomach the flash valet parking. Every time one of those jocks gets into my car, I die a little."

"Me, too."

They had driven from Duke's in their respective cars, Karen's a yellow XR3.

Drummond found himself almost constantly analysing his feelings about being with alone with her, his thoughts swinging like a metronome between awareness of her as a beautiful young woman, and of her professional role as a journalist, using the latter to appease the voice of conscience that whispered perpetual warnings in the labyrinths of his mind.

There was no denying the attraction. He liked everything about her, body and soul.

He said, "I'm going to start with the first of several embarrassingly trite questions, but I'd really like to know."

She smiled, a lazy, devastating smile that tripped his heart. "Do I come here often?"

"What brought you to the States – to LA? And 'How long have you been here?' and 'How long do you plan staying?' and 'Where did you live in England?' – that kind of stuff." There were other questions poking at his mind, but he shut them out.

"I've been here a year. I was working for *The Times* in London, reporting crime, and they decided to do a series on international crime prevention – a comparison of methods. I was sent here to report on the LAPD. I used *LA Times* resources, got to know a lot of people on the paper, and when the project was finished they offered me a job. So, here I am. How long will I stay?" She shrugged. "I don't know. I love the States. There's an *abundance* of crime to write about. So – "

Drummond frowned. "Why crime?"

"My father is a policeman. I was brought up on crime. It's in the Beal blood."

"Ah."

Their meal arrived, served by a beaming Signora Renata, a motherly soul, who fussed about them, murmuring Italian endearments, until all their immediate requirements were met, then bathed them in obvious compliments as she took her leave.

Drummond asked with grin, "What did she say?"

"Something to the effect that we grace her humble establishment and it is an honor to cook for us. She called us The Beautiful People."

"How nice. Well, she got half of us right."

Karen narrow-eyed him. "Which half?"

"Modesty forbids."

They tasted the food, pronounced it perfect.

"Drummond," she said. "That's a good old Scottish name."

"Yes, it is. My grandfather immigrated from Fort

William in the Twenties – or, rather, he was banished here by the family. Mad Harry Drummond, they called him. Quite a lad, by all accounts. Unfortunately, I never met him. He was shot to death in a poker game before I was born."

"How sad."

"He was a highlander, through and through, never happy at low altitude. He made a bee-line for the mountains of Northern California, made and lost several fortunes in timber, mining and heaven knows what, and, fittingly, died broke."

"How colorful. Do you take after him?"

He laughed. "In one respect – I love the mountains. I try to get home a couple of times a year. My parents live in Redding. Dad's a doctor. A *proper* doctor, my mother reminds me – an MD."

"You weren't tempted?"

"At first. I did two years' Pre-med. But once I got into Mind, that was it. The mind controls and influences the body, so what I do is preventive medicine, anyway."

"How do your folks regard hypnosis?"

He laughed. "With the greatest suspicion. I'm sure my mother thinks I turn people into clucking chickens for my own amusement. I'm afraid Hollywood and stage hypnotists have done hypnosis no favors."

"No, I'm sure. That's really all I know about it. What *is* hypnosis, anyway?"

Drummond smiled. "Have we started? Are you taking notes?"

"At the moment, mental notes. Ease me into it, it sounds complex."

"It is and it isn't." He laughed. "How's that for complexity?" He poured more wine into their glasses. "The truth is that, although the phenomenon has been known for thousands of years, we still don't know what hypnosis is. Certainly, it's a state of relaxation, with changes of

51

brain activity. But there's no such thing as a 'hypnotized feeling'. Most of my patients tell me after a first session, 'I never went under', and things like, 'I think my mind's too strong to be hypnotized', or 'It couldn't have worked because I heard every word you said'. And I sympathise and tell them to wait, see what happens."

"And what does happen?"

"They begin to change. Their thinking begins to change, and therefore their behavior. We are what we think. And we can become what we think. You are you because of the way you have thought and have been taught to think since the day you were born. Had your father been a Highland shepherd instead of a city policeman, you most likely wouldn't be sitting here now."

She laughed. "True."

"But there's an important distinction within Hypnotherapy. There is Suggestion Therapy and there's Analysis, and they're very different. Suggestion Therapy is fine for what are termed minor problems – nail-biting, smoking, weight control, pre-exam nerves, that sort of thing. Analysis is reserved for deeper psychological problems – anxiety states, compulsive behavior, phobias, etcetera. Now, I realise you're essentially interested in Forensic Hypnosis, which is something else again, but I think a general grounding in hypnosis won't be a waste of your time".

"Oh, I agree. I find it all fascinating. So, what actually happens in, say, Suggestion Therapy? How do the suggestions for change get locked into the mind?"

"We are creatures of habit. Habit makes life easier. Do a thing a few times, like driving a car, and habit takes over. The habit is locked into the memory bank, like information into a computer. Whenever you climb into your car, you automatically activate your computer. You don't have to think about what you're doing, it just happens.

"But instead of car-driving information, let's take self-denigration information – 'Mummy says I'm a bad girl, so I must be' . . . 'Daddy says I'm useless, so I must be' . . . 'Teacher says I'm stupid, so I must be'. Over and over, year after year, such information is poured into the memory bank, so what is the self-image that is formed?"

Karen nodded. "Bad, useless and stupid. So, in order to change the image, you change the information."

"You got it. And hypnosis hastens the process. In normal awakened state, the conscious mind acts as a guard dog. It analyses, sifts, questions, rejects. Tell that poor girl in awakened state, 'You're not bad, useless and stupid', and her conscious mind would fight you tooth and nail. How dare you challenge the habit of a life-time?

"But – put that conscious mind into a state of abeyance, call aside the watchdog that is guarding the doorway to the Subconscious, and you have direct access to the memory bank. Now you can begin to exchange the stored information for new information – 'You are good . . . you are resourceful . . . you are clever'. And, gradually, the new information takes over. That's what hypnosis does – it calls off the over-zealous dog that guards the subconscious mind."

"So, how come this isn't being taught in First Grade?"

Drummond topped up her glass. "Good question. What a different world it would be in just three generations if we hypnotized our kids – and they do respond wonderfully to hypnosis – and implanted 'Thou shalt not kill', or 'Thou shalt not steal' into their minds. Seventy-five years from now there'd be no LAPD, no crime reporters, no therapists . . ."

She smiled. "Maybe that's why it'll never happen – job protection. Seriously, d'you think it could ever happen?"

"Oh, yes. In maybe five or ten thousand years, when we've learned to control our old mammalian brain and use our new brain. It *won't* happen, of course, because long before then we'll have wiped ourselves out. Folks like Hitler and Stalin and Saddam Hussein will make sure of that."

"And Jack Crane?"

Drummond took a moment to answer. "I wonder."

They both eschewed dessert, not for any dietary reason but because Signora Renata's serving of veal had been generous, not to say effusive. Also, the conversation was such that food tended to get in the way.

By the time the coffee was finished they had covered hypnosis generally, the mystery of abreaction, the mechanics of the mind, and a couple of Drummond's more fascinating cases, but still hadn't touched on Forensic Hypnosis. Now the restaurant was filling up and proving too noisy for their purpose.

After Karen had winced twice at the clamor from the adjoining table, Drummond suggested, "Let's go somewhere quieter." He wondered, in the same instant: where? But he already knew.

Subconscious wheels had been grinding since the moment he'd spoken to her in Duke's, and now the knowledge loomed in his conscious mind with unequivocal certainty.

"I have a house in Malibu. We could sit on the deck and listen to the ocean while we talk."

"I'd like that."

As he climbed into his car, Drummond had the sensation of having crossed an important psychic line. He was experiencing feelings he had long forgotten. Starting the engine, he was aware that that 'one day' had arrived, more suddenly than he could ever have believed possible.

Chapter Five

Unlocking the street door, Drummond was awash with conflicting emotions. This would be the first time since Vivian's death that a woman, with the exception of Mrs Foy, had entered the house. In the restaurant, in the car, he had been carried along by excitement, by his feeling of the rightness of the moment. But now, on this threshold of his private past, he suddenly feared disaster. Karen Beal was no Mrs Foy. Karen Beal was a beautiful, desirable woman who, beyond any doubt, was sending out clear signals of her personal, as well as professional, interest in him. Once through this door, he knew, his feelings about the past would be changed forever. And that change, through guilt, might taint what was now developing between himself and Karen.

Sensing his hesitation, understanding his dilemma with a sensitivity that touched him, she said gently, standing behind him, "Are you sure this is what you want? We can go somewhere else. To my place?"

He shook his head. "Thank you, but it's okay."

He entered, turned a light switch to illuminate the garden and the steps, ushered her in, then led her down the steps and opened the front door.

The perfume enveloped him, but this time he found himself calmly acknowledging that it *was* floor polish. It was a very significant acceptance.

In the living room, Karen said, "It's beautiful, Paul."

"Thank you. I – I've been thinking of selling it, just haven't got around to it."

"No." Her tone told him she understood why.

He drew the drapes and slid open the glass doors, letting in the distant sound of the ocean. "Let's sit out here, I'll get some wine."

When he returned, they sat in silence for a while, looking at the moonlight on the water, getting used to each other all over again in this difficult place.

"I lost my mother a year ago," she said eventually, "Just before I came out here. It was cancer, but she died incredibly quickly. I didn't know what to do. I wanted to run away and stay away. I felt I had lost control of my life. I couldn't accept that I would never, ever see her again. After the cremation, I could not believe that the person who had been *my* mother no longer existed on this earth."

Drummond said, "Thank you," almost inaudibly.

"If you'd like to talk about her, I'd like to hear."

It took a moment. "We," he cleared his throat, "We met at USC. We were both doing clinical psychology, but Vivian's speciality was children. She'd been a battered child, herself – rich family, psychotic mother, a faded film star who took her anger and frustration out on a five-year-old kid. Viv was truly wonderful with children.

"We got married, set up practice on Wilshire Boulevard, did well. Her mother died and left Viv enough money to buy this house, and for five years life was perfect. Then one night, two years ago, Viv had been working late, by herself, I was away at a conference. She left the clinic to collect her car, and was mugged in a street off Wilshire. The kid, out of his mind on PCP, had seen her leave the clinic and thought we had drugs there. He tried to force her back into the clinic with a sawn-off shotgun, and when she resisted, tried to explain that we carried no drugs, he blew her head off."

Karen shut her eyes, "Dear God."

"Like you, I felt I had totally lost control of my life. I hated the clinic, hated this house, but I couldn't abandon either. Eventually, I worked out a weird sort of compromise. I bought a place in Palm Desert, set up a practice there. Now I spend three days here, the rest there, and spend all of the time wrestling with complex mind-games that include guilt and indecision and anger and – well, you know the games, you've played them to perfection."

"Yes, I have. I was the Guilt, Indecision and Anger Champion of Great Britain for a while. Even now, every time I think of my father, all alone over there, I want to take the next plane home. Yet I know it wouldn't do any good. He's lost an irreplaceable partner, as you have, and nothing can change that. You may – will – find another, but it won't be Vivian. That piece of your life will always be separate, cocooned, precious. And, in time, you'll start to build another."

He gave her an appreciative smile. "You'd make a great therapist. You have terrific insight, great intuition. In all seriousness, the experience of the death of somebody close does help to make one a better therapist. You can empathize with real pain when you see it, as I did today in Tom Keegan."

"I'd like to hear about Keegan. What happened today?"

"If you'd like to take notes, I'll talk about Forensic Investigative Hypnosis at the same time."

"Sure." From her copious shoulder bag she produced a tape recorder, set it on the low table between them, turned it on. "The lazy journalist's shorthand pad. It has a sensitive directional mike; so just speak normally."

"Okay. Well, for a start Forensic Investigative Hypnosis is such a mouthful I'm going to refer to it as FIH whenever possible."

"Fine."

"And if you have any questions, just ask them as we go along, don't feel you're interrupting."

"I have one already."

"What's that?"

"May I have some more wine?"

He laughed. "Of course. When I get on to the subject of Memory, I tend to forget everything else. How's that for a paradox?"

"I *could* recommend a good therapist."

When he had refilled the glasses, he said, "Forensic Hypnosis – FIH – is a special science, and needs special training."

"Where did you do yours, Paul?"

"At The New England Institute of Forensic Hypnosis. And, for the record, I'm a member of The International Association for Forensic Hypnosis, and The Society for Investigative and Forensic Hypnosis."

"Why does the training have to be special? Couldn't any hypnotist do it?"

"No. It has to be special because – particularly in criminal cases like the Mar Vista bank job – we are involved with the Law, and the process has to be very precise. But I'll get back to that in a moment.

"Firstly, let's talk about what FIH is, and what it isn't; what it can do, and what it can't do. Hypnosis is *not* a truth detection device. Anyone in hypnosis can lie, so all evidence must be corroborated. Even if I could have gotten Tom Keegan to give me the most detailed description of the two bank robbers, it would only have been a guide for Dick Gage, not absolute proof. Though, certainly, since he has absolutely nothing to go on, it would have been a great help.

"So, hypnosis cannot be used to determine truth." Drummond grinned. "In the civil sector, I've had calls from suspicious wives, husbands and lovers, asking me to hypnotize their partners to get at the truth. The public has some pretty exotic ideas about what hypnosis can do."

"You said 'in the civil sector'. As distinct from the criminal sector?"

"Yes. FIH is used in all kinds of situations. I've worked for attorneys, insurance investigators, safety and security directors, and private citizens."

"Doing what kind of work?"

"Always one kind of work – refreshing memory. That's what FIH does, Karen. It refreshes memory. I have used it on attorneys' clients, on employees, witnesses, and private citizens who have been in accidents, misplaced documents, money, jewelry, you name it. There's no end to its uses."

"But it requires special training?"

Drummond nodded. "It sounds simple, I know. You put someone into a light trance, ask the questions, get the answers. But it's a lot more complex than that. For a start, you must know *how* to ask the questions. Leading questions must be avoided like the plague. In criminal cases, particularly, every interview must be conducted as though the results will appear in court."

"Have you appeared in court?"

"Many times. I've appeared for both the prosecution and the defence as an expert witness, and believe me, it's a hot seat. The main aim of the opposing counsel is to destroy the credibility of the expert witness. If the hypnosis session hasn't been conducted with absolute professionalism, if there are any leading questions, if the video or sound quality is poor, the opposing counsel will go for the jugular, and the hypnotist – and probably the case – will be laughed out of court."

Karen shook her head. "I've been around the crime scene quite a while, but never knew this aspect of it." She smiled, sipped her wine. "We're not very big on hypnosis in England. Americans are so much more adventurous about mind matters. We still think 'shrink' is something that happens to our socks in hot water."

Drummond laughed. "I like that. May I use it at my next Association dinner?"

"Please. So – what happened today with Tom Keegan?"

"Yes, poor Tom," Drummond said reflectively. "He was very nervous when he arrived – understandably. He'd been through a terrible ordeal, been hospitalized for two weeks, and brought to a police station for a process he didn't understand."

"Will you describe him – so I can get a mental picture?"

"He's six feet tall, strong-looking, with short-cropped graying hair. He was wearing a dark-blue pin-stripe suit dating back to the Seventies. I'll tell you who he reminded me of – Boo Radley in *To Kill A Mocking Bird*. Did you ever see the movie?"

"About eight times. And you're quoting Robert Duvall again."

Drummond laughed. "Yes – coincidentally. Now, I'm not saying Tom Keegan is mentally deficient, far from it, but he had the look of Boo about him, physically strong but extremely vulnerable, pathetic."

"Got him."

"Well, I thought I had. Judging from his clothes, his weather-beaten appearance, and the fact that he earns a living doing odd laboring jobs, I had him slotted into the poorly educated category. But he surprised me. The man is not what he seems."

"How can you tell?"

"His accent. But I'm jumping the gun. To give you some technical details: the video camera and separate tape recorder were switched on when he entered the room. I got him settled into a recliner chair and asked him, before hypnosis, what he remembered about the day of the robbery. This is done so that the effect of the session can be calculated. He said he remembered nothing. I then put him into a light trance with Progressive Relaxation."

"What's that?"

Drummond smiled. "I won't tell you, I'll show you – later. Have you ever been hypnotized?"

"No."

"Would you like to be?"

"Sure. Anything to help the story."

"It will help."

"And how did Keegan respond?"

"Like a dream. Because of his nervous state, I thought I'd have some trouble, but he went into trance beautifully."

"And?"

"Everything went fine until I tried to regress him, take him back to the day of the robbery. All I said to him was, 'I'd like you to go back now . . .' and his reaction was devastating. He snapped out of trance, shot bolt upright in the chair, his entire body quivering, stiff as a board, an expression of stark terror on his face."

"Good Lord."

"I've never seen anything like it."

"Did it scare you?"

"Yes, it did. I was afraid for him. A convulsion like that is very dangerous, can even be fatal. In the days when they used to treat schizophrenia with ECT – Electro-Convulsive Therapy – patients were known to snap bones."

Karen grimaced. "What happened then?"

"I told him to return to the present, and he went back into trance and total relaxation as though nothing had happened. I ended the session then, I wouldn't risk another attempt, and when I brought him out of hypnosis, he didn't remember a thing."

"How incredible."

"The mind is incredible. Science is only just beginning

to realise how incredible. We know as much about its workings as Stone Age man knew about the microchip."

She drank some wine, looked out at the moonlit water. "No wonder Dick was disappointed. But from what he said in Duke's, I gather you're going to keep on trying with Keegan?"

"Yes. The guy's in a really bad way. His amnesia may extend beyond the robbery, may even be total, and if it is, he's walking around in a nightmare. I'm giving him a week at home, see what memory returns in familiar surroundings, and I'll start treating him next Monday. With luck, I'll be able to help him and get something for Dick."

"Why," she asked pensively, "would Keegan react like that, so violently, to being asked to go back into his past? Was it re-living the horror of his bank robbery experience that he feared? Or something else? Now, I find that *very* intriguing."

Drummond laughed. "The journalistic mind at work – or is it the journalistic nose? But I agree. I find it intriguing too. And, my dear Watson, be sure I shall not rest until I have solved the mystery."

It was midnight when she took her leave. They had talked about hypnosis, analysis, journalism, crime, the Coachella Valley, and other things, moving indoors as the sea air cooled, talking across the kitchen counter top while Drummond brewed coffee, talking in the living room before the gas-log fire, easy with each other, and in themselves, each aware of the significance of her presence there, of the changes it implied.

"Before I go," she said, as he held the suit jacket she had long since removed, "do you have a photograph?"

"Photograph?"

"For the article. I'm going to write it around you. The readers will want to know what you look like."

He frowned, uncertain.

"Why the hesitation?"

"I don't know, just a feeling."

"It'll be good for business."

"Perhaps that's what I don't want, Karen. I've . . . just about decided to quit LA for good, practice only in the Valley."

"Has anything that's happened today hastened that decision?"

He met her warm green eyes, saw her understanding. "You know it has. I've known for a long time that I have to cut from the past, start afresh, but while I live in this house and practice from the clinic, I'll never do it. You, being here, have brought it all into perspective. You've triggered the decision. I'm going to sleep on it, but I know now that I'm going to sell the house and close the clinic."

"But, Paul, you enjoy the forensic work so much."

"Yes, I do. It's a welcome break from dealing with neuroses all the time."

"So – can't you come in from the Valley to do it?"

"Of course. But I'd need an office. Not all interviews are conducted at police stations."

"And that's what you don't want, isn't it – tangible roots in the city that's broken your heart?"

He smiled. "That's nicely put – and absolutely right."

"But, surely, you can be selective about the forensic work you accept?"

"Yes."

"So – enjoy the best of both worlds. Live and practice in the Valley, come in for forensic when you feel like it. Paul, please let me personalize the article, let me have a photograph. You'll like what I write, I promise you."

With a sigh, he capitulated. "All right – but on one condition."

"What's that?"

"That you come out to the Valley this week-end."

Her eyes lit up. "Really? I'd love to."

"It's disgraceful that you've been here a year and haven't seen Palm Springs."

"I agree, I agree."

"Okay, it's a deal." He crossed the room, rummaged in a bureau drawer. "Here's one I had taken for the brochure I send out in the Valley. I even have the negative here."

"Wonderful." She took the photograph and studied it, smiled at him, teasingly. "Very Richard Crenna."

He accompanied her out to her car. "We'll have some fun this weekend, just relax in the sun, swim, if you like, do exactly what you like, no formality."

She turned to him, offered her hand. "Paul – thank you for a lovely evening, I've enjoyed it so much. And for the information."

He was conscious of the warmth of her hand, and of his reluctance to release it. "And I thank you. I'll call you."

"Please do."

He watched her drive away, waving from her window, then walked back through the garden, and was overwhelmed by an ache in his throat that was unbearable.

He stopped and touched the petals of a pink azalia that she had planted, remembering how she had called him from the house to see it. "Paul . . . Paul . . ."

Gone is gone.

"Goodbye, old girl," he whispered, and, entering the house, turned off the lights in her garden.

Chapter Six

Wednesday.

Drummond awoke at six and took to the beach. Walking along the water's edge, he viewed his elevated house with an awareness of a difference of feeling towards it. Changes were underway, prompted by his relationship with Karen Beal.

One of his principal approaches to therapy was to explain the mechanics of mind to his patients – how and why they thought as they did – using the analogy of a computer to get across the message. He was now beginning to program his own subconscious computer with new material, with a vision of a new life after Vivian's death, and with permission to live it.

Deep within his being he could feel the shadow of guilt at his own survival receding as tangibly as an ebbing tide, and had he been a believer in the paranormal, he might have given more than a passing thought to the notion that Viv's silent voice was urging the change.

It was a beautiful day, the sky clear, the air cool. He stopped and faced the ocean, stretched his arms wide, embraced the world. Thoughts of the week-end in the desert with Karen quickened his heart. He felt terrific.

Returning to the house, he showered, dressed in a dark-gray business suit, white shirt, blue silk tie. Then he made coffee, put two eggs on to boil, and did something he rarely did – switched on the kitchen TV set. He loathed morning television, preferring to catch up with the news in the paper he bought from the stand on Wilshire.

But Alan Forrest, the politics hot-shot, had got to him, had planted a seed of interest in Jack Crane in his mind, and he now felt an almost irresistible urge to catch up on the presidential candidate's latest doings.

The news boomed out at seven: "Governor Jack Crane accuses Senator Milton Byrne of being in league with criminals, national security saboteurs, and environmental rapists.

"In a speech to the Police Benevolent Association in New York last night, Republican candidate Crane flayed Democrat Byrne . . ."

As the newscast went to film and Crane's features filled the screen, Alan Forrest's words echoed in Drummond's mind, "Any day now, Crane will go on the offensive . . . he's an opportunist and a thug . . . Crane's fire-storm attacks . . . Byrne will be slammed back on the defensive, and he'll never recover."

Crane's physiognomy was military, the kind of face cartoonists draw to exemplify the archetypal stonewall, can-do, bomb-the-bastards general. Square-jawed, hard-mouthed, with close-cropped, graying hair, he appeared to have been chiselled from rock. Only the eyes, bright blue and alive with energy and fervor, humanized what might otherwise have been a cyborg construction.

In his close presence, even though televized, Drummond felt the power of the man. Had he been a legitimate screen actor, rather than a political one, Crane could have portrayed an incredibly threatening villain. As it was, because he espoused national ideals rather than criminal ambition, the emanation of threat became the power for good, the strength to subjugate America's enemies, the force necessary to restore her internal values, and her standing in the international community.

66

Or so a great many Americans thought, mused Drummond.

As he prepared the eggs and toast, he listened to, rather than watched, Crane. The man had an excellent, theatrical command of his voice, which was wide-ranging in tone and pitch, now granite-hard and witheringly acerbic, now deep, warm and appealing.

An actor.

"The guy's a pig, Doc. He's got a mouth like a Brooklyn hood. In public he comes on like the Messiah . . ."

"All over this great, great country of ours, young policemen are dying . . . are being *slain* in the line of duty . . . by creatures who do not deserve the appellation 'human being'. These . . . *animals* – though I hesitate to call them that because animals have dignity and their own righteous code of behavior – this non-human garbage, ladies and gentlemen, is often better armed than my boys were in Vietnam!"

Thunderous applause in appreciation of his recognition of police danger – and of his war record.

"And faced with this war on our streets, faced with a national escalation of crime that is going through the roof, what goodies do we find in my *opponent's* policy pail? Why, we find proposals forbidding American citizens the right to bear arms . . . we find proposals for better prison conditions and shorter prison sentences . . . we find proposals for massive expenditure on rehabilitation programs . . . in short, ladies and gentleman, we find Senator Milton Byrne doesn't give a damn about young police officers slaughtered on duty . . . doesn't give a damn about the innocent victims of robbery and rape and murder . . . doesn't give a damn about the hard-working American tax-payer. Well, what *else* are we to assume? Senator Milton Byrne is obviously in league with the criminals!"

Wildly supportive applause, and over it, Crane bellowing, "Milton Byrne will hand America over to murderers, drug pushers, rapists and child molesters . . . but JACK CRANE AIN'T ABOUT TO LET IT HAPPEN!"

Further edited clips of the speech showed Crane vilifying Byrne on national security and environmental issues, losing no opportunity to tell America that JACK CRANE AIN'T ABOUT TO LET IT HAPPEN!

In what appeared to Drummond to be an attempt at impartiality, the network went to coverage of a speech by Milton Byrne at a civic gathering in Illinois, the coverage succeeding, albeit unwittingly, in vividly demonstrating the contrast between the candidates, in Jack Crane's favor.

By comparison, Byrne, looking every inch the Ivy League professor he had once been, graying, bespectacled and distinguished, speaking of the importance of education to America's future, sounded erudite, sonorous, and boring.

In another film clip, Byrne, interviewed after his speech and asked for his opinion of Crane's campaign of attack, replied with a dismissive smile, "Jack Crane has never been overburdened with good taste. Nor with a true appreciation of America's mind and heart. Fear not, the people know dirt when they see it. I don't recall Crane discussing one substantive issue throughout this campaign. Wait until the television debates. The man's rabble-rousing rhetoric will not serve him there, I promise you."

From the newscast, the network went to political forum, to four experts aglow with morning TV self-importance and the rightness of their opinion.

"Crane is going too far. He's showing himself to be master of the world-class cheap shot."

"He's giving TV what it most adores – the sound bite. The cameras *love* that guy – and this election will be won on the six o'clock news."

"You've got to admit – Crane's got one helluva management team behind him. Didn't they work together on the Nuremberg rally in Nineteen Thirty-three?"

"Byrne's pinning his hopes on the TV debates – and he's right to do so. But does he *seriously* think Jack Crane will dispense with his rhetoric? Any takers for how many times he works in 'Jack Crane Ain't About To Let It Happen'? Along with tax-deferral, child-care and health plans?"

"Crane has TV locked up. How can Byrne possibly challenge that impact?"

"He *could* make his next speech stark naked?"

Drummond switched off the set.

The clinic at Wilshire and Bundy was contained in a two-story Spanish-style office development that boasted a court-yard with a playing fountain, wrought-iron verandahs, and a plethora of flowering shrubs. Though barely removed from the bustle of the boulevard, it offered a sanctuary that was perhaps more psychological than factual, and was an ideal city setting for the therapeutic sciences. Osteopathy, chiropractice and homeopathy were other branches of alternative medicine offered within the enclave.

Drummond parked his car on a trusted lot on Bundy, collected a copy of the *Los Angles Times* from a dispenser on Wilshire, and entered his ground-floor suite at nine-thirty.

The door from the courtyard led into what, when Vivian had practiced there, had been a reception area, but was now Drummond's waiting room. Two rooms to the left of reception had been Vivian's; the two on the right Drummond's. As with the house, the suite was cleaned and aired every week after his departure for the Valley.

Drummond passed through his outer office, which accommodated file cupboards and the telephone with recorder, and into his consulting room, furnished simply with a modest wooden desk, a reclining chair, an armchair, and shelves of books and recording apparatus. A window, shaded with a Venetian blind, offered a view of an adjoining blank wall in extreme close-up.

69

Turning on obligatory lights, Drummond settled into his desk chair, discarded the main international portion of the heavy *LA Times*, discarded the Sports, Business, Calendar and Classified sections, and unfolded the Metro section – Local News, Weather, Editorial.

And there he was, front page, center stage, a huge piece occupying four of the five columns, his enlarged photograph dominating the top right corner.

He muttered, "Good God," frowning, smiling, astounded.

The headline blazed: "FORENSIC HYPNOSIS: CRIMINALS BEWARE." The article began, "Forensic Investigative Hypnosis is one of the latest weapons to be added to the crime-fighting armories of the nation's police forces . . ."

Drummond read avidly, silently applauding Karen Beal's accuracy of detail, her balance between her need for drama and restraint regarding the limitations of hypnosis.

But half-way through the article he stopped applauding and went cold.

He could not believe what he was reading: "Typical of the difficulties encountered by the police is the witness whose imperfect memory probably holds the key to the solution of a major crime. Tom Keegan, recent victim of abduction and violence at the hands of the Mar Vista bank robbers and murderers, was such a witness whose memory Dr Drummond is attempting to restore."

Drummond flushed with anger. Grabbing up the paper, he stormed into the outer office, picked up the phone, found the number for the *Los Angeles Times* and stabbed it out. A moment later Karen Beal was on the line with a smile in her voice.

"Good morning. Have you seen the piece?"

"Just now."

"Well, what d'you think?"

"I think it's one of the most irresponsible pieces of journalism I've ever read."

70

Her astounded gasp, then bewildered laugh came down the line. "Paul . . .?"

"What is your circulation figure, Karen?"

"Our – it's one and a quarter million. Paul, what – "

"Double it for readership, that's two and half million people who now know that Tom Keegan is a prime police witness in the Mar Vista case, and that I am trying to extract information from his mind that will put those killers behind bars. Jesus, don't you see what you've done? You've hung him out to dry. You've put Keegan's life in jeopardy!"

"Paul!" she cried out in protest. "For God's sake, no! Do you honestly think I'd do a thing like that?"

"Do I think . . .? Karen, you've *done* it. I have it here in my hands."

"What? What have you got there, Paul? Read it out to me."

He fumbled with the paper, hands shaking. "Half-way through the piece . . . 'Tom Keegan, recent victim of abduction and violence at the hands of the Mar Vista bank robbers and murderers, was such a witness whose memory Dr Drummond is attempting to restore'. If that isn't telling the world . . ."

"'*Was* such a witness.' *WAS*, Doctor Drummond – past tense."

Drummond stopped as though he'd hit a wall.

Karen broke the silence, her voice very quiet, very earnest, and very English. "Doctor Drummond, I am a professional and a responsible journalist. Do you imagine I would have used Tom Keegan's name without first clearing it with the police? I wanted to use it because his name has already, recently, appeared in the papers in connection with the crime, so is fresh in the public's mind . . . and therefore more graphically illustrates the importance of the work you do.

"Since we had discussed Keegan at great length, and

since you had uttered no warning about using his name, I felt that police clearance would be all I would need. So, I phoned Dick Gage yesterday. Dick was out of town. When I told the station what I wanted, I was routed to Press Relations in the Parker Center, and after a very long wait was told that someone would get back to me. Later in the day I found a note on my desk saying that Tom Keegan was no longer regarded as a reliable witness, and, furthermore, that since two suspects for the Mar Vista job had been apprehended in San Francisco, I was cleared to use Keegan's name."

Drummond was nonplussed. He drew a deep breath, said contritely, "Karen, I'm sorry. I could say I should have known better, but I guess we don't know one another very well yet – and my faith in journalistic integrity, especially in this town, is not exactly profound. My first thought was for Keegan's safety."

"Of course. Quite rightly."

"But I find the situation odd. Why wasn't *I* told that Keegan was no longer regarded as a reliable witness?"

"Perhaps, knowing that Dick brought you in, they were waiting for his return, so he could tell you?"

"But who told you? Who sent you the note?"

"I don't know. It was on my desk. And, frankly, I was so tight to deadline, I didn't bother to question it. I was just so pleased I wouldn't have to take Keegan out."

"Okay. I'll check with Dick. Karen – look, I'd hate this to spoil your visit to the Valley. Do you still want to come?"

"Of course. For a minute I was mad at you, questioning my ethics, but you're right, we don't know each other very well yet, and we newshounds do have a ruthless rep. Perhaps by next Monday we'll know one another a little better."

"Count on it. I'll call you."

Drummond rang off, dialled Dick Gage and was told

72

he wouldn't be in till later. Drummond left a message for him to call.

With quieter mind he returned to his desk and re-read the article, acknowledging that it was both well-written and written with heart, by someone who liked him and respected the science of forensic hypnosis. Karen Beal had wanted to help both causes, and he had responded by attacking her professionalism. He was overcome with contrition.

The phone rang. It had a six-ring delay before the recorder cut in. Thinking it would be Gage, Drummond moved to it and caught it on the fifth ring, announcing the number.

A resonant, meticulous male voice enquired, "Doctor Drummond?"

"Speaking."

"Ah. Doctor Drummond, my name is Teffler . . . Andrew Teffler of March, Kemp, Teffler and Vigo, Attorneys At Law in Santa Barbara. I've just read the article about you in the *Los Angeles Times* and would like to consult with you about a client we are representing in an automobile accident case. Perhaps we could meet some time next week?"

By lunchtime Drummond's answerphone had logged twelve such calls; by the end of his working day a further eight.

Dick Gage's call came at five o'clock. "You left your phone off the hook or what?" said the message. "I've been trying for an hour."

Drummond called him. "Hi, it's me. You read the article yet?"

"Just now. Is that why I couldn't get through?"

"It's unbelievable. Twenty calls. I wanted to talk to you about Keegan . . ."

"Not now," Gage interrupted, his tone guarded. "Will you be at the house later?"

73

"I'm going home now."

"I'll be there at seven."

As Drummond, puzzled, replaced the receiver, the phone rang for the twenty-first time. He allowed the recorder to take it. "Doctor Drummond, this is Frank Delaney of the Delaney Detective Agency in Sacramento. I've just read the article in the *Los Angeles Times* . . ."

Drummond transcribed the details onto a legal pad, locked up the office and headed for the door. Out in the courtyard, he heard his phone ring again, and pondered with some disquiet, for the twenty-second time that day, the changes taking place in his life.

Just after seven Dick Gage announced himself over the intercom at the street door, and Drummond released the electric lock.

"Got a cold one waiting," he said, as Gage came through the yard.

"Make it three, it's been that kinda day."

They headed for the kitchen counter, their invariable gas-and-guzzle spot.

"You've been out of town?" said Drummond, taking four canned Buds out of the refrigerator.

"Yes, San Francisco. The SFPD picked up two armed guys loitering in an alley behind a Savings and Loan, ran a computer check on them and came up with a couple of similarities to the Mar Vista job. I went up to check it out."

"And?"

Gage shrugged, swallowed half his beer. "I don't know. It's vague. The Mar Vista punks were driving a blue Chevvy, so were these guys, but what does that mean? There must be forty million blue Chevvies in LA alone, and in any case, our punks would've ditched theirs after they threw Keegan out. Both pairs of men were wearing denim, but again – so what? We've had so many conflicting eye-witness descriptions of height and weight, they can all be discounted. They were wearing ski-masks, and only Keegan saw their faces. Without him, we've got nothing."

"And yet . . ."

"I know – and yet," Gage cut in vehemently, finishing his beer, snapping open another. "They've rejected Keegan as a reliable witness. I spoke to Karen, heard you had a bit of a tussle."

"I went off half-cocked when I read the article, saw Keegan exposed. But she explained about the clearance and we finished up okay. Dick, *who* has rejected Keegan, *who* gave Karen her clearance, left a note on her desk?"

Gage was shaking his head, his expression grim, thoughtful. "I don't know, Drum. There's something funny going on, I can smell it."

"What d'you mean – 'funny'?"

"Something about this whole Keegan thing is not kosher. The guy gets caught up in a bank heist, is thrown through a window, loses his memory. I call you in with hypnosis. And suddenly there are all kinds of top brass, *anonymous* brass, interested in the case. Drum, so far this year there have been five hundred bank robberies and more than a thousand homicides in this city. How many d'you suppose have received the personal attention of top brass?"

"I could not hazard a guess."

"Go ahead – hazard."

"None?"

"That would be my hazard, too. So, what is it about this particular case that interests the Parker Center – and God knows what other center? Okay, let's accept that there *is* something here worthy of their attention. They witness your attempt and failure to regress Keegan – just one attempt. At your own expense you volunteer to try again, but before you can get to it, Keegan is tossed out as a reliable witness. Someone gives Karen clearance to mention Keegan's name, and as a reason for doing so they use the fact that two guys have been arrested in 'Frisco for the Mar Vista job . . . when no one worthy of the name 'cop' would assume their culpability on such flimsy evidence. Now, what does that say to you?"

Frowning, Drummond snapped open his second beer. "It could say several things. One – that someone has screwed up badly in the Parker Center bureaucracy. Karen said her request was routed from West LA to Press Relations, and she had to wait all day for a response, which arrived in the form of a note just before her deadline. Who knows how many in-trays her request dropped into, and how many distortions it suffered, during that day?

"Two – it could say that someone has over-reached themselves by prematurely judging the culpability of the guys arrested in San Francisco – or they've suffered a *grand mal* attack of wishful thinking or desire to clear up the Mar Vista case in a hurry."

Gage said, "Like I said, no cop worthy of the name would do that."

Drummond smiled. "Are you saying there are no cops *unworthy* of the name, Richard?"

Contrite, Gage gulped his beer. "Nope. Carry on, Smartass."

"Three – and this is preposterous . . ."

"I knew you'd get around to it."

". . . someone, for some reason, has deliberately exposed Tom Keegan to the danger of annihilation by the bank robbers, should they still be at large, before his memory of them can be restored."

"Bingo," nodded Gage. "If I didn't know better, and I certainly don't, I'd say that 'someone' is using this opportunity to get that poor dumb schmuck out of the way. But who? And why? Tom Keegan, f'Crissake! Why should a guy like him interest top brass?"

76

Drummond's frown intensified. "Maybe the answer to that lies in not what and who Keegan is now, Dick, but what and who he was? The guy struck me as being a paradox. He looks like a laborer, works as a laborer, but speaks as something else. Let's take a flyer at something . . . you want another beer?"

"I'll take a flyer at that, sure."

Drummond crossed to the fridge, brought two back. "Two weeks ago, Keegan was a nobody, maybe totally amnesiac, socially a non-person. Then he gets caught up in a bank raid and homicide, and his name is all over the newspapers. 'Someone' says, 'so that's where old Tom Keegan got to'. Or – maybe they knew where he was all the time, and were happy with his amnesiac condition?"

"Go on."

"Keegan is hospitalized for two weeks. Medical reports say he's amnesiac about the bank job. Good, maybe he's still amnesiac about a lot of other things. But what's this? Lieutenant Dick Gage is bringing in a hypnotist to help jog Keegan's mind about the bank job. What if he jogs too much and brings up the other stuff? We'd better attend the session and see what comes to light."

"Hence the anonymous oversight committee," nodded Gage. "Carry on, you're doing real good."

"Drummond fails, and the session succeeds beyond their wildest dreams. Keegan is allergic to regression. Why?"

Gage shrugged. "You assumed it was the horror of his bank heist experience."

"But say it wasn't – or wasn't *only* that. Say Keegan has, sometime in his past, been *programmed* to violently reject attempted regression."

"You mean with hypnosis?"

"Yes."

"But he said he didn't know anything about hypnosis."

"Say he'd been programmed to believe that?"

Gage grimaced, swallowed beer. "Jesus."

"Let us proceed. At the end of the session, they hear Keegan plead with me to help restore his memory, and hear me accept him as a private patient. They also know Keegan is being discharged from hospital. As far as you know, he lives alone on Lomita Street – alone and vulnerable. Would it not, perhaps, serve their – whoever the hell 'they' are – their purpose to make sure Keegan does not begin therapy with me?"

"Perhaps."

"But how do they prevent it happening? They have a week to mull it over – they heard me tell Keegan next Monday for his first appointment. And then, out of the blue, an unexpected break. Karen Beal, a respected and influential journalist on the *LA Times*, actually requests permission to publish Keegan's name in an article linking him and the Mar Vista bank job with me and memory refreshment. You happen to be in San Francisco, checking on two suspects who *may* be the wanted guys, so why not use that as a reason to clear Karen? Hey, presto, open season on Keegan by the real robbers."

Gage drained his third can and crushed it flat. "Brilliant. Except for a couple of things. How come you presume those two Mar Vista assholes can even *read*, let alone that they ever read the *LA Times*? And, secondly, what if the punks I saw in San Francisco really *are* the Mar Vista boys? They're arrested, out of it, no threat to Keegan."

Drummond's frown came down, wiping all levity from his expression. "I've thought of that, Dick. I think the odds against the robbers reading the article are astronomical, and I don't think it matters whether the men you saw are the Mar Vista robbers or not. What I do think is that the robbers – or friends of the robbers, or relatives of the robbers – could be used by 'them' as the cause of making Tom Keegan permanently amnesiac. Hell, it's a gift for them. And for the press. Except for

Karen. See the headlines: 'Amnesiac witness to Mar Vista robbery/homicide slain before memory restored.' Sub-head: 'Tom Keegan, named in a recent *LA Times* article . . ."

"I take your well-grounded point. But there's a pile of presumption and a cartload of conjecture here. Why do you feel so all-fired strongly that Keegan's continued amnesia is so vital to 'them'?"

"Huh! Why do *I* feel . . . Dick, you were the one who clammed up on the phone, you're the guy who thinks something funny's going on, you're the fella who's puzzled by the attention Keegan's getting from top brass!"

"Sure I am, Drum, but there's a heap of difference between 'funny' and 'puzzled', and thinking somebody's out to whack the guy."

"Are you prepared to take a chance on there being a difference, Dick?"

Gage stared at his friend, drew a sigh. "What are you proposing? I know you've got something in mind."

"I'm proposing we both dig into Keegan's background; you in your way, I in mine. And I propose doing my digging in the Valley. I want to take Keegan out there, if he's willing, put him up at a motel, give him concentrated attention."

"You're a good man, Drummond."

"I feel partly responsible for his exposure in Karen's article. I should've told her the Keegan stuff was off the record, and didn't."

"Okay – so, when d'you want to get into this?"

Drummond checked his watch. "Right now. It's eight o'clock. I'll get ready to leave for the Valley now, you come with me to Keegan's place, maybe help convince him to come with me, at least look his apartment over, maybe pick up some clues to his past."

As Drummond headed for the bedroom, Gage called after him, "You sure you want to do this tonight? I kinda

79

promised Anne I'd be home for dinner. I try to get home for dinner at least once a year. She keeps squinting at me as though she's trying to recall the face."

Drummond turned at the bedroom door. "Call her, give her your apologies and my love."

"Oh, that'll do it. Drum, couldn't I just put Tom Keegan on a bus tomorrow?"

"No." He disappeared into the bedroom.

"Oh," Gage muttered to himself. "Well, don't sugarcoat it, pal, give it to me straight. One thing I can't stand, it's a ditherer."

Chapter Seven

Although Hollywood is world-renowned as a place of glitz and glamor, the district of that name covers a vast area, and much of it is seedy, bearing as much resemblance to its movie persona as a cellar does to the upstairs ballroom.

Driving their respective cars – Gage's a silver Volvo estate – they drew up to Keegan's apartment building just before nine. Too close to the roar of Venice Boulevard, the building was a two-story, prefabricated structure, ageing badly, its stucco stained and cracked, its pathetic plantings dust-smothered, dying or dead. The sidewalk and the short flagged path leading to the entrance were littered with husks from two spindly palm trees that stood, drooping like wounded sentinels, loyally guarding the place to their dying breath.

Drummond and Gage crunched up the path to the recessed door, the Lieutenant using his flashlight to check the names on the mailbox-and-bell panel.

"He's not here."

"You didn't get an apartment number?"

"We got dick from this guy except four-five-nine Lomita on a hardware delivery slip."

"But on Monday, at the station, you said you'd send somebody home with him, see if you could locate a relative to look after him."

Gage pushed a button. "I did. I sent a uniform, but I went up to San Francisco and haven't spoken to the guy since."

"Yeah?" The distorted, metallic demand crackled from the speaker.

"I'm sorry to disturb you, sir . . ."

"You bein' funny, asshole?"

"I beg your pardon, ma'am. Could you tell me which button to press for Mister Keegan?"

"Don't know any Keegan."

"Tom Keegan . . . six feet tall, strong-looking, short gray hair."

"I tol' yuh, I don't know any Keegan."

"Ma'am, this is the police . . ."

"Apartment six, out back."

"Thank you so much."

Drummond laughed. "Gage, you sure have a way with women."

"Public relations," sighed Gage, pressing six. "Time was, back in the good old days, when you could kick their door down, snap a coupla ribs, shoot the dog . . . now it's please and thank you. I tell you, Drum, all the *fun* has gone out of the job."

The speaker scratched again. "Yes?"

Gage glanced at Drummond. The totality of human fear seemed encapsulated in that one word.

"Mister Keegan . . . Tom? This is Lieutenant Gage . . . from West LA station?" There was a lengthy pause. "Tom?"

"What do you want, Lieutenant?"

"I have Doctor Drummond here with me. We'd like to speak to you."

"Doctor Drummond?" Keegan sounded incredulous.

Drummond moved closer to the speaker. "Tom, we have something to say to you. May we come in?"

The door-lock buzzed and clicked open.

There are many Los Angeles apartment buildings that are bad on the outside, better on the inside. The owner has just so much money, and what there is, is spent for the tenants' pleasure, not on external cosmetics. Four-five-nine Lomita was not one of these buildings.

"Jesus Christ," Gage muttered as they entered the hallway.

It was a small square, lit by a single naked bulb, featureless except for the concrete stairs on the left, and the reeking bags and boxes of garbage stacked and strewn beneath them. As Gage played his flashlight over the mound, something unseen scuttled away, claws scratching for purchase on plastic.

"It must be trash collection day," said Gage. "Looks like they've collected for the street."

A narrow corridor faced them. They went down it, Gage using the flashlight on door numbers. The odor of cooking and the stench of other things thickened to a choking miasma as they reached the end and found Keegan's door.

"God bless America," murmured Gage, rapping the door. "Not two miles from here, people buy diamond earrings for their poodles, and go into trauma if a fingernail breaks."

"Who is it?" Keegan's question came through the insubstantial door.

"It's still Lieutenant Gage, Tom."

As dead-bolts were thrown back and a chain released, pathetic precautions since one good kick would have disintegrated the hardboard paneling, Gage arched expressive brows at Drummond. "Scared shitless. The bank trauma or something else?"

"I shall do my best to find out."

The door peeked open. Keegan's haunted eyes checked them out, underwent a transformation to relief as they alighted on Paul Drummond.

He opened the door wider, and they entered, each reacting to the other with subtle expressions of surprise, bewilderment, and dismay as they quickly scanned the apartment, a sad euphemism for a single twelve-by-twelve

83

room, with a bathroom to the left, which they could see through its open door, and an integral kitchenette barely bigger than a clothes closet.

The living room was a tip; accommodation reflecting a mind in disarray. A single iron-frame bed, occupying the wall facing the door, obviously also served as a seat, since there was no chair in the room. A scarred coffee table, littered with debris – beer cans, fast-food containers, an overflowing tin ashtray – sat beside the bed. To the right, an ancient TV set perched upon a chest of drawers. Also to the right, a shallow clothes cupboard intruded into the room.

All this the two men took in instantly, but it was the wall behind the bed that captured their attention. It was covered entirely, floor to ceiling, side to side, with photographs, obviously gleaned from books and magazines, of the Vietnam war.

Staring at it, Drummond and Gage exchanged glances before turning to Keegan.

Drummond smiled. "Hello, Tom, good to see you."

As they shook hands, Drummond studied the man. Keegan, wearing a red-check shirt and jeans, was barefoot, unshaven, his features creased, as though he had been awakened by their arrival. His eyes, while no longer so specifically fearful, still held the tormented look Drummond had seen at the police station, the look of a man who had somehow lost control of, and tangible contact with, his environment.

Drummond had witnessed a not-dissimilar look many times, among schizophrenics in psychiatric hospitals, and this affliction now presented itself to him as a possible cause of Keegan's demeanor, and of his traumatic reaction to regression. Then again, having difficulty with concentration, schizophrenics did not usually readily accept hypnosis, as Keegan had done. So maybe there was nothing there.

Increasingly, Keegan was becoming not only a man Drummond wanted to help, but a case of irresistible interest.

He said, "Tom, I have a proposal for you. You've asked me for help, and I'm going to give it to you. But I don't want to leave our first session until next Monday, I want to start right away. I have a practice in Palm Desert, near Palm Springs in the Coachella Valley. I'd like you to come with me now. I'll put you into a comfortable motel near my office, and see you every day. Is that possible for you?"

Keegan stared blankly at him. "Now?"

"Yes, I'm driving there tonight, it's a two-hour drive. Are you working at anything, d'you have a job?"

Keegan shook his head. A light of understanding and pleasure appeared in his eyes. "Sure, I'll go with you, Doc. How long will it be for?"

"I don't know, depends on the progress you make. Is there anyone you need to tell about going away? A friend . . . a relative?"

The lost, uncertain look returned. "No."

"Okay, get your stuff together, whatever you need."

The prospect of leaving the place, of solid support, of immediate treatment, transformed and galvanized Keegan. Bustling, he opened the tall cupboard, took out a cheap cardboard suitcase, packed the few sweaters, shirts and underwear contained in the chest of drawers, put on a pair of socks and battered moccasins.

Drummond said, "Tom, d'you have a garbage bag? You may be away a while, we'd better clear this stuff away."

"Sure." Keegan brought one from the kitchenette, swept up the debris from the table, returned to the kitchen and emptied the tiny refrigerator.

During this activity, Drummond was noting Keegan's revitalized spirit, his co-ordination. He was functioning perfectly, without a hint of spasticity. Because, thought Drummond, he's functioning in the now, totally focussed on the present. It was the past that caused Keegan's problems. And the past that had to be revealed.

"The bathroom, Tom . . . shaving gear, toothbrush? And maybe you want to take a pee before we hit the road?"

"Sure."

Keegan went in, closing the door.

"Neat," smiled Gage. "The power of suggestion."

"I didn't want to say this in front of him." Drummond indicated the wall of photographs. "What d'you make of this?"

Gage shrugged. "An interest in the war."

"It's a bloody obsession. Check for army service, Dick, get details, call me. This could be a good place to start looking for his past, maybe the only place we'll need."

"Will do. Jeez, the change in this guy when you said you were taking him out of here."

"Because I excited him, gave him hope. And that gives me hope. His mind's all screwed up, but I feel there's nothing intrinsically wrong with him. He'll be okay if he can get his memory back, I'm sure. And maybe he'll nail the Mar Vista boys for you yet."

The lavatory flushed and Keegan came out with a plastic bag, threw it into the case and snapped the locks. "I'm ready."

Drummond asked, "How many door keys d'you have, Tom?"

Keegan frowned. "Two for the main door, two for this."

"If you give a set to the Lieutenant, he'll keep an eye on the place for you. Is that okay with you?"

"Sure."

Behind Keegan, Gage grinned and nodded, applauding the move. In Keegan's absence, he'd be able to search the place at his leisure.

Keegan handed over the keys.

Drummond said, "Nothing else you want to take with you?"

Keegan looked around the room, his gaze lingering for the briefest moment on the wall of photographs, and shook his head. "No."

"Okay, let's go."

In the car, on Interstate Ten, Drummond quickly became aware of a dichotomy in Keegan's behavior, in his attitude towards Drummond, or to being alone with him. Accepting the fact that people interact differently in a twosome than when in a threesome, he had expected his relationship with Keegan to change after they left Dick Gage, but did not anticipate such a radical change. The man beside him was patently nervous, as though afraid of him or something he represented, and yet Drummond sensed that Keegan wanted to be there.

Recalling his own feelings when, as a student, he would suddenly find himself alone with a teacher or an eminent psychologist, how different from sharing the man's presence with other students, how unnerving to be the focus of his attention, Drummond sought a way of breaking down whatever barrier his own persona – and perhaps title – was creating for Keegan.

"Ever been to Palm Springs, Tom?"

"No, I haven't, Doc."

Drummond glanced at him, smiling. "Paul. We're going to be spending a lot of time together, I want us to be friends. 'Doc' sounds kinda formal, hm?"

Keegan gave a nervous, acquiescent smile, but the hands in his lap continued their anxious washing.

"Ever been in the desert at all?"

"No." Then, a beat later, with a quickening of breath and a panicky edge to his voice, "I don't remember."

Drummond said quickly, soothingly, "Just relax, Tom, I'm not out to quiz you. I'm just making conversation. If you don't want to talk, that's fine, and if you'd rather I didn't talk, I'll shut up. But it's a longish drive and . . ."

"I don't mind you talking. It's just that . . . I don't know anything . . . can't remember anything . . ." Again, the hysteria, always there, barely below the surface, theatened to erupt.

"That's all right, just relax." He put out his hand and gripped Keegan's arm reassuringly. "Listen to me – I'm not going to ask you any more questions about the past, about what you've done or where you've been or what you know, okay? That way, you won't have to worry about finding an answer. I'll just talk, tell you about things, and if and when you feel like talking, go right ahead."

They drove in silence for a while, the Daimler purring along the freeway, which had grown quiet now that they had cleared the city.

"Beautiful car," Keegan said eventually, interrupting Drummond's reverie.

"Glad you like it," smiled Drummond, and almost asked, 'Do you drive?' but checked himself. "It was made for American freeways. If we had no speed limit, I could get home in an hour."

They lapsed into silence again, the comfort and smoothness of the heavy car soporific. Drummond glanced at Keegan and saw that his eyes were closed, head tilted back against the support.

As he invariably did with patients in hypnotic trance, he felt sympathy for Keegan's extreme vulnerability, sadness that a human life had gone so disastrously wrong.

Questions about the purpose of life had plagued him since youth, and while finally accepting the purely scientific explanation of chemical interaction for its development, he nevertheless believed that it was intended to be enjoyed, not lived in a state of fear, worry, panic and terror.

People were not affected by events or circumstances,

but by their attitude, their reaction to those things. It was all in the mind. Keegan's mental condition, his reaction to something in his past, was creating his private hell. It was up to Drummond to reveal that something, and to help Keegan to change his attitude towards it.

Keegan came awake with a startling jerk, eyes staring straight ahead at the illuminated road. "Up there with the gods . . . with magic eyes . . . he's the healer . . ."

Drummond shot a look at him, saw the rigidity of muscle, the quivering tension, not as chronic as in the hypnosis session, but bad enough. "Tom – are you awake?"

"Of course I'm awake. He can heal with his magic eyes . . . through the television. He cured him."

"Who cured who?"

"You don't believe it, do you? They're a great bunch of people here. You think they're stupid, but they're not. You should come and sit with them, talk to them, you'd learn something."

"Where are they, Tom? Who are the people?"

"My friends. They want to take me in, help me, so screw you."

"Tell me about your friends, describe them. I'm very interested."

"You're just saying that. You're patronizing me."

"No, really, I'm . . ."

High-pitched laughter. "There's golden father. There're two fathers . . . dozy father and golden father. You're like golden father. Why don't you wear gold? Gold heals everything. I want a golden tooth. I'm going to have all my teeth out and have gold ones put in. I've got no clothes. Those bastards have stolen all my clothes."

"Which bastards, Tom?" asked Drummond, convinced now that Keegan had flipped from sleep straight into psychosis, into an unreality that might or might not have its origins in fact.

Suddenly, the prospect of schizophrenia loomed large

in Drummond's mind, and with it the possibility that in taking Keegan to the Valley, he was wasting time and ought instead to be heading for a hospital.

But then: "Could we get some music on the radio, Paul?"

Drummond glanced at him. Keegan looked fine, the rigidity gone, features calm.

"Sure thing." He pressed buttons, got an easy-listening station, quiet instrumental with lyrical guitar. "What kind of music do you like?"

"Most. It relaxes me."

It did indeed relax him. Keegan resumed his head-back, eyes closed position, hands at peace in his lap.

Drummond took a chance at a question. "Want to tell me about your friends, Tom? I'd really like to hear about them."

"I haven't got any friends."

"The ones you mentioned a moment ago, when you woke up."

Keegan shook his head, eyes still closed. "I must've been dreaming."

Something clicked in Drummond's mind. Perhaps Keegan's illogical outpourings had not been psychotic after all. Maybe they were memories of real events, repressed in wakefulness, alive in sleep.

Drummond subscribed to Jungian theory that dreams were a process employed by the psyche to balance itself. Supposing Keegan *had* been programmed to forget certain aspects of his past, it was possible that his psyche was making an effort, through dreams, to counteract the deleterious effects of the program. Keegan's dreams might prove to be a major clue to his past.

"Do you dream much, Tom?"

"All the time. I have nightmares."

"What about?"

"I can never remember. Sometimes I wake up soaked in

sweat, and for a moment I can remember the dream, and I say to myself I'll remember this in the morning because it's so vivid, but in the morning it's gone."

"I want you to do something for me. I'm going to give you a pad and pen, and if you wake up from such a dream, I want you to write it down right away, no matter what the time. Put the light on and write it down. Will you do that? It could be very important to your recovery."

"Okay, Doc . . . Paul."

Drummond grinned. "Good, you're getting the hang of it. You just relax there, listen to the music. We're half-way to the Valley. Sleep, if you want. Maybe you can get a good dream in before we reach Palm Desert."

The miles slid by, devoured silently and effortlessly by the powerful car. The music continued with minimum interruption until eleven o'clock, when there was a break for news.

Drummond's mind focussed as the headlines opened with an update on the presidential campaign.

"Speaking to an audience of two thousand auto workers in Detroit tonight, Republican candidate Jack Crane continued his attack on the policies of his opponent Milton Byrne, accusing him of being a marshmallow towards the criminals, and rock-candy towards the tax-payer."

The newscast went to Jack Crane in fine, stentorian voice, "You good people know the value of money. If I were asked to give a representative example of an American tax-payer, I would, without hesitation, say the Detroit auto-worker. He works darned hard for what he gets, pays every last cent of his taxes as he goes, and is entitled to ask: what do I get for my money? Well, my friends, let me tell you what you'll get from Senator Milton 'It-Ain't-*My*-Money' Byrne . . ."

Drummond became aware, on the edge of his vision, of a sudden restiveness in Keegan. Apparently asleep, he rolled his head and grimaced as if in torment, trapped in a

91

nightmare. He groaned, murmured protestingly, worked his hands into knotted fists. Then, with a suddenness that startled Drummond, his eyes flew open, stared maniacally into Drummond's, and with a lightning movement he shot out a hand and snapped the radio off.

"Jesus," Drummond gasped, his involuntary jump swerving the Daimler across the lane.

Steadying the car, Drummond looked at Keegan who was now huddled forward, rocking against the restraining seat belt, his hands clamped over his ears with a fearful intensity.

"Tom . . . what happened? Come *on*, speak to me, tell me what scared you. Was it a dream . . . a nightmare?"

Keegan, still covering his ears, gave a faint headshake. "No. I don't know." A sob broke from him, an awful sound of desperation and despair. "My mind's all fucked up, Doc! I don't know what's happening to me!"

"Okay, Tom, take it easy, it's going to be all right, I promise you. Just lie back and try to relax. Come on, lie back."

With a sigh of capitulation, Keegan flopped back, eyes closed, cheeks wet with tears.

Drummond said, "Listen, I had planned to put you up in a motel near my office, but I've got a better idea. I've got a spare bedroom, a guest bedroom behind my house, it's really nice, very comfortable. If it's okay with you, I'd like you stay there."

Keegan whispered, "Sure. Anything, Doc. Just fix my goddamned head." He seemed to drift into an exhausted doze, repeating the plea. "Just fix my goddamned head."

From then until they arrived at the house, Keegan slept, silently and unmoving. And throughout that hour, Drummond's mind hummed and buzzed with theory, speculation and indecision. What precisely had triggered Keegan's reaction to the radio? Had it even been the radio, or something in a dream? *Was* Keegan psychotic,

92

schizophrenic? Should he now be in the care of a clinical psychiatrist?

Arriving at the house, he still hadn't come to any firm conclusion about any aspect of this sad, tormented man.

Regarding himself in the rear-view mirror, he did something he often did in times of indecision and dilemma – he asked his subconscious mind for guidance. In moments, his inner voice told him: cool it. Work on Keegan for forty-eight hours, see what happens.

Satisfied, he gently shook Keegan awake.

Chapter Eight

The guest bedroom behind the double garage was a spacious eighteen by eighteen feet, with a bathroom and a mini-kitchen, which made the room completely self-contained, and suitable as staff accommodation.

Sliding glass doors opened to sun terraces on two sides, the southern aspect facing the Santa Rosa and San Jacinto mountain ranges, the eastern terrace capturing a daylight view across the Ironwood Country Club and Living Desert Reserve.

The furnishing and decoration, typical of Valley homes, was uncluttered and colorful, the fabrics of bedspread, chair coverings, and drapes done in cream, sand, turquoise and terra cotta, the traditional Navajo colours.

It was almost midnight when Drummond unlocked the door, turned on bedside lights from a wall-switch, and started the air-conditioning to freshen the room.

Tom Keegan remained by the door, still dazed by sleep, his expression a compound of admiration for the room and inability to believe his good fortune at having it at his disposal.

Drummond grinned. "Will this do?"

"*Do*? It's beautiful."

"Well, I want you to make yourself at home, Tom." He placed Keegan's suitcase on the bed. "The bathroom's through there. Tomorrow we'll stock the kitchen, so you can make a drink or snack when you want, when I'm at the office. There's a bedside radio . . . TV over there." He pulled aside one of the sun-proof drapes, indicating the sliding doors. "Sun chairs out here to relax in and look at the mountains. That's what I want you to do – relax, make like you're on vacation. I don't want you to worry about a thing, and certainly not about hypnosis. We'll go at your pace, won't do anything you don't want to do – okay?"

Keegan heaved a sigh, of physical weariness, of mental exhaustion. "Fine, Doc. I don't know how to thank you . . ."

"Don't. And it's Paul – remember? Try and get a good night's sleep. If you need me, dial nine on the phone, it'll ring by my bedside. If you want a shower, the water's always hot, it's electric. If you want TV . . . have you used a remote control?"

"No."

Drummond took the control from the top of the set, pointed it, showing Keegan the buttons. "Press this for on and off." The set hissed to life. "Then these buttons to change programs." He zipped across the channels, bringing up a game show, a sitcom, a religious program, a Bogart movie, a newscast.

He paused at the newscast. The image of Jack Crane, in mid-close-up, standing at a podium, was haranguing his audience, ". . . his support for gun control. Is he not aware that hunting is as much an American tradition as apple-pie? Does Milton Byrne not *know* that hunting is as instinctive and necessary as breathing to millions of honest, hard-working, God-fearing Americans? . . . and that in this state, to name but one, *sixty percent* of adults hold hunting licenses? Well, folks, I'll tell you right now, if Milton 'Sock-it-to-America' Byrne gets his way, you'll be taking to the woods with sling-shots and bee-bee guns . . . and I wouldn't even bet on the bee-bee guns!"

Over roars of laughter and derisive hooting and whistling,

Crane was bellowing, "But you *can* bet on this – JACK CRANE AIN'T ABOUT TO LET IT HAPPEN!"

From his immersion in Crane's performance, Drummond became aware of its effect on the man standing beside him. Keegan was staring, saucer-eyed, at the screen, the by now familiar rigidity taking hold of his body, sweat glistening on his face, that hunted-animal aspect Drummond had witnessed in the hypnosis session now very evident.

Drummond shot a glance at the image of Jack Crane, then back to Keegan, connecting this reaction to what had happened in the car, to the fact that Crane had been speaking when Keegan had snapped off the radio.

He demanded, "Tom, what is it? What's upsetting you? Is it this man? Is it Jack Crane?"

As though with an effort to break a hold the televised image had over him, Keegan wheeled away, clutching his head, made for the bed and slumped down there, bent over, rocking, covering his ears as though to shut out the sound of Crane's voice.

Muting the TV sound, Drummond went to Keegan, crouched down beside him, urging him, "Tom, come on, talk to me. Is it Crane? Was it his voice on the car radio that upset you? Do you know this man?"

Sobbing, his voice breaking with hysteria and frustration, Keegan croaked out, "I don't *know*. It's my head. Something . . . happens."

"*What* happens? Can you describe it? Is it physical . . . like a pain? Or something that happens to your mind . . . a certain thought, a fear?"

All Drummond got was more head-shaking.

He switched off the TV set. "All right, Tom, it's gone, the threat has gone. Clear it from your mind. I'm going across to the house to get you something to help you sleep. You get into bed, I'll be back in a minute."

When Drummond returned, Keegan was lying in bed,

staring at the ceiling, his features fixed in that lost, bewildered expression from which they so seldom strayed.

Drummond placed a small writing pad and pencil on the bedside table, offered Keegan two capsules, went to the kitchen and drew a glass of water.

"The pad is for any thoughts at all, Tom, not just dreams. Write whatever you feel like – fears, impressions, feelings, anything at all. Dial nine if you need me, any time, don't be afraid to disturb me. Tom, listen to me – you're no longer alone. You've got help. You're safe here. We're going to work together to get to the root of your problem, so just try to relax, and give yourself a chance, okay?"

Keegan nodded.

"Goodnight, then. We'll have breakfast on the terrace, looking at the mountains. There is nothing like mountains to put things into perspective."

Closing the door, Drummond angled across a wide paved path to his kitchen door, the garage being set back from the house to clear the view for the kitchen window. Entering, he made a mug of weakish instant coffee, took it through into the living room and sank wearily into a deep armchair.

"Brother," he sighed aloud, "that was one helluva trip to the city."

His thoughts wandered sequentially over all that had happened. The forensic session, Keegan's incredible reaction, meeting Karen Beal, inviting her to the Malibu *house*, f'Godsake, and to the Valley, reading her article, the business response to it, the improbable conversation with Dick Gage, his own decision to bring Keegan to the Valley, Keegan's apartment with its wall of Vietnam photographs, and Keegan's weird reaction to – what? – on the journey in.

Some trip.

Keegan and Crane.

Could there possibly be a connection between a mentally disturbed maybe-laborer and the incumbent governor of California and Republican presidential candidate?

Was it the voice and/or image of Jack Crane that had triggered such a violent reaction in Keegan?

Was it that Crane's voice reminded Keegan of someone else or of a past event, and so caused the reaction?

Certainly, there appeared to be one source of common ground worthy of investigation – Vietnam. Keegan's wall plastered with photographs of the conflict . . . Jack Crane, a revered hero of that same war.

Drummond experienced regret that he hadn't paid more specific attention to those photographs, and a sudden urge to do so. Still, he had asked Dick Gage to check Keegan's background for military service. Perhaps a connection between Keegan and Crane would come to light in that material.

Meanwhile, he mused, finishing the coffee, he would dig away at Keegan's confused and tormented mind, see what came to light in *that* material.

Thursday.

Drummond awoke at seven, showered, dressed for a day of consultation in a dark blue business suit, one of eight suits in varying shades of blue and gray in his wardrobe, and, in shirtsleeves, prepared breakfast of fresh orange juice, cereal, scrambled eggs, grilled bacon, coffee and toast. This he transferred to a glass-topped, wrought-iron table on the rear terrace of the house, the eggs and bacon to a warming trolley beside it.

There was no response to his knock on the guest-room door. Opening the door, he saw Keegan, up and dressed in jeans and a blue denim shirt, sitting on the terrace overlooking Ironwood. Studying him, Drummond saw in his posture and expression the preoccupied bewilderment a man who has suffered a terrible psychic shock, who has

98

lost something vital to his life, and cannot believe it has happened.

Drummond called, "Good morning," and crossed the room to the open door.

Keegan turned, smiled, though he seemed nervous in this new environment. "Good morning."

"Admiring our view, huh?"

"It's beautiful. I watched the sun come up. It reminded me that I hardly ever see a sunrise in LA"

Drummond smiled. "Sounds like we have the makings of a desert convert. What you're looking at there is the Ironwood Country Club, beyond that the Living Desert Reserve. It has a zoo we'll take a look at some time, if you like animals. This is country-club country, there are dozens of them in the Valley, it's a golfer's paradise. Some incredible houses, too, with model homes we can look at, if you're interested in that sort of thing."

Drummond was doing some subtle probing, trying for reaction from Keegan on a variety of interests. But Keegan continued to gaze out across the broad, flat valley as though he hadn't heard.

He asked, "What mountains are those?"

"The San Bernadinos. That whole area is the Joshua Tree National Monument. Pretty rugged place, very popular with campers and hikers."

Keegan turned to face the mountains that rose close behind the house. "And these?"

"This first range is officially known as the Santa Rosa National Scenic Area. The taller range behind it are the San Jacinto Mountains – pronounced as an aitch, spelled with a jay – but usually they're all referred to as the San Jacintos. You like mountains, Tom?"

Gazing up at the five-thousand feet peaks, their stark granite faces sharp against the deep blue morning sky, Keegan nodded. "They're . . . solid."

"Yes. Dependable?"

"Yes, dependable. They'll be here tomorrow – right?"

Studying him, Drummond nodded. "Count on it. Come on, breakfast is waiting. I hope you're hungry, I've cooked up a mountain of eggs and bacon, kinda goes with the territory."

Keegan ate well, but with the air of absorption that accompanied all his activity, rather than with concentration on the good food.

Thoughout the meal, Drummond kept the conversation light and general, talking about the Valley and its people, slipping in the occasional probing question in attempts to draw from Keegan clues about his background, but eliciting nothing.

Finally, Drummond decided on a more direct approach.

"My office isn't far from here, about a mile, on El Paseo. I've got appointments this morning, Tom, but I'll be back for lunch, then I'd like you to come down with me this afternoon, make a start. Is that all right with you?"

Keegan brushed at his mouth nervously with the paper napkin, crushed the paper into a ball. "Sure, that's fine. I want to start. I want to get better, Paul. This . . . thing . . ."

"What exactly is 'this thing', Tom? Can you try to describe it? I'd like you just to talk about it, about yourself, your thoughts, feelings, dreams. We'll be doing this in hypnosis, but I want to hear it without hypnosis, to compare the two. Did you dream last night . . . did you write anything down?"

Keegan nodded. "I dreamt about the house again . . ."

"Again? You've had the dream before?"

"Yes."

"How often?"

"A lot."

"Tell me about it. I'll read what you wrote later."

"I'm in this house. It's old. Well, part of it's old, part

100

of it's new. It's a weird place, new on the outside, old and crumbling on the inside. I'm inside it, downstairs. And a fire breaks out, in the attic. The whole of the top floor is an inferno, and I know I have to get out but I can't. I'm trapped in there, and I know the fire's going to get me and I'm going to die, but I can't find the key to the door."

"And what happens?"

Keegan shrugged. "I wake up. The fire never gets to me, it's just there, roaring away, flames shooting down the stairs. It's terrifying. Does it mean anything, Paul, or is it just a crazy dream?"

"I think it means a great deal, but we'll talk about it later. The most important thing I want to know from you, Tom, is the current extent of your memory. I believe it's already beginning to improve. At the West LA police station – and in your apartment – you told me you couldn't remember anything. I presumed you meant before you woke up in hospital?"

"Yes. I remember everything since then."

"And yet you've just told me you've had the fire dream a lot of times. Surely that means you remember having had it *before* you woke up in hospital?"

Keegan stared at him. "Oh, wow. Yes. I . . . I haven't had it since then . . . so it must have been before."

"Good. So, there you are, you've remembered something. I told you your memory would probably start to return once you were back in familiar surroundings. Now I want you to get familiar with these surroundings, feel at home and safe here, Tom, just relax, enjoy the sun and the mountains, and we'll get you remembering more, I promise you."

Keegan's heavy frown signified his intense frustration. "It's like you feel when you try to recall somebody's name . . . someone you know so well . . . and it's ridiculous that you should forget it. You *know* their name, goddamnit, but it won't come. I have feelings like that about the whole of my life – before I woke up in hospital. I can't remember anything, Paul . . . my past life is like a big black hole. I don't know who I am . . . or what I've done . . . if I've got any family . . ."

"Tom, listen to me. Let's go back to that somebody's name we can't remember. Or the telephone number. Or a dream. What do we do about it? If we push for it, it seems to slip further and further away. But if we let it go, relax on it, chances are it'll suddenly pop up from our subconscious mind. Always trust your subconscious; it's there to serve you. Stop trying so hard, Tom; you're driving memory away. A moment ago, without trying, you suddenly recalled having had the fire dream in your pre-hospital life. It has happened once, it'll happen again. So, let go – and trust."

Keegan glimmered a smile. "Okay. Thanks, Paul."

Drummond checked his watch. "I must go. You can do the dishes. The house is yours, wander where you will. I'll be back at one."

On the drive down to his office, Drummond thought about Keegan's dream. The problem for the analyst with dreams was that, since they were invariably presented to the consciousness of the dreamer in symbolic form, the symbolism had to be interpreted, and was therefore subjective, open to differing opinions. Nevertheless, certain symbols were generally accepted within the fields of Psychiatry and Psychology, and Drummond felt privileged to have been privy, in Keegan's dream, to outstandingly clear-cut, and immensely revealing example of symbolism.

To dream of a house is to dream of oneself. Any simple drawing of a house, a child's for instance, takes on anthropomorphic features, with windows for eyes, a door for the mouth, the pathway a tongue. Keegan's dream house was new on the outside, old and decaying on the inside. This, to Drummond, was how Keegan saw himself – externally a young, physically strong man, internally a decrepit mess.

In his dream, it was the attic, the top story, that was ablaze. For attic, read head, brain, mind. His mind was aflame and out of control, theatening the entire structure, his very life. He knew it and tried to escape, but could not . . . because he couldn't find the key – because he couldn't understand what was wrong with him.

But more revealing to Drummond than this classically straightforward interpretation was the fact that Keegan had experienced the dream *before* hospitalization, *before* the trauma of the Mar Vista violence. In other words, Keegan's mental instability, and possibly his amnesia, had resulted from a previous experience, and had probably only been exacerbated by the kidnapping.

This proof, this vital clue, gave Drummond a more specific time-frame in which to search for the source of Keegan's malaise. For the time being, at least, he could set aside the Mar Vista experience, and concentrate on Keegan's past.

Intuitively, Vietnam loomed large as a direction for his search. That wall of photographs spelled obsession, and, like dreams, obsessions were signposts pointing to wellsprings of anxiety.

So, Vietnam it would be.

Vietnam . . . and a hero of that war.

Jack Crane.

Governor Jack Crane.

Presidential candidate Jack Crane.

Come November seven, more than likely President-elect Jack Crane.

And in January, Jack Crane – President of the United States.

Wheeling the Daimler into a parking space behind his office, Drummond cut the engine and sat there for a moment, pondering the improbable – a link between Tom Keegan and the future president.

Improbable, but not impossible.

Nothing in life was impossible, not even where presidents were concerned.

In principle, Watergate should have been impossible, but wasn't. It happened.

Drummond frowned, stirred by a sense of unease that he should think of Watergate. Where had that nudge come from?

Dismissing it, reminding himself that flights of presupposition had no place in factual analysis, he locked the car and headed across the lot.

Chapter Nine

Returning to the house at one, Drummond found Keegan lying on the bed in the air-conditioned guest room, his mood as relaxed as Drummond had ever seen it, which was not saying very much, but at least he appeared to have settled into this new environment, and to have been mentally preparing himself for treatment.

"I've just been lying here, trying to blank my mind, shut out the fear, just let the thoughts come. But it's hard. I feel as though there's an invisible threat, something like one of those metal balls that knock down buildings, suspended over my head, ready to drop and squash me if I think the wrong thoughts."

Drummond sat on the edge of the bed. "Do you have any idea, any feelings, about the subject you mustn't think about?"

Keegan shook his head. "It's a feeling that I mustn't think about anything, except what's happening right now. It's okay to think about anything that happened since I woke up in hospital, but not before."

"And if you do try to think about the past?"

"Something terrible will happen. The ball will drop . . . but it isn't really a ball. It's . . . death. A thunderbolt. I don't know what, but I know it'll kill me."

Drummond patted Keegan's shin. "Okay, Tom, just relax. Huh, I keep telling you to relax as though you wouldn't if you could, but I want you to try and keep as calm as possible, allow your subconscious to help you.

Come on, we'll have a bite to eat . . ." Drummond started to get up.

"I remembered another dream."

Drummond sat down again. "Great. Is this another you've had a lot of times?"

Keegan's brow furrowed. "I don't know. What I mean is – I don't know whether it's a dream or a movie I've seen or something I remember. God, I hate being so vague."

"Don't worry about that, just tell me what it's about."

"It's kind of in slow motion . . . weird. There are a lot of green men . . . in a garden . . . and they keep falling down and getting up, laughing, really laughing, falling down in hysterics, acting like they're crazy.

"That's it?"

"That's all I remember."

"Can you describe the men? Are they full-sized humans, real people?"

"I think so."

"What d'you mean by green, Tom?"

"It's what they are – green all over."

"Like soldiers . . . in camouflage?"

Keegan's hands made an almost involuntary movement to clasp his head. "Maybe. I don't know."

Drummond could see the tension surge through him, as though an electric current had been activated, and he responded quickly to stop the flow. "Tom, forget the dream. Clear it from your mind. I want you relaxed for this afternoon. We'll talk about it later. Come on, let's eat. How does mushroom soup and a chicken sandwich grab you?"

By three o'clock Keegan was stretched out on the couch. The blinds were closed, the room dim, temperature-controlled to a comfortable seventy degrees. Drummond had covered him with a paper-thin blanket, more a psychological than a physical comfort, a kind of woven womb

106

that patients in the vulnerable hypnotic state, particularly women, found reassuring.

On a table near Keegan's head stood a small battery-operated alarm clock, its tick metronomic and hypnotic, surprisingly audible in the silence of the room.

Drummond allowed Keegan time to settle, to adjust to the room and to the prospect of hypnosis, before beginning.

"All right, Tom, let's take it nice and easy. As I did before at the station, I'm going to ask you some questions before I hypnotise you, and repeat them in hypnosis. If at any time you don't wish to answer a question, just say so or say nothing. You're under no obligation whatsoever. I'll be recording all the sessions we have here, and the machine is running now. Tom, what is your full name?"

"Thomas Connor Keegan."

"How old are you?"

"I don't remember."

"When is your birthday?"

"I don't remember."

"It's all right, take it easy. That may be the answer to a lot of my questions, so don't let them get to you. 'Connor' and 'Keegan' sound Irish. Was your father Irish?"

"I don't remember him."

"Do you remember any of your family?"

"No. No one."

"You have no photographs of any of your family?"

"No."

"But you have a lot of photographs of something else."

Hesitation. "Yes."

"What are they of?"

"You saw them."

"I want you to tell me."

"The . . . Vietnam war."

"Did you collect them, cut them out, stick them on the wall?"

Hesitation. "Yes. I mean, it must have been me, I don't remember doing it."

"Why do you think you did it?"

Signs of discomfort now, hands shifting beneath the blanket, breathing irregular. "I . . . I'm interested in the war."

"Any particular aspect of the war?"

"No."

"Just a general interest?"

"I guess so."

"Were you in the services, Tom?"

"No! I mean, I don't remember. Sometimes I . . ."

"Sometimes you what?"

"Sometimes I get the feeling I *was* in the army . . . when I look at the photographs. It's like I was there."

"In Vietnam?"

"Yes. But it's like a dream. It's like that dream of the green men . . . or perhaps it was a movie. Christ, I don't *know*, Paul!"

"You will, I promise you. Okay, that's enough questions to be going on with. I'm going to relax you into hypnosis now. I want you to clear your mind, consciously settle down and listen to the ticking of the clock . . . just listen to the clock, Tom, and think of a windshield wiper. A slow . . . windshield wiper . . . moving . . . to the rhythm . . . of the clock . . . side . . . to side . . . back . . . and forth. Now, close your eyes . . . and concentrate all your attention . . . on the top of your head, on the muscles in your scalp . . ."

By the time Drummond had reached the toes, Keegan was deeply relaxed, breathing slowly and regularly, seemingly at peace.

"Good. I want you to talk to me, Tom, to tell me the earliest thing you remember."

Keegan made to speak, cleared his throat, licked dry lips, spoke in a husky, sleepy voice. "The nurse . . .

black nurse . . . bending over me, saying, 'wake up'. Didn't know where I was . . . what had happened to me. Couldn't remember."

"Anything earlier than that?"

"Dreams. It's all dreams . . . movies . . . playing in my head."

"Tell me about the dreams."

"I told you. The house on fire . . . the green men in the garden, laughing."

"No other dreams?"

"No."

Drummond repeated the questions about age and family he had asked before hypnosis, but got the same responses.

Then came his first surprise.

"I want you to go deeper, Tom, and tell me about the pictures in the apartment."

"What pictures?"

"The photographs."

"What photographs?"

The hairs stirred on Drummond's neck.

"I want you to describe your apartment at four-five-nine Lomita to me, in detail, from entering the door."

"It's just a room . . . bathroom and kitchen on the left . . . wardrobe cupboard on the right. There's a bed, a coffee table . . ."

"Let's stay with the bed a moment. What is behind it?"

"A wall."

"What is on the wall?"

Hesitation. "Paint."

"Nothing else?"

"No."

"No pictures?"

"Used to be."

"What used to be?"

"It was crap . . . picture of a laughing clown. I couldn't stand looking at it . . . threw it out."

"What did you put in its place?"

"Nothing."

Denial, mused Drummond. A psychological response to an unpalatable situation or event. Here was a mind which, in normal consciousness, was obsessed with the Vietnam war, but in hypnosis was denying the interest.

Dig deeper.

"Tom, tell me what you know about the Vietnam war."

From the reaction he got, Drummond might well have yelled "Fire!" in Keegan's ear.

"Nothing!" Keegan's body went rigid, then he shot up into sitting position, trembling and shaking, staring wide-eyed at the wall, hands clawing at the blanket, sweat glistening on his skin. "I know nothing! Can't talk . . . mustn't talk . . ."

"Why not? Who says you mustn't talk about Vietnam?"

"It'll hurt." Keegan's face crumpled with agony. "Not a word . . . it'll hurt . . . don't know anything." His hands came up and slapped against his head, covering his ears. He shook his head violently, as though shutting out Drummond's voice.

"All right, Tom, forget I asked the question. I didn't ask the question. Relax. You're safe. Lie down and relax."

Keegan underwent the remarkable transformation Drummond had witnessed in the forensic session, suddenly shedding all signs of anxiety, deflating like an untied balloon, folding backwards into complete repose.

So – the word "Vietnam" was a trigger. Convinced now that Keegan had been programmed to react with terror to any attempted recall, by hypnosis, of at least certain aspects of his past, and undoubtedly his military past, Drummond knew that the restoration of Keegan's memory would be very difficult.

110

Whoever had done the programming had done a first-class job; Keegan's terror was intense and real, and, to judge from his bug-eyed expression and the plea "It'll hurt", possibly coupled with some form of nightmare hallucination involving pain.

Drummond was now faced with the dilemma of how to help Keegan, without causing him awful distress and possible mental injury. Too many precipitations into the terror state might send him into permanent psychosis, and yet to do nothing might achieve precisely the same result.

Action had to be taken, and until Dick Gage came through with details of Keegan's military record – the existence of which Drummond now felt certain – he decided the best direction would be to test Keegan's reaction to different levels of hypnosis, and, in the process, to try to unearth any other trigger words.

To begin, he chose a circuitous route. "Tom, I want you to listen intently to my voice . . . to the slow . . . steady . . . ticking of the clock . . . and go deeper . . . much deeper . . . into relaxation."

Drummond worked for fifteen minutes, his voice a somnolent drone, inducing feelings of sleepiness, drowsiness, heaviness, evoking imagery of a peaceful, bucolic setting, of trees and flowers and grass.

"You are in a garden . . . your garden. Do you see it, Tom?"

"Yes."

"Who else is there with you?"

"Nobody."

"Can you hear laughter?"

Hesitation. "Not here."

"Where is it you hear the laughter?"

"Another garden."

"Go there. Tell me when you are standing in that garden."

Drummond watched the change take place, from total

relaxation to the stirring of discomfort, the frown of disconcertion ruffling the smoothness of the brow.

"I'm . . . there."

"Describe what you see."

"Men . . . green men . . ."

"How many?"

"A lot."

"Ten?"

"More."

"Fifty?"

"More."

"What are they doing?"

"Laughing . . . acting crazy . . . falling down . . . killing themselves laughing."

"How are they dressed?"

"In green . . . and black."

"Describe their faces."

"Green and . . . dirty . . . like clowns."

"Like the picture of the clown you threw away?"

"He was laughing . . . hated him . . . couldn't look at him."

"Because he reminded you of the laughing men?"

"Yes. Hated them."

"Are they laughing at you?"

"No."

"What are they laughing at?"

"Nothing. They're just crazy . . ."

"Are they drunk?"

"No."

"Who *are* they, Tom?"

"Don't know."

"They're soldiers, aren't they?"

"No!"

"They are soldiers in camouflage."

"No!"

"And you are one of them."

"No! I'm not one of them."

"But you *are* a soldier. You're in the *army*."

"NO!"

With a cry of protest, Keegan shot upright, locked in shaking trauma.

Drummond said, "Tom – clear that garden from your mind! Return to the first garden . . . the peaceful garden. Lie down again . . . and relax."

Again, Keegan settled, as blissfully as though nothing had happened.

"Vietnam" and "army". Whoever had programmed Keegan had made certain that, even in deep trance, he would never reveal whatever it was he had witnessed or had participated in during his service. The laughing green men could not be taken at face value. They appeared in this form in Keegan's dream, and therefore were probably symbolic of something else. Drummond felt an even greater impatience to hear details of Keegan's army service, and would call Dick Gage later, from the house.

Meanwhile, he decided to try for one more trigger word from Keegan, then call it a day. This kind of probing would have to be taken very slowly.

"Tom, I want you to go deeper still. I want you to imagine that you're standing at the top of a long, golden staircase in a beautiful house . . . and with every step you descend, you will go deeper and deeper into relaxation . . . deeper and deeper into peace and tranquility. There are twenty steps down, so start down now . . . nineteen . . . eighteen . . . seventeen . . ."

When Drummond reached five, he said, "Stop here for a moment. Look across the white marble hall to the front door. There's a man standing there. He has come to visit you. It's the man whose voice you heard on the car radio . . . the man you saw and heard on television last night . . ."

Signs of agitation, a body spasm that jolted Keegan from deep inertia.

"Do you know this man?"

Labored breathing, a spastic shake of the head.

"Have you ever *met* this man?"

"No!"

"Do you know his name?"

Silence, yet in it Drummond sensed affirmation.,

"Can you tell me his name?"

Another headshake, a determined tightening of the lips.

"Tom, say his name."

Silence – and growing terror.

"Will you cross the floor to meet him?"

"No!"

"Tom, this is very important . . . *have you ever met Jack Crane*?"

Keegan exploded a cry of protest, "NO! I DON'T KNOW! LEAVE ME ALONE!"

"All right, no more questions. The man has gone. You're safe. You're on the staircase . . . walking back up to peace of mind. Six . . . seven . . . eight . . . becoming calm and very relaxed with every step you take . . ."

At the count of twenty Keegan opened his eyes, turned his head and gave Drummond a wintry smile. "Was it okay? Did I go under?"

"What d'you remember?"

Keegan shrugged. "Not much. I felt very relaxed. Did you ask me any questions?"

"This was kind of a test session, to see how you took to hypnosis here."

"How'd I do?"

Drummond smiled. "You're a natural."

Drummond managed to connect with Dick Gage around six. The Lieutenant came on out of breath, shouting something unintelligible and laughing to someone across the room.

"Gage."

"That's life in the LAPD – just one long office party."

"Hi, Drum. Are you kidding? We're allowed one laugh a week and you just heard it."

"Did you get it?"

"What? Did you crack a joke?"

"Keegan's army record. He does have one?"

"Oh, sure. I've got it here somewhere. I was going to call you tonight. Here y'go. Thomas Connor Keegan served four very undistinguished years in the army, three in Vietnam, as a box pusher – a supply clerk. He was a private going in and a private coming out. In 'Seventy-two he suffered a nervous breakdown, and was given a psychological discharge. It all fits, huh?"

"Yes, very neatly."

"How's it going out there?"

"With difficulty – but very interesting. On the freeway, he got panicky when I questioned him about his past. I just can't ask him a direct question without him threatening to blow a fuse. Then a couple of weird things happened. He'd fallen asleep, then he woke up suddenly and started talking about someone being 'up there with the gods', having 'magic eyes' and being a healer. He said 'they're a great bunch of people here' and 'you think they're stupid, but they're not', meaning that *I* thought they were stupid. Then he went on about there being two fathers, a dozy father and a golden father, and some bastards had stolen his clothes."

"Jesus. What d'you make of it, Drum?"

"Schizophrenia sprang to mind, psychotic rambling, but then I wasn't so sure. Now I've heard his army history, I think the ramblings could have a basis in fact."

"How come?"

"If he had a nervous breakdown, he's been hospitalized. I'd like to find out where, for how long, and what his treatment was. Is there anything in his record about medical treatment?"

"No, just the bare bones of rank, postings, job, and discharge."

"That doesn't surprise me. They wouldn't release intimate medical stuff for a general police enquiry. But I'll bet he's done time in a psychiatric ward – and that could account for the ramblings."

"In what way?"

"His terminology – 'magic eyes', 'healer', the 'great bunch of people that I think are stupid, but aren't'. I think he's talking about a doctor, probably a hypnotist, who worked on him, and the great bunch of people are his fellow patients. They tend to get protective of one another in psychiatric wards, feel the outside world thinks of them as being stupid, and, with good cause, resent it."

"What about the stolen clothes bit?"

Drummond smiled. "In psych wards they do it all the time, borrow things without asking, wear each other's gear. It's a form of bonding, reassurance."

"You seem to be tapping into something here. What else happened. You said a couple of things . . ."

"The next was incredible. Keegan snapped out of the rambling as quickly as he'd gone into it, and asked me to find some music on the radio. He fell asleep again, the guy's mentally drained, Dick. Then the music cut to a newscast, to Jack Crane making a speech in Detroit, ranting about Byrne, as usual, and suddenly Keegan went berserk. He came out of sleep as though someone had stuck him with a knife, shut the radio off, and sat there rocking and holding his head like it was going to explode."

"Brother. What d'you think caused it?"

116

"I think the voice of Jack Crane caused it."

"*Crane*? Why Crane? I mean, I know he's not everybody's ideal presidential candidate, and some, including me, think he's an overbearing asshole, but . . ."

"Hang on a minute, Dick . . . are you all right for time, here?"

"Sure, go ahead, I'm finished for tonight, heading for Duke's."

"I need to get this all out, because there's something I want you to do for me."

"Surprise, surprise. Go ahead, I wouldn't miss this for the three cold Buds that're waiting for me."

"Okay. As you know, I was going to put Keegan up in a motel, but in his mental state I decided to put him in the guest room, back of the garage. I got him settled in, and was showing him how the TV remote control worked, turned on the set, and who should appear on the screen, but . . ."

"Jack Crane."

". . . Jack Crane. You really should've been a detective, Gage."

"Flatterer. So, what happened?"

"Exactly the same. Keegan flipped. I asked him questions – was it Crane's voice that was doing it? did he know Crane?"

"And?"

"He doesn't *know*."

"Meaning – he can't remember."

"Right."

"But there has to be something there, huh? Otherwise, he wouldn't have flipped."

"Right again. And you have just put your digit on a very vital point in this whole Keegan scene. No matter how much you mess with the human mind – and I'm now convinced Keegan's has been messed with diabolically – there always seems to be a certain core, a central essence,

117

that fights tooth-and-nail to preserve its integrity. Are you with me?"

"All the way. Keegan's mind is fighting for its life, throwing out clues . . ."

"Correct. First came the Jack Crane thing. Next came the dreams. He has two recurring dreams, one about a house being on fire, which is about himself. The other is about laughing green men in a garden, which I'm sure relates to soldiers in camouflage in the jungle."

"Vietnam."

"For sure. Where Governor Jack Crane made a big, big name for himself."

"Yes, *sir*."

"Another interesting bit, Dick – in hypnosis, I had Keegan at the office for a session today, he denies the existence of those Vietnam photographs he plastered all over his apartment wall. So here again we have a dichotomy of mind – part of it denying he was a soldier, denying he was in Vietnam, and another part needing to hang *on* to Vietnam, for a reason vital to its own preservation.

"So, where do we go from here, Drum?"

"What I'd like you to do is . . ."

"Cross-check Crane's and Keegan's army history, see if they overlap?"

"My God, you're good. *And* I want you to check Keegan's pre-army history, find out where he lived, if there's any family, and especially about his education. It shouldn't be difficult now you have his army record. About Crane – a short-cut for you might be to ask Karen Beal for help. The *Times* will have a ton of stuff about him in the morgue."

"Will do. How do I get this stuff to you? Mail it? Fax it?"

Drummond smiled. "No. Karen's coming here for the week-end. Give it to her."

"Oh, yeah? Well, well, well."

"Strictly business, Gage. I'm interested in Forensic Hypnosis in England, and her father, being a cop, might be able . . ."

"She told you that?"

"What?"

"That her father's 'a cop'?"

"I believe she used the term 'police officer'. Why? Isn't he?"

Gage chuckled. "Her father, old sport, is Sir Edward Beal, England's 'top cop'. He's the head of the CID."

"Oh."

"Happy hunting, Stanley."

"You, too, Ollie."

Drummond put down the phone, thinking of the god-like man with magic eyes, the golden father who cured "him" through the television. "You're like golden father. Why don't you wear gold? Gold heals everything. I want a golden tooth".

Somewhere there was a man like himself, a hypnotist, who had a golden tooth, and who, with the aid of hi-tech equipment, destroyed the minds of men who knew too much.

Chapter Ten

Friday.

Drummond was busy with regular clients throughout the day. Week-ends, with their potential for boredom and loneliness, posed an additional threat to those suffering from deep-rooted anxiety and lack of confidence, and an eleventh-hour session of analysis helped to carry them through till Monday.

It was seven o'clock and dark when he arrived home for dinner. He had seen Keegan briefly at breakfast, but had not returned home at mid day. Keegan had slept moderately well, undisturbed by bad dreams. He looked relaxed and stable, not least due, Drummond felt, to having somebody to talk to.

Entering the house by the kitchen door, he found Keegan in there, looking well-scrubbed and renewed, as though he had just stepped out of the shower, his blue summer shirt and cream cotton slacks smart and well-pressed. He was putting the finishing touches to a bowl of salad, and two peppered steaks lay waiting for the grill.

Drummond, delighted by the man's apparent transformation, grinned. "Hey, hey, what's this?"

Keegan smiled, self-consciously. "I found the steaks in the freezer, took the liberty. You're doing so much for me, you shouldn't have to cook as well. Hope you don't mind."

"*Mind*? I really appreciate it. I'm getting mighty sick of my own cooking. Fancy a beer?"

"Yes, sir, thank you."

They ate in the dining room which was integral to the living room, the sliding doors wide open, the night air wonderfully cool but smelling of warm earth.

"Yuh done good," said Drummond, cutting into and tasting his steak. "You enjoy cooking, Tom?"

And the frown was there, always waiting to make its entrance at the sound of a question relating to the past. "I guess I do".

Drummond brought him quickly back to the present. "What did you do today?"

"Sat, mostly. Looked at the valley and the mountains, let the thoughts come, as you said. I like this place. It's peaceful."

"That it is. *Did* any thoughts come?"

"A lot of thoughts, but no memories."

"They will. Tell me what you were thinking."

"Oh, just vague stuff, feelings, more than specific thoughts. It's hard to describe. I feel I'm in limbo, that I'm only two weeks old, that my life began when I opened my eyes and saw the black nurse. And yet part of my mind knows there's a ton of stuff back of that, just out of reach. When I do reach for it, it moves further away, and stays there, tormenting me, daring me to catch it."

Drummond nodded. "Years ago, I had a dog. He loved to be chased. He'd sit there, daring me to catch him. He'd let me creep up on him, and at the very last moment, as I stretched out my hands to grab him, he'd dart away, and sit there again with a superior, teasing look on his face. But I worked out a way to catch him."

"What was that?"

"I ignored him. Made like I was interested in something else, not his silly game. And when he was off-guard, I'd pounce. The mind's like that, Tom. What's going on in yours is a contest between the conscious and the subconscious functions. Memory is stored in the

121

subconscious region. If it were stored in the conscious part of the brain, we'd be able to recall anything at will.

"Take that name or phone number we talked about. When it finally pops into your conscious awareness, where does it come *from*? It's as though there's a little guy down there in the subconscious, in charge of a roomful of filing cabinets. And when you need to remember something, you send down a message, 'Hey, Joe, get me the name of that girl I used to date at school.' And Joe, like the efficient, dependable worker he is, starts working through the files. But if you bug the guy, put pressure on him, keep sending down increasingly impatient messages, 'Joe, f'Crissake, come *on*, I want that name *now*,' he gets rattled and freezes up."

Keegan smiled, nodded. "It's a good analogy. But in my case, it looks like either Joe died on the job two weeks ago – or that someone destroyed the files."

Drummond stopped eating and looked at him. "What makes you say that, Tom?"

"What? that . . ."

"That someone destroyed the files? Do you feel that someone *has* done something to your mind?"

The frown again. Keegan shook his head. "I just don't know. It seemed an obvious thing to say."

But it had to come from somewhere, thought Drummond.

He said, "I'd like to try something, a little dinner-table game. It's called Word Association. I say a word, you associate it with another word, the first word that comes into your mind. Don't intellectualize it, just say it – okay?"

"Sure."

"Gods?"

"Glass." Keegan grimaced. "Glass? Where in hell did that come from?"

"Don't question it, this is very valuable. Next word. Magic?"

"Black."

"Eyes?"

"Black."

"Gold?"

"Glass." Again Keegan grimaced.

"Father?"

"White."

"Dozy?"

"Strong."

"Stupid?"

"Mad." Keegan passed a disconcerted hand across his brow. "Why am I saying these things?"

"Don't question it, Tom, this is exactly what I want to hear."

"But they don't make sense. If I had more time to think . . ."

"That's precisely the point, you mustn't *consciously* think. These responses are coming from your subconscious, and to me they're clues to what is buried there. Look, I don't want to spoil your dinner. If you find this distressing, we'll leave it till later."

"I think I'd rather."

"Fine. This is a great steak, let's talk about something else. When we've finished eating, I want to take you down to the office for another session. Maybe we'll do some more Word Association down there. But it's always what you want and can stand, Tom. I'm working in the dark, have to try different approaches. If anything distresses you too much, we'll stop. Now, forget all this mind-stuff and eat your steak."

It was several minutes later, when Drummond was talking light-heartedly about the celebrities who lived in the Valley, that he notice the sudden change in Keegan's expression.

"What is it, Tom?"

"That last word you gave me. You said 'stupid' and I said 'mad'."

123

"What about it?"

"I thought I meant 'mad – crazy'. But it's been playing over and over in my mind. I didn't mean 'crazy' at all."

"What did you mean?"

"I meant 'angry'. People who call other people stupid make me very angry. But how do I know that? That's got to have come out of . . . before I woke up in hospital."

Drummond grinned. "Indeed it has. That, Tom, is a conscious memory – the first crack in the dam that's blocking the flow of your past into your present. Great! Now we work on that tiny crack, make it bigger. So, let's get down to the office and start packing a bit more Word Association dynamite in there."

Drummond started the recorder and identified the session. The following day he would transcribe the pertinent points of the session onto a computer disk, from which he could call up or print out the information as required. This system was particularly useful in analysis when it was necessary to review a client's recollections, perhaps a hundred or more over a period of time, in order to check for repetition and emphasis, the clues to repressed anxieties.

Keegan was now settled on the couch, looking more relaxed, through familiarity, than he had the previous day. The second visit was invariably more relaxed than the first.

"Before I hypnotise you, Tom, I want you just to close your eyes, empty your mind, and respond to the words I give you without any conscious thought. Don't question your replies, and don't worry about them. Just say the word. Are you ready?"

"Yes."

"Knife?"

"Fork."

"Left?"

"Right."

"Up?"

"Down."

"Garden?"

"Green."

"Green?"

"Black."

"Black?"

"Red."

"Red?"

"Blood."

"Blood?"

"Garden." Keegan shifted uncomfortably. "I . . ."

"Don't question it, let it go. Next word. Friends?"

"Laughter."

"Television?"

Tenseness. Hesitation.

"Television?" Drummond repeated.

"Entertainment."

Drummond knew the answer was an intellectualized evasion. He let it go.

"Sparrow?"

"Crumbs."

"Eagle?"

"Soar."

"Pigeon?"

"Race."

"Flamingo?"

"Pink."

"Crane?"

An in-drawn breath, tension.

"*CRANE*?" insisted Drummond.

"Nothing. I can't think of anything."

"What does the word *Crane* mean to you, Tom? It must mean something, it's a common word."

"I can't think of anything! I don't . . . want . . . to think . . ."

"All right, let it go. Relax. I have some very good news for you."

"What's that?"

"You remember a whole lot more than you think you do."

"I do?"

"Sure. How else could you tell me that eagles soar, flamingos are pink, and pigeons race?"

"My God, that's right! It just came out!"

"And a lot more will come out before we're done. You're doing fine. Let go, and trust your subconscious. Okay, I'm going to hypnotise you now, see what else we can come up with."

Over dinner, Drummond had decided to try to take Keegan to a much deeper state of hypnotic trance. Hypnotists generally accepted that there were four stages of trance, each of which encapsulated a number of symptoms.

The first stage, covering the Hypnoidal and Light Trance depths, required of the patient such undemanding symptoms as relaxation, closing of the eyes, limb catalepsy, and general lethargy. This stage was attainable by almost all people, the exception being those who, through handicap, drugs or alcohol, suffered diminished mental capability.

The second stage, known as the Medium Trance, brought about complete muscular inhibition, sensory illusions, and partial amnesia. Many people were capable of entering this stage.

The third stage, called the Deep or Somnambulistic Trance, attainable by far fewer people, produced dramatic symptoms, such as complete anaesthesia, positive and negative visual hallucinations, and control of organic body functions.

The fourth stage, the Plenary Trance, attainable by very few people, resulted in a stuporous condition in which all spontaneous activity was inhibited.

Drummond reasoned that if Keegan had been programmed so effectively to forget his military history, it would have been done at the third, or possibly the fourth stage. In order to access that programming, he, Drummond, would have to duplicate the stage.

The difficulty of attaining this would depend not only on Keegan's hypnotizability, but also on whatever blocks had been set up during the programming. It was possible that, in addition to a range of trigger words or phrases, such as "I want you to go back", "Vietnam", "army", and "Crane", a depth control had been planted that would eject Keegan from the hypnotic state and prevent any other hypnotist duplicating the deeper levels. If this were so, the investigative process might well be impossible.

But there was only one way to find out.

Drummond worked on Keegan for half an hour, beginning with Progressive Relaxation, then deepening with backwards-counted numbers, then through the second stage with the extensive use of imagery, sending Keegan into outer space on a journey to the stars, then bringing him back down to earth for a colorful and sensual mind-trek through desert, ice-field and, finally, lush jungle valley.

By then, Drummond was sure Keegan was in third stage trance, and that no depth-control block had been instilled.

However, before beginning the questions, there were a couple of tests to do. From his desk drawer he took a cellophane packet containing a sterilized needle, tore open the packet and took out the needle. Then he stood, facing Keegan.

"Tom, when I count to three, you will open your eyes but you will remain in deep hypnosis. One . . . two . . . three . . . open your eyes."

127

Keegan did so.

Drummond leaned close, observing the fixed stare and dilated pupils.

"Tom, your right hand is getting cold . . . very cold. When I count to three it will be so cold there'll be no feeling in it whatever. One . . . two . . . three. Your right hand is now so cold there is no feeling in it whatever. It is like a block of ice. I am going to touch your right hand now and you will feel absolutely nothing."

Watching Keegan's face for change of expression, Drummond pricked the hand with the needle, several times. Keegan gave no sign that he had felt it.

Drummond resumed his seat. "On the count of three, your hand will return to complete normality. One . . . two . . . three. Your hand is now normally warm and comfortable. Close your eyes, Tom, and listen to the sound of my voice. I want you to return to that jungle valley, the one you were in a moment ago. Are you there?"

Keegan's response was a croaked whisper. "Yes."

"We're going to play a game. It's called 'making a movie'. I want you to imagine that you are an actor and I am the director, and I'm making a movie. This is not real, it's just pretend. Okay, I think I'll make a movie about . . . soldiers. There's a big basket of uniforms over there under a tree, all kinds of uniforms. You go over and choose one for yourself and put it on. Tell me when you're ready, so I can check it out."

Keegan took a moment, then said, "Ready."

"That looks good. You'll have to help me out here, Tom, I've never made a movie about soldiers in a jungle before. I'd like to hear your opinion about things as we go along. Is that the right color uniform for the jungle?"

"Green, sure."

"What army would be fighting in the jungle?"

"The Marine Corps."

128

"Good. I've got some more actors coming along, about a hundred of them. You can hear them now, coming through the trees, laughing. I want you to help me, Tom, to be my assistant. I want you to talk to these men, tell me what they have to say. Here they come now. Go to them, mix with them, tell me about them."

For a full, long minute Keegan said nothing, yet Drummond could see he was reacting to the group. He mouthed silently, grimaced, twitched and jerked.

For Drummond, the value of any product from this exercise was doubtful; in order to circumvent a negative reaction from Keegan to a real-life military scenario, he had concocted a pretend one, and so could expect a pretend outcome. Nevertheless, whatever the product, it might yield clues to what had really happened to Keegan in Vietnam.

Keegan blurted excitedly, "Marty's here!"

Drummond's pulse leapt. "Who is Marty, Tom?"

"Friend."

"What's his second name?"

Keegan frowned, struggling with memory. "Don't know. Can't remember."

"Is he a good friend?"

"The best."

"How long have you known him?"

"Since . . ." The anxiety building now. "I can't *remember*."

"Is Marty a soldier?"

"No. Yes. He's here."

"What is he wearing?"

"Green."

"What is he doing now?"

"Laughing. Singing."

"What is he singing?"

Keegan broke into a tuneless, rhythmic chant. "Trice . . . trice, twice as nice. Trice, twice, nice, ice."

"What are all the other men doing?"

"Happy. Laughing. Singing. Pick it up . . . pick it up. All together. In a trice . . . in a trice. Laughing. Falling down. In a trice, it will be nice. Get it going. Stand up, fall down. Ho, Ho, Hee, Hee . . . Marty's climbing up a tree. In a trice, it will be nice . . . Charlie will be put on ice. Going home, guys. In a trice, it will be nice . . . Charlie will be put on ice. Going home, going home, going . . ."

Keegan gave a violent shudder, and in the next instant was overwhelmed by visual horror. "Jesus Christ! Marty . . ."

"What's happening, Tom?"

Keegan rolled his head. His face was creased with anguish. Tears squeezed from his tight-shut eyes and trickled down his cheek. "Oh, Jesus, no, no, no."

"Tom, what is happening?"

"Green . . . and black. Black. Black, black, black."

"What is black, Tom?"

"Guys. Black guys. All the guys are black."

"Is Marty black?"

"In a trice, it will be nice . . . Charlie will be put on ice."

Drummond sensed a breathless desperation in the chant now, as though Keegan were using it, like whistling in the dark, to block out terror.

"What are the guys *doing* Tom? What is Marty doing?"

A defiant, indomitable shaking of the head, his breathing chaotic, hyperventilating. "In a . . . trice . . . it will be . . . nice, Charlie will . . . be put on . . . ice. In a . . . trice . . ."

"All right, Tom, the game's over, the movie's finished. I want you to take off the uniform, leave the jungle. Relax . . . relax. Come back to the present. You are here in my office, safe and secure. In a moment I'm going to count you slowly up from one to five, and when I reach the count of five, you will wake up

130

completely, feeling rested, confident, and very good. One . . . two . . ."

On five, Keegan opened his eyes, blinked a lot, frowned, looked down at his shirt, and said, "Jesus, what happened? I'm wet through."

"Yes, I think you had a bad dream."

Keegan turned his head to look at him. "Did I fall asleep?"

"What d'you remember?"

"You saying something about stars . . . outer space."

"Nothing after that?"

"No."

"Nothing about making a movie?"

Keegan smiled. "A movie? No."

"Tom, who is Marty?"

Keegan thought, frowning, before shaking his head. "Don't know any Marty."

"Does this mean anything to you – In a trice, it will be nice . . . Charlie will be put on ice?"

A longer, more thoughtful, different tone of pause this time. "Sounds crazy. Did I say that in my sleep?"

"It means nothing to you?"

"Nothing. Not a goddamned thing!"

But it did. Recognition, perhaps only the merest vestige of rememberance and significance, was evident to Drummond in the unconscious shadow of fear that passed over Keegan's face, and in the slight over-emphasis of his denial.

"Tom, in that recurring dream you have about the men in green, laughing in the jungle . . . do they sing as well as laugh?"

"Sing?"

"Chant."

"No. They just act crazy, giggle and laugh like guys do when they fool around."

"Does anyone climb a tree?"

Keegan closed his eyes, the effort of recall showing on his face. "I . . . I don't know."

"The guys what colour are they?"

"I told you – green."

"But are they Anglo-Saxon or Negroid?"

"Anglo."

"Then what is it about them that is *black*?"

"Blood!" Keegan shot up into sitting position, eyes staring, chest heaving. "No! Can't be blood. Blood is red. Dirt. Dirt is black."

And so, thought Drummond, is dried blood. And so might blood appear as it seeped through olive-drab combat material.

In Word Association, Keegan had linked garden to green, green to black, black to red, and red to blood.

If it hadn't sounded so bizzare, Drummond might have suspected that Tom Keegan had been witness to a crowd of people who had, literally, killed themselves laughing.

"Okay, Tom, that's enough for tonight."

Heaving a distraught sigh, Keegan, hunched over on the edge of the couch, asked, "Paul, are we getting anywhere?"

Drummond said confidently, "Yes, sir, I think we are," and switched off the tape recorder.

Chapter Eleven

When they arrived at the house, Drummond suggested a beer or a hot drink, but Keegan declined, saying he was tired and preferred to go to his room.

Studying him closely, looking for signs of adverse reaction to the hypnosis session, and detecting in Keegan a deep and abiding weariness, Drummond accompanied him to the guest room and said goodnight.

Returning to his kitchen, Drummond made tea, so deeply immersed in thought that he was virtually unaware of what he was doing.

The word *attrition* came repeatedly to mind. Keegan looked as though he were being worn away from the inside. As a therapist, Drummond had witnessed many times the terrible effect of unrelenting stress on the human organism. Stress had, literally, the capacity to kill.

Supposing that Keegan's malaise did refer back to Vietnam, it meant that he had been carrying this enormous mental burden of memory-, and therefore identity-loss, for almost twenty years.

Attempting – and at very best that was all it was, an attempt – to empathise with Keegan's condition, Drummond tried to imagine the nature and extent of the war being continually waged in Keegan's head.

But with all his knowledge and experience of other people's stress, and even of his own after Vivian's death, he knew he could not begin to imagine what Tom Keegan had suffered, and was still suffering. The miracle was that the man was still alive, still fighting to regain control of his mind.

Carrying the tea into the living room, intending to sit out on the deck for a while, he saw the incoming-message light on the answerphone flashing, and pressed the button.

Dick Gage's voice said simply, "Call me, huh?"

Drummond settled into an armchair and dialled Gage's home number.

Anne Gage, a stunning brunette of twenty-eight, an ex-nurse, now mother of two, whom Dick had met in hospital the time he was shot in the thigh by a punk with a zip-gun, answered.

"Hello?"

"That's an incredible voice. I'll bet you're a real looker."

"I am. Your voice is pretty nice, too."

"What d'you want to do about it?"

"Meet me tonight, midnight, Santa Monica pier."

"Aren't you married?"

"Oh, sure, but he's a washed-up cop."

Drummond could hear the Lieutenant in the background. "She means I'm doing the dishes!"

"Oh, hell, he heard. Call me some other time, stranger."

Gage came on. "Whoever you are, my wife ain't available. Not tonight. Friday night, she irons my shirts. If Monday's okay, we'll talk price. Ouch! Stop that! Madam, I must caution you that it's a criminal offense to grope a police officer while he's on the phone – kindly wait till I've finished. Ooh, on second thoughts . . ."

"When you're both finished . . ." laughed Drummond.

"Oh, it's *you*, Drum." Gage became serious. "Glad you called, got a coupla somethings to tell you. I've given Karen written notes on this stuff to bring to you, but I wanted to talk it over because it's *ve*-ry eenteresting."

"Good. Shoot."

"First off – yes, Jack Crane and Tom Keegan were in the same theater of operations in Vietnam at the same time, but a closer connection between them than that isn't evident from the details I've managed to get hold of so far, and will probably be impossible to establish or prove."

"Why d'you say that?"

"Because, old buddy, I have the gravest suspicion that Tom Keegan's army record has been falsified, and whatever it says he did, and with whom, he probably didn't do at all."

"*What*? Why? How d'you know . . .?"

"I don't *know*, Drum. I'm just suspicious. Let me start at the beginning. I've managed to track down details of Keegan's family life and scholastic record. He was born in Northridge, in the San Fernando Valley, May Nineteen-forty-six. His father, Michael, owned a drugstore there, and was a qualified druggist. His mother, Alice, died of meningitis when Tom was six years old, and he was brought up by an aunt, Cissie, Michael's spinster sister, who moved in with them from Ventura where she was living with her parents. I got a lot of this stuff from a Northridge cop who knew the family well."

"You're good, Gage."

"I know. Young Tom, it appears, was *ve*-ry bright. Attended local schools and college, straight A's across the board, with a special aptitude for . . ."

"Chemistry?"

"You're not so bad yourself, Doctor. Yep, chem. and phys. So good that he won a scholarship to Cal. State University in San Fernando, Northridge, a few blocks from home. He graduated with honours in Nineteen-sixty-eight, and went straight into the army to do his draft stint."

"And became a 'box-pusher', a supply clerk."

"Man, you are good. Right. And if that doesn't stink, horse-shit smells like fresh-baked bread."

135

"Question: why did Keegan wind up doing four years in the army instead of two?"

"Don't know. My Northridge cop says Michael Keegan died during Tom's first year in the army, the business was sold, and Aunt Cissie moved back to Ventura to be near the ocean. She was born in Dublin and couldn't stand to be land-trapped."

"Your cop is a mine of useful information."

"His name is O'Reilly."

"Enough said. So he lost touch with the family – what was left of it?"

"Not entirely. He gets a Christmas card from Cissie every year."

"She's still alive?" Drummond asked excitedly.

"Absolutely. Thought that might please you. Karen will have Cissie's address and phone number with her."

"Good man. You haven't tried to contact Cissie?"

Drummond heard the change in Gage's tone. "No, I haven't. As I was leaving the station tonight, I was told I've been taken off the case. In fact, it's been transferred out of West LA to FBI jurisdiction."

"You sound funny."

"I feel funny. Keegan's army record isn't the only thing that stinks around here."

"How so?"

"I'm being asked questions, Drum, about Keegan and you. All kinda casual, like, but underneath as subtle as a boot in the balls."

"What kind of questions?"

"Do I know if you are still treating Keegan? Have you been able to help Keegan regain any memory? Where *is* Keegan? Is he out there with you?"

"Who's asking the questions?"

"Ostensibly, the captain. But the questions are coming from the Parker Center, bet your ass. And my guess is they're being relayed by the Center from somewhere else."

"Why?" mused Drummond. "Keegan's all washed up as a witness, so it has to be something in his past that somebody is frightened of."

"Have you managed to uncover anything yet?"

"I'm not sure, Dick. I got some interesting responses in a couple of Word Association sessions, with and without hypnosis, and some pretty hairy stuff from hypnosis imagery. There's no doubt in my mind that he witnessed something terrible and bloody in Vietnam. It has been blocked from his conscious mind, but comes out in weird fragments from his subconscious. Tonight he was repeating an incomprehensible couplet that obviously had great significance for him at one time."

"What was it?"

"'In a trice, it will be nice . . . Charlie will be put on ice'."

Gage repeated it. "What in hell could that mean?"

"It's obviously linked to that dream he has of the green men, laughing in the jungle. In the imagery I gave him, he had them all chanting it, as though they were learning something by rote. I'll keep working on it. One thing just hit me."

"What's that?"

"If 'they' are asking you where Keegan is, they know he's not at home. Someone's been to four-five-nine Lomita to check up on him."

"Right."

"I wonder what they would have said – or done – to him if they'd found him home?"

"Good question."

"Speaking of which – how did you answer the captain's?"

"Me? I'm just a poor dumb overworked cop, I don't know anything. In any case, what goes on between a doctor and his patient is privileged information. Drummond would only tell me stuff that related directly to Mar Vista."

"So, they don't know Keegan's out here?"

"Not from me."

"Okay, Dick, I'll keep you posted. While we've been talking, I've had an idea. I sure would like to talk to Aunt Cissie. She could give me Tom's background, something solid to work with over the weekend. I could maybe drive in early tomorrow, drive back with Karen. I'll call Karen now, get Cissie's address and number, arrange a visit. If anything new develops, I'll phone you Sunday night."

"I'll be here."

Drummond rang off, looked up Karen's number, dialled it. He got a machine, and a beautifully modulated English voice that was sexy as hell without trying to be. "This is Karen Beal. I'm awfully sorry I'm not in at the moment . . ."

At the tone, Drummond said, "Hi, Karen, this is Paul Drummond . . ." and she picked up instantly.

"Hello, Paul, it's me."

He laughed. "You must've had the phone in your lap. How are you?"

"Great. Looking forward to the week-end. Oh! I hope you're not calling to cancel it?"

"No, ma'am, but I may suggest a slight re-timing. I've just spoken to Dick. He told me about Tom Keegan's Aunt Cissie . . ."

"Yes, isn't that exciting?"

"Yes, it is. And I want to talk to her. The background stuff she could give me on Tom could be immensely helpful in treating him. What I thought was, provided it's all right with her, I'd drive in early tomorrow morning, see her, pick you up on the way back. There's no point in using two cars for the weekend. I'll be back in LA early Monday morning as usual, in time for your work."

"Great idea. But I have a better one. You pick me up *before* you visit Aunt Cissie. I want to meet her."

"You do?"

"Paul, this whole Keegan thing is *very* peculiar. Dick has voiced his suspicions to me, off the record, and from what you've told me, I smell a story here. Now, although you absolved me of endangering Keegan's life with my article, I still feel a twinge of guilt that I didn't check with you first, and I'd like to make amends. If I, through the paper, can help Tom Keegan's case in any way, I'd be happy to do so. I'd really like to work closely with you on it – and no journalistic tricks, I promise."

"Nothing would give me greater pleasure. I think, with your resources, you might be a tremendous help."

"Good. Now, you want Cissie Keegan's address and phone number."

"And your address. I don't know where you live."

"That," she smiled, "must be rectified."

She came back a moment later with the details.

Drummond said, "Thanks, Karen. I'll call her now, let you know what happens. If it's a no-no for tomorrow, we'll revert to Plan A."

"Roger."

"And out."

Smiling, conscious of the pleasure it gave him to talk to her, he depressed the cradle button and dialled the Ventura number.

On the sixth ring he felt the onset of disappointment.

Hope and excitement had begun to crystallize within him since the moment Dick Gage had revealed the existence of Aunt Cissie. He felt, no, *knew*, that her knowledge of Tom's past was the key to much of the mystery that surrounded him.

Ten rings and no answer. He checked his watch. It was ten thirty, a not-unreasonable time to call an elderly woman.

He was now experiencing an impatience to talk to her that bordered on desperation. He had seen it in his mind's eye – call Cissie, make the appointment, drive in, pick up

Karen, talk to Cissie, drive back to the Valley with Karen, armed with the information that might help speed Tom Keegan back to normality. And here, at the first stage of the plan, he was stymied.

Fourteen rings, still no answer.

Awful possibilities loomed. Cissie had moved. Cissie was ill. Cissie was dead!

Dick Gage's Northridge contact had mentioned only receiving a Christmas card from her, and that was ten months ago. Cissie had to be in her seventies, so anything, including death, could have happened to her in that time.

Eighteen rings. Enough. There was no one there.

He would try again early tomorrow, but in his mind he was already preparing for disappointment.

He removed the receiver from his ear. His finger hovered over the cradle button. And in the split-second before he depressed it, he heard a scratching in the earpiece.

He rushed the instrument back to his ear, his pulse leaping. "Hello?"

"Hello?" The voice was female and faint, not from distance but from sleepiness, and in just that one word Drummond could hear the pathos and lyrical gentleness of old Ireland.

"Miss Cissie Keegan?"

"It is."

"Miss Keegan, my name is Drummond – Doctor Paul Drummond. I'm speaking from Palm Desert, California, and I do apologise for disturbing you, but it's about your nephew, Tom."

It took a moment to register. "Tom? Oh, God, what's happened?"

"Now, please calm yourself, Miss Keegan, I didn't mean to frighten you. Tom's all right. I mean, he's not physically ill. I'm a clinical psychologist, not a physician, and I'm helping Tom with certain problems."

"Ah, he has plenty of those, poor soul."

140

"That's exactly what he is, Miss Keegan, a poor soul. How long is it since you've seen him?"

"It's been years . . . years. I can't remember how many. Where is he now?"

"He's here in Palm Desert with me, at my home. Miss Keegan, in order to help him, I need to know as much as possible about his background. I'm afraid Tom has lost all memory of his life prior to a few weeks ago, and that includes memory of you and his family. I would very much like to talk with you, hear about his past from you."

"Well, of course. When would you like . . .?"

"Tomorrow, if that's possible."

"Entirely. I'm here all the time, never go out. Come when you like, and welcome."

"Thank you. It'll probably be mid-morning. And I'd like to bring somebody with me, a young lady who's helping me with Tom."

"Bring whoever you like – and bless you for helping him. It's time somebody did."

"I'll do my best. Thank you, Miss Keegan. See you tomorrow."

Elated, Drummond rang off and dialled Karen. "It's on. I'll be at your place about nine, we'll get to Ventura about eleven."

"How does she sound?"

"Very cooperative. She blesses us for helping Tom, says it's time somebody did."

"I think this is going to be a very worthwhile visit."

"So do I. See you at nine."

"I'll have breakfast waiting."

"You cook, *too*?"

"Listen, I've won *prizes* for my cornflakes. Goodnight, Paul."

Drummond sat there for a while, drinking the tea, letting thoughts come. The image of Karen Beal was persistent. He had liked her on sight, and the feeling was growing. She

141

was a great-looking woman, but there was more to it than that. There was a quality of sense and sensibility, a depth, that appealed to him enormously. Perhaps it was her cool, calm Englishness; he wasn't sure. But whatever, he found himself looking forward to being with her, with the kind of anticipatory tingle he hadn't enjoyed for a long time.

As his thoughts ranged over the coming visit to Aunt Cissie, they took a sudden detour into the conversation he'd had with Dick Gage, into the questions Dick had been asked, and back to his own supposition that, in order to know Tom Keegan was not at his apartment, 'they' must have been there.

What followed next was not the outcome of logic, but a sudden flash of intuition as strong as his imperative need to speak with Cissie. He felt a compulsion to see four-five-nine Lomita, to check Keegan's effects, to study the Vietnam photographs and just to be there, he didn't know why or for what, but just to be there. Perhaps it was a subconscious urge to gather as much information about Keegan, now that Cissie promised so much, as he could get his hands on. Information was the therapist's bread-of-life, and in Keegan's case he was greedy for it.

Whatever the source, the compulsion propelled him from the room, across the drive, to the guest room door. The light was still on. Tapping lightly, he eased the door open, saw that the bed had been used but was empty, then heard the toilet flush, and waited by the door for Keegan to emerge.

He tapped again, as though he had just arrived. "You there, Tom?"

"Sure, come in."

Keegan was standing by the bed in his shorts.

"I saw the light, just wanted a word. You okay?"

"Fine. Just needed to pee. I think I'll be able to sleep."

"Good man. Tom, I need to go into LA early tomorrow,

142

but I'll be back before dark. I'd rather you stayed here. Will you be all right?"

"Of course."

Drummond smiled collusively. "I'll be bringing a very pretty lady back, to spend Sunday with us. You'll like her, I promise. Tom, I was thinking – while I'm there, why don't I check on your apartment, make sure everything's okay?"

Keegan shrugged. "If you want to. But I thought the Lieutenant . . ."

"He's out of town. If you'll let me have your set of keys . . .?"

"Sure." Keegan collected them from the dresser. "Thanks, Paul."

"I'll be off early, so I won't disturb you. The house will be open – help yourself to anything you want. Get a good night's sleep, have a nice lazy day tomorrow, and we'll be back around six."

"I'll have dinner cooking."

"Tom, you don't have to, you know."

"I want to."

"Okay. Surprise us. Phone the market and order anything you like, impress the lady for both of us, hm?"

Keegan grinned. "Okay, you got it."

Closing the door, Drummond glanced back and saw Tom Keegan deep in thought, but for the first time it seemed a pleasurable process, not the morbid preoccupation with self that had so far dominated his mind.

Seeing this, Drummond sensed that the process of healing had begun, and felt an even greater impatience to learn whatever secrets Aunt Cissie and four-five-nine Lomita had to offer.

Chapter Twelve

Karen Beal lived in Santa Monica, in a third-floor, ocean-front apartment that looked out across the green sward of Palisades Beach Road with its towering palm trees, to the Santa Monica State Beach and the Pacific Ocean. There were islands out there that should have been visible from such a vantage point, but as coast-dwellers complained, most days the smog was so bad they were lucky to see the palm trees.

Drummond, wearing a gray, pin-stripe suit, arrived early, eight-thirty, smack in the middle of the morning rush, and was lucky to find a parking space a block from the apartment. Walking back, seeing the crush, hearing the noise, smelling the fumes, he wondered how he had existed in Los Angeles all those years, or survived the deadly poisons.

The apartment building was, like most, security guarded. He pressed a button, announced himself, and walked into a splendid hallway done in pale pink marble and tall smoked mirrors. A dainty elevator, dressed in matching pink, lifted him to the third floor. Somehow he couldn't imagine any male inhabiting the building.

Karen, a morning vision in a white silk blouse and black tailored skirt, her blonde hair billowing to her shoulders, was waiting at her open door.

"Good morning. You made it."

"Almost didn't. Had to park in Bakersfield, I've been walking since three."

She laughed. "I *adore* hyperbole. Come in, coffee's on."

He followed her down a small hallway, catching the wake of her perfume. Admiring the liaison between perfect figure and perfect tailoring, delighting in the squareness of her shoulders, the delicacy of her ankles, the movement of her hair, he knew he was going to enjoy this day with her, and probably many more.

The living room was spacious, done in chrome and pastels, generously windowed for the view. Deeply-cushioned chairs and a sofa faced a white marble fireplace on the right. The open kitchen, with bar-stools and counter-top, set for breakfast, was on the left.

Karen went into the kitchen and busied herself.

Drummond crossed to the window, then turned to admire the room. "Beautiful."

"Art deco meets Miami Vice," she smiled. "I love it. I was brought up on chintz and furniture engineered from petrified oak . . . back-breaking chairs that scream at you 'don't you dare throw me out, I'm only four hundred years old!' I love the impermanence of all this, love the way Americans sell their furniture with the house. It's a refreshing change from 'this piece has been in the family for two thousand years.' and everybody's thinking, 'for God's sake, why?'."

Laughing, Drummond crossed the room and sat on a counter stool, watching her deftly whip eggs in a bowl.

"You didn't tell me your father was Sir Edward Beal."

She narrow-eyed him. "Blabber-mouth Gage has been talking. Why should I have told you?"

"Why not?"

"Because it would've sounded pretentious."

"Not to an American ear. We love it."

"I want America to appreciate me for *me*, not for who my father is. He's not at all pretentious, bless him. He thinks of himself as a policeman first, everything else second."

She poured the eggs into a pan, clicked down the toaster, dispensed juice into glasses, then returned to the eggs, working with neat, graceful coordination.

Drummond said, "Tell me about your mother."

She drew a tiny sigh. "They met in Hong Kong. Mother's people were in banking, shipping, everything, out there. Dad was with the police. Later, they travelled the world, Dad studying the international crime scene and investigative methods. I was born in England, but didn't live there much. I had a wonderful childhood, saw wondrous things. Mother was a highly intelligent and very accomplished lady. She sang beautifully, played the piano, sculpted, painted, rode, flew a plane, and read, read, read. It was through her influence that I fell in love with language; through my father's interest in crime that I became a crime journalist. She was the world's best mother – and wife. And we both miss her abominably."

She pulled warm plates from the stove, heaped fluffy scrambled eggs upon them, set them on the counter. A plate of hot sausages, crispy bacon, grilled mushrooms and grilled tomatoes followed.

Drummond laughed as she added hashbrowns, buttered toast, English marmalade, juice, and two mugs of coffee. "You did mention something about cornflakes."

"Oh, you want cornflakes, too?"

"No!"

She came round and took the stool beside him. "Did I forget anything?"

"Well, the kitchen sink's still over there . . ."

"That's for dessert. Help yourself, there's no English formality here, it's the butler's day off."

Grinning, Drummond asked, "Did you ever have one – a butler?"

"Many. Some were my closest friends when I was little."

"You've lived quite a life already."

"I've been very lucky, Paul. Exceptionally lucky."

"And now you want to give something back."

She glanced at him, frowning, thinking about it. "Tom Keegan? I don't feel guilty about my good luck, if that's what your psychoanalytical mind is thinking."

"It isn't. It's thinking about . . . fairness."

She gave an approving nod and bit into a piece of toast. "Thank you. With due modesty, I'll buy that. I think it's a very unfair life, and it tends to get me mad. The circumstances of birth can be *very* unfair. Go a few miles east or a few more miles south of here, and life can get bloody unfair. I've witnessed chronically unfair life in Africa, in the Far East, even in England. And I've got a feeling we're going to find that whatever it is that happened to Tom Keegan's life, it falls squarely into that catagory, too."."

"What makes you think that?"

"Don't you?"

"I want to hear your summation. Incidentally, these eggs are unbelievable."

"My mother was a cordon bleu cook."

"Of course."

"Here is a man who was a very clever boy, a straight-A student at high school and college, a chemistry and science scholarship student at university, who ought by now to be running the Rand Corporation or MIT, but is, in fact, living in squalor, earning a crust doing odd laboring jobs, and unable to remember the least thing about his life prior to two or three weeks ago. Now, whatever caused that turn-about has got to be chronically unfair."

"The trauma of the Mar Vista experience?"

She shook her head, cut into a sausage. "He was living in squalor before that."

"The nervous breakdown that resulted in a psychological discharge from the army?"

147

She nodded slowly. "That puzzles me. I mean, I don't know the first thing about US Army procedure, but if Keegan was as bad as this at the time of his discharge, I'm surprised they let him go. Surely he should have been hospitalized until his memory returned?"

"Good thinking. I'd have thought so, too, unless . . ."

"Unless someone with enough clout, and with enough interest in keeping Keegan amnesiac, ordered that he should be let go."

"Bravo. Will you be wanting that last sausage?"

"Heaven forbid. In which case, we are not only neck-deep in unfairness here, but in criminal negligence. I suppose it is just possible that we're getting paranoid, and that what has happened to Keegan is the result of simple negligence, of plain old ordinary bureaucratic inefficiency, and not some unimaginable conspiracy?"

"Perhaps. But what of Dick's suspicion that Keegan's army record has been falsified?"

"That means nothing." She snapped a piece of bacon and crunched it between snow-white teeth. "It is only a suspicion. And even if it were true, there may be a dozen good reasons – national security, for instance – why they did it."

"Okay – what about all the questions Dick is being asked, about Keegan's whereabouts, his state of memory, whether or not I'm still treating him?"

She arched an eyebrow at him. "I didn't say we *were* paranoid. I merely put forward the possibility."

"And you don't believe we are?"

"No, I don't."

"Neither do I. I have some Keegan material you don't yet know about. I've done a couple of Word association sessions and a hypnosis session, and some interesting stuff has come out. I'll tell you about it in the car. I also have the keys to Keegan's apartment, and his permission to be there. After we've talked with Aunt Cissie, we'll pay a visit to four-five-nine Lomita, see what we can find. Maybe you'd like to bring a camera along, just in case."

Karen smiled. "I never go anywhere without it." Twenty minutes and a range of subjects later, she asked, "Had enough to eat, Doctor?"

He gave a mock groan of abundant repletion. "I have to tell you, I'm disappointed about the cornflakes."

"Next time. I'm still learning."

She took the dishes to the sink.

"Let me help with those, hm?"

She tapped a dishwasher with her foot. "We'll let the butler do them."

The dishes and pans disposed of, she disappeared down the hall, reappearing minutes later, wearing the jacket of the suit, carrying a capacious overnight bag, a camera slung on one shoulder, a tape recorder on the other.

Drummond grinned. "Vogue Business Woman of the Nineties. Ready for all eventualities. Beal, that's what I call style."

She dropped a curtsey. "Thank you, sir. Now, if you can manage to get off that stool, let's go see Aunt Cissie."

"Now, *that*," said Karen, "has character. I adore it. It's going to smell of the sea and lavender polish, and don't be surprised if Doris Day, wearing bobby socks and toreador pants, is cooking brownies in the kitchen."

The house was a turn-of-the-century, two-storied structure, built of gray-and-white painted clapboard, with generous, multi-paned windows, and a deep, sun-screened verandah.

It stood on a bluff overlooking the coast road and the ocean in an area of haphazard development, its neighbours a mish-mash of architectural styles, graceless and upstart by comparison. There was something matriarchal and self-assured about its bearing, untouchable either by passing years or the madness of modernity. It was a house that knew who it was, and liked itself.

"It kind of looks like Aunt Cissie sounds," said Drummond. "Substantial, old-world dependable, last of a great breed."

He turned the Daimler into a steep driveway and parked at the side of the house.

They took their time mounting the wooden steps and crossing the porch, looking about them, getting a feel of the place, exchanging smiles at the wooden rocker and the swing seat, relics of a byegone age, quite at odds with the roar of coastal traffic and the thud and thump of passing vehicular stereo.

"Yes," said Karen. "There he sits. Gordon Macrae in bow tie and skimmer, playing his ukelele and singing, 'By the li-ght . . . of the silvery mo-on . . .'"

Drummond laughed. "Beal, you are an unqualified romantic."

"Guilty as charged. I'm an Edwardian at heart, born seventy years too late."

Drummond pressed a huge, highly-polished brass bell button and heard it ring inside the house. Moments later the white lace curtain covering a glass door panel inched aside, deadbolts were withdrawn and the door opened.

Cissie Keegan, like her house, looked of another age. Diminutive and frail, her hands gnarled with arthritis, she wore an ankle-length print dress with a high, white-lace collar, her abundant gray hair fashioned in an Edwardian roll with a bun at the crown. Although her features were plain, and always had been, gentleness and kindliness radiated from her welcoming smile and from eyes as green as Galway grass.

"Miss Keegan? I'm Paul Drummond . . . and this is Miss Karen Beal."

Cissie stepped back, offering her hand as they entered.

150

"You had no trouble finding me? I'm getting a bit lost in all the building that's going on around here."

Drummond smiled, delighting in the charm and lilt of her accent that must not have diminished one iota since the day she left Ireland. "No trouble at all. Your home stands out like a beacon of good taste in a darkness of mediocrity."

Cissie laughed, her eyes twinkling mischievously as she shook hands with Karen. "This man will have to be watched. He has the silver tongue. Are you sure he isn't Irish?"

"He's a Scot, Miss Keegan – a mountain man."

"Heaven help us. Well, come in and welcome. We'll sit in the parlour and take tea. I'm sure you must be thirsty after your long journey."

As she led off down the hallway, Drummond and Karen spoke silently to one another, sharing the feelings of delight and sadness that Aunt Cissie and her home evoked in them both.

From the wide, high-ceilinged hallway, with its polished oak staircase, they entered a large room on the left whose bay window overlooked the front porch and distant ocean view.

The room was a museum of Victorian memorabilia, its furniture solid yet comfortable, the brown leather chairs adorned with embroidered antimacassars, the upright piano complete with a sheet of long-forgotten music.

Cissie said, "Make yourselves comfortable, I'll get the tea," and wandered away towards the back of the house.

Gazing around the room, Drummond said, "Turn your back to the window and tell me what year it is."

Karen nodded. "It's Nineteen-oh-one and the queen has just died. Or Eighteen-eighty and Garfield is about to be elected US president. It's incredible."

They circled the room in silence, studying the paintings

151

on the walls, the china in cabinets, the objets d'art and bric-à-brac on mantel, table and shelf.

Drummond paused at a silver-framed photograph of a man and a boy in his early teens, posing before a lake, an arm about each other, a big trout held aloft by the boy in triumph. Father and son. Michael and Tom Keegan, though the boy was barely recognizable as the same person living in Drummond's house.

Behind Drummond, Karen asked, "Why do old photographs always make me feel sad?"

"You, too?"

"There has to be a psychological explanation."

"Probably fear of one's own mortality. Or they're a reminder that life is rushing by and we'll never have enough time to do all the things we want to do." Hearing Cissie approaching, he replaced the photograph, and they both sat in armchairs.

Tea steeping in a silver pot, bone china crockery as delicate as rice paper, assorted cakes on a matching plate, arrived on an antique serving trolley, its rubber tyres squeaking on the polished wood floor as Cissie rounded the corner and entered the room.

Karen came to her feet. "May I help, Miss Keegan?"

"Bless you, no, it's so seldom I get a chance to entertain, I enjoy the privilege. Is it milk and sugar for you both?"

While she poured and dispensed, handed out cake plates and starched napkins, and entreated them to eat, she talked about the house.

"It is just Victorian, built in Nineteen-hundred by a retired New York businessman who had a great love of the sea and for peace and quiet, and in those days got plenty of both here. I have an old photograph somewhere of the house just after it was built, and there's nothing around it at all, except miles and miles of California."

She seated herself facing them, her cup and saucer rattling in an unsteady hand. "My mother and father came to America from Dublin when I was ten, seventy years ago. I had three brothers, all older than me, but one died at birth and another died in a riding accident when I was twenty, and that left just Michael and me."

Drummond said, "May I ask what your father did, Miss Keegan?"

It was the signal for her to get up and produce photographs. "Da was a chemist. He'd had a small shop in Dublin, and opened another in Los Angeles, in Pasadena, when we arrived. Later on, Michael, always the clever one, joined Da after university, and they ran it together until Da retired in ill-health in Nineteen and forty. That's when he bought this house."

She returned from a sideboard with a thick, leatherbound album, opened it on her knee and turned pages, extracting several photographs, all black-and-white, explaining each as she handed them around.

Drummond asked, "Was Michael married when your father retired, Miss Keegan?"

"No, he was not. The Keegans have always tended to marry late – " she gave a shy, regretful smile, "or not at all. Michael did not marry until Nineteen forty-four, when he was thirty-six years old. Alice was a gorgeous girl, from Northridge, I have a photograph of her here with Michael, taken in Yosemite."

"Was that when Michael moved to Northridge?" Karen asked.

"Indeed it was. Alice's father was a builder, and he'd just completed some new shops, one of which was to be a drugstore with a pharmacy. Since Northridge is much nearer here than is Pasadena, Michael decided to move. That way, Alice could stay close to her parents, and we could see much more of Michael."

Drummond said, "So, up to that time you had always lived at home, Miss Keegan?"

"Yes. After Frank died in the riding accident, Ma

153

seemed to need me terribly. Then Da's health began to fail and . . ." she gave a tiny, fatalistic shrug. "There was a man . . . but he was from the East, and I didn't have the heart to leave them. Still, that's all a long, long time ago."

"And Tom . . . he was born in Nineteen forty-six."

The mention of his name seemed to transport her cruelly from wan but fatalistic reminiscence into a new dimension of concern, as though a line between past and present had been crossed.

Noting the change, Drummond supposed its basis lay in the fact that all the people she had talk about thus far were dead, beyond the pale, suitable only for nostalgic remembrance. But Tom, and his circumstances, was alive, and therefore worthy of much more active concern.

The brightening of her eyes and the slight furrowing of her brow were indications that, at eighty, she was girding herself for battle, and in that instant Drummond knew that this gentle, genteel creature was possessed of an underlying passion that deserved the appellation 'Fighting Irish'. For all her apparent frailty, Cissie Keegan was a tough old bird.

"Poor Tom. Your telephone call came as such a shock. I'd virtually given him up for dead, yet I feared to hear it said."

Karen said, "Miss Keegan, now that we're talking about him, would you mind if I recorded what you have to say?"

Cissie glanced at the recorder, her mind elsewhere. "Not at all. I've been dreading the news for a long, long while."

Drummond urged gently, "If we could start at the beginning, we'd like as full a picture as possible."

"Of course. I just get so angry whenever I think . . . but as you say, to the beginning. Yes, Tom was born in Nineteen forty-six. And he was the delight of everyone's eye, a wonderful boy, so bright and quick."

As she spoke, she was turning pages of the album. She took out several photographs of young Tom with members of the family, on the beach, riding a pony, playing soccer with his grandfather.

"I swear he gave Da and my mother a new lease on life. They adored having him here. Those were good years for us all. And then . . . dear Alice went so suddenly. With meningitis. So very suddenly."

"Tom was six when it happened?" said Drummond. "We got a little information from a family friend in Northridge, a retired policeman named O'Reilly."

"Oh, Gerald, yes, we've known him for many years."

"So, you elected to live with your brother in Northridge, help raise Tom."

She nodded sadly. "Indeed. With my parents' health much better, I felt Tom needed me more. Michael was well established there. Tom had started school; it seemed the best thing for him."

Drummond smiled. "It obviously was. We hear he did very well at school."

Cissie's eyes lit up with pride. "Ach, what a student he was, right from the start. Chemistry and science were his delight. Of course, Michael was thrilled, and taught him so much more than he was learning at school."

"He won a scholarship to Cal. State."

"That and more. He won prizes galore. I suppose he should have gone to one of the Ivy Leagues, and certainly he could have, but he wanted to stay near home."

"He graduated in 'Sixty-eight, then. What were his plans for the future?"

"He wasn't sure. Michael, of course, would have loved Tom to join him in the business, but knew he was far too bright to be dispensing medicines in a drugstore. However, that dreadful Vietnam war was on, and Tom wanted to do his bit before deciding on a future. He felt that if he enlisted before he was drafted, he might have more control over his time in the army, maybe be able to do something that would enhance his scientific future."

Drummond nodded and said, more to Karen than to Cissie, "Which explains why he did four years instead of two. He probably negotiated a kind of short-term contract with the army."

"Indeed he did," said Cissie. "He had heard that the army employed chemists, and felt he could learn some valuable specialized knowledge from the military. And he had several interviews with that intention."

"Where were the interviews held, Miss Keegan?"

"Oh, all over. He had to fly to Washington for one of them. But he didn't talk about them much." She gave a disturbed frown. "In fact, he said almost nothing at all. When he'd done them, just before he signed the contract, Michael and I could see he was troubled about something, but he wouldn't talk. It was as though he'd been sworn to secrecy or something. It wasn't like him, because he was such an open boy, shared everything with us, but we didn't press him. He was old enough to make up his own mind."

Karen asked, "Where did he begin his service, Miss Keegan?"

"He started at Fort Bragg, but he wasn't there long. He had his first furlough after three months, and in that short time he seemed to have changed."

"In what way?" asked Drummond.

"He seemed quieter, preoccupied, as though he were struggling with a dilemma. When I asked him what the matter was, he said that if the army had always been as disorganized as it seemed, he was amazed America had ever won a war. He said there'd been an administrative mix-up, that he'd signed on for service in science and technology and had been allocated a job as a supply clerk. He was bitterly disappointed."

"What happened then?" Karen asked.

156

"He returned to Bragg for posting and we didn't hear from him for some weeks. Whether worry over him, thinking he'd gone to Vietnam, brought on Michael's heart attack, I couldn't say for certain, but it surely didn't help. Michael had been complaining of indigestion for some time, and then one morning I didn't hear him in the bathroom and went up to see if he was awake, and found him unconscious on the bedroom floor. He died in hospital later that same day."

Karen said, "How awful for you."

Cissie nodded solemnly. "It was a terrible time."

"Did Tom come home for the funeral?" asked Drummond.

"He did. And I hardly recognized him. Oh, not physically, he looked well enough, but he seemed . . . strange. There's really no other way to describe it. There was something different about him you couldn't put a finger on. He'd grown spiritually older, as though he'd seen things no man should ever see. He seemed . . . scarred."

"And you detected this, even allowing for the shock and sadness of his father's death?" said Drummond.

"Oh, yes. The two things were entirely separate."

"Did he talk about his army experience at all . . . give you any clue as to where he'd been and what he'd been doing?"

Cissie shook her head. "Very little. He apologized for not writing more, said he'd been moved around a lot, and that really there hadn't been much to write about. But I felt he meant he wasn't allowed to write about where he was and what he was doing." She breathed a small sigh. "To be sure, I felt I'd lost him for ever, even then. Lord God, how swiftly life can change from good to bad. One minute, a happy family, Tom promising so much, then Michael gone and Tom so changed."

Karen said, "Was that when you decided to return here, Miss Keegan?"

"Yes, my dear. Da was three years dead by then, and my mother had had nursing care for some time. I talked it over with Tom and he agreed we should sell up in Northridge, and I should come home to look after mother."

"How often did you see Tom after that?" asked Drummond.

"I didn't see the boy for two whole years. Here, now, let me pour you some more tea." While she stood and served them, she continued, "I'd had several letters, some with no address at all, a few from a place called Edgewood in Maryland, but none of them with any information as to what he was doing. Then one awful day I got his first letter from Vietnam, and my heart died in me. Every night the television was bringing us such awful pictures of what was happening over there, and the thought of Tom . . ." she left her feelings unspoken, finishing the sentence with a gesture as expressive as any words.

Drummond sipped his tea, put down his cup. "Can you remember when it was you received that first letter, Miss Keegan? I realise it's a very long time ago . . ."

"It is, but I remember that whole period as though it were yesterday. Tom was like my own son to me, and my only living relative by then. Mother died shortly after I returned here. So Tom was all I had to think about. His first letter from Vietnam came at Christmas, Nineteen sixty-nine. He'd been in the army sixteen months by then."

"What was the tone of the letter? Did he give you any real news, name any names?"

"No, he did not – and never did. He said he was fine and in no real danger, told me not to worry. But I'm sure all the boys wrote that kind of thing home."

"Did you get the impression that his job *was* providing supplies, as he'd said at the beginning, rather than actually fighting?"

She took a contemplative moment to answer. "I don't

think I ever believed that Tom spent those four years as a supply clerk. Right from the start there was too much . . . secretiveness about his circumstances. He was *far* too bright for a job like that. And there was the other thing . . ."

"What was that?"

"He was never promoted, not even to corporal. Now, Tom was officer material if ever there was such a thing. That always puzzled me greatly."

Karen asked, "Miss Keegan, when you wrote to him, what addresses did you send to?"

Drummond turned to Karen with a congratulatory smile.

"Always to one address – to a post office box in Edgewood, Maryland. And all his letters, even from Vietnam, had that address on them."

Drummond took over. "And he never mentioned any names? Jack Crane, for instance?"

Thoughtful, she shook her head. "No names at all, I'm sure of it. His letters varied very little, so much so that I felt they were being heavily censored, as if he was allowed to write certain stock phrases of reassurance, but no more."

"So – two years passed, which brings us to – when – Christmas Nineteen seventy-one or thereabouts?"

"Exactly so, Doctor. Tom had four weeks Christmas furlough, but he spent very little of it here with me."

"Had he changed very much?"

"Oh, God love him, entirely. He was not the same man. He was nervous, worried-looking. He slept badly, suffered nightmares. Of course, I knew from television and the papers that so many of our boys were returning in that condition, so I wasn't too surprised, just heart-broken."

"And he never volunteered any details of his experiences?"

"No. I tried to talk to him, ask him questions, but I

159

couldn't reach him. He was living in some awful nightmare world of his own."

"Do you know where he spent the remainder of his furlough, Miss Keegan?" asked Karen.

"No, my dear. Within a few days he became so restless, so nervous, I feared he was going to be ill. Then he said he wanted to get away, just drive where the fancy took him, and that was the last I saw of him. I had two more letters from him after that, both from Vietnam, and the next thing I heard was that he was in hospital, in a private clinic in Maryland, and that he'd suffered a nervous breakdown."

"Was the letter from Tom himself?" asked Drummond.

"No, it was from the clinic. They said Tom would write as soon as he was able, but he never did."

Drummond frowned at her. "You mean the last contact you had with Tom was in Nineteen seventy-two?"

"With Tom, yes. But I had a visit that summer from two men who said they were army doctors. They told me that Tom had suffered a terrible breakdown and had completely lost his memory. They said he was being well looked after, and hoped that in time his memory would return, but until it happened, there would be no chance of his returning home."

Karen asked, "Did you suggest visiting him, Miss Keegan?"

"Yes, of course, but they advised against it. They said that not only would it involve a very long journey, but Tom would not know me. They also said he was very unstable, given to violent outbursts, and might do me harm. So, against all my instincts and desires, I took their advice."

"And you haven't seen Tom since?"

Slowly, sadly, she shook her head. "The weeks and months passed, and became years. At first I received the occasional letter from the clinic, telling me there was no change, but eventually they stopped. I suppose in self-protection I gave Tom up for dead long ago. Continual futile hope can be so . . . soul-destroying. And then, out of the blue, your phone call, Doctor. I thought it was the call I'd dreaded for so many years, telling me that Tom was dead."

Drummond shook his head. "No, he's very much alive, but still amnesiac, I'm afraid. He was unwittingly involved in a bank robbery recently, as an innocent bystander, I hasten to add, and was injured. I was called in by the police to try to refresh his memory, get details from him about the robbers. Of course, I got nothing, but I've taken him on as a private patient to try to help him. He's with me now at my home in Palm Desert, a hundred miles from here."

Tears glistened in Cissie Keegan's eyes. "The poor, poor soul. And where has he been all this time, what has he been doing?"

"He's been living in Hollywood, doing odd laboring jobs, but for how long, we don't know. Until now, we've known very little about his past. What you've told me has been a tremendous help, Miss Keegan. At least now I know his amnesia is not just the result of his recent injury. And you've confirmed our own suspicions about his army service. We don't think he spent those four years as a supply clerk, either."

"Then – as what, Doctor?"

"I don't know. And it may well be we'll never know. But be assured we'll do our best to find out – and keep you informed of his progress." Drummond stood. "Thank you so much for your hospitality and your help."

"And I thank you both for yours. In my heart I knew he was alive. Pray God I can see him soon. If he should need anything, Doctor – he has a lot of money here. Michael left everything to him. Let me know how much he needs."

"I will indeed. Just one more thing before we go, Miss Keegan. It's a very long shot, but worth a try. Did you ever hear Tom speak of or recite this couplet

161

– 'In a trice, it will be nice . . . Charlie will be put on ice'?"

Frowning, she shook her head. "I don't think so. When he came back from Vietnam, he talked a lot in his sleep, often cried out and woke up bathed in sweat, but the words were always unintelligible. What on earth does the couplet mean?"

"We don't know, but I believe it had great significance for Tom, and if we can find its meaning, we'll probably know what happened to him in Vietnam."

Drummond signalled to Karen who switched off the tape recorder. "Thank you again, Miss Keegan. We'll return Tom to you just as soon as we can."

At the open door, as they started towards the car, Cissie called, "Doctor Drummond . . . how is it the army never let me know Tom had been discharged from that clinic? How could they do such a terrible thing?"

Drummond turned, nodded in agreement. "It was terrible. And it's one more thing we intend to find out."

Chapter Thirteen

"The *bastards*."

Drummond smiled at the vehemence of the expletive, delivered in such a classy, ladylike accent. "Anyone in particular?"

They were in Pacific Palisades, heading for 459, Lomita in South Hollywood.

"The army! The industrial-military complex. The politicians. Anyone who turns two innocent lives into nightmares of anxiety and grief and madness. How *dare* they treat a woman like Cissie Keegan like that – to say nothing of Tom. All those years, not knowing whether he was sane or insane, alive or dead. My God, who *are* these people?"

"The people who control our destiny. The nameless, faceless guys who own the world. The megalomaniacs who talk in terms of acceptable losses instead of human lives. To someone, or a group of someones, Tom Keegan was an acceptable loss, and Cissie was of no consequence whatever. Expediency rules – okay?"

She looked at him, her expression angry and determined. "How can we stop them, Paul? Surely they can be stopped, exposed, made to pay?"

"You and your paper stand a better chance than most. These people have power. They give power to one another in the guise of government regulations, military protocol. They operate in a twilight zone called national security where the rules of behavior are as flexible as a potentate's whim. I suspect that more crimes have been committed against Americans by Amercians, in the name of national security, than by any alien nation. And the same is probably true for all nations, your own included."

"Oh, I'm sure it's true of mine. It's there in the insanity of the First World War. My father used to say power without wisdom was a child playing in a crowded room with a live grenade – it was only a matter of time before someone got awfully hurt. I'm also sure you're right about my paper. It has the kind of power needed to fight their power. But how do we go about it? How can we expose 'them' when we don't know who 'they' are? Back at the house, I thought you might have asked Miss Keegan if she still had those letters from the private clinic in Edgewood, Maryland, just as a starting point. We have so little to go on."

"I did think of it. But even if she still had them, it was such a long time ago, the contents would be meaningless now. If we started an inquiry there, I really can't see anyone admitting: 'Oh, yeah, I remember kicking Tom Keegan out while he was still amnesiac. What would you like to know, folks?'"

She gave a rueful smile. "You're right. I'm grabbing at straws."

"Whatever was done to Tom Keegan was done for a purpose, Karen. If there's any information to be had, it's going to have to be dug out and fought for. Whoever is asking Dick Gage questions about Keegan and me does not want that information made public. Keegan's exposure in the press with the Mar Vista thing sent up a warning flare to someone with a very long, very powerful arm – powerful enough to be able to jerk the LAPD around. And you can be absolutely certain a polite inquiry to a private clinic in Maryland will get you nothing but a bill for the phone call. One thing you can do, though."

"What's that?"

"Use your contacts to find out what the hell is at Edgewood, Maryland. I've got a feeling that place could be the heart and soul of the Tom Keegan mystery."

"I can do that right now." She indicated the car phone.

"Sure, go ahead."

She pressed buttons, said, "Hi, this is Karen Beal. Could I have the morgue, please?" Then, "Hello, Fran? Karen Beal. Is Alex there?" With her hand over the mouthpiece, she told Drummond, "Alex Jarmand is a twenty-year-old computer whizz-kid. If a thing is findable, he'll find it. Especially for me. I think he's just a teensy bit in love."

Drummond grinned. "Impossible. No twenty-year-old man could be just a teensy bit in love with you."

She eyed him comically. "Was there a compliment in there somewhere? Hi, Alex . . . Karen. I wonder if . . . well, I'm fine, thank you, how're you? Uh huh. Well, it's very nice of you to say so." She arched a brow at Drummond. "Alex, could you do something for me? There's a place in Maryland called Edgewood. It has an army or other military connection, but I don't know what. I'd like whatever you can find on it. I'm in a car, heading for Hollywood. I'll be in and out of the car all afternoon, so if you'd keep on trying? That's very sweet of you. Here's the mobile number . . ."

When she rang off, Drummond, teasing, asked, "What was it that was very sweet of him to say?"

"He *said* that it was always a pleasure to hear my voice, that he could listen to my English accent all day, no problem, and that it made up for him having to work Saturday."

"Huh. And from stuff like that you deduce the guy's a teensy bit in love with you?"

"I realise I may be reaching a bit, Doctor, but when a girl hits twenty-six, all such stuff is grist to her mill."

He laughed. "Poor guy. Can there be a more miserable human condition than to be twenty years old and madly in love with an unattainable goddess?"

She gave him the askance look again. "Who says I'm unattainable?"

It was two-thirty when they drew up outside 459 Lomita and Karen said with dismay, "He lives here?"

"Oh, this is neat, clean and respectable. Wait till you see inside."

Drummond locked the car, unlocked the front door of the building and they entered the hallway. The mound of garbage had been removed, but the odorous memory lingered on.

Karen wrinkled her nose, gazed about her. "Aunt Cissie would die if she knew."

Drummond led her down the corridor, unlocked the apartment door, switched on the light. "My God."

Behind him, Karen said, "What's the matter?"

"They've been here – in spades."

Drummond moved to the center of the room. Karen entered and closed the door. Now it was her turn to say, "My God."

The apartment was wrecked. Every inch of it, bathroom, kitchen, living room, had been picked over. Cupboard doors hung open, their contents checked, strewn, torn and spilled. The drawers had been removed from the chest and tossed aside. The back had been removed from the television set. The iron bed was thrown up against the wall, and kapok from the slashed mattress covered the floor like dirty snow.

But it was the wall behind the bed that riveted Drummond's attention. It had been stripped naked. The Vietnam photographs had been ripped off, leaving only the corners taped to the painted plaster wall.

He was suddenly aware of the thudding of his heart.

166

Catching his transfixed expression, Karen said, "You've gone pale."

He gave a nod, said tightly, "Now I'm worried. Up till now it has all been nebulous. Despite those men being at West LA station, and the questions Dick was asked, it's all been speculation, supposition, possibly our over-active imaginations and the ramblings of Keegan's psychotic mind. This makes it real, Karen – and frightening. What in *hell* are we into here?"

She was moving slowly about the room, picking her way through the debris. "What were they searching for?"

"My guess is, an indication that Tom Keegan is not totally amnesiac. And my next guess is they found it."

"What makes you think that?"

He gestured at the wall. "The photographs. To have collected them, Tom must have remembered something about Vietnam. Whether there was anything specific amongst those photographs that frightened them, I can't say, but maybe it wasn't necessary. Maybe just this indication of *some* recollection was too much for them."

She was peering intently at the wall, at the plaster behind the leaning bed frame. "There's something here, Paul."

He went to her, pulled the frame away, bent to see what she was indicating. Scratched in the painted plaster, by someone as they lay in bed, was the couplet, "In a trice, it will be nice – Charlie will be put on ice."

Drummond stared at it, then gasped, "Oh, Christ."

"What?"

He stood abruptly. "Keegan came out with this couplet in deep hypnosis. When I brought him out of trance he knew nothing about it. But he undoubtedly scratched this here, with an iron nail or whatever,while he was fully conscious. Or at least when he was not hypnotized."

"Maybe he did it in his sleep?"

He stared at her. "Possibly half-asleep. A drowsy state

167

is similar to a light trance state. But I doubt if 'they' would know that, or attribute this scratching to sleep activity."

"Meaning what?"

He was already moving towards the door, his urgency pulling her with him. "Meaning that between the photographs and the couplet, they have more than enough to convince them that Tom remembers too damned much about Vietnam."

They didn't speak again until they were speeding down Venice Boulevard, heading for its nearest junction with the I-10.

Drummond indicated the phone, "Try and raise Tom at the house." He gave her his Palm Desert number. "You'll get the machine, but if he's there he'll hear you. Tell him to pick up the phone."

When she got through, she said slowly, clearly, loudly, "This call is for Tom Keegan. If you're there, Tom, please pick up the phone."

When she shook her head at Drummond, he reached out and took the phone, "Tom! This is Paul. If you can hear me, pick up the phone. I have something very important to say to you."

Cursing under his breath, he handed the phone back to her. "There's an extension in the guest room, but if he's there he won't hear the machine." He checked the time on the dash clock. It showed three-fifteen. "I told him we'd be back before six. He said he wanted to cook dinner for us, so any time now he ought to be in the kitchen. He'll hear the machine from there. Keep trying the number, every five minutes."

"You're very sure he's in danger, aren't you?"

He drew a sigh. "Karen, I just don't know what the hell to think. I'm flipping between certainty and self-ridicule every seven seconds. Just when I'm sure we've got more than enough evidence to place Tom in danger, that pesky

168

voice of sweet reason whispers, 'Come *on*, Drummond, this is real life, not a B-movie. Things like this don't happen in real life."

"But they do."

"But, by God, they *do*. And I'd never forgive myself if something did happen to him and I could've prevented it."

She said, "I think you're absolutely right to react the way you are doing. Listen, I know you see a pretty grotty side of life in therapy, but for living proof of real human weirdness, try crime journalism for a while. I promise you, that pesky voice of sweet reason will soon shut the hell up and never bother you again."

He smiled at her. "Thanks, I needed that."

"I mean it. You were talking about the megalomaniacs, the power brokers, the men who own the world. They exist, Paul. They are real people, not characters in a B-movie. And they gain their power and continue to exist because of millions of people like you and me, people who are blessed – or cursed – with that voice of sweet reason that won't allow them to *fully* accept, even when the evidence is there in the newspaper or on the TV screen for them to see, that such brutal, callous, greedy, ambitious bastards are a living, breathing reality. Unfortunately, it's only when the daughter of the nice family is raped, or Granny is mugged on the street for three bucks, or Daddy is shot down in a store stick-up, that the facts of life strike home. Then, by God, you've got one helluva convert. That's why so many cops burn out. They *know* the crap is for real."

They were joining the I-10, and with a tremendous burst of acceleration that seemed an acknowledgement of her support for the legitimacy of his fears, Drummond flashed across into the fast lane and brought the speed up to eighty-five.

The phone rang, making them jump.

169

Karen picked it up. "Hello? Alex . . . what've you got?" She listened in silence for a while, shot a meaningful glance at Drummond. "Alex, thank you so much, you're a dear. I owe you a coffee break."

She replaced the receiver. "Well, now. What we have in Maryland is the Edgewood Arsenal. And what we have in the Arsenal . . . is the Edgewood Army Chemical Center."

Drummond nodded, his expression grim. "Jesus."

"Which just about confirms that Private Tom Keegan was never a supply clerk, was never a private after boot camp, and that his army record is total bullshit."

"And his 'nervous breakdown'?"

"Is more of the same."

Drummond said, "Try the house again." And brought the Daimler up to a hundred and ten.

Chapter Fourteen

Long before they reached the turn-off for Palm Springs, Drummond was suffused with the premonition that something bad had happened to Tom Keegan. There had been no reply to Karen's continual phoning. And despite her varied attempts at justification – "He may have fallen asleep . . . gone for a walk . . . be sitting outside . . ." Drummond knew none of these alternatives was possible. Keegan had been too enthusiastic about cooking dinner, as a gesture of gratitude, to be doing anything but that, and if he'd been in the kitchen there was no way he could not have heard the repeated calling of his name on the machine.

A tout silence had begun to envelope them as call after call went unanswered. Drummond had driven very fast, one eye constantly on the rear-view mirror for the Highway Patrol, and they'd been lucky. In under an hour, from joining the I–10, they were turning onto the State 111, and barely slackened speed until they entered the outskirts of Palm Springs.

He turned to her with an apologetic smile. "I'd hoped to introduce you to the Valley in happier circumstances. I had nice plans for the week-end."

"There'll be other week-ends, Paul. I haven't yet given up hope that Tom has fallen asleep or something. You said yourself the man's mentally exhausted, disoriented. I mean, he *could* have wandered off and been unable to remember his way back."

"Anything's possible," he said, without conviction. "Keep your fingers crossed."

"I've had fingers, toes, and everything else crossed for the past half-hour."

They passed quickly through Palm Springs, Karen barely giving the lovely, tree-lined town and its smart shops more than a glance. On down the One-eleven, now called Palm Canyon Drive, through Cathedral City and across the boundary into Palm Desert.

Only now, as they turned right and began to climb towards the house, did she acknowledge the beauty of her surroundings. But "Oh, those mountains," was all she said.

Drummond skidded the Daimler to a halt in front of the garage and hurried from the car, Karen following him at a run as he went down the path, threw open the kitchen door and strode inside, shouting, "Tom! Are you here?"

Quickly he covered the entire house, checking the living room, both bedrooms, bathrooms, then out to the rear deck, almost colliding with Karen as he wheeled about and made for the kitchen again, crossed the path and opened the guest room door with a perfunctory knock.

For a moment he stood there, scanning the room, listening for sounds, noting the empty, made bed, noting the open glass doors leading to the side terrace.

"TOM!"

He strode across the room, stepped outside, checked the side and rear of the house, came back in, and found Karen behind the kitchen counter, staring down at something with a look of puzzlement and growing horror.

"Paul, come here."

He joined her at the sink. The aluminum bowl was filled with water. Bright pink water. It had been turned pink by the blood seeping down from the tile surround on both sides of the bowl.

172

Drummond whispered, "Dear God."

He looked down, and around, seeing the water under their feet, seeing now a trail of it marking the carpet between the kitchen and the door, seeing now the twin tracks across the carpet as though made by dragging heels or toes.

"Oh, Christ, no."

"What have they done to him?" Karen was shaking, her voice quavery.

Drummond moved back to the sink, spread out his arms, held his hands above the concentration of blood, and inclined his body and head towards the bowl of water. "The bastards have tortured him. They've held him here . . . cut him . . . drowned him."

She gasped. "Oh, *Paul*. Oh, God, I can't believe it. Maybe . . . maybe he did this himself, tried to commit suicide . . . got afraid and . . . ran off."

He took her by the arm. "Look at these. They're tracks, Karen. Heels or toes. He was dragged out of here. Look at the trail of water. He was dripping water." He was urging her towards the door. "Look! That's blood . . . and here and here."

Now they moved out of the room, followed the blood spots down the paved path to where the Daimler was parked, and there found several spots clustered together, where Keegan had remained stationary while someone opened a car door and bundled him in.

"So he was alive when they took him away," Karen said, her tone an amalgam of dismay and hope. "Otherwise they'd have carried him, wouldn't they? And it had to be more than one person, you said Tom was strong, like Boo Radley. And he's not bleeding that much, Paul . . . I mean, they didn't intend killing him, just hurting him, frightening him . . . d'you think?" Her words tumbled out, seeking confirmation, from a racing mind, stunned by the discovery.

"Probably." Drummond, equally stunned, headed back to Keegan's room.

There he paced about, trying to think clearly, to calm his pounding heart. Observations, deductions and rhetorical questions emerged in bursts from a distraught and disbelieving mind. "They probably came early, caught Tom here in this room. There's no sign of a struggle in the kitchen, in the house. Two questions: how did they know he was here? How did they know he'd be alone?"

"Dick didn't tell anyone he was here," she stated.

"No, he didn't. Was it a guess on their part? Would they take that kind of chance – on Tom being here, and on me *not* being here, even if Tom was?"

"Perhaps they didn't care whether you were here or not. Maybe they'd have been prepared to dispose of you to get Tom."

He frowned at her, paced away, to the open door and back again. "Why did they torture him? Obviously for information. About what? About what he'd told me. And what would Tom be able to tell them? Practically nothing. He'd tell them he couldn't remember anything . . . and they wouldn't believe him because of the Vietnam photographs and the couplet scratched into the apartment wall . . . so they'd go on drowning him and cutting him until . . . why did they stop?"

"They were interrupted?"

"By what or by whom?"

"By someone calling at the house?"

He shook his head. "I never get callers . . ." He stopped, clicked his fingers. "The market. When Tom volunteered to cook dinner for us, I told him to cook what he liked, order it from the market."

"Which market?"

He shook his head. "I don't know. There's a whole bunch of them in Palm Desert. Anyway, it wouldn't help us any to find out who delivered."

"Why not?"

"Because whoever was here didn't answer the doorbell. There are no groceries here or in the house."

"Maybe the delivery man saw a car . . .?" She dismissed the thought with a shrug before it was completed. "So – he saw a car here, so what? He rang the bell, got no answer, cursed, and drove away."

They both took up pacing, Karen stopping Drummond as he again reached the open glass door. "Paul . . ."

"Hm?"

"There's one thing that Tom would've been able to tell them, and probably did."

He turned. "What's that?"

"That you'd had him in hypnosis sessions – at your office."

He stared at her, then smote his own forehead and groaned. "Oh, God." He headed for the opposite door. "Come on!"

As he threw the Daimler down the hill towards El Paseo, Karen said shakily, "This is unreal. I've been to a lot of scenes of crime, seen a lot of blood, but somehow this is different. Maybe it's because there's no body. Maybe it's the vagueness of their reason for doing what they've done. Almost always it's something tangible, like drugs or revenge or territoriality. But to torture and kidnap a poor guy who can't remember a damned thing . . . I mean, who is Tom Keegan going to harm, even if he could remember what happened to him in Vietnam?"

Drummond swirled into the almost deserted parking lot behind his office block. "A very wise old guy named Epictitus once observed that a person is not affected by a situation, only by their interpretation of that situation. It's not what Tom Keegan knows and how much damage he could do with the knowledge, it's what somebody *thinks* he knows and *believes* is the damage he could do."

"And that means they could now think the same thing about you."

He braked to a halt and cut the engine. "Let's find out how much they think I know."

They climbed the external stairs, went along the corridor to the outer glass doors of Drummond's suite. At this hour on a Saturday afternoon the building was deserted, and he was aware of a sudden hush as they lost the sound of traffic along El Paseo. He was not comforted by the comparative silence.

He took keys from his pocket and approached the door, inserted a key, but peered through the glass into the outer office before turning the key. On the far side of the office, a window faced a blank white wall of the next building. Rays from the setting sun burnished the wall to brilliance, and the light of their reflection through the window enabled Drummond to see every detail of the room clearly. It looked and felt as it should.

Turning the key, he pulled open the door and went in, gesturing to Karen to wait at the door until he checked the inner office.

His call, filled with dismay, came a moment later. "Karen!"

She hurried in. He was standing in a room more brutalised than Keegan's apartment had been. Hardly a square foot of floor was visible beneath the devastation that covered it. Files had been pulled from two metal cabinets, their contents strewn to the furthest corners of the room. A large wooden bookcase stood empty, the books ripped apart and flung to the floor. The drawers of Drummond's desk had been jimmied open, and lay upside down on the desk. And the leather couch, slashed along its entire length, looked like a bursting cotton pod.

Drummond, however, seemed focused on a tall metal cabinet that stood beside the bookcase, its doors flung wide, its shelves empty.

"Those evil sonsofbitches. They've taken all my computer disks and audio tapes. Now they *know* what Tom Keegan told me."

Stepping through the debris, Drummond picked up the phone and held it to his ear. "At least they spared this."

While he punched out a number, Karen, standing shocked and helpless, made a reflexive move to pick up a sheaf of file papers.

Drummond, with an acerbic smile, said, "Honey, thanks, but don't bother. I'm going to have to load this lot into a dumpster and take it up to the house. It'll take a month to sort out."

"West Los Angeles Police Station."

"Yes, Lieutenant Gage, please."

"I'm sorry, sir, Lieutenant Gage is not on duty."

"Thank you." To Karen he said, "Dick's off duty, I'll try him at home."

"Your lovely books . . . and the couch." She sounded close to tears of anger. "They had no need to do this."

"I think they did. This was more than a search, it was a warning. First the blood at the house, which they could've cleaned up; now this. They're telling me to drop the Keegan case or else . . ."

"Hello?"

"Hi, Anne . . . Paul. Is he there?"

"What – no seduction? Am I losing my appeal?"

"Sorry, I've just been raped – metaphorically."

"You sound raped – physically. Hang on, he's right here."

Gage came on, serious, picking up his wife's tone. "Yes, Drum?"

"I'm calling from my office in the Valley. Karen and I went up to see Cissie Keegan in Ventura today. Tom was strongly connected to a place called Edgewood in Maryland. On the way back Karen did some checking over

177

the car phone. Guess what? The army has its *Chemical Center* at Edgewood."

Gage muttered an appreciative, "Uh huh."

"I'm trying to stay cool and give you this in sequence, but it's testing my control."

"Why, what in hell's happened?"

"Let me do it my way or I'll fall apart. Towards the end of Tom's stint in the army, Cissie was notified from a private clinic in Maryland – Maryland again – that he'd lost his memory. She had a couple of early letters from the clinic, then nothing more all these years. They never told her he'd been discharged."

"Jesus wept."

"On the way back, we checked out Tom's apartment on Lomita. I had his permission, he gave me his keys. They'd been there, Dick. The place was wrecked. And the Vietnam photos had been ripped off the wall. And – we found that 'trice-nice-ice' couplet scratched into the plaster, which worried me, because except in hypnosis, Tom denied knowledge of that couplet. But its being there obviously didn't worry me half as much as it worried our friends."

"How d'you know?"

"Now we get to it. Tom's gone, Dick. We got back to the house and found blood. We think he's been tortured and kidnapped."

"Oh . . . Christ. Drum, are you *serious*?"

"Entirely."

"I didn't mean that. I mean what in hell are you *messing* with here?"

"I don't know, but it's getting bigger by the minute. We have to figure that the Vietnam photos and the couplet in the plaster led our friends to think Tom remembers a whole lot more than he does, and they tortured him to find out. Well, he must have told them I've given him hypnosis sessions . . . because at the moment I'm speaking to you

178

from a once neat and orderly office that now resembles Omaha beach on D-Day plus five."

"Dru-um!" It was a cry of protest, of concern for a friend's life. "Will you get the hell out of there now . . . and get back to LA where I can give you some protection?"

"Thanks for the offer, but I don't think it's necessary. They've got what they wanted – Tom Keegan and all my audio and computer records. By now they'll know what he gave me in hypnosis."

"And what was that?"

"Practically nothing. Unintelligible ramblings about green men in a garden and that 'trice-nice-ice' thing."

"But you don't know what that means to them, do you? You just said the photos and the couplet worried them enough to come after Keegan."

"That's my guess, yes."

"But now they know *you* know about it. Why shouldn't they come after you, too?"

Drummond sighed. "Well, for one thing, I don't have Keegan's Vietnam experience. All I have is the green men and the couplet, which by themselves are meaningless. For another thing, I'm not an amnesiac borderline psychotic with no social pull or connections. For a third thing, they've already delivered their warning to me to stay out of the Keegan case – the blood up at the house, and my trashed office. What more would they want to do to me?"

"Who the fuck knows *what* these guys want? We don't even know who they are! Maybe *they're* psychos who enjoy torturing people and trashing offices. Maybe they don't *want* to think that you know nothing."

"Meaning what?"

"Meaning, you naive asshole, that maybe they won't be satisfied until they do to you what they've done to Keegan!"

179

"Dick, thanks for the concern, but I think you're overstating the case."

"And *I* think you could be in very deep shit. Do me a big personal favor and get back to LA."

"I can't. You should see this office . . . all my files are screwed up . . ."

"Screw your screwed-up files. They won't be much good to you when you're buried in the desert out there."

"I'll think about it."

"At least get Karen out of there, huh?"

"I intend to. I'll rent a car for her, send her back tonight."

Karen frowned at him, shook her head.

Drummond said, "She's telling me no, but I'll tell her what you've said. Dick, what are we going to do about Keegan?"

"What can we do? We have no police jurisdiction out there, and the local cops are a very small force. If you call them in, show them some blood and your trashed office, tell them the Keegan story, what are they going to do? Call in the Feds? And what are they going to do? Drum, we don't know how big this thing is. Where are the orders coming from? Those guys at the forensic session – maybe *they* were Feds. You go blowing the whistle and you could find yourself so tied up in investigative shit you wouldn't have time to take one, never mind run a business."

"So you're saying forget about Tom Keegan being tortured and abducted?"

"I'm telling you to. I'll put out feelers, see if I can pick anything up. Meanwhile, watch your ass, buddy . . . Anne and I are too fond of it to lose it."

"Okay, Dick, thanks."

Drummond put down the phone, turned to do battle with Karen.

"I'm not going back tonight."

"Dick thinks I'm in danger. And you, too, being

180

here. I think you ought to go, Karen. I'll rent a one-way car."

"May we go back to the house? This place upsets me. Can't I help you tidy it, Paul?"

"No, thanks all the same. If I do it myself, slowly, I'll be easier. I'll do it tomorrow. Come on, let's get you a car."

By eight o'clock they were back at the house, in the kitchen, Karen nursing her second vodka tonic while Drummond grilled two steaks and prepared salad. Both were aware of functioning on two levels of consciousness, a superficial level which enabled to them to trade some banter and talk of inconsequential things; and a far deeper, more intense level, a consuming preoccupation attributable to shock, neither of them being fully able to believe what had happened to Keegan and was happening to them.

"You toss a mean salad, Doctor."

"I read a book. 'Three Hundred Things You Can Do With A Lettuce'." He threw down the salad servers, leaned on the table and looked at her. "Some week-end, huh? The best-laid plans of mice and psychotherapists. Tom was . . ." he shook his head.

"Was what?"

"Was so excited about doing dinner for us." He suddenly exploded. "God*damn*, those bastards." He struck the table with his fist, making her jump. "I'm sorry."

"Don't apologise. I feel the same way and I didn't even know him."

"Dick wants us to lay off, do nothing. But I can't just let it go. The guy was *my* patient. He was tortured in my home, abducted from my home. I can't just walk away from this, forget I knew him. And what about Cissie? We can't leave her expecting progress reports, expecting him home. She's been through that once, I won't put her through it again. She has a right to know. And yet what, and how, can we tell her?"

"We can't assume anything about Tom yet, Paul. Not until he surfaces . . . or his body turns up."

"And what if he – or his body – doesn't? How long do we keep her in the dark?"

Both became immersed in thought, Drummond resuming work on the salad, turning the steaks. When they were done, he said, "Shall we eat outside? I feel I need air."

"Me, too. I'll set the table, you bring the food."

Out on the deck, she laid a cloth over the slatted table and lit candles in red glass jars. For a moment or two they ate in silence, their minds still occupied with thoughts of Keegan.

"I've got an idea," she said eventually. "That trice-nice-ice couplet. It was obviously very meaningful to Tom . . . so meaningful he carved it into his wall, so meaningful that it broke through his amnesia, or what was possibly a deep hypnotic block. Okay, what if . . . what *if* Tom Keegan is not the only person who knows what the jingle means? You told me he'd linked it in hypnosis with those green men in the garden, that they were chanting it, as though learning it by rote?"

"That's right."

"And in his dream or hypnotic recall, there were maybe a hundred or more men involved?"

"Yes."

"So that could mean that one hundred people out there know what the jingle means."

Drummond smiled with approbation. "She is not just an exceedingly beautiful face."

"So why don't I," she went on, pretending to ignore him, "write a piece, naming the jingle, and asking anyone who knows what it means to contact me at the paper?"

Drummond's smile faded. "And put yourself in the same danger that Dick believes I'm in? No, certainly not."

"Oh, Paul, I wouldn't *be* in the same danger. Once that couplet goes into print, I've got the protection of the paper. If a journalist got whacked every time a scandal or a crime was exposed, there'd be none of us left. The villains might try to shut us up *before* publication, but there's no point doing it afterwards."

"They could try to stop you receiving the information, after publication."

"No point. Somebody else would take up my cause. They'd have to dispose of the entire *Times* staff."

Drummond thought about it.

"You know it makes sense," she insisted, smiling at the severity of his expression. "Don't look so worried, nothing's going to happen to me. I'm Sir Edward Beal's daughter, they wouldn't dare."

"We have so little else to go on," he reasoned, almost to himself.

"That's right. And you said it yourself – it takes the power of a paper like the *Times* to fight the power of these people. And I've got access to that power. Paul, it'd be a crime not to use it. It's probably the only way we have of finding out what's happened to Tom – or why it's happened. And maybe, in the long run, preventing it happening to someone else."

He gave a capitulatory nod. "Okay, let's run it. But give yourself protection. Write it in such a way that the villains know the meaning of the jingle will be known by other people on the staff, not just you."

"Trust me." She cut into her steak. "I don't want them coming after me. But if they did . . ." she added with a teasing smile, "boy, what a story."

183

Chapter Fifteen

Up to the final moment before her departure, Karen was resisting his decision. It was almost ten o'clock, and they were standing in front of the garage, the engine of the rented compact Buick ticking over, as she said, "Paul, this is ridiculous. Why do I have to go back tonight? What can possibly happen to me between now and Monday morning?"

In part-answer, Drummond glanced meaningfully at the blood spots on the concrete near her feet, and reflexively she shifted away from them. "Dick's right. Whoever did this to Tom may well be psychotics who enjoy hurting people. I'm not willing to take the chance of it happening to you."

"And what about you?" She looked about her, at the darkness of their surroundings and the black loom of the mountains behind the house. "You're so isolated up here."

"I can look after myself. I'll lock up when you've gone. But I've got to sort the office out tomorrow. I've got clients next week and I need their files."

She offered him a wry smile. "I think you're just trying to get rid of me. Twelve hours together and already you're tired of me."

He looked at her intently, said quietly and seriously, "Dear girl, nothing could be further from the truth." Then he took her face between his hands and gently kissed her on the mouth. "Nothing."

As he released her, she looked up at him, into his eyes, the expression in her own telling him she liked the kiss, liked him, wished even more now that she was not leaving. "When will I see you?"

"I'll be in Monday morning, as usual. But call me when you get home. I want to know you're safe."

"All right." She climbed into the car, closed the door, lowered the window. The final look she gave him said much more than the words she spoke. "Take care."

"You, too."

With a wave, she drove away. Drummond stood there for a while, following the progress of her taillights, already feeling bereft of her presence before they disappeared.

Alone, he became more aware of his isolation than ever before. Now, in that place, with its darkness and the pressing black mass of the mountains, everything that had happened since they entered Tom Keegan's apartment got to him – the violence they had witnessed there, the more shocking, bloody signs of violence in the guest room, and the brutal devastation of his office. Suddenly, he was afraid.

Quickly, he turned and entered the kitchen, closed and bolted the door. As he moved through the house, checking all windows and the sliding glass doors in the living room, drawing the drapes, Dick Gage's warning rang in his head. Why hadn't he listened to it? Why hadn't he told himself "screw the screwed up files", and gotten the hell out of there? At that moment he could have been driving back with Karen in the Daimler, could have been with her, where he wanted to be, not stuck up on a mountain, alone and vulnerable, unarmed and unprotected, running around locking glass doors and windows that they could bust through in a second if they . . . if *they* . . .

In the middle of the living room he stopped himself, aghast at how spooked he was.

They didn't want him. They had to know from the audio

185

tapes that the information about the green men, and the couples was meaningless to him.

Wandering aimlessly into the kitchen, so deep in thought he was unaware he was there, Drummond sat down at the table and tried to recall exactly what had transpired, what both Keegan and he had actually said, in the making-a-movie hypnosis session.

After he'd set the scene in the jungle, he'd asked Keegan about the color of the uniforms and which army would be fighting there . . . then Keegan had blurted out about his friend Marty . . . and then had gone into the trice-nice-ice thing in a big way, and about the guys laughing and falling down . . . and then into the black, black, black business.

But then, out of hypnotic trance, Keegan had denied knowledge of everything. No, not *every*thing. He'd asked Keegan about the men, were they Anglo or Black? Keegan replied "Anglo". Then Drummond had asked "Then what is it about them that's black?" and Keegan had exploded, "Blood!"

Would that, to the minds of the kidnappers, constitute a threat? Would it indicate sufficient rehabilitation of Keegan's memory to cause them trouble – either from Keegan or himself, or both?

Dick Gage's warning echoed again in his mind. "Maybe they don't *want* to think you know nothing. Maybe they won't be satisfied until they do to you what they've done to Keegan! Maybe they're psychos who *enjoy* torturing people . . ."

Maybe . . . maybe . . . maybe. He was neck-deep in that world of supposition, speculation and doubt again, balancing on the edge of a credibility gap that was the mind's natural defence against the shocks and horrors of a violent and unpredictable life.

What *was* the truth of the situation? Where should he look to find it?

After a moment, as though his body was acting on its own volition, Drummond found himself standing up and moving towards the kitchen door, unbolting it, heading out across the path to the guest room, entering it, switching on the lights, and standing there, shaking, staring at the bloody sink.

He had asked questions, and his subconscious mind had answered them. *Here* was the truth of the situation. *Here* was where one looked to find it. This was Tom Keegan's blood.

Again unbidden, his body moved. His hand reached out, a finger dipped into a palm-sized pool of gore, and came away contaminated. He rubbed the blood between finger and thumb, feeling the awful reality of it, sticky, thick and drying. This was Tom Keegan. This blood had flowed in his veins until someone had severed them. Until someone – under orders from somebody else – had come here, had grabbed Tom Keegan, had held him here, had cut his wrists, had forced him to watch his own life-blood flowing into the water in the sink, and then had plunged his face into it, drowning him in his own blood.

An act of awful, calculated brutality.

Performed by whom?

Ordered by whom?

Originating from whom?

Possibilities tumbled through his mind.

The people who had falsified Keegan's army records.

Someone at the Edgewood Army Chemical Center.

Someone Keegan had served with in Vietnam.

Someone associated with the private clinic in Maryland.

The faceless men who had attended the West LA session.

All of the above.

Some of the above.

None of the above.

From a cupboard beneath the sink, Drummond took

a plastic bowl, a bottle of disinfectant cleaner, and a washcloth, and for an hour scrubbed at the sink, its surrounds and the floor until they shone.

For a moment after, he stood looking at the place, then around the room, only now remembering Keegan's meagre possessions. Crossing to the closet, he opened the door, found it empty, went to the bedside drawers – empty – into the bathroom stripped. Nothing of Tom Keegan remained. Not one damned thing. Securing the sliding door, he turned out the lights, locked the outer door, and returned to his kitchen.

It was there that the name leapt into his mind as an addition to the list of possibilities.

Jack Crane.

It now occurred to him that Karen had brought with her, and taken back with her, the details of Crane's army service which Dick Gage had given her, and that they'd never had a chance to discuss Crane at all. When she phoned, he would ask her to read out the details and he would record them. Not with the slightest hope, in view of the falsification of Keegan's records, of linking the two men in Vietnam, but perhaps of gaining better insight into the man whose name and voice had disturbed Keegan so.

With this in mind, he entered the living room, attached the suction microphone of a portable tape recorder to the answerphone, and returned to the kitchen to make a mug of coffee.

With uncanny synchronicity, the phone rang almost immediately.

Frowning, Drummond checked his watch. It was an hour and a half since Karen had left. Unless she'd driven very fast, it was unlikely to be her. Unless . . .

His heart increased its beat.

Unless she'd had trouble on the way . . . car trouble . . . accident trouble . . .

The answerphone was on its fourth and final ring as he reached it. The automatic recorder cut in. There was silence for a moment while his out-going message played, then the beep sounded. He was reaching for the phone, anticipating her voice, when a male voice stopped him. The voice was deep and resonant and gentle – and the most threatening Drummond had ever heard.

"Please pick up the phone, Doctor Drummond, I know you're there."

Now Drummond's heart leapt. For several moments his mind panicked. It was as if the caller could see him standing there! His gaze flashed to the glass doors, but the drapes were drawn. The image of a hidden camera haunted him.

"Doctor Drummond, please, don't let's waste time. I know you can hear me."

Presence of mind now broke through the anaesthesia of shock. The portable tape recorder was attached to the phone. Drummond reached down and pressed the record button, then picked up the receiver.

"Who is this?"

"Think of me as a friend. Friends look out for one another. They care about such matters as health and safety. I care about yours."

"What do you want?" Drummond could barely speak for the constriction in his throat, the pounding of his heart.

"My needs are simple. I want you to forget that you ever met Tom Keegan, that you ever spoke with him, and to forget everything he has ever said to you in hypnosis."

"Or what?"

The caller gave a small, disappointed sigh. "We could have taken her before she reached the freeway . . . or on the freeway . . . and might still do it before she reaches her apartment in Santa Monica. At this moment Karen Beal, in her rented Buick, is, perhaps coincidental to the timing of this call, perhaps not, on the I-Ten in South Hollywood, a few blocks from Lomita. What was your question again, Doctor Drummond?"

"You bastards leave her alone. She has nothing to do with this."

"On the contrary. She accompanied you to Ventura this morning when you spoke with Cissie Keegan, then to four-five-nine Lomita. Karen knows as much about Keegan as you do. Do warn her to stop meddling in our affairs. I know you'd hate to have to clean up her blood, as you've cleaned up Keegan's."

Drummond, aghast, momentarily lost control again. They knew! They were watching his every move!

"Nothing to say to that, Doctor? No macho stance or counter-threat? Listen to me very carefully, Drummond, I shan't be calling again. You are meddling in things which don't concern you, and you are completely out of your depth. Drop it – or we'll drop you, or perhaps the girl. Take warning from what was done to your office. But if that isn't enough, check your freezer."

The caller hung up.

Legs trembling so much he could scarcely stand, gut-twisted, hands shaking so badly he tried three times to replace the receiver, Drummond moved from the living room to the kitchen and stood staring at the refrigerator. It was a big Westinghouse, right half fridge, left half freezer. It had suddenly taken on the threat of a vampire's coffin.

He tried to recall if he'd opened the freezer while preparing dinner, and decided he hadn't. The steaks had been in the fridge, the remainder of a pack Keegan had opened for that dinner.

What in hell could be in the freezer?

Dreading the discovery, he reached out and eased the door open, stomach nerves tight with anticipation. He pulled down the flap of the top section, peered in. Six

190

packaged frozen dinners. Everything quite normal. Next section: bags of vegetables. Nothing out of place. Third section: tubs of icecream. Fourth section: empty. Fifth section: empty.

Nerves now stretched to screaming pitch, he pulled out the bottom basket and fell back, nauseated, gagging, crying out in protest.

It was a rat. A foot-long, long-dead rodent, its body bloated and burst, its guts smothered in a mound of hideous, fat, frozen white maggots.

There was a message. Simple, yet terrifying. It was attached to the rat's tail in the form of a small leather luggage identification tag.

The name and address on the label was Karen's.

Chapter Sixteen

First things first.

He'd had to regain control of his logical mind. For the past nine hours, since he had opened Keegan's apartment door and seen the devastation, he'd been spooked, been firmly in the grip of the old mammalian segment of his brain that demanded an emotional fight-or-flight reaction to everything that had happened. It was time to pry it loose.

It was ironic that a man who spent much of his time apprising patients of the structure and mechanics of mind, and educating them to their use, should become so ensnared by runaway emotion that he had to make a strenuous, conscious effort to extricate himself from it. But perhaps, he reasoned in his own defense, this said more *for* the power of the ancient brain than *against* his abilities as a psychotherapist.

And again, these people who were doing the frightening were undoubtedly very experienced and able psychologists in their own right. They knew all the psychological pressure points that triggered fear and panic, and how to exert maximum pressure upon them. In their own dark field of endeavor, they were very professional indeed.

Take the rat. There was a piece of imaginative obscenity worthy of an A-plus grade. It struck at numerous pressure points simultaneously. Not only did the corpse itself strike deep into ancient human fear and repulsion of death, decay, and being eaten by worms, but its positioning in the freezer also triggered the fear of being poisoned by contaminated food (never again would he eat food from that refrigerator), and a feeling of chronic insecurity, deriving from the fact that someone, with impunity, had entered and desecrated his home.

The caller had been right. He'd said, "Take warning from what was done to your office. But if that isn't enough, check your freezer". Implying: that'll do it. Knowing, with certainty, it would do it.

It was half-past midnight when Drummond thought these thoughts. He was seated in the living room beside the phone, waiting for Karen's call. He had tried her number once, got the answerphone, and left a message for her to call him immediately. He had also tried to reach Dick Gage, and had been told by the babysitter that Dick and Anne were out to dinner and wouldn't be home until one.

In the past half hour he'd spent all the emotion he could afford, beginning with the utter revulsion of removing the rat and burying it at the bottom of the rear yard, and continuing with anger, fear and uncertainty as he replayed the caller's tape time and time again.

Now, by virtue of the "physician, heal thyself" lecture he had given himself, and some concentrated self-hypnosis, he felt calm and detached, more in control, able to review the tape yet again, to analyse and assess the contents that had initially so appalled and frightened him.

So, what did the content of the tape really mean?

For a start, the voice itself. Calm, gentle, and educated. Well-chosen for the job of frightening a professional man. They had guessed, correctly, that a collegiate voice would carry more impact for Drummond than a deze-dem-and-doze accent because it implied intelligence which, coupled with violence, was far more frightening than raw brutality.

Then came the assumption: "Please pick up the phone,

Doctor Drummond, I know you're there." And later: "I know you can hear me". Okay, think that through. Unless the house was bugged, there was no way for certain that the caller could know Drummond was within ear-shot of the phone. Quite possibly the house was under surveillance, but with the drapes closed Drummond's immediate location could only be guessed at. And that was probably what the opening bit had been – a guess and a lucky hit. But psychologically devastating.

Then the really scary bit: Karen. They knew about the rented Buick, that she'd left the house, and was on the freeway, heading for her apartment in Santa Monica. The part about her being adjacent to Lomita may have been total bullshit, just to plant the thought in his mind that someone was dogging her, every foot of the way.

Then the clever bit about the caller knowing Drummond had cleaned up Keegan's blood. Another lucky guess?

He didn't doubt that Karen and he had been under surveillance since their arrival in Ventura, that they'd been tracked to Lomita, to the Valley, to the office, to the car rental place, and back to the house. And he wouldn't bet money against the house and the phone being bugged. He didn't, couldn't, deny that the caller and his pals, however many, were bold, ruthless and determined people. But one thing he now emphatically denied – that they were going to stampede him into blind panic.

His animal brain activity had now been relegated to moments when it could be of use, not a detriment. From here on, it was going to be a thinking man's war.

The phone rang. He didn't wait to hear who was calling, he picked up and anounced his number. It was Karen.

"Hi, it's me."

"You got back safely?"

"Sure. Just got in."

"No trouble along the way?"

"None. Should there have been?"

"I've had a phone call." He kept his voice calm, factual, yet concerned. If they were listening, he wanted them to know, for Karen's sake, that he'd got the message and respected it.

She asked, "From whom?"

"From them. They've warned us to drop the Keegan case, forget everything, and I think we should."

"You . . . Paul, you can't mean that."

"I do! Karen, listen to me. These people know everywhere we've been and everything we've done since I picked you up this morning. They have terrific resources and a very long arm. The caller said I was completely out of my depth on this, and he's right. So are you. Now, please, do as they say and forget it."

When she spoke again, he could hear in her tone disappointment with him, and disbelief that he could say such a thing. "And what about Cissie? Are we going to leave her in the dark?"

"Yes! We're going to leave everything, right now."

"And what about the idea we had . . ."

"Karen! Let it go! I don't want to hear another *word* about Tom Keegan."

There was a prolonged silence. Drummond could visualise her frowning at his abusive tone, with dismay, bewilderment, and then with growing understanding that he feared they were being overheard.

Eventually, with a capitulatory sigh, she said, "All right, Paul, if that's the way you want it."

"*I* don't want it that way, *they* want it that way. And they have the power."

"Yes. Right. Well, call me sometime. Maybe I'll see you in Duke's."

"Sure. Goodnight, Karen."

He put down the phone. Smart girl. She was telling him not to call her at the apartment. The reference to Duke's was to the safe pay phones there that the police used for sensitive calls. She was saying: I know we're both bugged.

Dick Gage's call came ten minutes later.

"What now, buddy?"

"Karen left at ten. She just called from Santa Monica."

"Good. Now I want you in."

"There's no need, Dick. I'm dropping the Keegan case. For me, the guy never was."

There was the same kind of pensive silence Karen had given him. "Something happen?"

"I had a call."

"Uh huh. Tell me about it."

"I'd rather not. I've got a lot of other patients to take care of, and I can't afford to endanger my practice. I've had fair warning and I'm heeding it. I've already forgotten Keegan. I won't even bill West LA for the forensic session."

"As you wish. Personally, I think you've made the right decision. Some things are better left alone. See you around, huh?"

"Yeh, take care, love to Anne."

Drummond rang off, knowing Dick had also got the message. His last response had been ludicrously formal, totally uncharacteristic. Dick Gage had never said "as you wish" in his life.

So, where did they go from here? Part of what he had told Dick was true, he did have other patients to take care of, and to do it he needed his files reassembled. He would get up early, spend the whole of Sunday in his office, drive to Malibu Sunday evening instead of Monday morning.

And in the time between, he would work on a code he could use to direct Karen and Dick to safe pay phone numbers from which they could plan their strategy.

This would be his first move in the mind-war he was about to wage against the bastards who had destroyed Tom Keegan – and desecrated his Westinghouse refrigerator.

196

Chapter Seventeen

Sunday.

Midnight.

Malibu.

Drummond sat watching Politics Today, an in-depth media discussion of the presidential nominees and their vice-presidential running mates. The panelists were journalists on the *Chicago Tribune*, the *Atlanta Constitution*, and the *Orlando Sentinel*.

The discussion centered on the up-coming television debate between Jack Crane and Milton Byrne, scheduled for the following Sunday at the Pauley Pavilion on the UCLA campus. It was the only debate to which Jack Crane had agreed.

Chicago was saying, "And Byrne is lucky to get this one. Crane doesn't have to debate. What governs a candidate's decision whether to debate, and under what terms, is a very simple one: who is ahead in the race and who is behind? As of today, Crane is ten to twelve points ahead. Why should he take the risk?"

Atlanta came in. "And it will be a risk. Strategically, Byrne has been backed into a corner. He's been overwhelmed by the power of Crane's personality and the bulldozing tactics of his campaign – not least by the onslaught of his negative TV commercials. It is now *imperative* that he meets Crane face-to-face, and demolishes him in debate, if he's to stand a chance in this election."

Orlando: "Byrne could do it, too. He is, by far, the better debater. On the stump, he's not in the same league as Crane. He is mild-mannered Clark Kent compared to Crane's war-hero Superman. But Byrne is intellectually superior. He's extremely knowledgeable about a wide range of issues, and a stickler for facts. If he plays his cards right, he *could* make Jack Crane look a blustering, know-nothing bully-boy up there."

Chicago: I think you're missing the essential point about TV political debates here, Frank. They are a modern phenomenon, have a character all of their own, and shouldn't be confused with any other form of political interface. What the voting viewers take away from a presidential debate is *not* the specific answers on complex national and international questions, but an *overall impression of the debaters*. Which of the candidates will appear more *sincere*, which more *charismatic*? These are the judgements that could determine the vote of millions of Americans, who are too preoccupied with other matters to follow the campaign on a day-to-day basis."

Atlanta: "I have to agree. The debates *have* become a crutch for voters who are too busy, lazy or disinterested to follow the campaign. And considering that the answers given in TV debate are seldom more than a rehash of boilerplate responses given on the stump, they're not very satisfactory as a means of deciding the outcome of a general election. Seen in another light, they might even be dangerous. Because they *are* the single most sustained dose of candidate exposure most voters are likely to get, they've begun to assume enormous importance in the eyes of the voter, far greater importance than their intrinsic worth."

Orlando: "Okay, I go along with those comments, but they don't detract from what I said about Milton Byrne. I still maintain he has a good chance to pull back percentage points in this debate. Jack Crane will undoubtedly come across as usual as 'Stonewall Jack', the charismatic hero-warrior-saviour of America, the tough-ass who's going to kick crime and drugs into touch, and restore old-time Norman Rockwell values to America, and Milton Byrne will be standing there looking like a profoundly knowledgeable wimp – unless . . . *unless* he can come up with a question, a line of attack, *something*, that will rock Crane back on his heels, undermine his confidence, knock some of the iron-clad stuffing out of him."

Atlanta: "And what might that be, Frank?"

Orlando: "Well, I've no idea. But if I were managing Milton Byrne, seeing political oblivion staring my candidate in the face, right now I'd have my team of guys taking Jack Crane's political and private life apart, searching every closet for a potential skeleton. The debate next Sunday, the *only* debate these two will have, is conceivably the one and only chance Milton Byrne will have of getting into the White House. Yes, he has the knowledge on a broad range of issues to undermine Crane's TV persona, make him look politically ignorant, but it may not be enough. What Byrne needs in his armory is not only the blunt instrument of superior knowledge, but a stiletto he can slip between Jack Crane's armor and make him howl. Hell, this is TV. Come on, Milt, give the folks a show!"

Chicago: "Do you think Byrne capable of such tactics, even if this 'stiletto' came to hand? The guy's a gentleman. I really can't see him fighting dirty, even if it means the White House."

Atlanta: "I think it would depend on the nature of the weapon. If it was merely personal dirt – no, Byrne wouldn't stoop to using that. But if it was something indicative of a dangerous flaw in his opponent's character or political ability, something that might conceivably be detrimental to the nation, I think he would. Milton Byrne may appear excessively ethical, to the point of political naivety, but he's certainly no fool. He wants the White

House. He thinks he can be good for America. And so do I. Personally, I hope he finds his stiletto before next Sunday."

From the almost reflexive nods that Chicago and Orlando gave, it appeared they were in agreement.

As the discussion moved on to an analysis of the vice-presidential candidates, Drummond switched off the set.

Curious.

According to the polls, Jack Crane was ten to twelve points ahead of Byrne in voter popularity, and yet without exception the political pundits Drummond had viewed or listened to favored Byrne. Did they, like Drummond, sense something unpalatable in Crane's makeup that the average voter didn't? Was the public, as Chicago suggested, blinded by Crane's TV charisma?

Beware the cult of personality, a wise man once said.

Getting up from the armchair and heading for the bedroom, Drummond found himself hoping that Milton Byrne would find his weapon. But finding it and being capable of using it were two different matters. Little David had his stone and his sling, but if he hadn't let fly, Goliath would've made hamburger out of him.

Come November 8, Milton Byrne was going to have to bring down his own Philistine . . . or wind up on a bun.

He was entering the corridor leading to his bedroom when he heard it – and froze. Heart pounding, he turned towards the source of the sound, towards the sliding glass doors of the living room. There it was again, the unmistakeable tread and scuff of footsteps on the wooden sundeck.

Quickly, he moved back across the living room, searching for a weapon, seeing the heavy brass poker in the fireplace, going for it, grabbing it, moving now to stand beside the floor-length drapes, listening, his heart rocking his body as he heard the locked door being tried.

He tried to think clearly, to reason, to subjugate panic.

Who could it be?

Them?

Had they trailed him from the Valley?

If so, why try to break in now? To do what? They could've visited him in Palm Desert, stopped him along the way, or come two hours ago.

Burglars?

But they could see the glow of the room lights through the drapes. Would they take such a chance?

The door was tried again. And then – a soft knock!

Drummond grabbed a drape and flung it back.

He was staring into the face of Dick Gage.

Drummond opened his mouth to speak, to curse, to protest, but Gage raised a finger to his lips, motioned Drummond to open the door.

Drummond slid it back. Gage waved him outside onto the deck, telling him to shut the door.

"Christ, Dick, what's going on? You scared the crap outta me."

"The house is bugged. I spoke to Karen this morning, in person, not by phone, hers is bugged, too. She told me what had happened in the Valley. Man, you're both into something really serious here, and I want you to get out of it right now. I didn't believe that shit you gave me over the phone about forgetting Keegan, but you've got to. The people you're messing with are major league, Drum, big enough to tail you and Karen all over California, to abduct Keegan, trash your office, and bug your phones."

"How d'you know they're bugged?"

"Because I've had one of our guys check them out. I called on Karen this morning, took Joe Stills with me. He's an old buddy, does all our electronic sweeps for us. He found a room bug in Karen's phone."

"How could they get into her apartment? It's a secure building."

Gage sighed with exasperation. "Jesus, you still don't

get it, do you? These guys are *pros*, Drum. They have access to any nefarious talent you can put a name to – house-breaking, alarm by-passing, bugging, undetectable surveillance, and all kinds of fucking murder and mayhem. After I'd seen Karen, I brought Joe over here. You've got bugs all over the place, buddy – phones, kitchen, and bedroom. You can't take a piss without them hearing it."

Drummond leaned on the rail and looked out over the moonlit beach and the black, shimmering ocean. Despite his resolve not to be panicked, he was shaking.

"How did you know I was here, Dick? I haven't told anyone I was coming in tonight."

"I've had the patrol boys keep an eye on the place, as a personal favor. I got a call at home around ten that the Daimler was here."

Drummond looked at him. "That was good of you. I appreciate it."

"Someone's got to look out for you, you dumb bastard. And if I didn't, I'd catch hell from Anne."

Drummond smiled his appreciation.

"Tell me about the phone call from our friends."

"A real smoothie, voice like Vincent Price, quiet, genteel, frightening. Told me to forget Tom Keegan or else. Implied something bad would happen to Karen. Then told me to check my freezer."

"Your freezer?"

"There was a dead rat in the bottom drawer. It'd been dead about a week, if you get my drift."

Gage pulled a face.

"There was a luggage tag tied to its tail. It had Karen's name and address on it, was probably hers. Now I know how they got it."

Gage sighed deeply. "You have to give them credit for one thing, they're giving you two plenty of warning. And I just *know* you're going to take it."

"Did Karen mention her idea about the trice-nice-ice thing?"

"No – what?"

"She's going public with it in an article this Wednesday, trying to find someone else who knows what it means."

Gage exploded, *sotto voce*, "Is she crazy? Has she got a death-wish or something?"

"She's a journalist, Dick, and smells a good story. Maybe even a big one. She's also incensed by what has happened to Keegan, and to Cissie, and wants to do something about it."

"Well, that's fine, but does she fully realise the danger involved, what kind of people she's messing with?"

"I gave her the same lecture. She said that once the piece was published, there'd be no point in anyone coming after her."

Gage repeated his sigh. "Drum, do you recall a journalist named Dorothy Kilgallen?"

"I've heard the name, sure."

"She was a syndicated columnist, much more prominent than Karen, probably as well known as Johnny Carson. In Nineteen sixty-five, Kilgallen interviewed Jack Ruby in his Dallas cell. She was the only major journalist permitted to interview him. She told a few people that, from the stuff she'd gotten from Ruby, she was able to obtain further information that would blow the John F. Kennedy assassination case sky high. A few days later, Kilgallen died of a massive overdose of barbiturates combined with alcohol. Her apartment was found in a shambles. I repeat: like Tom Keegan's apartment and your office, her apartment was torn apart. The transcripts of her interview with Jack Ruby were missing. And guess what? Her death was ruled a suicide. I sure would hate to see Karen end up the same way, *especially* when, unlike Kilgallen, she doesn't even know what kind of story she's chasing."

"Dick, she's aware of the danger. Hell, she saw

Keegan's blood. She's going to include safeguards in the article, make it plain she's not working solo on this, that other *Times* staff are involved. Once the piece is published, there'll be no point in anyone coming after her. Obviously, Dorothy Kilgallen's mistake was talking about the information before she published it."

"And you think it's worth the risk – to yourself as well as Karen?"

Drummond, staring out at the glittering ocean, was pensive for a moment. "The word 'cause' has kind of fallen into disrepute lately, hasn't it? It sounds old hat, naive, silly. This country, maybe the whole damned world, is in the hands of the grabbers. I get so sick of this 'Gotta win' mania . . . 'number one is everything, number two nothing'. Christ, Dick, the world's full of number twos. Do they get nothing? Tom Keegan was made a number two by the grabbers, and that's what he got – nothing. Not even a life. I think it's time the number twos got together and made their presence felt."

"In other words, you're going through with it."

"Yes. Let's see what reaction Karen's article gets."

"Okay. I'll do my best to keep an eye on her – on you both."

"Thanks, Dick."

"Drum, I get pissed being jerked around, too. Keegan was my witness. I was taken off the case. Those two suspects they picked up in San Francisco? They let them go. It was all bullshit. The case is closed and the Mar Vista killers are running around loose. I'll do what I can for the number twos." Gage checked his watch. "Jesus, I must go."

"Thanks again for everything, Dick."

"Just watch your ass, kiddo."

At the top of the stairs leading down to the beach, Drummond said, "One thing, Dick . . . the stuff you gave Karen on Jack Crane, we didn't get a chance to go over it. Can you remember the gist of it?"

"Sure. Nineteen sixty-nine, Crane was a major in the Marines. He led a daring-do helicopter rescue mission behind VC lines and brought back more than a hundred American prisoners. He made six trips personally, got shot down on two of them, was badly injured on the last. Real Rambo stuff, won a bunch of medals. After that he transferred to Military Intelligence, then to the CIA. He resigned from the CIA to run for office."

"More than a hundred prisoners?"

"Is that significant?"

"I don't know. A hundred-plus soldiers featured in Keegan's dream and hypnosis recall."

"A coincidence?"

"Maybe. Maybe."

"Take care." With a wave, Gage went down the stairs.

Drummond followed his progress along the beach, saw him cut up between two houses to where he had parked his car.

In the living room, doors again locked, drapes drawn, Drummond felt the cold touch of unease that came with the knowledge of their electronic presence. This was invasion of privacy at the grossest level. His home now felt as spoiled and polluted as had his refrigerator. Until this thing was over, he would have to guard every word uttered, every act performed in this house.

Until this thing was over.

What thing?

A soldier comes home from Vietnam, has a nervous breakdown, is placed in a private clinic, and is discharged without memory. Many years later his name appears in a newspaper, he goes into therapy, babbles about a hundred green men in a garden, recites a rhyming couplet, and is disturbed by the voice and image of Jack Crane. Jack Crane is a hero of Vietnam, wins medals for bringing a hundred men out of the jungle, joins Military Intelligence and then the CIA.

Crosschecks:

Vietnam in the same time-frame.

One hundred-plus men in the jungle.

The CIA bug phones, carry out surveillance, make people disappear.

Jesus Christ, it wasn't possible.

And neither was the assassination of President Kennedy.

And neither was the death of Dorothy Kilgallen.

"In a trice, it will be nice . . . Charlie will be put on ice."

What if . . . there *was* someone out there who knew what the jingle meant?

And what if its meaning opened up a can of worms as awesome as Kennedy's death – and came into his and Karen's possession?

What then, huh?

Making his way towards the bedroom, Drummond found his heart pounding again.

Chapter Eighteen

Monday.

Ten am.

"*Los Angeles Times*, good morning."

"Karen Beal, please."

"One moment."

She came on. "Karen Beal."

Drummond said, "You remember where they called us The Beautiful People?"

There was a small hesitation, then a smile. "Of course."

"Can you meet me there at twelve-thirty?"

"Yes." Serious now.

"Tell no one."

"All right."

Drummond hung up. He had used a pay phone on Wilshire, half a block from his office. He had no idea whether Karen's office phone was tapped, but had to assume it was. He was taking Dick Gage's lecture to heart; these people were pros and had to be treated as such.

Walking back, he was conscious of a growing nervous condition brought on by all that had happened over the weekend, a kind of fizzy sensation affecting his entire body. It was not altogether unpleasant. He felt more alive than he had for a long time. His senses seemed keener. He was constantly aware of his environment, of cars on the street, of the people around him.

With a touch of satirical humor, he surmised that this must be how under-cover agents felt, spies in a foreign city, and thought he now knew why they did those jobs. There was something primeval and exciting about being under threat, of pitting one's wits against a dangerous adversary. It took a situation like this to reveal just how primitive *homo sapiens* still was, beneath his thin veneer of social sophistication. What was shocking was the revelation that it applied to *himself*, to Doctor Paul Drummond, as much as anyone. What price the New Brain when the dogs of war were loosed?

Karen looked a dream in a sage green suit and cream silk blouse when she entered Casa Renata. Mama greeted her like a long-lost daughter and escorted her to Drummond's table, reiterating, in a potpourri of Italian and fractured English, that she looked like an angel and how wonderful it was to have The Beautiful People grace her establishment again.

Disappointing Mama, who had wanted to place them at a window table to show the passing world the quality of her patrons, Drummond had insisted on a table at the rear of the restaurant, away from prying eyes and possibly from prying parabolic microphones. Though far from knowledgeable in such hi-tech matters, he'd seen enough movies to know equipment existed that could pin-point and pick up individual conversations in rooms more crowded than Casa Renata.

Karen joined him, smiling. "Hi."

"Hi, yourself. Mama's right, you do look angelical. Vodka tonic?"

"Please."

He ordered two and Mama departed.

Drummond smiled at her, enjoying the sensation of warm affection that coursed through his body at the sight of her, at the closeness of her. He wanted to reach out and touch her face, to kiss her beautiful mouth again.

208

"What?" she said, arching a brow, knowing full-well what, but playing her woman's game.

"Nothing. I was just sitting here, trying to remember the phrase they use in England to describe a girl like you. A 'cracking bird'?"

She laughed. "And you? How about 'cool dude'?"

He nodded. "Right now, I'm feeling pre-tty cool."

Their drinks arrived. They ordered antipastas and a light fish entrée.

Karen asked, "Did you come in this morning?"

"No, last night. I worked at tidying my office all day yesterday, got it fairly okay, left about eight. I needed to get out of the house, the Valley."

"They've spoiled it for you, haven't they? You loved it so much there. Can the house ever be the same?"

He shook his head. "No. But that's okay. I can sell it, buy another. I was never that attached to it, only to its isolation. There are plenty more to choose from."

"Tell me about the call."

"It was creepy. Quiet and threatening. They threatened me with your . . . well being."

"You mean with my life."

"Implied, not specified. I believe we were very lucky deciding to eat dinner out on the deck, rather than in the kitchen."

"Why? Oh, what we talked about. You think the kitchen was bugged?"

"Very likely. If they'd heard about your trice-nice-ice article in the kitchen, you might not have reached LA. The caller claimed to know exactly where you were on the freeway, said they could have taken you at any time after leaving the house. Now I'm inclined to believe him."

"Why now?"

"I had a visit from Dick last night. He came in from the beach and frightened the hell out of me, knocking on the living room doors. We talked out on the deck. He told me he'd visited you with Joe Stills, checked your apartment, found the phone bug. After your place, they checked the beach house, found bugs in all the rooms. If they've done it to the Malibu house, they've done it in the Valley. I've also got to assume my office here, and maybe even your office phone are bugged. Dick went to great pains to impress upon me the extent of their reach and capabilities. So, yes, if they'd heard about your article, I believe you might not be sitting here now."

The hors d'oeuvres arrived and they began to eat, but without particular enjoyment. It was not an occasion for culinary appreciation.

Drummond asked, "How's the article coming?"

"It's written – and approved. I worked on it all day yesterday, showed it to my editor this morning. I had a long talk with him, told him everything that had happened – to Tom Keegan, to us. He was appalled. Like us, he feels there could be something terrifically big behind this, for them to go to all this trouble – to say nothing of the violence – and he smells a huge story. He's backing me all the way."

"Good. But we've got to be very careful, trust no one we don't have to. We don't know who these people are, or where they are. If they can pull rank on the cops, they can pull it anywhere. Dick reminded me of the death of Dorothy Kilgallen. Do you know about that?"

"Of course. Every journalist worth the name does. It was infamous."

"So – who killed her and stole her transcripts?"

She nodded. "There are some very creepy people around, Paul. Right now, I could go to the phone and arrange to have somebody killed for a thousand dollars."

He frowned at her. "Are you serious?"

"Perfectly. You'd be amazed what you can buy for a thousand bucks in LA."

210

He shook his head. "Speaking of phones, I got your message about using Duke's."

"They're safe. Joe Stills sweeps them every few days."

"But it's not a very satisfactory arrangement, is it? If we want to contact each other in a hurry . . ."

"I know, I've thought of that. I talked with Joe about it, asked him about us using cellphones, but he said there isn't a phone in existence that can't be tapped into, provided the tapper has the frequency. Unless the phone is attached to a scrambler, of course, but that's impractical for us. All phones operate by radio waves, and radio is public domain."

"So, okay, we'll just have to be very careful what we say to each other. I've given this some thought. We'll choose public pay phones at maybe six locations, near our offices and homes, and number them. If you have something urgent to tell me, you call me at my office or home from wherever you happen to be, and simply say: one, two or three, and we'll agree a time. Then I go out, find a payphone, and call you at that number at that time. The same applies to me with four, five six. If I happen to be in session and you get my answerphone, leave a 'Hi, it's me' message and I'll get right back to you. How does that sound?"

She laughed. "Brilliant. You know, I think you're actually enjoying some of this."

He gave a conditional smile. "Some of it. I enjoy the mind-game, out-thinking these bastards. It's the violence I loathe."

They dispensed with talk while the waiter removed plates and served the main meal.

Their privacy restored, Drummond said, "We didn't get a chance to go over the Jack Crane material Dick gave you. But he gave me a brief resumé of Crane's military career, and I did a lot of thinking last night. Well, perhaps

211

not so much logical thinking as listening to the voice of intuition."

"And what did it tell you?"

"I can't shake their Vietnam connection, Karen – Keegan's and Crane's. It simply won't go away. As a psychologist, I'm a profound believer in the workings and the existence of the subconscious mind. It's there for a purpose." He gave a smile. "Like the LAPD claims with its motto, it's there to protect and to serve. I believe that somebody went to a great deal of trouble to obliterate Tom Keegan's memory, but for all their efforts, a certain level of his mind remained untouched.

"Keegan had dreams – a subconscious function. He dreamt of green men in a garden. In the hypnotic state, when his subconscious mind was exposed, he recalled one hundred-plus soldiers, laughing and falling down, in the jungle . . . and he recalled the trice-nice-ice couplet. And Dick tells me Crane earned his hero rep by rescuing one hundred-plus US prisoners from behind enemy lines. He was shot down twice during the rescue, and wounded. He transferred to Military Intelligence and later joined the CIA. Now, in view of all that's happened since the Mar Vista bank job, what possibilities come to mind?"

She drank some vodka. "Was that rhetorical or do you want my opinion?"

"I want your opinion. I'm sick of hearing my own, I was listening to it most of the night."

She put down her glass. "Okay. In some capacity or other, Tom Keegan is in Vietnam at the time Major Jack Crane performs his heroics and brings a hundred or so prisoners back to freedom. This would account for the men laughing and falling down. They'd be delirious happy to be rescued, and they'd probably be in a weak physical condition, maybe even wounded."

"Right! Which would also account for Keegan's recall of their uniforms being green and *black*. He emphasised

212

black a lot, even linked it to blood in Word Association. So, okay, let's suppose he was there when the boys arrived back, weak, wounded, undoubtedly filthy dirty, which could also account for the 'black', but deliriously happy. Incidentally, in hypnosis he also recalled a friend, Marty, who climbed a tree, fell out of it, and injured himself. How badly, I don't know, but Keegan got very distraught about the incident. But it perhaps gives us an idea of the state of elation among the men at that moment. So, go on, what happened after that?"

She frowned in concentration, stared at the table cloth, visualising the scene. "Major Crane is brought in, wounded. Or maybe he's flown straight to hospital. Either way, he's the hero of the hour. Later on, he's awarded medals, his name appears in the papers back home. He transfers to Military Intelligence. And then . . ." She paused, searching.

"And then?"

"Something happens. Tom Keegan hears something, learns something, witnesses something."

"What kind of something?"

"Something detrimental to Hero Crane. Something about the rescue mission? Perhaps Crane didn't plan and execute the rescue at all? Maybe it was somebody else, but Crane grabbed the glory. It wouldn't be the first time that's happened in war, in moments of great confusion, fire-fights, helicopters being shot down, people dying. I've just had a thought . . ."

"Tell me."

"What if . . . Tom Keegan was the real hero of the action? What if Tom was there serving under Crane, planned and led the action, got wounded, and lost his memory? Major Crane takes the credit, the medals, the publicity. Later on, Keegan's memory returns, he makes a protest, which threatens Crane's career. By now, Crane is with Military Intelligence. He has the power to pull strings, to get Keegan shipped to the private clinic in Maryland, to alter his military record . . . and to make sure Tom gets treatment at the clinic that will ensure his memory is gone for good."

Drummond was nodding, seeing it. "Tom is eventually given a psychological discharge. He is amnesiac, no further threat. Crane moves to the CIA where he has the power and the resources to keep an eye on Keegan, and take action should Tom's memory return. Crane progresses into politics, but retains all his connections with the Intelligence communities, both Military and Central. He is a man of burgeoning status, with a great deal of power and an eye on the White House."

Karen picked up the scenario. "And then one day, out of the blue, here's Tom Keegan again, victim of a street crime, still amnesiac, thank God, but about to be interrogated by a forensic hypnotist at West LA police station . . . at the very moment Jack Crane is about to become president-elect of the USA! Panic stations. Get a couple of the boys over to the station, find out what Keegan remembers. Whew, nothing. That's a break. But what's this? Doctor Drummond is taking Keegan on as a private patient and will use his considerable expertise to restore Keegan's memory . . . and there you have it. Keegan is tortured and disappears, your records are stolen, our phones are bugged, and you are threatened with my life. What more can there be?"

Drummond put down his knife and fork, the meal finished. "A perfect scenario – almost."

"Oh." She gave a pretend pout. "What's wrong with it?"

"The time-frame. Dick said Crane performed his Rambo act in Nineteen sixty-nine. Keegan had been in the army a year then, but came home okay for his father's funeral. He couldn't have been wounded and lost his memory in that engagement, because Cissie had

214

her first letter from him from Vietnam at Christmas of that year."

"Shit." She pushed her plate away.

"But I don't think you're all that wrong. With the exception of that one point, the occasion when it happened, I've got a feeling you were right on the button."

"Then what occasion, Paul?"

He smiled. "'In a trice, it will be nice . . . Charlie will be put on ice'. Find the meaning of that, and I think we'll have our occasion."

Chapter Nineteen

Wednesday.

Karen Beal and *The Los Angeles Times* had done a great job.

Drummond bought the paper from the bin on Wilshire and opened it on the street.

Her article dominated the front page of the Metro section.

Headlined: "IN A TRICE, IT WILL BE NICE . . . CHARLIE WILL BE PUT ON ICE", and sub-headed: "Mar Vista bank robbery victim pleads for help. Do *you* know the meaning of this rhyme?" she had written it as a continuation of her previous article about Forensic Hypnosis, now focusing on the unfortunate Vietnam veteran Tom Keegan and his fight to regain his memory, proposing that a full recovery might well be triggered by an explanation of the mysterious couplet. Drummond was relieved to see that she had ended it with the safeguard, asking that information be given to any staff member on the Metro desk through the *Times* general phone number.

The article had a general appeal – to Vietnam veterans, to the general public as both a human interest story and an intriguing mystery, and to the crime buffs who devoured the Metro section. It was cleverly written, and Drummond phoned her from his office immediately to compliment her.

"Good work, lady."

"Thanks, Paul. Now we wait. Where are you calling from?"

"My office. No calls so far?"

"Not about the jingle. The desk has taken a couple of sympathy calls about Tom's amnesia from people who've suffered," she said, reiterating the safeguard, "also a somewhat belated protest about the Vietnam war, and one from an avant-garde homeopath who recommends Tom Keegan stand on his head for four hours a day. I had no idea my readership was so eclectic."

Behind the humor Drummond could sense her nervousness at the likelihood of his phone being tapped. He asked, "Will I see you later?"

"I'd like that, very much. But won't you be returning to the Valley?"

"No. I've decided to stay over, see what happens, maybe go in tomorrow morning. If events warrant it, I'll re-arrange my Valley appointments and stay longer."

"That would be nice."

"Shall we meet in Duke's for a drink? Six o'clock? We can eat out later."

"Six is fine. Thanks for calling, Paul. I needed it."

He rang off, heard his first client of the day – an anxiety-prone female – enter reception, and struggled to focus his attention on her well-being.

The struggle became more acute throughout the day with successive clients, his mind straying constantly to Karen, to the Metro desk, to the possibility that a call had come in that explained the meaning of the rhyme, and to the possible consequences of the call.

Finally, his working day was ended, and with a cauldron brew of excitement, impatience and trepidation bubbling in his heart, he made his way to Duke's.

Chapter Twenty

The tavern was doing brisk business. The stools along the bar were filled, and at most of the tables off-duty cops were washing away memories of another shift with good-tasting ale and good-humored banter.

Drummond stood inside the door, searching the room and experiencing a pang of concern that Karen wasn't to be seen. Although it had only just turned six, and there were plenty of legitimate reasons why she should be delayed, where she was concerned he was now programmed to be vigilant, and to anticipate trouble.

Something hard and pointed pressed into his back and his heart ran riot as a voice growled in his ear, "Freeze. This is an up-stick. Damn, will I ever get that line right?"

He whirled. "Jesus, Dick, are you *trying* to finish me?"

Gage grinned disarmingly. "Just practicing. When I retire as a cop I'm turning robber, the pay's better. Karen not here?"

"Don't see her. You know she's coming?"

Gage brandished the rolled-up copy of the Metro section he'd used as a gun. "I called her about this and she said she was meeting you at six. Let's get a booth."

Drummond ordered four beers and a vodka tonic for Karen, a talismanic assurance that she would turn up.

He hoisted his beer to his friend. "Life."

"Amen to that." Gage took a hungry swallow.

"What time did you speak to her?"

"About noon."

"Any reaction to the piece?"

"None that'd help. Lots of vet sympathy calls, apparently, personal and organizational, but none from anyone who knows what the jingle means. Still, there's plenty of time. It doesn't have to come today, y'know. People read papers days, even weeks after they're published, or maybe the answer will come from someone who's told about the article days from now, or read it today and has to think about it. All kinds of possibilities."

Drummond nodded. "Yeah, I know. But I wanted it to happen today. Somehow I got it fixed in my mind that the call would come an hour after the paper hit the street. Quite irrational, but I'm so geared up on this Keegan thing now, I want the impetus maintained and a positive conclusion. If it drags on, it'll die. The people responsible for Keegan *want* it to drag on and die. They know that without solid new information we've got nothing but guesses and supposition."

The Lieutenant took another deep swallow of beer. "You sound as though you believe there's some kind of deadline involved here."

"I do. I can't shake the Keegan-Crane connection, Dick. I talked it over with Karen on Monday. She came up with a scenario that wasn't accurate but had its merits. Based on what we know, we think Keegan learned something in Vietnam that was detrimental to Hero Crane, and could threaten his political future right now, and that the trice-nice-ice jingle is the key to that something. Yes, I think there's a deadline here – November eight, election day, three weeks from now."

Gage stared at him, then exploded an astounded laugh. "Christ, Drum . . ." He shot a glance around the room, lowered his voice to a hoarse whisper. "Are you saying this thing could maybe kick Crane out of the race?"

"Scandals have ended political careers before, and they'll sure as hell do it again."

"Boy, wouldn't old Milt Byrne love to get his hands on something real juicy right now, just in time for the TV debate next Sunday?" Gage frowned, deep in thought. "Who'd take over if Crane got the boot? His running mate? Man, what a mess if it happened." He looked at Drummond, very serious. "Now it all makes sense . . . why all these major league players are involved, why the Parker Center asks 'how high?' when somebody says, 'jump', why Keegan's disappearance, why the phone taps."

"It's still speculation, Dick. It was only a scenario."

"Yeh, but it smells right. It has to be something that big."

"I only hope we're not chasing air with this jingle thing. It'd be a hell of a let-down if no one comes forward, or if they do, and it turns out to mean nothing."

Drummond, his eyes almost permanently on the door, saw Karen enter. She waved and came across the room. He followed her progress, knowing from her expression that no one had come up with the explanation.

"Hi, guys," she said wearily, managing a smile as she slid in beside Gage. "This my drink? Bless whoever, I need it. Cheers."

She was wearing a beige dress in fine wool and might, to Drummond's eye, have just stepped off a Paris catwalk, rather than out of a hectic newspaper office.

He said with a compassionate smile, "No calls, huh?"

"Plenty, but none about the jingle. You know, I didn't realise so many kind people still existed. I thought they were a dead breed. We've had so many calls offering help for Tom – advice, jobs, money. I got the feeling a lot of the calls came from people who'd lost relatives in Vietnam. That war left a terrible scar here that isn't healed yet."

The men nodded agreement.

Karen went on, "As the calls came in, I found myself getting madder and madder about what has happened to Keegan. Except for my editor, no one at the *Times* knows

220

he's disappeared. It felt weird thanking people for their help, telling them we'd pass their offer on to Tom, knowing he might very well be dead."

Gage said, "I wondered about that, the way you've written the piece as though he was safe and sound in Paul's care. A full, shit-hits-fan exposé must have occurred and appealed to you."

"It did, both counts. But I rejected it. Firstly, where's our evidence? I can't go on the rampage about Intelligence plots and suspect presidential candidates without it. The *LA Times* does not deal in fanciful speculation. Secondly, if I'd submitted such a piece, the paper would've insisted on firm corroboration all along the way, which would take a lot of time, which we don't have, and would've alerted *them* to our intentions, which would put everybody in jeopardy, even Tom Keegan. I still have slender hopes that he's alive, and may be released after the election, *if* that's what this is all about. Doing it this way," she tapped the rolled-up Metro section, lying on the table, "It's little more than a human-interest piece, but it could provide the evidence for an eventual exposé. Oh, believe me, Dick, I am *aching* to write the full story. Woodward and Bernstein, move over. This could make Watergate seem like a society piece in the *Cape Cod Crier*."

"And if nobody comes forward to solve the jingle mystery?" asked Gage.

She lifted her shoulders, heaved a sigh. "I don't know. I guess the bad guys will win – again. Tom Keegan *may* reappear, wandering down some lonely country road, his memory really fixed this time. Paul could go to work on him again, maybe get him to recall what happened. But it would all be too late. Right now is the only time this thing is ever going to work." She drew a breath, reviving herself. "What the heck, I'm going to buy you guys a drink. If we can't get famous, at least we can get happy."

She looked across the room, saw a waitress with a

221

loaded tray heading through the crush in the direction of the booths, and waved her over.

The woman, blonde, middle-aged, and running to weight, said breathlessly, "Yeh, it's for you, you must be psychic," and moved off to serve the adjoining booth.

Karen stared after her, back at Drummond and Gage, then spun out of her seat. "Ellie . . . what's for me?"

The waitress jerked her head towards the bar. "Phone call. I thought you heard it. You wanted drinks? I'll be right with yuh."

Karen whirled back to the men. "It has to be the desk. Order for me. Make mine a double. Either way, I'm going to need it!"

They watched her as she shot across the room and disappeared behind a partition that housed the phones.

Gage held up crossed fingers, compressed his lips. "Then again, I'm not sure I want it to be *the* call. That intuitive voice you're always going on about tells me you and Karen ought to get out of town right now, go play nice games up in the mountains until November nine."

Drummond nodded. "I hear the same message. But we both know it ain't going to happen."

He looked across at the partition. Gage did the same. Ellie came and interrupted their vigil, took their orders. Then they were right back at it.

They caught sight of her as she rounded the partition, disappeared for a moment behind behind a wall of cops, then came into view again around their flank.

Gage muttered, "Uh huh, just look at that goddamned grin. She's got something, Drum."

Drummond's pulse tripped. He suddenly knew what it felt like to win the lottery.

She sauntered the last couple of steps, slipped into her seat, eyed them both with a mock-smug smirk, enjoying their pent expressions, then turned the smirk into a genuine, joyous grin. "Bingo!"

222

Chapter Twenty-One

"That," she said, flushed with excitement, "was Bill Ryman, Metro desk. "He took a call ten minutes ago, from a man. Bill said he sounded middle-aged and black. He recorded the call, I've had the desk record everything that came in. I wanted to make sure, if a call did come in, that we get everything that's said, and be able to go over it, maybe do a voice-analysis, if necessary, to test for lie-stress or hoax or whatever."

Gage made a face at Drummond. "Smart."

Karen went on, "Bill played the tape back to me, it's very short. The man asked for me, and when Bill said I wasn't available, the caller said something like, 'I knew Tom Keegan in 'Nam, and I know about the Trice jingle. I'll tell Miz Beal what I know, but she does it my way because it's dangerous and she doesn't know what she's messing with. Tell her to be sitting in her car at nine tonight and I'll call her then'. And then he rang off."

Drummond frowned. "He knows you've got a car phone?"

"He's obviously taken the trouble to find out. It wouldn't take much. I'm listed."

Gage asked, "What did you think of the voice?"

She shrugged. "He sounded genuine . . . very cautious. With due allowance for human weirdness, I don't think a hoaxer would've taken the trouble to trace my mobile number. And there was something in the way he said the words "Nam' and 'Trice jingle' that sounded as though he used them with familiarity. If you remember, I never used that abbreviation in the article. I always wrote 'trice-nice-ice'."

Trading looks with Drummond, Gage said, "She'd make a great detective."

"And a damned good behavioral psychologist."

"Aw, shucks, fellas." Karen spotted Ellie approaching. "This wouldn't be because I'm buying the drinks, would it?"

"That helps," said Gage.

When Ellie had gone, Drummond raised his glass to Karen. "Here's hoping."

The Lieutenant said, "Well, hell, me too, but let's be careful here. Let us suppose . . . no, let us *assume* that our friends have read the article. Right now, they're jumping up and down and gnashing their teeth that you've out-foxed them. You've ignored their warnings, you've opened up the Trice jingle to public scrutiny, but you've covered yourself by making the thing a human interest cause, with the entire Metro desk taking the calls. Or *are* they gnashing their teeth? Do they *care* that the Trice jingle is public knowledge? In other words, can there *be* anyone else out there who knows what it means?"

Drummond said, "From their point of view the possibility must exist – otherwise they wouldn't have continued to pressure me to lay off after they grabbed Tom."

"Right. Okay, I'm putting myself in their place. I'm the head villain for a minute. What can I do about this situation? There's no point in taking you and Drum out of the case, because the damage is done. Dead or alive, I've got Tom Keegan. The possibility exists that someone else, another Tom Keegan, another poor slob with enough memory left to hurt me, will answer your appeal for information. So what do I do?"

Drummond winked at Karen. "Do tell us, the suspense is killing us."

"*I* get in first. I concoct a righteous-sounding but harmless story, get an appropriate-sounding guy – a middle-aged black veteran, for instance – to deliver it, and the Trice jingle business fizzles out as the ravings of an amnesiac, psychotic veteran. In Intelligence circles, it's called disinformation. Tell enough of the truth to make it sound plausible, but alter the core of the matter."

Karen said, "Hm. But what happens if a genuine witness also comes along?"

"Then whose story are you going to believe? Or, to further confuse you, I'll send in a third guy, with yet another version, and maybe a fourth and a fifth. By the time you're finished, you won't know which way is up."

She looked at Drummond, back to Gage, drank some vodka. "You just made my day."

Gage said, "Hey, I'm just airing possibilities. Maybe this guy *is* genuine. I'd like to hear that tape."

"Bill Ryman's sending a copy here by motorcycle courier."

"The lady thinks of everything."

"Not about disinformation. I guess I got carried away."

Drummond said, "Dick's right, this guy could be genuine. We'll just have to be careful, wait to see if we get any more calls."

"Wait how long?" she asked in a tone of self-annoyance.

Drummond reached over and touched her hand, the intimacy of the contact and the kindness behind the gesture diluting her mood. "Listen, we'll go with what we've got. Maybe the villains aren't as smart as Boy Wonder, here. Maybe they *are* just gnashing their teeth and praying you get no calls – and if you do, they'll be ready with all kinds of denials or law suites . . . *or* some disinformation *at that point*. They are also possibilities, hm?"

She smiled at Gage. "Boy, does he know how to cheer a girl up?"

"He's the king, all right."

Drummond said seriously, "One thing, though – from now on you do nothing, meet no one without me being there, and without letting Dick know what's going down. Understood?"

She snapped a compliant salute. "Yes, sir."

Gage said with a sigh. "Which means, of course, that he'll be obligated to spend a great deal of time with you. Man, the sacrifices Drummond is prepared to make in the cause of justice jurst bring a lump to mah throat."

The tape arrived at seven.

Karen delved into her shoulder bag for the tape recorder, but Gage said, "Not here. Whose car is closest?"

Karen said, "Mine's right outside. Ben Teague was pulling out as I arrived."

"Let's do it there."

They paid their tabs, left Ellie, a policeman's widow, a generous tip, and went outside.

Gage squeezed into the rear of the yellow XR3i, and Drummond took the front, adjusting the passenger seat to accommodate his long legs. It was Drummond's first time in the car, but not the Lieutenant's. Gage had go-betweened its purchase from Teddy Macklin, an auto genius who serviced the cruisers and staff cars at West LA station, and Karen had rewarded him, Gage, with rides home from Duke's on a couple of occasions when his beer consumption had transcended clear judgement.

The car was a peach, not at all what it seemed. Macklin had done wonderful things to the engine and the suspension to make the machine perform more like a Porche Targa than a production-line Ford.

Karen had added the quad stereo that now reproduced the tape message Bill Ryman had recorded.

"Metro desk . . . Bill Ryman speaking."

"Yeah." That one word bespoke Black. There was a hesitation, a faint rustling of paper, as with newspaper.

226

"I'd like to speak to Miz Karen Beal?" Polite. Gentle. A request.

"I'm sorry, sir, Miss Beal is not in the office at this time. May I help you? What was it in connection with?"

"It's about her piece in the *Times*."

The voice, deep, raspy, tired-sounding, wore a Californian accent with a hint of country South. It was also nervous.

Ryman said, "Yes, sir. You have some information for Miss Beal?"

"Yessir, I do."

"If you'd like to give it to me, I'll see it's relayed to her immediately."

Another hesitation, more rustling. "I knew Tom Keegan . . . in 'Nam. An' I know all about the Trice jingle, what it means." Now a long hesitation, labored breathing.

Then the caller and Bill Ryman began to speak simultaneously, and Ryman said quickly, "I'm sorry, sir, go ahead, didn't mean to interrupt."

"I said . . . gotta work this out right. Damnedest thing, all these years, now suddenly . . ." The voice trailed away. The man's perplexity was obvious and seemed genuine.

He came again in a burst of now-or-never determination. "Listen, you gotta tell her this is dangerous and has to be handled just right. She . . . Miz Beal don't know what she's messin' with, for sure. I'll give her all I know, but she's gotta do it my way. Tell her to be sittin' in her car, nine tonight, I'll call then."

And the connection was cut.

Gage said, "Play it again, hm?"

They listened to it twice more.

Gage said, "That *sounds* like one scared cat. Or a very good actor. And there are plenty of those in LA. What d'you think, Drum? You're the psychologist."

"Sounds promising. The voice-age is right, the nervousness. I'd say it sounds genuine, but I'm waiting for the other shoe to drop."

"The next call?" said Karen.

"According to Sherlock, here."

"Well, until it happens, we'll go with this." She plucked her car phone from its holder and punched a number. "Bill Ryman, Metro, please." Ryman came on. "Bill, Karen, thanks for the tape. Yes, it sounds good. It is now . . . seven thirty. If anything else comes in, will you call me on the mobile? But not between a quarter to and a quarter past nine. I don't want to be engaged when he calls. Thanks, Bill."

She rang off.

Gage said, "Guys, I have to go. What are you planning to do?"

Karen conferred with Drummond. "Shall we cruise?"

"Yes, I'd feel better on the move."

Drummond got out to let Gage out, then resumed his seat.

"Keep me posted," the Lieutenant said through the open window. "If he suggests a meet tonight, get the details and phone me at home. Don't go anywhere until I can arrange some back-up."

Drummond asked, "Who can you trust?"

Gage smiled, patted the bulge of his shoulder holster. "Coupla pals of mine . . . Mister Smith and Mister Wesson."

With a wave he was gone.

Karen started the car, the exhaust emitting the throaty, bubbling rasp of a vehicle of far superior class.

Drummond glanced sidelong at her. "Always meant to ask you, what've you *got* under there – a Vee Twenty-four?"

She grinned, "I think it came out of a T-bird . . . or was it a tank?" To prove the point, she gunned away from the curb, throwing Drummond back into his seat, but slowed immediately, laughing. "If you ever want to up-grade that lumbering Daimler, go see Teddy Macklin at the West LA

228

garage. A day with him and you could do one-twenty-five, easily."

"The Daimler can already do one-twenty-five," he said, pretending miff.

"In first gear?"

Drummond laughed and shook his head, his eyes straying, finding the movement of her legs beneath her skirt, as she went through the manual gears, compulsive viewing. She drove expertly, all of her movements – hands, feet, eyes and head – neat, conservative and graceful. She seemed incapable of clumsiness. "Did you ever study ballet?"

She shot a quizzical glance. "At school. Why?"

"It shows."

"Was that a compliment? Or d'you mean I walk with my feet at ten-to-two?"

"It was a compliment. Your walk, like all your movements, is a joy to watch."

The corner of her mouth twitched in a smile. "Well, thank you. I had, in fact, noticed you ogling my legs."

"I was not ogling."

"Please don't apologise. Every girl enjoys an ogle if she likes the ogler and she deems the parts he's ogling worthy of an ogle."

"Well, they are. But I wasn't. I was . . . admiring."

"Oh." She did her pretend pout again and sounded disappointed. "How . . . bland."

"All right, if it makes you happy, I was ogling."

She flashed her gorgeous grin. "Thank you."

"You're a shameless hussy."

"Thank God he's noticed."

She was so easy to be with. She possessed that rare female quality of managing to combine physical beauty and grace and intelligence with a sense of humor, and a practicality that bordered on earthiness. Images of Grace Kelly and the young Katherine Hepburn came to

229

Drummond's mind, and with them the word "class". There was probably no more misused word in the American lexicon than "class". It was as indefinable as "glamor" and "sexy", but you knew it when you were in its presence. There, in the car, watching her drive, smelling her perfume, swapping banter that was something more than that, he was assuredly in the presence of class. Right then, there was nothing he wanted more than to be as close to her for the rest of his life.

"Penny for 'em, Doctor."

"I . . . was just wondering where we're heading."

"Oh, really?"

They were in Santa Monica, on Olympic Boulevard, near the ocean front.

She said, "I think I must have been a lemming in a former life, I seem to head inexorably for the sea."

"Find the pier and a hotdog stand, I'll spring for dinner."

"Deal."

By eight thirty they were parked on a lighted terrace just south of the pier, overlooking the beach and a barely visible ocean. Early evening, a weather front of heavy gray clouds had rolled in from the Pacific, obliterating the moon and dropping the temperature to the low sixties. It was not yet raining, but it was up there, threatening.

They ate hungrily, enjoying the fat, juicy hotdogs and the fun of picnicking in the car. Background music played softly from the stereo. They talked of family and youth and other things, yet were always conscious of progressing time.

Karen sipped from a straw embedded in a can of Coke. "Did you ever visit Scotland?"

"Twice, as a boy. My Uncle Bruce and Aunt May still live in the ancestral home. It's a rambling Georgian manse in the lee of Ben Nevis, four hundred acres with cattle, sheep and horses. A magical place for a lad."

"The mountains are in your blood."

"I'd die if I lived in Texas or Kansas. Even a seascape unsettles me. I must have inherited Mad Harry's genes."

"This kind of sky and temperature unsettle me. They remind me of England. A lousy, unpredictable climate, England has. Even after a year here, I get a charge seeing the sun every morning, knowing it's going to last all day, knowing exactly what to wear. At home we get four seasons in one morning, sometimes within the hour. It's so exasperating."

"You'd love the Valley, despite your introduction."

The way he said it, the something in his tone, made her look at him. "Yes, I'm sure I would."

"Maybe, when this is over, we can take a fresh run at it, try to forget . . . well, hardly forget, but place things in perspective. I will sell the house. I'd like your help in choosing another. I'd like that very much."

"So would I."

Though the dash clock was plainly visible, Karen checked her watch, a nervous gesture. It was ten to nine.

She drew a sigh. "This has to be for real, hm? It can't be a hoax. Or them? We've had no more calls."

"It sounded right."

"I'm standing on the edge of that credibility gap again. I can't believe that he'll call, or if he does that anything will come of it. There has to be a catch."

"Why?"

She smiled softly. "'Cause there always is."

Reaching into the rear seat, she brought her shoulder bag onto her knee, took out the recorder, moistened the sucker microphone and stuck it behind the earpiece of the telephone.

"Well, *I'm* ready, buster. Come on, strut your stuff."

The luminous minute hand on the dash clock flicked up to eight to nine. A taut expectancy settled on them

231

now. Karen noisily sucked her Coke tin dry and gave a laugh.

"Takes me back. I can hear my mother saying, 'That's an indelicate sound, Karen. If you must drink out of a tin, leave a drop in the bottom.'"

Drummond smiled. "Yours, too? Sounds like we had the same mother."

"Somehow you don't feel like a brother."

The clock whirred softly in the ensuing silence.

They watched the minute hand click up to five.

She whispered, "He won't call. He died of nerves ten minutes ago. They've caught him. He's rolling on the floor somewhere, laughing."

"Nil desperandum."

"Did you take Latin?"

"Took it and left it."

"Me, too. I was a straight Zee student. 'Non nobis solum sed toti mundo nati'."

"Very good."

"I'm cheating. It was my school motto, one of them."

"Do you believe it?"

"What?"

"What it says."

"What does it say?"

"'Not for ourselves alone, but for the whole world'."

"Hey, come on, Drummond . . ."

The phone buzzed and she screamed.

"Oh, my God . . . steady . . . steady . . . I am calm, I am *calm* . . . start the Goddamned recorder, Beal . . . now, pick up the phone."

Her hand was shaking so much she almost dropped it.

"Hello?"

"Miz Karen Beal?"

"Speaking." She mouthed, "It's him!" to Drummond.

"Miz Beal, I do have the information you want. But I want something in return."

232

"Oh? And what is that?" She rolled her eyes at Drummond, telling him here came the catch.

"I want five thousand dollars. Cash. In twenties."

"Uh huh."

"And right now you're thinking: this is a con . . . this man will take my money and peddle me bull-doody . . . if this man really knew Tom Keegan in 'Nam, he'd be glad to do this for an old army buddy for free . . . stuff like that am I right, Miz Beal?"

"May I have a name, sir?"

"Call me Ambrose. It ain't my real name, but it's memorable."

"Well, you are not wrong, Ambrose. I admit that kind of thing was passing through my mind, plus a few others. However, don't let my suspicious journalist nature prevent us from discussing this further. May I ask why you *are* asking for five thousand dollars?"

Drummond smiled and nodded at her, indicating comprehension.

"Certainly, you may. Because I'm broke."

"That's a pretty good reason. And why only five thousand dollars?"

"Because I ain't greedy. And because I figure *The Times* can afford it, but maybe wouldn't go for much more."

"You're very astute, sir."

"An' you talk real nice. Thank you for bein' polite."

"You're welcome. All right, say we could come up with five thousand dollars, what do we get for our money?"

"A tape. An audio tape. With information about the meaning of the Trice jingle, like you asked for."

"And how would I know that the explanation wasn't a complete fabrication, something you just made up?"

Ambrose thought about it. "Well, now, you got me there. I just don't know how I could guarantee it's genuine . . . 'cept I wouldn't do such a thing to a 'Nam

233

vet, specially not to one who's hurtin' like Tom Keegan, an' specially not to Tom himself."

"How can I be sure you even knew Tom Keegan, Ambrose?"

Ambrose gave a small, throaty chuckle. "My, you're just full of good questions, Miz Beal. Tell the truth, I didn't even think about them, so I don't have any answers right now. I just saw the piece this mornin' an' . . . well, this is something I've been wanting to spit out for a very long time. When I saw that Trice headline, I couldn't believe my eyes. An' Tom's name. Often wondered what happened to Tom Keegan." A sudden change of tack. "Miz Beal . . .?"

"Yes, Ambrose?"

"Is this call bein' traced?"

"No, it isn't. It's being recorded for my own use, but not traced."

"Are you alone?"

"No. I have Doctor Drummond with me, the psychologist who's helping Tom. Ambrose, we want to meet with you. We have a number of questions . . ."

"No, ma'am." The response was very emphatic. "That is not possible. Miss Beal . . . you just don't know what you're dealing with here." Ambrose's voice had suddenly taken on an uncharacteristic edge of authority, quite possibly the tone of military command. "Please understand this – the Trice matter is far reaching. It involves people who are God . . . damned . . . dangerous. There is only one way this can be done – and that's *my* way. I will not reveal my identity over the phone. I've already put it on tape with what I know about the Trice jingle. It's here if you want it, and if you can raise five thousand dollars. That's the deal. No meetings, no interview, no questions, just the tape. Take it or leave it."

"I'll take it. How do we negotiate?"

"I'll give you twenty-four hours to raise the money.

234

I'll call you on your car phone at nine tomorrow night. Be prepared to drive around town. When I judge the moment to be right, I'll stop you and do the deal. Is that understood?"

"Perfectly."

"Please, Miss Beal, let's keep this simple and honest, and just between us. The Doctor can be with you, but nobody else. I'll be watching you. I don't want to see cops or cameras. If I do, the deal is off. This is for Tom. Use the tape as you see fit. But no tricks."

"You, too, hm?"

"You'll get none from me." Ambrose rang off.

Karen went, "Phew," hung up, and rewound the tape.

Neither of them said a word until she had played the tape through.

She asked, "What d'you think?"

"Interesting, his switch of character. Starts off kinda corn pone and ends up drill sergeant."

"Yet rings true?"

"Yes. Yes, he does. This guy's angry, he's been hurt. This isn't just for Tom Keegan, it's for him, too. And maybe for a lot of other people."

"Like maybe a hundred green men in a garden . . . and for Marty who fell out of a tree?"

"It has that feel."

"So – how do we handle it, Paul?"

He breathed a sigh. "It's a risk. You – we – drive around town tomorrow night with five thousand in small bills. He could direct us anywhere, a nice isolated spot, open up with an Uzi . . ."

"I know. It happens all the time in drug deals."

"Well, the same option applies to us as to him – any sign of funny business and the deal's off. No isolated spots, no dark alleys. But if we don't take some risk, it's a stand-off. Nobody gets anything."

"I know. I say we go for it."

235

Drummond smiled. "Of course you do." He reached for the phone, punched out a number. "Dick . . . he called. We've got it on tape. Okay, fifteen minutes."

He hung up. "He said what's keeping us, the beer's getting warm and the pizza's getting cold."

They were at the Gage's house in twelve.

Chapter Twenty-Two

Thursday.

 Santa Monica.

 8.55 pm.

Once more, they occupied the XR3; again watched the luminous minute hand of the dashboard clock click upwards, again leapfrogged through the gamut of emotions from doubt to hope to the excitement of expectation, and back again. Both now clung to the very rim of the credibility gap by their psychic finger tips, ready to believe the entire episode was nothing but wishful thinking or a mutually-shared dream, with no basis whatsoever in reality.

The truth was, they had sat there too long. Over-anxious that Ambrose would call earlier than nine, and that they should do all and more of what was required of them to secure the tape, they had taken up position outside Karen's apartment house by eight o'clock, and by now the minutes were dragging by like tranquilized snails, stretching the nerves, creating delusions, giving birth to emotions that had them ready to believe everything and believe nothing.

The past twenty-four hours had not helped. They had talked with Dick and Anne Gage until two in the morning, playing and replaying the telephone tape, sifting, analysing, speculating, theorizing. They had covered the entire Tom Keegan episode in minute detail, sifting, analyzing, speculating and advancing theory on every aspect of it from Tom's involvement in Vietnam to the political implications of a stand-down by Jack Crane. And, in the process, they had imbibed a little too much beer.

Later in the day they had been involved with the Lieutenant again. Unwilling to reveal details of their proposed deal with Ambrose to anyone on the force, he had at least provided them with a powerful police hand radio, his intention being to shadow them at distance on their night journey around town, at least to be there in the vicinity, armed, should anything go wrong.

Early evening, they had done a trial run, testing the radio communication, Drummond transmitting the briefest details of their location while Karen drove, Gage responding with a single-word acknowledgement. To anyone listening on their insecure frequency, the exchanges were minimal and, they hoped, meaningless: "Arizona and Twelfth." "Roger." "Wilshire and Yale." "Roger."

And now it was five . . . no, four minutes to nine, and everything that could be done, had been done. The car was fully gassed. Drummond and Karen were appropriately dressed against the rain that had fallen all day, in jeans, sweaters and anoraks, in case they were obliged to quit the car. All that remained to do was . . .

Wait.

Karen muttered, "Damned rain. Of all nights."

The engine was ticking over to operate the demister, but still the side windows were steaming up with the warmth of their breath. She wiped at her window with her sleeve.

"I wish I had a gun."

Drummond grinned. "Can you shoot one?"

"Of course. I'm Sir Edward Beal's daughter."

"I'm sorry, I'd forgotten. What have you shot?"

"All kinds. Handguns, rifles, shotguns, automatic weapons . . ."

"No, I meant what living things have you shot – you know, ducks, deer, moose, men . . ."

"Oh, I haven't shot *living* things. I wouldn't. Couldn't. But I've scored maximum points over iron sights at five hundred yards."

"That's terrific. But I don't quite follow from that your desire for a gun in this particular situation."

"I just wish I had one. Has that clock stopped? That clock has stopped."

As they studied it, the minute hand jerked up to one minute to nine.

She looked at him, the street light through the windscreen and through the rivulets of rain, engraving his face with squiggly patterns. "I don't suppose you have a gun?"

"I have one, but not on me. Dick wouldn't permit it."

"What living things have you shot?"

"I once shot a sparrow, in the garden in Redding. I was nine years old. I shot it with a friend's bee-bee gun, and sat there watching it twitch and flutter. It took a very long time to die, and when it did, I knew I'd never, without provocation, shoot another living thing."

"Without provocation. That's the thing, isn't it? I've seen so many awful things, people who've been shot, I just don't know if I could do it to save my own life."

"You could. So could I. But I hope we never have to put it to the test."

As the hand hit the hour, the phone buzzed.

Karen gasped, "My God, he's punctual."

"Military training."

"Hello?"

"Miss Beal . . . you have it?"

"Yes."

Drummond and Karen had provided the money. They had discussed this at length at the Gages'. Five thousand dollars was either a modest amount of money or a lot, depending on how you looked at it. The *Times* was likely, under the circumstances, to see it as a lot.

Karen knew she could provide no assurance that the tape would contain anything of value to the paper. Despite her editor's personal interest in and support for the Keegan story, she expected problems raising the money, and problems meant meetings, and explanations, and delay. So, assured that the *Times* would readily reimburse them should the tape prove newsworthy, they elected to provide the funds themselves.

"Is it in cash . . . used twenties?"

"Yes."

"Good. Who is with you?"

"Doctor Drummond."

"Let me speak to him, please."

Karen handed over the phone.

"Drummond."

"Good evening, Doctor. I read what you're trying to do for Tom. Don't be surprised at what's on this tape. It's the truth, as I know it. Use it the best way you can. Will Miss Beal be driving?"

"Yes."

"Then you answer the phone. Where are you now?"

"Santa Monica. On the front at Montana."

"Facing north?"

"Yes."

"Start driving. Stay on the coast road."

The line went dead.

Drummond replaced the phone and picked up the walkie-talkie. "It's a go. Coast road, north."

The radio crackled. "Roger."

Drummond nodded at Karen. "Drive on, stay on the coast road."

Within five blocks they had cleared the boundary of the district of Santa Monica and also the city limits of

Los Angeles. From here on, the land rose sheer to their right, mostly solid cliff face, with only occasional roads leading in and up from the coast highway into the maze of development surrounding Palisades Park.

Throughout this area, there was little of the orderly grid planning typical of most American cities. Here the hill-and-canyon topography enforced a policy of build-where-you-can, the result being a confusion of twisting, turning, rising, dropping streets, avenues, roads, drives and crescents that were difficult enough to locate and to drive at high noon on a clear sunny day, and almost impossible on a black, rainy night.

The phone buzzed. Ambrose said, "Take Chautauqua Boulevard," and rang off.

Drummond told Gage. "Chautauqua Boulevard."

Gage said, "Shit, not in there."

Karen, face pressed almost to the windscreen to peer through the rain and the licking wipers, said, "I know Chautauqua. It cuts right through to Sunset Boulevard. I just hope we stay on it. It's a real cow's guts in there."

"Well, we're not getting into any canyon cul de sac. We stay on well-lit roads or we go home."

"Here we go." She turned right, dropped a gear and accelerated as the road rose steeply off the highway, the relative darkness and quietness of the boulevard a profound contrast to the headlighted brilliance and rainy swish of the coast road.

Chautauqua took a sharp bend to the left, then to the right. All about them lay a brooding blackness. Roads ran off into the night, and hazy house lights hung surrealistically in the over-abundance of dark, towering trees.

"Cree-py," Karen murmured.

"If he says stop here, we don't."

"The park's over there on the left. You don't suppose . . ."

"No way. Even with Dick behind us, we don't go into any park."

She glanced into the rear-view mirror. "I don't see his headlights."

"He's got a difficult job. He'll stay as close as he can. How far now to Sunset?"

"About half a mile. I'll be so glad to be on it."

The phone buzzed. "Turn left at Borgos Place, left again at Toyopa."

Drummond transmitted to Gage.

"Roger."

Karen was at the windscreen again. "God*damn* this rain. Look, there're the lights on Sunset."

"And here's Borgos."

"Damn him, where's he taking us?"

"He could be checking to see if we have a tail."

"But where is he?"

"He could be anywhere. Or nowhere. He could be sitting at home, directing us from a map, having fun."

She turned left into the short Borgos Place, then almost immediately left into Toyopa.

Drummond said, "We're going back the way we came. This runs parallel to Chautauqua. He's running us in circles."

"I'll have to be careful I don't run into Dick." She gave a nervous laugh. "Wouldn't that be something? God, I hate this place. Let there be light!"

At the bottom of Toyopa, they hit a tee junction. Left led into Chautauqua, to start all over again. But the phone went, sending them right into Corona Del Mar, into Alma Real, riding the boundary of Palisades Park now, the blackness of the night and the loom of tall, wet trees unnerving, threatening.

The phone again, and into a circular route called, appropriately, El Cerco, then off at a two o'clock tangent into Pampas Ricas Boulevard, and at its end, blessedly, the lights and traffic flow of Sunset Boulevard.

"Whee," went Karen, stopping at the junction. "It's like coming out of a coalmine."

"If he sends us back in there, I'll refuse."

The phone buzzed. "You're now at Sunset."

"We are."

"Turn left."

"Turn left," Drummond told her.

Karen gunned the XR3: into a break in the traffic while Drummond radioed Gage.

"West on Sunset."

No response.

"West on Sunset."

Drummond shot a glance at Karen.

"West on Sunset."

"Roger, roger. Dropped the freakin' radio."

"Where are you?"

"Christ knows . . . missed Pampas Ricas, going round in circles. Can you slow down?"

"Difficult, the traffic's heavy."

"Do your best. I'm back on Chautauqua, I'll catch up."

From this point, some three miles from the ocean, heading west, Sunset Boulevard changes its broad, elegant city-dude persona and becomes a narrower, meaner, switchback ride of a road that plunges and twists its way down to sea level, following the contours of the hills and canyons of the Castellamare district, and taking a wild loop around Santa Ynez Lake. In a fast, sporty car, the kind that seemed to be the most typical user of this stretch of Sunset, it is a zoomy, exhilarating drive, and heaven help the straggler. Caught up in the mad gallop for the sea, it's almost impossible to drop below sixty.

Karen tried it and got a fanfare blast of horn for her trouble.

Drummond said, "Don't worry, Dick'll catch up at the lights at the bottom. Just go with the flow."

243

They were on the ocean front in three minutes.

The phone went.

"Turn right, now. Go north on the coast road."

Drummond replaced the phone. "Turn right. He knows we're here. He can see us."

"A lucky guess?"

"No, he knew. The way he said it"

The junction was a bad, busy one. When the lights changed, everybody moved, no exceptions. Karen was swept into the northbound traffic, back on the coast road, maybe two miles north of where they'd left it to enter Chautauqua.

Reflexively, and uselessly, Drummond peered about him, somehow expecting to see a middle-aged Black man staring intently at them from one of the dozens of cars that jammed the intersection, either waiting for lights or going with them.

He activated the radio again. "North on the coast highway."

"Christ, I've only just made Sunset!" Gage's voice was faint and breaking up, the signal affected by distance and the intervening hills. "Can't you slow down?"

"He knows we're here. I think he's following us now."

"Shit. Be careful, Drum, I . . ." The rest was lost in a screech of static as lightning lit up the ocean.

"Say again, I lost it."

No response.

"Say again, Dick . . ."

Thunder detonated above their heads.

Karen laughed, appalled. "I don't believe it. This only happens in movies! The storm breaks, the radio won't work, and everybody goes yeh-yeh-yeh."

"Come in, Dick. Are you there?"

Crackle, screech, blah. "I'm doing . . . traffic . . . going . . . careful."

They were in Pacific Palisades now, perhaps five miles

from Malibu and Drummond's beach home. The crazy notion entered his head that Ambrose was directing them there, then doubted that Ambrose knew where he lived. He, Drummond, wasn't important to Ambrose in all this. The money, the tape, and Karen were important, in that order.

Drummond wondered where Ambrose would make his move. This seemed an unlikely place. The coast road changes its face along this stretch, its multi-lanes now undivided, now divided. Here, between Pacific Palisades and Malibu, it is undivided. The blank walls of beach houses and other buildings line much of the road on the ocean side. On the inland side, houses perch precariously on the very lip of the sheer hillside from which the road has been cut. Except for the turn-ins that lead up to these houses, there are few places of sufficient dimension to allow for safe parking off the paved road.

To Drummond, it seemed likely that they would now continue unchecked beyond Malibu where the road widened and offered greater opportunity to pull over.

Of course, it was always possible that Ambrose would get them to swing inland on the Twenty-three to Thousand Oaks, or have them carry on to Ventura, Santa Barbara, or fucking Canada! It was now almost ten o'clock and he was losing patience with the game. If Ambrose hadn't signalled a stop by the time they reached the beach house, he had it in mind to pull across and call it a night.

Then Karen went, "Uh uh," her eyes on the rear-view mirror.

"What?"

"Cop. Motorcycle. He's flashing me to stop."

Drummond swung in his seat. "Damn. We weren't speeding." He turned to the front. "There's a driveway coming up, pull in there."

He tried the radio again, all caution abandoned now. "Are you there, Dick? Come in, for Crissake."

Gage came in, loud and clear. "Where are you, buddy?"

"Still on the coast road, about four miles from the house. We're being stopped by a motorcycle cop. We've pulled into a driveway."

"Stopped for why?"

"I don't know. Where are you?"

"At the lights at Sunset. This is okay, it'll give me time to catch up. If Ambrose is following, he'll cool it till the cop's gone, maybe run past you, then pick you up down the road. See what this asshole wants, maybe he's lost and needs directions. If he makes trouble, call me up, I'll speak to him."

"Roger."

"Hey, that's my line."

Drummond switched off and turned to watch the policeman approach. Karen was using the rear view mirror. Though there was little detail to see through the rain-streaked rear window; no more than a silhouette against the winking lights of the motorcycle and the blinding heads of the oncoming traffic, it was obvious the man was huge.

Nearing the rear of the car, he momentarily obliterated all direct light, then released it again as he came up to the offside of the car and filled Karen's window with the weatherproofed bulk of his girth.

An enormous black hand made a fist and knuckle-tapped gently on the glass. As Karen lowered the window, the cop lowered his head to fill the space. Beneath the helmet visor was a massive, handsome face, the eyes humorous and intelligent.

Karen found herself smiling in response. "What's the trouble, officer?"

"Will you turn off your engine, please?" He had to speak up against the roar and swish of the traffic close behind him.

246

She did so.

"Did you know you had a tail-lamp out, ma'am?"

She frowned. "I do? Then it must've happened in the past couple of hours. I checked the car thoroughly . . ."

"May I see your driving license, please?"

"Sure."

She reached for her bag on the rear seat, went into a side pocket, produced a wallet, extracted the license, handed it to him.

Using a flashlight, he checked it, compared her features with the photograph. "Karen Beal?"

"That's me."

The flashlight flicked over to illuminate Drummond, then into the rear compartment, searching it, then back to Drummond.

"And Doctor Paul Drummond, I presume."

Stone silence from them.

Drummond's pulse erupted.

Karen jerked an astounded look at him, then back to the cop.

The cop made a move, slipped a hand inside his waterproof, as though reaching into his left breast pocket. "Have you got the money?"

Both stared at him.

The hand withdrew from the waterproof, holding a cassette tape wrapped in plastic. He leaned down, forearms on the window frame, his hands inside the car, the tape virtually under Karen's nose. "This is what you want."

With his face pressed so close to her, his bulk now seemed oppressive, threatening. Reflexively, she moved away from him, and towards Drummond.

Drummond said, with an edge on his voice, "We expected someone else."

The cop smiled with his eyes. "Ambrose? I'm his messenger."

Drummond frowned. "Hell, I don't like this. He should've told us. He . . ."

The cop's face set, the eyes lost their humor, and suddenly it was the most threatening physiognomy they'd ever seen.

"Listen, do you want this tape or not . . ."

In the next instant, the question was moot.

To the rear of the car, on the paved surface, they heard a squealing skid, the metallic rush and thud of an opening door, and a thin, explosive burst of noise, almost lost in the swish of speeding traffic, yet still identifiable as the sound of automatic gunfire.

Many things happened in the next three seconds. The cop was first thrown hard against the car, his helmet smashing into the top of the window frame, and while he hung there, held there by the hail of bullets that slammed into his massive body, his fingers extended in the rigor of shock and released the cassette tape into Karen's lap.

Two seconds into the action, he began to twist clockwise, his back turning towards the hood of the car, his arms slowly withdrawing from the window frame. Now, also, the realization of what had happened and was happening had begun to penetrate the frozen, dumbfounded minds of Drummond and Karen, and as he roared, "Get out of here!" she was already turning the ignition key, shoving the gear shift into first, flooring the accelerator, and throwing the car hard into the near-side lane, empty now, blocked by the assassin's vehicle.

The acuteness of her angle of departure carried the falling body of the policeman half-way into the near-side lane. The speed of her acceleration dumped it directly in the path of the shooter's vehicle.

Drummond spun in his seat. Half-blinded by its head-lights, he caught the impression of a white van, saw the silhouette of a figure jump out and bend to the body of the cop, then lost it completely as cars veered from the outer lane to the inner, slowing to view what they probably thought was an accident, seeing the cop's motorcycle parked on the verge.

Karen was now doing seventy in the fast lane, driving by instinct, hands white-knuckled on the wheel. "Are they following?" Her voice was choked, tremulous, barely audible.

"They were searching the cop." Drummond's voice was not much stronger.

"For this." She dipped her chin towards the tape in her lap.

"No doubt about it." He reached for it, slipped it into his pocket.

"Paul, what're we going to *do*?"

"First thing, get off this road. When they don't find the tape, they'll be coming for us fast."

"Get off where?"

"This is one lousy road to *get* off. There's only the Twenty-three to Thousand Oaks. If we could get over into the other lanes, head back to the city . . ."

"Hold on!"

She hit the brakes, did something miraculous with accelerator, clutch and handbrake, flung the car in an anti-clockwise skid into a minimal gap in the on-coming traffic, and boosted the vehicle up to flow speed without attracting so much as a protesting horn hoot.

Drummond, hauling himself upright, gaped at her. "Where did you learn that?"

"Evasive driving course . . . England."

"Thank God for Sir Edward Beal's daughter." He felt down the side of his seat, under it, came up with the radio, activated the switch with trembling hands. "Dick, are you there?"

"Goddamned hold-up, Drum, looks like an accident up front."

"It's no accident. It was a hit team, they killed the cop."

249

"*What*? What cop?"

"The guy who stopped us. He was working for Ambrose. He had the tape."

"Jesus Christ, I don't believe this. What happened?"

"He was leaning in the window, holding the tape, asking for the money, when they came up behind him and opened fire. Karen got us out of there. We're heading back towards the city."

"Did you get a look at their vehicle?"

"A glimpse. Looked like a white van. I saw somebody searching the cop, obviously for the tape. They'll be coming after us now."

"Why?"

"We've got the tape. He dropped it in Karen's lap."

"Okay, I'm going to radio this in. Listen to me, those guys will have a back-up vehicle, so don't bother looking for a white van on your tail. Oh, brother . . ." Gage was thinking on the run. "Listen . . . get the hell off the coast road . . . find somewhere safe . . . don't go home . . . get out of the city . . . got any ideas?"

"Yes."

"Don't tell me! Just head there. Find a secure way of letting me know where you are. Question is – how did those guys know where to find you and the cop tonight? They've had you two – him – pinned like bugs on a board every step of the way. Okay, Drum, get going. Don't trust *anybody*, y'hear? Good luck. Over and out."

Drummond switched off and threw the radio into the back seat.

Karen said, "The lights at Sunset are coming up. Do we turn?"

"No, carry on into Santa Monica."

"What's the idea you have, Paul?"

"We're going home."

She frowned at him. "But Dick said . . ."

"Not LA home."

"Valley home?"

"No, home home. Redding home. Mountain home. If these bastards want a fight, we'll do it in my terrain, not theirs. We need some breathing space, time to listen to the tape, maybe make plans, take action. If this tape is worth killing a cop for, it's dynamite. Dick's right, we can't trust anybody – down here. But there are a lot of people I can trust in Redding. And we're going to need help."

"Sounds good to me. So – where do I head for?"

"The I-10, through to Boyle Heights, then the I-5, all the way up to Redding."

"How far and how long?"

"Five hundred and fifty miles . . . about ten hours. Well, say, eight in this little monster. Listen, I have to tell you, I am knocked out with admiration for the way you handled the situation back there. If you hadn't reacted so fast, we'd be dead, for sure. You saved our lives."

She gave a fluttery sigh. "Well, thanks, but I think that poor policeman saved our lives. If he hadn't been so big, shielded us, we'd have taken some of those bullets. It . . . it really hasn't struck home yet, you know. I may appear cool, but don't be surprised if my driving goes haywire an hour from now. I'm still numb with shock."

"I know. So am I."

"God, I hope that tape is worth it."

They were well into Santa Monica, nearing the pier, ready to turn inland and negotiate that jiggle around City Hall that would feed them onto the I-10, when the phone buzzed, startling them both.

Karen gasped, "Jesus, I'd forgotten about him."

Drummond let it ring.

She asked, "Aren't you going to answer it, tell him what happened?"

Drummond, grimacing, shook his head. "Let's ask ourselves Dick's question: how did those killers know

251

where we were? And where the cop would stop us? We were giving our movements to Ambrose."

She stared at him. "D'you think this phone is bugged? Or Ambrose's phone, maybe? Or both?"

"Anything's possible. But let's ask a few more questions. Who *is* Ambrose? Who was the cop? Who the hell is anybody? And, most importantly, what's on the tape? Maybe when we hear it, we'll get answers to all those questions. Until we do, we take Dick's advice and stay away from unsecured phones and radios."

The phone stopped buzzing.

"So – when are we going to listen to the tape?"

She had negotiated the chicane of street turnings around the City Hall and Court House complex, and as she tore up the ramp and accelerated into the fast lane of the Interstate Ten, Drummond, reaching into his pocket, said with a smile at her impatience,

"Right now."

Chapter Twenty-Three

Drummond switched on the car's interior light, slid the cassette from its plastic box and inspected it. It seemed an ordinary Sony HD-F-90, Type 1 tape, its identifying label blank. The tape was wound for A-Side playing. The B-Side label was also unmarked.

Turning off the light, he slid the cassette into the stereo system and pressed the Play button.

He was conscious of his own excitement, and aware of Karen's. He looked expectantly at her. She gave a tight-lipped grimace and made a fist, urging Ambrose to do his stuff.

There was a tense ten seconds of hissy silence from the speakers. Drummond reached out and turned the volume down a touch, expecting Ambrose's voice to boom out.

What they got was the driving, thumping, pounding opening bars of a piano piece, the unique technique instantly recognizable to Drummond as that of Errol Garner, the number, 'Please Don't Talk About Me When I'm Gone', also very familiar to him, evocative, speeding him back twenty years to see himself at the piano in the front room in Redding, desperately trying to emulate Garner's bold, outrageous style, wonderful chords, and transitions from pure power to moments of incredible, feather-like delicacy.

For a brief while he was lost in the magic of the playing, in memories, then suddenly came out of it, realizing Errol Garner was not what they had expected to hear, not what they'd been prepared to pay five thousand dollars for, not what a policeman should have died for, and not the reason they should be speeding out of the city, their lives in jeopardy.

Karen was alternating her bewildered glance between the road, the stereo player, and him, her mouth open, loath, yet, to voice the fear that had begun to pervade her, too.

After the strident, bellicose opening, Garner had swung into his enthralling admixture of pulverizing base chords and right-hand air-brush strokes, taking the listener now deep into the belly of the dragon, now up into an ethereal fairy world, toying with the senses, confusing expectations, mezmerizing with his artistry and keyboard command.

In her expression, beneath the amazement, disappointment and growing dread, Drummond could see a reflexive appreciation for Garner's sound. It was as though his playing had created in her mind a dichotomy: wanting to listen, desperately wanting to end it and hear something else.

"What *is* this?" she demanded.

He knew what she meant, but answered obliquely, his tone telling her he shared her fears, that he also was praying the music would end any second and Ambrose would speak to them.

"Errol Garner. Have you heard of him?"

She answered distractedly. "I . . . think so."

"He wrote 'Misty'."

"Yes, of course."

"He's dead now. He was a giant here in the Sixties and Seventies. Perhaps he wasn't so well known abroad. I had this number on a ten-inch LP at home. 'Please Don't Talk About Me When I'm Gone'. I used to try and play along with him. Nobody could play along with Garner."

"Paul . . ." There was protest in her tone.

"I know, I know. Let's just hear the tape through.

254

Maybe he put this at the beginning for a reason, in case somebody else played it accidentally. Maybe he has a weird sense of humor."

"And maybe the whole damned thing's a con," she said angrily. "Maybe that policeman died for nothing . . . and maybe we're running for our lives for nothing. Oh, Paul, if it's so . . ." She lapsed into silence because she couldn't think what the outcome would be if it was a con.

With Drummond, she reverted to hope and patience. Gradually becoming more engrossed in the music, she asked, frowning, "What's that sound . . . in the background? Sounds like somebody muttering."

Drummond smiled. "That's Garner. He makes that noise on all his fast numbers. He's either muttering to himself or humming, I could never decide which. I played that LP over and over, trying to hear what he was saying, but never could. I think he just used to hum to himself."

The piece was a long one. When it finally ended, and in the ensuing silence, they braced themselves with renewed expectation, willing Ambrose's voice to come in, to speak to them, to tell them what they wanted to hear.

But it was Garner again, with another up-beat number, and with the opening chords of 'That Old Black Magic' Karen gave a despairing groan.

"Paul, we've been had. Well, thank God at least we didn't hand over the money. But that cop . . ."

"If he was a cop."

She glanced at him. "You think he mightn't have been?"

"Uniforms can be borrowed, stolen, made. When you think about it, we saw very little of it, just a bit of helmet and his weatherproof."

"What about his motorcycle?"

"We saw even less of that. Police lights could be rigged on any kind of bike. Like all good confidence tricks, a lot is left up to the assumptions of the victim."

She digested this, went on to other thoughts. "I wish we could call Dick. He'd know by now if the guy was a cop."

"We will as soon as we can."

"His being a cop or not could make a difference to our situation. You know how the police react when one of their own gets killed. It could weaken the control these people appear to have at the Parker Center . . . maybe give Dick more power to help us directly. But if the man wasn't a cop, our situation remains the same."

They were silent for a while as Garner thumped and tinkled and muttered his way through the classic number. By the time it had ended, they were into the interchange at Boyle Heights, transferring to the I-5 and heading due north for Redding.

Their new direction triggered an awareness that their departure from the city had, psychologically, really now begun. With it came a need to analyze their situation in the light of their growing belief that Ambrose was a conman who had never known Tom Keegan, had never heard of the Trice jingle before Wednesday morning, and that there was nothing on the ninety minute tape but some very talented piano playing.

As Garner broke into a spectacular arrangement of 'How High The Moon', Karen drew a deep, determined breath and asked semi-rhetorically, "Okay, where do we go from here? Let's try to recap what's happened so far – with alternative assumptions. Let's assume the villains have somehow managed to tap into the frequency of this phone. I know the instrument itself isn't bugged because Dick had Joe Stills sweep it."

"What about the car itself?"

"Likewise. The car's clean. But who is to say we weren't followed from Duke's last night and listened to from a distance? I don't pretend to know much about state-of-the-art surveillance equipment, but I do know that

almost every week something new and utterly fantastic –
and I don't use that word lightly – is being invented, and
that there's really no place left on earth where people can
have a conversation without being overheard."

"Okay, we'll assume our conversations with Ambrose
were bugged."

"That tells us that Ambrose had nothing to do with
them, that he's merely a conman who tried to make
an easy five thousand. Otherwise, they wouldn't have
killed Ambrose's messenger for a tape of Errol Garner
classics."

"Right."

"But how did the villains – let's call them the V's – how
did they know the cop – or pretend cop – had the tape?
Okay, the V's were listening in to our phone exchanges
with Ambrose while he sent us around the houses, stayed
at a discreet distance, were right behind us on the coast
road, saw the cop pull us over. But how did they know it
wasn't a legitimate roust? Paul, they came screaming up
behind him and opened fire almost before they'd stopped!
They couldn't possibly have seen the tape in his hand, or
him offering it to me, because they searched his body in
case he still had it on him. So how did they *know*?"

As Garner continued to fly exuberantly to the moon
and play liltingly among the stars, Drummond shook his
head. "Unless somehow they got a line on Ambrose,
found out who and where he was . . . and tapped into
his communication with the cop."

"Possible. But why should Ambrose communicate
with him? They were working together. The cop would
know where Ambrose was directing us. All he had to
do was wait on the coast road and pick us up after
Sunset."

Drummond shook his again. "I just don't know. It's
almost as if they were listening in to the cop's conversation
with us."

She looked at him. "How could that be? The car's clean. Unless . . ."

"What?"

"No, it's rubbish. I'm getting into fantasy now."

"What? Tell me? Isn't everything goddamned fantastic right now?"

"What if the cop was, you know, a kind of double agent, pretending to work with Ambrose, really working for the V's, telling them he'd hand the tape over to them after he picked it up from Ambrose, then deciding he'd like five thousand bucks instead?"

"Hm. Good try. But if they knew who and where Ambrose was, why didn't they just kill him and grab the tape instead of killing the cop? Or why didn't the cop kill Ambrose for them? And how come the cop didn't know, and tell them, that the tape was a phoney and the whole thing was a scam?"

She groaned. "Enough! I told you it was rubbish. I think the shock is just beginning to hit me."

"Want me to drive?"

"No, I'm okay for a while. Are we planning to reach Redding tonight?"

"Not necessarily. We're probably both much more stressed and tired than we realise. Stockton is a little over half-way, inland from San Francisco, we'll see if we can make there. I'd prefer a biggish town if we have to stop over. Don't care much for the idea of a Norman Bates-type motel in the middle of nowhere."

Again she looked at him, her eyes radiating her concern. "You think they're still after us, don't you?"

"They know we have the tape, and they believe what's on it is worth killing for. Yes, they're looking for us."

She made a fist and struck the steering wheel, a gesture of frustration and disappointment. "Goddamn it, all this for nothing. Can't we let them *know* it's only Errol Garner? Hell, Paul, I don't mind dying for a good cause, but not for a guy playing 'Fly Me To The Moon' and chunnering to himself." She frowned at the sound coming from her quadraphonic speakers. "Ambrose, you bastard, at least you might have made a decent recording."

Drummond grinned. "What's wrong with it? It's sounds exactly like mine used to on my old player."

"That was twenty years ago. Ambrose probably recorded these numbers off the same old ten-inch LP's as you had."

He frowned at her. "Why d'you think that?"

"Well, listen to the crummy quality, all that background noise. It's like somebody's doing a whispering sing-a-long with Errol."

Drummond laughed. "Yes, well, to tender ears attuned to the state-of-the-art CD perfection of the Nineties . . ."

"Ambrose probably has one of those old radiograms, what d'you call them here – phonographs? – with a pick-up head that weighs four pounds and uses steel needles. Still, I suppose we ought to be grateful we got anything on the tape at all, he might just have sent a blank tape."

"He might."

Slowly, simultaneously, the import of what they had just said penetrated the gauze of shock and confusion that cocooned their minds, causing them to look at one another, Karen then voicing their common question. "Why didn't he?"

Drummond nodded, repeating, "Why didn't he?"

He reached out and snapped up the volume too loud, making them wince, lowered it, tilted his head to a listen, closed his eyes in concentration, inclined an ear towards the nearest speaker, murmured breathlessly after a moment,

"I'll be damned."

"What?" she asked excitedly, weariness gone now.

"I think we may owe Ambrose an apology."

"*Why*? Drummond, if you don't tell me . . ."

"It's a subliminal recording! There's a voice behind Garner, recorded almost too high to hear. It's a technique used in hypnotherapy. The subconscious mind can hear the message, the ear can't. My God, that's clever. He's chosen Garner deliberately, because he mutters to himself, to cover the whisper. Now, who the hell is Ambrose to think of this . . . to be able to do this kind of recording?"

"Is it difficult?"

"No, but you need to know how. What does this tell us about Ambrose? That he knows something about psychology? Hypnosis? Recording equipment? I think he's done this for me, because I'm a hypnotist and he thinks I'm treating Tom Keegan with hypnosis."

"But you could easily have missed it."

Drummond shook his head. "Not if the cop had had a chance to tell us. Remember what Ambrose said to me? Don't be surprised at what's on the tape. He also warned us that the situation was dangerous, that we had to do it his way. This was a safeguard, Karen, in case the tape went astray. And I think as soon as we handed the cop the money, he would have told us about the subliminals."

"Can't you hear anything of the background?"

"No, it's too faint, too high a register. But I know somebody in Redding with the equipment to pull it out."

"How exasperating. It's there and we can't hear it."

He laughed, at her impatience, and with relief that their efforts had not been a failure after all. "We'll know soon enough."

"This puts a different complexion on the cop's death, doesn't it? He really was working for Ambrose. I wonder who he was, whether he was a real cop?"

"We'll find that out soon enough, too, either from Dick or your paper."

"It's a pity we didn't get around to working out that coded payphone idea of yours, and letting Dick in on it.

How are you going to be sure you're both on a secure line when you call?"

"I'll think of something. The trick will be to give him the number I'm calling from, without giving him the number. I'll work out a code based on birthdates, anniversary dates, that sort of thing. Karen, you'd better call *The Times* tomorrow, let them know you'll be away for a while."

"Yes. But – how long a while?"

Her tone told him the buzz she'd received from the discovery of the subliminals was wearing off, replaced by over-riding concern for their situation. He was aware of the re-emergence of his own concern.

"I don't know. I'm sure it depends entirely on what's on this tape. If it *is* dynamite, and we can get it to *The Times*, we'll be out of danger . . . provided, of course, that they're willing to publish it."

She frowned at him. "Why shouldn't they?"

He gave her a smile and said with a confidence he didn't feel, "Oh, I'm sure they will. Anyway, let's not speculate, let's first hear what we've got to offer them."

It was a long twenty seconds before she said, almost to herself, "It never occurred to me – that they mightn't publish it. That would leave us out on a limb, wouldn't it – privy to dangerous information no one will touch?"

"Hey, now, don't jump the gun and start worrying about that before we even hear the tape. Let's just try and relax and . . ."

"I wonder if that happened to Dorothy Kilgallen?"

"You wonder if what happened?"

"The story was that she'd told 'a few friends' that from her interview with Jack Ruby she'd obtained evidence that would blow the Kennedy assassination case sky high. But she was a renowned, syndicated columnist. Why did she give that incredible information to a few friends, instead of filing the story?"

261

"Well, I don't know . . ."

"My point is, Paul – maybe she did. And maybe someone said this stuff is too hot to handle, or found it expedient to suppress it, and passed the word that lead to her transcripts being stolen, and to her death."

"Karen, will you please forget the tape until we get to Redding?"

"I'm only asking: What If?"

"Well . . ." He shrugged. "I don't *know* what if."

The Garner tape came to an end. Drummond reversed it and pressed the Play button. It was more of the same, with the subliminal hiss continuing in the background.

Karen said, "Well, if length is anything to go by, we've got one helluva story. You know, Paul, I'm beginning to get the feeling . . . to truly believe . . . that within a few days everybody in the entire world *will* know what Ambrose is saying. And we will be responsible." She looked across at him. "Isn't that just a little bit scary?"

He smiled but said nothing.

Yes, it was scary, but speculative, a possibility, not yet proven. There was still the chance that Ambrose was a conman, a joker, a liar, or that he knew less about the Trice jingle than he'd have everyone believe.

For Drummond, there was something else, much more firmly rooted in certainty, to find scary, something that they had already discussed, but the importance of which Karen had somehow not quite locked onto. It concerned a question she had asked.

The question was: how did the villains know the cop had the tape?

He had commented that it was as though the killers could overhear the cop's conversation with them, at the car.

If so, how?

If the car and the phone were clean, *how*?

That unknown he found *very* scary.

262

Chapter Twenty-Four

Friday.

2.30 a.m.

Stockton.

Physically and emotionally depleted, they pulled into the covered way of the Rest-E-Z Motel on the northern outskirts of the city and roused the night manager from an armchair slumber.

Yawning and scratching, he checked them out through a wire security grill, deduced them respectable enough for his establishment, unlocked plate glass doors and admitted them into the office.

"We'll need adjoining rooms," said Drummond. "Ground floor."

The man, balding, late fifties, said, "Y'gottit." His expression questioned the economic wisdom and outmoded circumspection of renting two adjoining rooms when everyone knew they'd wind up together in one queensize bed. "Credit card or check?"

"Cash."

The guy smiled. Cash. Cautious. Nothing traceable. He took a closer look at the registration card Drummond had filled out, noting the California car tag. He handed Drummond two keys. "Fifteen, sixteen, right at the end. It's quieter down there."

"Thank you. May we take some coffee?" Drummond indicated the flask on the hotplate.

"Sure, help yourself, on the house. Donuts, too, but they ain't fresh."

"Just coffee's fine."

Karen filled and lidded two dixie cups.

Drummond said, "Thanks. Goodnight."

"Goodnight, Mister Ellison . . . ma'am. Sleep well – what's left of it."

They moved the car to the end of a two-story block of units. This late in the season there were few cars parked outside the rooms. Across the spacious yard was the pool advertised on the motel's illuminated sign, but it was covered, its sun loungers stacked at one end.

They inspected fifteen first, found it clean and presentable, everything functioning, and designated it Karen's. She then accompanied Drummond into sixteen, the end unit, flopping into an easy chair to drink her coffee while he did the rounds, checking that the lights, TV, shower, toilet and heater worked.

The place had seen better days. It had taken on that smell and patina of shabbiness peculiar to motels, but it was clean and the queensize beds were firm. Right then, that was all they were interested in.

Drummond tucked the canvas money bag into the closet and hung up his dark blue anorak. Around midnight they had briefly left the interstate at Kettleman City and found a late night drugstore for toothbrushes, shaving gear, and something to eat. Drummond now deposited his toiletries in the bathroom, came out and took the chair facing Karen at the small round window table. She had both hands cupped around the coffee container, her eyelids drooping as she sipped the hot brew, but managed a wry smile when he looked at her.

"Mister Ellison, I presume."

He returned her smile. "It won't fool anybody for long, but there's no point in advertising we've been here."

"Well, it gave the manager a little off-season thrill. I

264

could read his mind like *The Times*. I'll bet we're the first people to pay cash all year."

"Thank God we have it. Now we don't have to use credit cards or checks."

Her smile faded and the strain of concern etched her face. "How can they follow us, Paul? How can they possibly know which direction we took?"

"They can't – unless they were right on our tails after the shooting. Dick said they'd have a back-up vehicle, but where was it at the time of the shooting? If it had been close to the scene, the van would've put them on to us immediately, and we'd have been intercepted by now – or at least we'd have seen them. I was checking our backs when we came off the freeway at Kettleman City. No one followed us off. And if they were there, they wouldn't know for sure we'd get back on the freeway. They wouldn't risk just hanging around, waiting to pick us up."

"So, okay, they lost us on the coast road. So how can they hope to find us again?"

He shook his head. "Our problem is and will always be that we don't know who these people are, how many of them there are, and precisely how far-reaching their power is. *If* – and it's a big if – this thing has anything to do with Jack Crane and involves his old cronies in Military Intelligence and the CIA . . . and if, as Dick suspects, they have their hooks into the LAPD, then they could have the same kind of pull with other law enforcement agencies – local police, highway patrol, and sheriff departments. All they might have to do is scream 'national security threat' down the line to have every cop in California looking for us."

 Seeing her astounded look, he went on quickly, "Karen, I don't mean to frighten you, and I may be exaggerating wildly. This may be a very local thing, just within the Parker Center. But for safety's sake, until we can get that tape transcribed, and use it to protect ourselves, I think we've got to assume the worst. As Dick warned us – we trust nobody."

She was nodding, thinking. "Then we've got to lose the car, fast."

"We'll do that in Redding. I've got a Range Rover up there. We'll hide yours in a garage."

She heaved a sigh. "We really shouldn't have stopped, should we? It'll be much more dangerous in daylight."

"And just as dangerous to try for another two hundred miles as tired as we are. We'll get four hours sleep. Go on, off you go, I'll wake you at seven."

She stood, picked up her ubiquitous shoulder bag. "I need to record some notes. Even if Ambrose's tape turns out to be garbage, I'm going to get a story out of what's happened to us."

"Okay, but don't take too long." He opened the door for her, planted a kiss on her nose, making her smile. "Sleep tight, short as it is."

"Who's going to wake you at seven?"

"Hey, I'm the hypnotist, remember? I can program myself."

"Show-off."

He watched her enter her room, then closed and bolted his door.

Five minutes later, finished in the bathroom, he returned to the bedroom and switched on the television, finding a 3am newscast on Channel 7. There was a lot about Jack Crane and his runaway success in the presidential race, nothing at all about a police officer shot to death in Los Angeles.

Drummond lay down fully dressed beneath the covers and switched off the lights. In the event of any emergency during the next four hours, he didn't want to be fumbling around trying to get his pants and socks on.

What emergency?

Who the hell knew?

The old, tantalizing, frightening, recurring question presented itself for his consideration yet again: Who *were* those guys?

A scene from one of his favorite movies also played again in his thoughts. In "Butch Cassidy and the Sundance Kid", a posse tracks Newman and Redford uphill and down, endlessly, over the most impossible terrain, and every now and then, astounded by the expertise of the trackers, Butch asks Sundance, Who *are* those guys?

It was terrifying to be hunted, but at least Butch and Sundance knew more or less what their hunters looked like, how many of them there were, and the limit of the posse's powers.

He and Karen knew none of those factors.

What kind of machinery was in motion at that moment to find the possessors of the Ambrose tape? What exaggerations, fabrications and downright lies were being transmitted right then by radio and telecommunication link in order to prevent the content of the tape being made public?

"This is an APB on Paul Drummond and Karen Beal, known Communist sympathisers . . . enemies of the state . . . in possession of top secret information vital to national security . . . apprehend . . . arrest . . . shoot on sight . . . armed and dangerous . . ."

Ridiculous?

A man thought to possess the tape had been shot on sight that same night.

Preposterous?

Tom Keegan had been abducted, and probably killed, for just *possibly* being able to recall the meaning of the Trice jingle.

Unreal?

There were three bullet holes in the rear fender of the XR3i that were very real.

The challenge was: how to survive.

First requirement: expect the worst possible scenario to be probable.

Second requirement: get to Redding quickly and unobtrusively.

Third requirement: decode and transcribe the tape.

Fourth requirement: get the information into safe hands.

Fifth requirement: Stay alive long enough for it to bite.

Well, once they got to Redding, that last requirement wouldn't present the problem it did right now. Redding was mountain country, and Redding was home. Just north of the city lay the Shasta-Trinity National Forest, a vast tract of wild and rugged terrain, with peaks rising to fourteen thousand feet, which the Drummond family knew as well as anyone, local police included.

Mad Harry had been a Highland hunter and had raised his four sons to be the same. Paul's father, the doctor, had eschewed killing, but had "shot" more than his share of animals all the same – through the lens of a camera. Throughout his childhood and youth, Paul had accompanied his father on his photographic expeditions into the wilderness, knew how to survive in the mountains in all kinds of weather, knew places to hide where no policeman or CIA hitman would ever find them.

All they had to do was get to Redding safely.

The sweep of headlights through his curtained window jerked him from reverie, heart leaping. In two seconds he was up at the window, peering past the curtain's edge.

Illuminated by the lights in the court, he could see the vehicle but not its occupants. It was a two-berth camper van, painted metallic brown, with brown smoked-glass windows which made it impossible to see inside, even in daylight.

The camper now drew into the parking space next to

the XR3 and to Drummond's mind seemed to do so with excessive quietness, possibly with stealth. The vehicle was expensive and brand new, but even allowing for a new, quiet engine, it seemed to make too little sound as it coasted to a halt outside unit fourteen.

Drummond heard the engine die, saw the headlights go out. Then . . . nothing. No door opened, no movement was made.

Were the occupants checking the XR3, planning strategy?

Standing there, heartbeat rocking his body, he realised how totally vulnerable he and Karen were. She had been right, they shouldn't have stopped. They should maybe have gotten off the freeway and into an isolated site – the entire area between there and Redding was riddled with lakeside campsites and recreation facilities – and caught a few hours sleep in the car.

But would *that* have worked? If the word had gone out to law enforcement agencies, wasn't it more likely they'd figure he and Karen would stay on the backroads, rather than take the freeway to . . . to wherever they were heading, and accordingly keep a close eye on the rurals?

God, he didn't know. He didn't know a damned thing. He was wallowing in a mire of speculation, projection, imagination and fantasy. He'd have given an arm for a few cold, hard, dependable facts.

Well, there was a cold, hard, dependable fact, happening right before his eyes – the driver's door of the camper was opening.

A man got out, huge, black-bearded, mid-thirties, wearing mountain clothes, a khaki weatherproofed jacket over a check lumberjack shirt. Silently, he pushed the van door to, without closing it, and stood looking at the XR3, inspecting it.

He bent down, peered into the passenger window, then stood erect and re-opened the van door, appeared to speak to someone inside the van. From his angle, Drummond could not see into the driving compartment.

The man turned back to the XR3, switched on a flashlight, directed the beam inside the car, worked it over the interior, across the dashboard, now began to move around the car, coming fully into Drummond's view as he played the beam around the exterior rear of the car, paused at the three bullet holes in the rear fender, and moved on to stand at the driver's door, his back to Drummond.

Drummond could scarcely breathe. His mind was racing with his heart. The man was a giant, six-five and two-eighty, solid as rock. *Now* Drummond wished he had a gun. He glanced quickly, pathetically, around the room, searching for a weapon, knowing there was nothing there he could use, throw, wield that would make the slightest impression on the guy outside – not to mention whoever else was in the van.

What did one *do* in a situation like this? Wait for whatever was about to happen, to happen? There was no way out of the room except through the door. And then what? Karen's door would be locked. The car was locked, and she had the keys. He could maybe make a dash around the end of the building, into the darkness, find some kind of weapon . . . and leave Karen?

As soon as he opened the door, the big guy would be after him like a hound after a rabbit . . . or would shoot him, as they shot the cop.

He was consumed by a paralyzing helplessness that infuriated him, attacked his male pride, reached deep inside him to excite a primal need to fight, to defend, to survive. And at that moment he knew with certainty that in order to survive, he, Doctor Paul Drummond, rejecter of violence, could kill.

Rigid with tension, unaware that the hand holding the curtain ached with the intensity of his white-knuckled grip,

270

he watched as the giant shook his flashlight beam at the opaque windows of the van, and the passenger door began to open.

On the far side of the van, out of Drummond's sight, someone stepped down, rocking the vehicle.

For an endless moment, Drummond waited for the figure to appear around the rear of the van, anticipating someone as threatening, as lethal-looking as Giant, perhaps carrying the automatic weapon that had slain the cop. Perhaps more than one person had stepped down, there was room in the van for eight.

A lone figure emerged into sight.

Drummond felt the rush of intense relief and utter foolishness flood his mind and body.

It was a woman, five-foot-two, a hundred-and-ten pounds, wearing white jeans and a floral parka.

She came up to Giant in a playful crouch, peering at the car, pausing to stick her finger in one of the bullet holes, to whisper something, then to slip her arm around his waist as they inspected the interior of the XR3 and exchanged whispered comments.

Drummond released the curtain and his pent breath simultaneously. Just two innocent, thoughtful travellers, aware of sleeping people, perhaps contemplating buying a small car like the XR3.

He lay down again, concentrated on getting his breathing and heartbeat normal, his mind relaxed for sleep.

Two innocent travellers – this time.

But what if they hadn't been? What if it had been them?

He didn't feel foolish now. An analysis of his reaction and feelings was vital. He'd been right to feel helpless, because he'd been helpless, right to feel panicked and scared, because he'd been those things too. For a few moments there, he had lost control – of his, and Karen's, safety, of their lives.

271

He thought again about his desperate, reflexive search for a weapon, and his spontaneous readiness to use it. Now, out of immediate danger, he wondered again whether, if he had possessed a gun, he would have been able to pull the trigger and end the giant's life.

Unfair, unfair, logic whispered. Then, yes; now, no.

Responsibility insisted that he picture Karen and himself in another "then" situation, maybe later that same day, or the next, or the next. How prepared would he be in the future to protect and preserve their lives?

He had access to weapons. Even on photographic sorties into the mountains, he and his father had always carried weapons. You didn't co-habit with bears and wild boars and mountain cats without the means to defend yourself.

What was required now was a conscious decision, visualization, permission.

Constantly, in Suggestion Therapy, he offered patients the dictum: "What the mind can conceive, and believe, the mind can achieve." He now offered it to himself.

Settling, he entered into a process of deep rhythmic breathing and progressive relaxation, retaining sufficient control of his conscious thoughts to conjure up a vision of himself and Karen in a situation of mortal danger . . . seeing himself there, armed, threatened, without alternative.

He then visualized himself aiming, pulling the trigger, and sending a bullet into a human body.

Now, prepared, he knew he could do it.

Now, prepared, he programmed his Subconscious to wake him in precisely four hours, and in a moment was asleep.

Chapter Twenty-Five

Friday.

8.30 a.m.

Sacramento.

Fifty miles north of the Rest-E-Z Motel, in the heart of the state capital, a team of twelve people were assembled in the spacious dining room of the governor's official residence.

They were not there to eat.

In the past hour a radical rearrangement had been made to the dining furniture. A space had been created at one end of the room, into which had been introduced two large tables with chairs, and two wooden lecterns. A dozen other hardback chairs were scattered about, for general seating.

Governor Jack Crane sat off to one side, stonily watching the preparations, a two-inch-thick file of papers on his knee. Satisfied that things were moving along efficiently and precisely according to plan, he returned his gaze to the file, to the elaborate issues book that had been compiled by his team to bring him up to speed on all the subjects likely to be raised in the television debate on Sunday night.

Even though the polls placed him an average ten points ahead of Milton Byrne, and predicted a landslide victory, Jack Crane was taking no chances. In war, you took nothing for granted.

This particular precaution, this preparation, this war-game, was called Candidate School. In it, as accurately as possible, would be duplicated the experience the candidate was likely to encounter during the upcoming television debate. Crane was training for the fight as though he were preparing for a championship bout. The prize was the White House.

Although the television debate was a relatively recent phenomenon in general elections, and despite a degree of denial among political pundits that voters could be crucially swayed by a single by a candidate performance, its powerful potential to enhance or mar the chance of victory was generally accepted.

For ninety minutes the impartial, merciless eye and ear of the TV camera would bring a combatant's strengths and weaknesses of appearance, personality, knowledge and behavior into the living rooms of millions of voting viewers. There he'd be, in glorious close-up, warts 'n all, for all to see. How could they not be swayed?

There was an axiom to which all candidates were repeatedly exposed by their managers and trainers: the debate lasts ninety minutes; you only need thirty seconds to win it. Or lose it.

Jack Crane was aware of the threat posed by the debating expertise of his otherwise ineffectual opponent. Milton Byrne was an egg-head, a mild-mannered, non-charismatic Ivy League professor, who could not hope to compete with Jack Crane as a mover of people's emotions or manipulator of their minds, but possessed a vast knowledge of national and international matters, and was a calm, statesman-like debater.

Provided he, Crane, was sufficiently prepared, could field the challenge of facts and return it with interest, he had no doubt his superiority of personality, his firebrand magnetism would win the night.

The preparations had been profound. His team, his

"hired guns" were literally the best in the business. And money had never been a problem.

He looked up from the file and studied the activity. There stood the man chosen to be his opponent in this mock debate, the stand-in for Milton Byrne, a man so like Byrne in appearance, persona, coloring, education and political expertise that he might have been a laboratory clone.

And there, about to take their seats at the "press" table, were the four stand-ins who would represent the panel of three questioners and the moderator, all practicing journalists and broadcasters, primed to pose the kind of questions most likely to be thrown at the candidates in the Pauley Pavilion. His lieutenants were now setting the lecterns – exact replicas of those to be used on Sunday – in their correct positions. Other experts on his team would evaluate his appearance at the lectern with regard to lighting, with regard to Milton Byrne's superior height. If necessary, a wooden riser would be concealed behind his lectern to even that particular discrepancy.

Every aspect of the debate had been, and would continue to be, analysed in the minutest detail, and every advantage implemented to ensure a resounding success for Jack Crane on Sunday evening.

Political over-confidence on the eve of a general election was a two-edged sword that had slaughtered many a presidential candidate, but it wasn't going to cut Jack Crane down to size.

Nothing, absolutely nothing, would be left to chance.

Crane saw Karl Hoffman, his campaign manager and "top gun", break from the action and head towards him. Karl the Killer, Hoffman the Heavy were epithets used jokingly, but with justification, among his team. Of Teutonic origin, Hoffman had been with Crane in Military Intelligence, and had already served him spectacularly in politics. Come January 20, Crane had no doubt he would continue to do so as chief of his White House staff.

Hoffman hove to, huge and muscular, sweat staining his white shirt. "About ten minutes, Governor."

"Okay, Karl."

"I've been thinking about the riser behind the lectern."

"What about it?"

"Byrne's four inches taller, hm? You don't want to be seen *stepping* up to match his height."

"Then what?"

"A ramp. You approach the lectern, rise gradually, no sudden move."

Crane nodded. "Byrne's people will want to okay it."

"Leave them to me. When I've finished with them, they'll agree to him standing in a hole – or a four-inch amputation."

As Hoffman walked away, Crane had the impression of a wall receding. He wished he had more men of Hoffman's calibre behind him. With a small battalion, he could rule the world. Still, with the team he'd got he was doing pretty damned good.

He returned to his studies. Such a lot to learn, so much of it boring, intellectual crap – child care, medical insurance, college bonds, cleaning up the environment, social security, housing, farm subsidies, abortion – but stuff Byrne was very strong on. Much of it he, Crane, could wing. He had an armory of boilerplate responses he'd used a thousand times on the stump, and would use again and again.

But this was television, and on TV everyone wanted to be a star, especially those journalist assholes who'd be on the panel. Nothing would give them greater pleasure than to put Jack Crane on the spot with a question he didn't know the answer to. On the stump, you could pretend you didn't hear an uncomfortable question, or shout it down, roll right over it with the power of personality. At worst, you were playing to an audience of maybe a few hundred voters, so a gaffe didn't matter that much. But on TV you were playing in close-up to millions of voters and probably all of the delegates, and showing yourself to be an inept, unprepared prick was the last thing you needed.

The irony was, the average voter didn't *listen* to profound, knowledgeable, substantive responses. Only the media did that. The average Joe reacted to bumper-sticker language, to witty one-liners and smart-ass slogans. 'Jack Crane Ain't About To Let It Happen' had been the brain-child of one of his hired guns, an advertizing executive drafted for the campaign. It had been a runaway success. On the stump, you could precede a good slogan with a boxcar-load of high-sounding, rhetorical, meaningless shit, and bring the house down with the pay-off.

Voters didn't listen, they watched, and felt.

What applied now was not substantive issues, but the mechanics of politics – and personalities. Television had changed politics for all time. Television had become the arbiter of what was important enough to show to the viewers, the voters.

And what was important was the "sound bite", the interesting picture, the controversial image, the entertaining gaffe. A politician tripping up the steps to the rostrum was, for the cameras and therefore for the viewers, far more interesting and entertaining than the speech he made at the rostrum. It was "good television", and far more likely to go out on the six o'clock news than another, uneventful speech, regardless of content.

Jack Crane had learned this lesson well. His team were masters of the "sound bite". They had planned his entire campaign with a view to capturing as much airtime as possible. They had sculpted it into a speech-and-advertising onslaught against the left-wing liberal policies of an Ivy League professor who was too naive to appreciate what was happening, too much of a gentleman to respond with a negative counter-attack, and who wouldn't know a sound bite if it bit him in the ass.

Milton Byrne's strengths were congressional experience, and political knowledge. He'd do just fine as America's president. The panel of journalists knew this, and would try, through their questions, to show the nation Byrne's qualities, an opportunity Jack Crane had largely denied the voters with his overwhelming fire-storm campaign of negatives.

In this vital debate, substantive responses would only become an important issue if Byrne were allowed to make his opponent look ignorant, shallow, foolish.

And, his opponent mused, returning to his studies, Jack Crane ain't about to let it happen.

Several minutes later he again saw Karl Hoffman approaching and closed the issues book, fully prepared now to take the lectern and join the fray.

But Hoffman was shaking his head, then nodding in the direction of the telephones at the end of the room.

"Not yet, Governor, you got a call. It's Jackdaw."

Crane stared hard at his lieutenant, reading his eyes. "Is he secure?"

"Yes. Take it in your office."

Crane stood. "Does he sound happy?"

"No, sir. He's scared shitless."

Blood drained from Crane's face.

Jamming the file into Hoffman's midriff, he strode across the room, out of the door and across the hall. By the time he picked up the scrambler phone on his desk, he was rigid with rage.

"Tell me."

The caller cleared his throat. "No luck so far . . ."

"*Luck*! You incompetent moron . . ."

"They've gone to ground. They're not fools. They could be anywhere."

"You've checked his place in the Valley?"

"We've checked everywhere they use. I've got guys watching the Malibu house, his office, her office, her apartment. They just took off, didn't stop to pick up clothes, passports, anythin'. Shit, we've been searching all night, every direction, trying to pick up the beacon, but unless we get within range . . ."

"Shut the fuck up, I'm thinking. They're scared. They've got the tape. Whatever's on it, they'll be figuring how best to use it to save their lives. They'll need help . . . and time. They won't go to the police, their pal Gage has warned them off cops. You heard him tell them to trust nobody. They need a place to lie low, a safe house, people they can trust. For sure, they won't stick around LA. So where do they go?"

"Friends? Relations?"

"They saw the messenger killed. They know the same is going to happen to them. They're responsible people. They wouldn't involve friends, risk their lives."

"The same goes for relatives."

"Not necessarily. When people get into deep shit, their instinct is to go home, back to where everything's familiar, safe, dependable. Drummond and Beal will need a lot of help, and they can't trust anyone they don't know. They need to lose her car, find another vehicle, and they won't rent or buy one, leave a trail of checks or credit card vouchers for us to follow. They won't stay around the old homestead for long, but you could pick up their scent again there, wherever there is."

"She's English."

"Forget her, concentrate on Drummond. Use our pull at DMV, check back through his license applications, this guy's been driving since his teens. He's a PhD., check his professional license, also his home address at university. From there, go back through his schools. Check for passport applications, he may have

279

traveled abroad as a student. His next of kin will be listed.

"Will do."

"You sure as shit will do. When you find it, get four men there, even if it's fucking Alaska. I want that tape . . . in my hand . . . in forty eight hours. And I want them out of it. And Jackdaw . . ."

"Yes, sir?"

"If Trice gets out, you're a dead man."

Crane slammed down the phone.

He stood there for a long time, enraged, suffering the worst panic attack of his life, his heart bursting through his chest, bowels turning to jello. He was terrified.

He'd come so far, done a lot of covert, necessary things to get there. But he hadn't done enough. Put another way, he'd done too much of the wrong things – like trusting so-called fucking experts to do a thorough, professional job.

They said Tom Keegan was safe, wiped clean, all memory erased like a tape recording. And Ambrose, whichever one he was, was another. Two mistakes that could cost him everything.

In war, you leave nothing to chance. But he had. He'd let them live.

Jesus Christ, so close.

If he could keep the lid on Trice until January, he was home free. He could use the power of the presidency to pull all kinds of national security shit, suppress the tape, or, if it surfaced, dismiss it as the ravings of a vet psycho.

But now – the media would eat it up.

Ever since Nixon had tap-danced his way through the Sixty-eight campaign claiming he had a plan to end the Vietnam war, and then slammed the door on the issue when he entered the White House, the media had realised the imperative of forcing an answer to sensitive questions

280

before the insulation of the Oval Office engulfed the candidate.

If Trice got out, those bastards would bury him.

There was a knock on the door and Hoffman came in.

He took one look at Crane's face and said, "They're still loose."

Crane drew a breath, braced his shoulders, and marched to the door. "Let's get this done . . . though I'd hand Byrne this debate on a plate to know where those two are right now."

As he spoke the words, Drummond and Beal were passing within a mile of him, traversing Sacramento on Interstate 5, three hours from Redding.

Chapter Twenty-Six

They came off the I-5 at Colusa, fifty miles north of Sacramento, for gas and breakfast, and found a rustic restaurant in the recreation area near the Sacramento River.

The day was stunning, the sun warm in a cloudless sky and the cool fall air smelling pungently of pine.

Climbing from the car, Karen stretched, tilted her face to the sun, inhaled deeply, sensually. With the exhalation she said earnestly, "God, I love this country. I think I'm going to live here the rest of my life."

Drummond joined her, slipped his arm about her shoulder, gave himself for a moment to the sun and the river and the feel of her. "And I think I'd like that."

She smiled, fresh and beautifully as the morning, and put her arm around his waist. "I believe . . . I was born to live in America. I fell in love with it, with the land, when I saw my first cowboy movie. I used to think how lucky actors like James Stewart and Gregory Peck were to earn a fabulous living riding a horse through country like this."

"They'd probably agree with you. But wait till you see my mountains, they'll *really* send you. Come on, I'm going to buy you a genu-ine cowpoke breakfast – pancakes with maple syrup, a side order of crispy bacon, and a gallon of fresh-brewed coffee."

The place was pine-clad and smelled of it, and of grilling bacon and percolating coffee. Three or four of the red-gingham booths were occupied by late-season campers, all senior citizens.

Drummond chose a booth by a front window from where he could keep an eye on the approach road and their car.

Karen, noting his choice and the look in his eyes, said, "I'm sure no one followed us off the freeway. I was watching all the way here."

"Me, too. I'm sure we can relax for a while."

The waitress came and took their order, served their coffee immediately.

Drummond smiled at Karen over the steaming mug. "Cheers, pardner, or whatever cowpokes say. You should stick to four hours sleep, you look ravishing on it."

"Whah, thenk yuh, Rhett. And you . . ." she tilted her head at him, "look different." Her tone lost its banter.

"Oh? How so?"

"I don't know exactly. You *feel* different, as though you've been doing a lot of serious thinking. I mean extra serious."

"You're very perceptive. I have."

"About what?"

"Did you hear that van arrive last night, the brown camper parked next to the car?"

"Vaguely. I was bushed."

"I got up when I saw its headlights. A huge guy got out, started inspecting the XR3 with a flashlight, gave it a real going over – and damn-near gave me a heart attack."

She was staring at him.

"Oh, it was okay. He had a tiny woman with him, they were probably in the market for a small car and fancied yours. But it made me think. It might have been them – and we'd have been defenceless. I hated the feeling of being so vulnerable. I'm not going to let it happen again."

She narrowed her eyes, reading his. "You're going to get a gun."

"Yes."

"And you've prepared yourself to use it. That's what's different about you."

"It's called giving yourself permission."

She looked down at the checkered tablecloth, traced the squares with her nail. "What's our plan when we get to Redding?"

Drummond saw the waitress approaching with their meal. He waited until she'd replenished their coffee mugs and departed before answering.

"We'll be in Redding by one o'clock. Before we leave here I'm going to call a friend, Mike Fallon. He runs a hypnotherapy center in town. He also has a very comprehensive recording studio there, makes mail order self-improvement tapes, including subliminals. That'll be our first call. We'll drop the tape off, then head for my folks' place. My father practices in the city, but they live a few miles out, on Whiskeytown Lake."

She smiled. "Sounds gorgeous."

"It is. The whole region is lakes and mountains and forests . . . well, I won't attempt to describe it, you'll see for yourself. My folks have a big old wooden house, like Aunt Cissie's, on ten acres of woodland, fronting on the lake. We'll hide your car there, use the Range Rover. With due respect, I'll feel a whole lot happier when we get rid of Buttercup out there."

Karen looked out at her car. "She is rather bright. I've been told one doesn't drive a yellow car in LA, it isn't a 'power color', whatever that means."

He grinned. "I could never imagine you getting involved in LA psych-games. I doubt Sir Edward Beal's daughter ever had a confidence problem."

She demurred with a shrug. "Right now, I'm not so sure. I'd feel better knowing where the V's are, who they are, and how many. So, go on, we ditch Buttercup . . ."

"Then we kit up, head into Shasta-Trinity. It's Rambo

country, rugged as it comes, a whole mess of lakes, rivers, creeks and mountains. We'll keep in touch with Mike Fallon by radiotelephone. When he's transcribed the tape, we'll go in and pick it up. We can decide what action to take then, depending on what we've got."

She shook her head, disbelievingly. "'In a trice it will be nice . . . Charlie will be put on ice'. Words. One man, probably two, have already died because of what they mean. I wonder how many others are going to . . . well, if not die, at least have their lives decimated by them?"

"We have to be very careful about that."

She looked up at him. "You mean the people we now touch – Mike Fallon, your parents."

"Yes. Their involvement must be kept to an absolute minimum."

She searched his face. "You're afraid the V's know where we're heading, aren't you? . . . that they may be already in Redding, waiting for us?"

"It's a possibility."

"But how could they possibly know?"

"They won't *know*. But they may have made an educated guess. These guys are pros, and they're desperate. They've lost us. Since ten o'clock last night they've been doing a lot of head-scratching. They've applied psychology to the problem of finding us. Now, what's one of the first things the cops do when they're looking for a criminal, a suspect?"

"Check previous associations, previous hangouts."

"Right. When someone goes on the lam, he needs help, shelter, money, wheels, all kinds of things, and he heads for where he can get them. Automatically, the V's would have covered all the places we function in – our homes, offices – and will be working outwards from there. They *know* we've got to ditch Buttercup, get a replacement vehicle. They'll *assume* that we, knowing their police connections, won't be trading Buttercup in, or writing checks or using credit cards. Okay, they know we've got cash, but that alone won't buy what we need – some safe time. My guess is they'll use their resources to check on our previous associations and hangouts, and keep an eye on them. What can they lose? It's a better bet than aimlessly chasing all over the West Coast looking for us, and certainly worth a try."

"And that means your associations and hangouts. I've got none."

"Right."

"So they'll pick up on your parents' address from . . ." she was working on it as she talked, "what? – license applications? Next of kin requirements?"

"All kinds of places. These guys will flash a badge, mutter 'national security', and the walls of privacy will come tumbling down."

She frowned at him. "Then if you expect them to be waiting for us, why are we heading home?"

"First reason: I need Mike Fallon. I know of nobody else who could do this job, and quickly, and keep his mouth shut. Second reason: we need clothing, equipment, and weapons, and they're all there waiting for us. Third reason: if we're going to be hunted, I want it done in my own backyard." He smiled. "Don't worry, we'll be careful. In a way I hope they are there. I'm getting a stiff neck from looking over my shoulder."

He pushed his plate away. "I'm going to phone Mike Fallon."

Tension accrued as the miles to Redding diminished.

Affected by Drummond's hypothesis, they shared the expectation that at any moment they would run into a road block, be surrounded by a posse of howling police cars, be shot at from an overtaking vehicle, even descended upon by a machine-gunning helicopter.

As a thirty-mile marker from the city loomed, Karen

discovered a tendency to slow her speed, a reluctance to contemplate taking the eventual off-ramp. Every mile, being a mile closer to their goal, a mile closer to probable danger, engendered ambivalence.

"This is like standing on the roof of a burning building," she murmured, her eyes everywhere now. "You're damned if you don't jump, probably damned if you do."

"We have a couple of things in our favor. We *know* where we're heading, they can only guess. I can't believe they have unlimited men to expend on this thing, so they can't cover every eventuality. Since we hit the freeway this morning, I've begun to get a feeling about these people, to develop a theory."

"Tell it to me."

"They have power. They have connections. They have authority. But they have to be selective in how they use their resources, because what they're doing is illicit. It's as if they – or some *one* – is functioning on two levels, illicitly but within the framework of officialdom."

"Like Watergate."

"Right. Let's talk Jack Crane. As Governor, as war hero, as ex-Military Intelligence, as ex-CIA, he has power, connections, authority. If this does concern him, and if it was all above-board, we'd have been picked up hours ago. Every freeway in the state would've been swarming with Highway Patrol guys. It hasn't happened. We haven't even seen a cruiser since we left Stockton. So what he's got working for him is a limited team of official badges, operating privately and illicitly.

"When they encounter a problem, they have the muscle to solve it, no come-backs. The magic words 'national security' open most doors and close all mouths. But he's got to be careful. And, because of his limited manpower, selective. Right now, he may well have someone watching the house on the lake, but I'm sure he can't have a man parked at every interchange exit between here and Redding."

"How many alternative exits are there?"

"Four. The first is just before Cottonwood, the second just after it. We could take the second, then a tortuous rural route into Redding by the back door. The third interchange is Anderson. That's a humdinger. About four rural routes lead into the city from there. The fourth exit is on the north side of the city, we'd have to double back on city roads if we took that. So, you see, he'd need a fleet of cars and a dozen men to cover all the possibilities, and he can't even be sure we're heading this way."

"'He'. My stomach turns over every time I think of it possibly being Jack Crane. It sounds so . . . outlandish." She looked at him. "Okay, which exit do we place our bets on?"

"Anderson. It gives us a greater choice of rural routes if anyone should be waiting."

"How far to Anderson?"

"Twenty miles."

"Twenty miles . . . twenty minutes." She drew a fluttery sigh. "Okay, folks, bets down. Spin the wheel. Rien ne vaplus."

She brought their speed back up to sixty.

Chapter Twenty-Seven

Karen said, "Tell me about Mike Fallon."

They had come in on a minor road to the west of the I–5 and were driving through increasingly populous suburbs of tract housing and shopping malls, the high-rise buildings of the city now visible a few miles ahead. They felt safer here, had done since they'd quit the freeway. No car had followed them off. To make doubly sure, they had backed into a side street and waited there for fifteen minutes, taking note of the few vehicles that did come off the interstate, but seeing nothing remotely suspicious.

Karen felt comforted by Drummond's theory about the restrictions on the V's. Later on, they'd have to re-hone their vigilance, but for now they could afford to stand down from high-alert.

"Mike? You'll love him. Physically he's no Greek god. He's five-ten, average build, has red hair, poor eyesight, and freckles. But he's a charmer. And has a great voice. All his female patients fall in love with him."

"How long have you known him?"

"Sixteen years. We met up at UCLA, he was the first guy I spoke to on the first day of the Psych course, and we've been friends ever since. We both went on to USC for our doctorates."

"Is he married?"

Drummond smiled. "Not yet. He always seems about to but never quite gets around to it. He gets so engrossed in his work, I think he forgets there's a girl waiting somewhere for him. By the time he remembers, she's not there anymore."

"By work, d'you mean hypnotherapy, or the recording studio?"

"Well, now, that's an astute question, because with Mike there is a difference. It was the essential difference between him and me. I was always more interested in the human problem, he in the techniques for solving it.

"When I first met him he was already obsessed with the subject of hypnosis, with mind control. At eighteen he was already a good hypnotist. He used to work on the kids in the class, giving them Suggestion Therapy for confidence, pre-exam nerves, athletic improvement, and was so good at it that students from other classes started coming to him. That's when I gave him a suggestion. He was always broke, his folks had no money, and he was doing crummy jobs to pay for his tuition, so I suggested he charge five bucks a session. He pretty well hypnotized his way through college."

They reached an intersection. Drummond directed Karen across it. The houses and shops were getting more dense now. A sign read: City Center 2 miles.

Drummond continued, "By the time we graduated from UCLA Mike had written a book entitled 'Mind Control: Fact or Fantasy'. It was a remarkable effort, a seminal investigation into the history and potential of hypnosis, including its uses in Intelligence and in the training of assassins. It was published while he was at USC, and sold pretty well.

"He got deeply into technology then, began experimenting with recording equipment, with the making of subliminals, and decided that was the way he wanted to go – selling self-help hypnosis to the public, as well as establishing a practice.

"By that time we were like brothers. His parents lived in Brooklyn. He didn't go home much and loved California, so he spent most of the holidays with me at the lake. My father took a great interest in him, and when we graduated, Dad found premises for him in the same medical complex he practiced in. Dad, of course, wanted me there, too, in partnership with Mike, but I'd made plans with Vivian and opened up in LA"

Karen stopped for traffic lights. They were entering the city proper now, and she felt the creeping return of threat. Poor yellow Buttercup was just too conspicuous for their good.

"Does Mike know anything about Tom Keegan?"

"He called after your first article, joking about getting you to do a write-up about him and his Bettalife tapes." He smiled. "You may recall I wasn't too happy with the mention of Keegan that day, so I kept discussion about you and Tom to a minimum. When I spoke to him this morning I purposely kept it brief, just told him we were coming in and needed his help. Mike is lightning quick, doesn't need pictures drawing. He will have read the Trice article, maybe tried to call me in the Valley, expecting me to be there. All he said this morning was: Get here."

He pointed. "Turn right at the furniture store, go down two blocks, make a left."

Karen was relieved to quit the main thoroughfare. They entered a quieter, tree-lined street of porched, multi-storied houses, then turned left into a similar street dominated by a more modern office complex surrounded by a spacious parking area. The building was named Trinity House.

Drummond said, pointing at a pair of windows facing the street, "That's my father's surgery. Mike's round the back. Drive round, there's a rear entrance."

Karen drew into an area designated "Shasta Hypnotherapy Center". As she switched off the engine, she heaved a sigh of relief. "Well, we made it this far."

Drummond patted her knee. "Yuh done good, Scarlet. Let us go confer with genius."

She reached for her bag off the rear seat. "You've got the tape?"

He tapped the left breast pocket of his parka. "Next to my heart."

As they entered the building, an unmarked gray Plymouth sedan was entering the city limits on Interstate 5. It was occupied by two men, code names Albatross and Peregrine. Albatross, a White, was driving. Peregrine, a Black, was wool-gathering, wondering how long this crazy chase would keep him from the soft, warm body of his woman in San Diego. Both men were in their mid-thirties, supremely fit, and heavily armed.

Wearing business suits, neither was dressed appropriately for mountain work, and thought their immediate superior an inept asshole for rushing them north without due preparation. It did not inspire confidence to see one's boss in a shit-scared, flat-out panic. Whatever was on the tape must be a huge thumb up somebody's political ass. Jackdaw was always the picture of cool.

Beep.

It took a split second for them to react.

Beep.

Peregrine shot upright, staring at the tracker screen. "Fuckin' bingo!"

Albatross, a lugubrious blond, muttered viciously, "Got the bastards."

Peregrine snatched the phone from its cradle, punched a number. "This is Peregrine. Gimme Jackdaw."

Jackdaw came on. "Yeah?"

"We just picked up the beacon."

"Thank Christ. Where are you?"

"I-5. Elevated, half-way across the city."

"What's the range?"

"Two miles."

"Are they moving or static?"

"Can't tell yet."

"How fast can you get off the freeway?"

Peregrine consulted a state map. "There's an interchange about two miles on, we'll have to double back."

"Okay, hold on."

Silence for a long twenty seconds.

Peregrine said, covering the phone, "I think he's jacking off with happiness."

"Not possible. Somebody big chewed his family jewels off when we lost these two in LA."

Jackdaw came back. "You still got them?"

"Loud and clear, but the range is increasing, so they could be static and we're running away from them."

"Okay, get off the freeway and find them. Don't intercept without checking with me. They may be dropping the tape somewhere and we need to know where. I'm checking known associates. Find them and call it in."

"Roger. Peregrine out."

Mike Fallon, wearing a white clinical coat over a fawn tweed suit, thick-framed bifocals magnifying the staring intensity of his jade-green eyes, listened to the story of Tom Keegan and the tape with the total concentration he gave to all information that passed across his desk. It was this silence, this facility for conveying to his clients his undeviating interest in what they were saying, as much as his expertise as a hypnotist and therapist, that had built his immensely successful practice.

Rather than interrupt Drummond's flow, with occasional interjections from Karen, he would lean forward occasionally and jot down a note or question, then lean back again in his soft leather chair and resume his listening pose, hands clasped, fore-fingers steepled, their tips touching his lips.

Only when Drummond had finally finished did he allow his feelings to show, but then did so with such exuberance, with an exclamation of such astonishment, disbelief, dismay, that Karen jumped at the outburst.

"Jesus Christ, what are you guys into!?" He threw his hands in the air, brought them down with a resounding slap on the arms of the chair, guffawed an astounded laugh. "Oh, brother – and sister – have you got a rattler by the tail."

He shot forward, arms on the desk, hand open to Drummond. "Let me have the tape."

Drummond dug it out of his pocket.

Fallon looked at it, tapped it against a thumb. "Ninety minutes. You say the subliminals go all through?"

Drummond nodded. "Far as I can tell."

"I'll have to transcribe it myself, and my typing stinks. Ninety minutes could run to ten A-Four pages, double-spaced. We're looking at five hours work, easy. I'll have to do it tonight after work. Friday's always a bitch for clients, as Paul knows. Neuroses flare like brush fires at the weekend, it's the fear of being alone. I've got a full case-load till six."

Karen said, "If you could pull out the subliminals, I'd be glad to stay here and type it up."

Fallon shook his head emphatically. "No, honey, I want you both out of here in the next five minutes. Look," he spread his hands entreatingly, covered them both with a serious intensity of expression, "I know something about these guys. I wrote a book, did a lot of research . . ."

Karen said, "Paul told me."

"Right. Well, I came up with things I just couldn't believe. There is stuff going on in this country that *no-one* would believe. We're in the hands of the cryptocracy, Karen – people who thrive on secrecy, who believe they can do whatever the hell they want to do, because the laws that govern ordinary mortals don't apply to them.

294

Like James Bond, they've got a license to kill. Only they go a whole lot further. Their license is called the National Security Act, and if *they* deem a situation threatening to national security, they can gun you down in LA, turn you into a zombie without a memory, make you a spy, an assassin, plant you six feet deep in the desert, or put you on a rocket to the moon."

He sank back into the chair, holding the cassette, looking at it as though it would give up its secret visually.

"Jack Crane. Well, I for one do not doubt him capable of being behind this. Hell, he *was* a spook – MI and CIA – and once a spook, always a spook. Does anybody believe Crane won't use every advantage he can lay a hand on, every connection, every trick in the book to get into the White House – and stay there? If the Trice thing in any way threatens his chance of election – watch out. I'm sure you're right, Paul – if this wasn't an illicit, covert operation, there'd have been an army after you and you wouldn't have got out of LA. But, nevertheless, you're in deadly danger, and you have to get out of here now."

He pulled open his desk drawer, took from it a set of keys and tossed them to Drummond. "Take my Cherokee, leave Buttercup here. Go to the house, leave the Cherokee there, use your Range Rover and head for the hills. Phone me here at midnight. If everything's okay, you come in, pick up the transcript, and take off for LA. Now, get going, and for Pete's sake, keep your eyes skinned."

They got up. Karen held out her hand. "It's been a short, traumatic visit, Mike. I hope we meet again under happier circumstances."

Fallon got to his feet, came round the desk to see them out. "Absolutely count on it. If this tape is what we think it is, we'll be celebrating your Pulitzer."

Drummond said, "I was going to drop in and see Dad, but in the circumstances . . ."

Fallon shook his head. "You're dad's not here, he's at home. He doesn't work Friday afternoons anymore, likes to get in a long weekend. Paul . . . take care up at the lake, hm?"

Drummond nodded. "Absolutely count on it."

The phone buzzed. Peregrine picked it up.

Jackdaw said, "You found them yet?"

"Still looking. We're close, but this is a city, they could be tucked in anywhere."

"Are they static?"

"Seems so."

"Okay – known associate in Redding: father. Doctor Robert Drummond. Trinity House Medical Center, Trinity Street. You picked up a city map?"

"Just now."

"Check out Trinity House. If the XR3 is there, call me. I'll bring in Seagull and Blackbird from the lake with the van. I want a nice clean lift. If the car moves, call me. They'll probably be heading for the lake. Seagull and Blackbird will intercept."

Peregrine said, "Maybe they're dropping the tape off with his old man?"

"If they don't have it on them, ask the Beal girl where it is – nicely."

Peregrine sniggered a laugh. "Sure. Nicely."

He hung up, opened the city map on his knee, checked their position by street signs, found it on the map. "Okay, straight ahead four blocks, make a left, down two blocks, make a left. That's Trinity."

The Cherokee, a sturdy, off-the-road vehicle with a powerful engine and four-wheel drive, was parked three spaces from the XR3.

Drummond started the motor and backed out of the space.

296

Karen gazed mock-forlornly at her car and waved, "'Bye, Buttercup, see you whenever."

"She'll be safe here. We'll come back and get her when this is over, spend a few days at the lake."

Drummond drove across the lot, stopped at the entrance to allow a red Corvette to pass from the right, saw a gray Plymouth enter Trinity from the left and approach at a crawl, the Black passenger peering about him as though looking for an address.

Waiting, Drummond saw the Black point towards the Medical Center sign. The vehicle came to a halt.

Karen said, "They're coming in here."

Drummond turned into the street.

The tracking device was beeping frantically.

Wincing at the noise, Albatross told his partner, "They'll be round the back. Go take a look."

Peregrine got out, disappeared round the end of the building, reappeared a few seconds later, got back in the car.

"They're here."

Albatross muttered, "Thank Christ," and switched off the tracking device. "Call Jackdaw."

Peregrine eyed him laconically. "You must get real exhausted giving orders."

"I'm driving, ain't I?"

"Yeah, I forgot. That's real heavy stuff." He reached for the phone.

Jackdaw answered.

Peregrine said, "We got 'em. Medical Center."

"Good work. You seen them?"

"No, just the car, parked round the back out of sight."

"Okay, nail this tight. The van should be there in twenty minutes, tops. It's ten miles from the lake to the Center. If they appear, Taser the bastards, get them into the Plymouth and get out of there, meet the van later. If they don't have the tape, find out where they dropped it. It'll likely be with the father. I want them and the tape back here tonight. Don't screw up . . . or I'll use your balls for putting practice."

Peregrine parked the phone. "Drive in, get behind the XR3."

As Albatross slipped into the lot and took up position, Peregrine reached for a leather case on the rear seat. It contained two electric Taser guns.

The Taser is a close-range weapon which fires tiny barbs, linked to the gun by hair-fine wires. With the barbs embedded in flesh, the circuit is closed, and a devastating high-voltage shock, capable of climbing rapidly to fifty thousand volts, disrupts the nervous system and paralyzes muscular control.

If the gun is left on, the pain is unendurable. Albatross had no doubt that Drummond would *beg* to tell them where the tape was when he heard the girl scream.

He handed one of the guns to Albatross. "You take Drummond."

Albatross gave him a sneery look. "While you get to play with the cunt."

Peregrine grinned. "You think I do this shit for the pay?"

"No," said Albatross. "That thought has never crossed my mind."

Chapter Twenty-Eight

State Highway 299 comes into Redding from the east, from Alturas near the conjunction of the Oregon and Nevada borders. Five miles west of Redding, it passes through the town of Shasta, then, five miles further, through Whiskeytown.

It was in Shasta, on the 299, that they almost came to grief.

In the center of town, the traffic lights changed to red. Drummond braked, head of the line. The cross traffic began to move. Then suddenly, from the direction of Whiskeytown, the dark green, three-ton removal van was coming into the intersection against the lights, accelerating, horn blaring, weaving violently to avoid the cross traffic, the driver losing it, the van slewing into a clockwise skid, heading inexorably for collision with the Cherokee, Drummond seeing it, stamping the accelerator to the floor, cutting hard right into the empty cross street, feeling the chunk as the van's rear bumper clipped the Cherokee's, and going on a hundred yards until they could find a place to stop.

Karen gaped at him. "That was brilliant! Thank you for my life!"

Drummond made a face, whistled with relief. "Someone was sure in a hurry to move. Are you okay?"

"As soon as my stomach leaves my throat, I'll be fine. Let's go see who died back there."

No-one had died. There was no sign of the van, the traffic was flowing smoothly.

Drummond shrugged, turned right at the lights and drove on to Whiskeytown.

It was several seconds after Seagull regained control of the van, and Blackbird had hauled himself upright and was in the process of cursing his partner's insane driving, that they realized their tracker was beeping.

With the vehicle on even keel and barreling down the 299 to the city, they could afford the luxury of logical thought.

Blackbird, a small, thin, pugnacious individual who liked to shoot people, frowned at the tracker screen. "That don't make sense." He hit the instrument with the palm of his hand. "I reckon you shook it up, there's something loose in there."

Seagull, a red-faced, six-four country boy who preferred to use his lethal hands, said emphatically, "Bull . . . shit."

"Okay, how far've we come from the lake?"

"Five miles."

"So the Medical Center is still five miles ahead. How come we're picking up the beacon and it's showing one mile?"

"Maybe they're on the move."

Blackbird snorted. "Jackdaw would've called us. We're supposed to intercept if they head this way."

"Okay, you call him, check it out."

Blackbird reached for the phone, punched the number. "Fucking electronic shit. The Japs are still waging war on us an' we don't know it. Yeah, this is Blackbird, lemme speak to Jackdaw."

Jackdaw said, "What?"

"Listen, there's something screwy this end. We've just come through Shasta, five miles from the Medical Center, but we're picking up the beacon signal at one mile and stretching. You sure they're still there?"

Blackbird heard a terrible silence, then a gasped, "Jesus Christ," then a snapped, "Get back to you."

When the phone went, Peregrine was saying impatiently, "Come on, come on, you sweet young thing, let me zap you with my Taser. You ever do anybody with a Taser, bro? It's *fun.* 'Specially a girl with all that hair. It stands out like Elsa Lanchester's in Frankenstein's Bride." He picked up the phone. "Peregrine."

Jackdaw's voice carried barely contained hysteria. He spoke slowly and carefully, as to a child. "Peregrine, is the car still there?"

"Sure."

"Can you see it?"

"I'm looking right at it."

"And is your tracker beeping?"

Peregrine shot a glance at Albatross. "We . . . my partner turned it off. It was driving us crazy. I mean, there was no need . . . we'd tracked them right here."

"Peregrine, turn the fucking thing on, right now."

Albatross, who could hear the amplified phone signal, switched it on. He stared at Peregrine, open-mouthed, whispered, "Oh . . . shit."

Peregrine cleared his throat. "It's on."

"And?"

"Nothing."

"Nothing." Jackdaw's fury built like the take-off blast of a space rocket. "You asinine assholes . . . you worthless fucks . . . you unmitigated shitbrains . . . they're not there! They've gone! They're on their way to the lake! Seagull and Blackbird just picked up their signal in Shasta, five miles from where you haemorrhoids are sitting playing with your dicks."

301

Peregrine burst out in protest. "But the car's *here*. When we got here, the beacon was beeping."

"And no one's left the Center since you got there?"

"Nobody's come out of the door we're watching."

"And no vehicle has left the area?"

"No . . . yes." Peregrine threw an agonised look at his partner. "Yes, just as we got here, a . . . a Cherokee was pulling out of the parking lot."

"So," Jackdaw repeated unctuously, "a Cherokee was pulling out of the parking lot. And your tracker was beeping. And you let them drive right past you. And then you switched off your beeper. Hey, I must recommend you guys for some sort of reward."

Peregrine was sweating. "But how could it happen?"

"Because the beacon, you indescribable moron, is not in the car . . . it's on the girl! And if you'd had your tracker on, you'd have checked them driving away!"

Jackdaw withdrew himself from fear and fury and turned himself over to logic. For several moments there was a resounding silence over the line, then he spoke calmly and decisively.

"All right, I'll put Seagull and Blackbird on to them. You check for the tape. You're dealing with a doctor, so use your wits. He'll be a local celebrity, known to the cops, so take it easy. But find that tape!"

The phone slammed down.

Peregrine let out his breath with a rush.

Albatross gave a sardonic tut. "And you don't get to use your Taser."

Peregrine gave him a very evil look and said, "Oh?"

Seagull answered the phone.

Jackdaw said, "You were right, they broke loose. What does your tracker say?"

"They're behind us, heading northwest, about three miles."

302

"Turn around and go after them, they'll be making for the lake."

As Blackbird hit the brakes and slammed his partner into the door in a screeching turn, Seagull gasped, "How come they . . .?"

"I've got fools on my team, is how come they. Don't have me thinking the same about you. Get after them, they're driving a Cherokee."

"A Cherokee? We almost hit . . . I mean, we saw a Cherokee in Shasta a coupla minutes ago."

"Well, go get 'em! Use the Tasers, nice clean lift. Check them for the tape. Then call me, yes or no."

"Willco. Out."

Seagull decked the phone. "Can you fucking believe that? We almost had them back there. So how come they got away from the schmucks at the Med. Center?"

Blackbird, dismissing the question as rhetorical, stomped the accelerator to the floor and sent the supercharged van hurtling back up the 299.

Albatross and Peregrine got out of the Plymouth and walked back across the parking lot towards the main entrance. Peregrine looked up at the sky and shivered. In the past hour a front of dark gray clouds had come out of the north, driven by a freezing wind that smelled of rain, or something worse. To Peregrine it didn't feel like California any more.

He said, "I hate this job. I hate the north. Anywhere north of San Diego makes me very unhappy. I dig the sun."

"I can tell by your tan."

"I dig *heat*, man."

"You've got Africa in your blood. Were your folks slaves?"

"Only my father. He still wears his chains around the house, likes the jingle. Where're you from, Al?"

303

"Alaska."

"Fucking figures."

They pushed through swing glass doors into a vestibule, consulted a wall directory. Doctor Robert Drummond occupied Suite One on the first floor.

Through more swing glass doors they entered a reception area, with stairs and toilets and the desk on the right. On the far side, a long wide corridor of doors led through the building to a rear exit. With the exception of two female staff on the desk, the place was deserted. It was not yet two o'clock and the Center was still out to lunch.

Immediately on their left was a door designated: Suite One. Doctor Robert Drummond.

Peregrine nudged Albatross towards it.

"May I help you?" A gray-haired guardian regarded them over her glasses, affronted that they should even contemplate entering a doctor's office without her blessing.

Albatross said, "No," and pushed the door open.

"Er, excuse me!" She was after them.

Peregrine stopped her cold with an ID in the face. "Official business."

She squinted at the card, saw a photograph and something about the State of Maryland and backed off. "Oh."

Peregrine shut the door.

They were in a small reception, with a closed door to the left, and an open one behind the desk. Through it they could see an auburn-haired, middle-aged woman in a white smock standing at a metal filing cabinet, looking quizzically in their direction.

She came out into the reception, frowning, but smiling, knowing they'd made a mistake, wondering how they could have gotten past the desk. "Yes?"

Albatross said, "We'd like to speak with Doctor Drummond."

Her frown intensified. She was beginning to get vibrations. "Who are you?"

Albatross flashed his ID. "Official business." The card disappeared back into his breast pocket.

This one was not so easy. "I'm sorry, I didn't get to read that. What kind of official business?"

"That's okay. Is the doctor in here?" He made a move towards the closed door.

"No! He's not. Doctor Drummond doesn't work Friday afternoon. May I please see your ID again?"

Albatross turned his ice-blue eyes on her. "What's your name, lady?"

She stared at him, swallowed, retreated a step from those eyes, from his physical presence, felt the hot flush of fear. "M-Mrs Woods."

"Sit down, Mrs Woods."

As she lowered herself into the chair, Albatross moved round the desk to crowd her. Peregrine sauntered over to the closed door, opened it, looked inside the surgery, closed the door, returned to perch on the desk, crowding her from the other side.

Albatross lowered his face towards her. His smile was entirely humorless. "No need to be afraid, Mrs Woods . . ."

"I'll tell you right now," she said with laudable defiance, "there are no drugs in here. It's a Center policy . . . no doctor keeps drugs on the premises."

Albatross's lip curled in the semblance of a grin. "Do we look like druggies? Relax. We're not after drugs, we only want a little information. You give us the answers to a couple of questions, we'll go away. First question: what time did the Doc quit work today?"

Terrified but loyal and valiant, she looked from one man to the other. "Why d'you want to know?"

Albatross shook his head. "No, Mrs Woods, you got it wrong – we ask the questions, you supply the answers.

Now, what time did the Doctor leave?"

She compressed her lips, shook her head. "I'll tell you nothing. How dare you come in here . . ."

Peregrine cut her off. "Mrs Woods, do you know Paul Drummond, the Doc's son?"

She looked up at him, sensing in the Black a more reasonable man, and behind his question the possibility that something bad had happened to Paul. "Yes, I know him."

"When did you last see him?"

She thought about it. "About a month ago."

The men exchanged bewildered looks.

Albatross scowled at her. "A month? You saw him today. He was here half an hour ago."

She didn't like this man. "I'm not a liar. Paul hasn't been here today. Look, what's going on? Who are you men?"

Peregrine said solicitously, "Mrs Woods, we can't tell you. It has to do with national security. I'm afraid Paul has got himself caught up in something very nasty, and he's in terrible danger. He was supposed to deliver something to his father, here, today, and we were supposed to collect it from Doctor Robert. I'm sorry if we frightened you, but we're desperate."

Peregrine got up off the desk and moved away, giving her room, easing the pressure, seeing she couldn't be intimidated, and trying the charm, the help-me-I'm-Black bit.

He swung back to her, offering his open palms appeasingly. "Look, we shouldn't tell you this, it's top secret, but you're obviously an honest, reliable, professional woman, and I know this won't go any further. Paul, as you well know, does Forensic Hypnosis – for the police and all kinds of people. Well, he happened to learn something from a client, something very secret that has to do with the military, and he put it on tape. Now, a foreign power has learned about this tape, and they're out to get it . . .

306

and they don't care what they *do* to get it, if you get my drift."

Mrs Woods was gaping at him.

"Oh, I know it sounds incredible, but it's perfectly true. Paul is at this moment on the run. He contacted the police in Los Angeles who passed the information on to us. We arranged to meet him here, to pick up the tape and give him protection. Now, we know he arrived here, Mrs Woods. The car he drove up is out there on the lot, and the engine's still warm. So you can see how hard it is for us to believe he didn't come in here to see his father. Can you offer an explanation?"

She shook her head, shrugged. "What time did he get here?"

"Probably about one o'clock, a little after."

"Then he probably saw his father's car wasn't here and assumed the doctor wasn't."

"So Doctor Robert left before one?"

She nodded, giving in on the matter. "Normally he stays till one, but his twelve-thirty appointment cancelled and he left soon after." She frowned at Peregrine, ignoring Albatross, still hovering, playing his bad-cop role. "But you say Paul's car is still on the lot, so where can he be?"

"We believe he drove away in another vehicle. What car does Doctor Robert drive?"

"A Nissan Pathfinder. Sometimes a Range Rover. It's Paul's, but the Doctor runs it to keep the battery up."

"How about a Cherokee Jeep?"

"No, he doesn't own one of those."

Albatross came in. "We think he drove away in one. Whose would it be?"

She disliked this blond, pale-eyed brute intensely. "I wouldn't know, I'm sure. There are lots of Jeeps around here, this is mountain country."

"Maybe. But he wouldn't just dump his car, climb in the first Cherokee he saw and take off."

"Then maybe you're mistaken. You said you *think* he drove away in one, so obviously you didn't see him."

"We saw him."

"Then why didn't you stop him?"

Albatross realized his mistake and thought quickly to correct it. He was getting real pissed with this stubborn, nigger-loving bitch. "That is, we saw a Cherokee leaving as we arrived. We didn't know it was Paul driving, we've never met him. Since then, we've come to the conclusion it was probably him, and we wondered whose vehicle it was that he borrowed."

Liars, thought Mrs Woods.

Peregrine, the "good cop", took over. "Mrs Woods . . . Paul must've spent a lot of time here at the Center. Who else does he know in the building?"

She shook her head. "Paul has been in Los Angeles for a long time. To my knowledge he doesn't know a soul here besides his father and me."

Peregrine sighed. "Well, it's a mystery, all right. We arrange to meet him here, to give him protection. He arrives, doesn't come in here, doesn't know anyone else in the building, and yet he drives away in another vehicle."

"How do you know he drove away? He may have walked."

Peregrine smiled. "No, ma'am, he didn't walk. For certain he didn't walk." He gave a nod to Albatross. "Let's leave this dear lady in peace. Sorry to have frightened you, Miz Woods, but you can understand how concerned we are. We trust you'll respect the secrecy of what we've told you?"

"Of course."

"If you tell *anyone* about this conversation, it could put Paul in even greater danger."

"I shan't repeat it to a soul."

"I'm sure you won't."

308

Peregrine felt the comforting hardness of the Taser gun in his side pocket. But there were voices in reception as the Center stirred from lunch.

"Let's go," he told Albatross.

With the door closed, Evelyn Woods waited twenty interminable seconds to make sure they'd gone, then reached for the phone. Her hands were shaking uncontrollably as she pressed the buttons, mis-dialled, and started again.

Kay Conners answered. "Shasta Hypnotherapy Center."

"Kay, this is Evelyn. Is Doctor Fallon available for a few minutes?"

"He's got a client in fifteen. Evelyn, are you all right, you sound stressed?"

"I am. I have to speak to Doctor Fallon right away. Will you ask him?"

"Sure, hang on." She came back almost immediately. "Come on through."

Evelyn opened the door cautiously, peered into the reception. There were a dozen people there, but no sign of the two men. Slipping through the door, she locked it, crossed the reception hall and entered the far corridor. At its end she paused at the rear glass exit doors, cautiously checked the parking lot, saw the XR3 in one of the spaces reserved for the Hypnotherapy Center, saw Kay Conners's white Toyota Tercel, saw a number of cars parked way back against the right boundary fence, but because of sky reflection on its windscreen did not see the two men sitting in the gray Plymouth sedan.

Neither did she see any sign of Mike Fallon's Cherokee.

Opening a door to her left, she entered his reception.

Kay Conners, an attractive thirty-year-old blonde, was at her desk. She and Evelyn were business friends, took lunch together, swapped gossip. Her expression reflected her concern, but she knew better than to ask.

She got up, opened a door to Fallon's consulting room, ushered Evelyn in with a muted, "Speak to you later."

Fallon, at his desk, smiled a greeting while scanning her face, interpreting her body language. "Hi, what's the problem?" He gestured to a chair.

She sat, nervously. "I've just had a very weird experience."

Fallon sat motionless, fingertips steepled at his lips, while she related what had happened.

"But they were lying, I could feel it," she concluded. "It seemed to me they were taken aback by the fact that Doctor Robert wasn't there, and Paul hadn't been in, so they had to make their story up as they went along. And they made mistakes."

"Such as?"

"Well, as I said, first off they said Paul was to give the tape to his father and they were there to collect it. Then they added that they were there to protect Paul. Well, if they'd come to protect Paul, what would be the point of him giving the tape to his father? He could've simply given it to them."

"Smart lady. Anything else?"

"They kept pressing me about the Cherokee, asking me who owned one around here. So help me, I almost told them about yours, but something stopped me. I was getting very bad vibes from those two, the way they'd bulled their way in, refused to let me read their ID. Anyway, when I questioned their certainty that Paul had driven off in a Cherokee, they said they'd seen one drive out as they arrived, but couldn't be sure it was Paul because they didn't know him by sight. But why did they even *assume* it was him in the Jeep? Why did they assume he would be driving away in any vehicle when he was supposed to be meeting them here? You see what I mean?"

Fallon nodded gravely. "I do indeed."

310

"Another thing – they said Paul got here just after one o'clock. *They* arrived here about half after one, but didn't come into the office until nearly two. Why? It doesn't make sense. They arrive at half one, see the Cherokee leaving, think that maybe Paul is driving away in it, don't do anything to stop him, are supposed to meet him in his father's office to pick up the tape and protect him, but sit around for half an hour before they come in to do it. Why?"

Fallon smiled. "Evelyn, you'd make a terrific analyst." His smile faded. "Paul was here, of course. And he did take my Cherokee. He's with Karen Beal, the *Times* journalist who wrote that article on forensic hypnosis. And they are in trouble, but from the people those two men represent. They didn't come here to protect him, they came here to get the tape."

"You mean there really is one?"

"There's a tape, but what's on it has nothing to do with military secrets – at least, not the way they implied. Look, Evelyn, you've handled this terrifically well, but for your own safety I don't want you to know anything more about what's going on. Have you finished in the office?"

"I was just doing some filing."

"Leave it. Go straight home. I'm going to call Doc Robert right now. Paul and Karen are on their way up there. We'll tell you what this is all about when it's safe to do so. And thanks again."

When she had gone, Fallon sat thinking.

Question: Why did the goons suspect Paul and the girl were in the Cherokee, yet not intercept them?

Answer: They didn't suspect. They arrived, found the XR3, assumed Paul was with his father, and sat waiting.

Question: Waiting for what?

Answer: Waiting for Paul and Karen to appear? to zap them? grab them? Waiting for reinforcements?

Question: How did the goons know where to find the

XR3? Paul had stressed how carefully they'd checked their tracks.

Answer: The car was bugged.

Question: So how did the goons get onto the Cherokee?"

Answer: *They* didn't – otherwise they'd have followed it. Someone else did – and radioed the information to the goons.

Question: Who?

Answer: Other goons. The reinforcements? On a mission of this importance there'd be more than one team in action.

Question: Again, how did they get on to the Cherokee?

Answer: The Cherokee was bugged.

Ridiculous.

His intercom buzzed.

Kay Connors announced, "Mrs Shepley is here, Doctor."

"If she'd kindly wait one minute."

Fallon released the intercom and reached for the phone.

Robert Drummond's mellifluous voice answered. "Drummond."

"Rob – it's Mike. Has Paul been in touch with you in the last half hour?"

"Paul? No."

"He'll be there any minute. Look, I haven't got time to explain, Paul will fill you in, but he and the girl with him are in political trouble, in danger. Get the Range Rover warmed up, have some thermal clothing, food, and some weapons ready for them, and tell them to get away from the house fast. And hide my Cherokee."

"Mike, I . . ."

"Rob, I'm sorry to hit you like this, it sounds preposterous, I know, but it's for real. Tell Paul the *V's* were here and know about the Cherokee. Now, Rob, for their sakes, please don't ask questions, just do it."

"All right. I'm gone."

Fallon put down the phone, adjusted his mind, pressed the intercom button. "I'll see Mrs Shepley now, Kay."

An hour devoted to rich, bored hypochondria was exactly what he needed right now.

Out on the lot, Peregrine was telling Jackdaw, "The tape's not here. We rousted Robert Drummond's receptionist pretty good, she was telling the truth. Paul never entered the office. Robert left for home about twelve-forty-five. We got here one-thirty and heard the beacon. Figure Paul and the girl got here about one, what were they doing between one and one-thirty?"

"Organizing new wheels? The XR3 has a phone. Maybe Paul saw his father's car wasn't on the lot, phoned somebody?"

"How sure are we about the Cherokee?"

"We're not. Seagull is following but hasn't eyeballed them yet."

"Maybe the Cherokee's a false lead. The receptionist said she didn't know anyone here that ran one, said Paul didn't know anyone else at the Center."

Jackdaw said, "You sure she was telling the truth?"

"I'm sure. We laid it on that we were there to protect her master's son. She wouldn't lie and put him at risk."

"Okay, drop the Med Center. Get up to the lake and Taser those two, they've got the tape. Call up Seagull. Whatever vehicle Drummond is driving, Seagull should have it in sight any time now."

"Roger, out."

Peregrine dialled the van.

Seagull answered. "Yo."

"Peregrine . . . you on them yet?"

"Like a hound on a bitch, half a mile ahead."

"What vehicle?"

"Looks like a Cherokee."

"Can you pick up the license plate?"

"At half a mile? This road's like a freaking switchback – now you see 'em, now you don't."

"Get the plate as fast as you can. We're joining you."

"Make my day."

Peregrine rang off, told his partner. "Get going."

Albatross smiled. "Smart. Get the plate, get the owner."

Peregrine nodded. "Drummond had help here. Find the owner, we find out who."

"But if Drummond's got the tape, why worry where he got the vehicle?"

"Al . . . who says he's got the tape?"

"Jackdaw just said . . ." He saw the look in Peregrine's eyes and spat out of the window. "Yeh, sure."

Chapter Twenty-Nine

Drummond went "Uh-uh," and his cautionary tone and the direction of his gaze into the rear-view mirror sent Karen twisting in her seat to peer out of the rear window.

"What?"

"It's gone again. Wait till it tops the rise."

"What d'you think it is?"

"It's big and it's dark green and it's . . ."

"The removal van! I see it."

"It's coming at a helluva lick."

"It was coming at a helluva lick in Shasta. Nobody drives a van like that unless . . ."

"Yes, unless. Time we got off this road. Buckle your belt and hold on tight."

They were in the outskirts of Whiskeytown, deep into the Shasta State Historical Park, with the three-thousand-foot peak of Buckhorn Summit ahead of them, and the taller Bohemotash Mountain to their right. Over on the left they occasionally glimpsed the sheet-steel spread of Whiskeytown Lake through the trees. There were a lot of trees.

Drummond hurled the Cherokee into a left turn, towards the lake, ran along a suburban road of tract housing, cut right immediately, then left, zig-zagging, one eye on the mirror, looking for an appropriate place to stop and check their suspicions, finding it in a tar-strip road that led into a deserted picnic area.

Taking the road, which wound between stands of tall, spaced pines, he reached the empty car park and went on, riding over an earth-mound verge, winding between the trees to the table area, close now to the wind-whipped waters of the lake.

Here there was a small complex of brick buildings housing toilets and a refreshment stand, battened for the winter.

He ran the Jeep into the lee of the building, hiding it from the approach road, switched off the engine and got out, leaving the door open.

Moving to the corner of the building, he peered around it, seeing nothing, beginning to feel a little paranoid. Maybe it wasn't the removal van? Maybe it wasn't the *same* removal van? they usually went in fleets. Maybe it was the same asshole driver who'd forgotten something in wherever he'd come from, and was racing back for it?

Maybe . . . maybe . . . maybe.

But he didn't care. It was his responsibility to be cautious, over-cautious. Lives depended upon his total vigilance, including his own.

He glanced back at Karen. They exchanged shrugs and smiles that were a little self-conscious.

He returned to his watch, shivering in the icy wind that swept in from the lake, pulling the parka hood up over his head to protect his neck, thankful he'd decided they should wear weather clothing, even if it was only LA weather.

Still nothing. He'd give it thirty seconds.

His gaze drifted around the picnic area, through the trees to the lake. How desolate and forlorn such places looked in the approach to winter, how different from the colour and vibrance of high summer. He knew this place well, from childhood and from youth. One of the trees bore his initials, carved with a penknife when he was ten. It seemed a very long time ago.

A movement caught his eye.

He swung his gaze fully back to the gravelled road that ran past the tar-strip road. There! Between the trees. A solid block of dark green, moving very slowly, the cab concealed by bushes and small trees, only the top half showing, but it was undoubtedly the van.

Now it stopped, at the beginning of the tar-strip road, at the entrance to the car park. Drummond knew it wouldn't, couldn't venture into the car park, there was a six-foot-six steel barrier guarding the entrance, to prevent motor homes and caravans using the site. But its occupants might well come in on foot.

The van was not moving. Somehow the V's – and he was positive now it was them – knew they were there. It was decision time.

He turned back to the Jeep. Karen had seen the van, she was staring, stricken, in its direction.

As he climbed in, she said, "It has to be them. It's just too coincidental that they should take the same twisty route you took here."

"It's them."

"But how did they *find* us? There were a dozen alternative streets and tracks you could've taken since we left the two-nine-nine, yet they came straight here."

"I don't know, but it worries the hell out of me." He started the engine.

Karen asked, "What are you going to do?"

"Give them a run for their money."

He turned the Jeep away from the buildings, headed directly for the lake, using the buildings to conceal them from the road until the terrain began to slope down to the water's edge and they were lost permanently to the V's sight.

Now Drummond cut to the left, using the Jeep's power and four-wheel drive to plough through the soft loam bordering the lake, its nubby tires slithering and sliding, but biting and hauling them out of the mush time and again.

"Thank God Mike drives this instead of a Merc." He shoved headlong through a dense clump of bushes, the Jeep bouncing so high as it rode the hump that their heads made contact with the roof.

He shot a glance at Karen, had to grin at her boggle-eyed expression. "Keep your tongue behind your teeth or you'll bite it off."

She grabbed for the side of her seat to hold herself down as they hit another clump, leapt high, swung wildly to the left to avoid a pine tree, then right to miss another.

Now Drummond began to work upwards from the lake, hitting firmer ground, but more trees, having to throw the vehicle about in a giddy slalom . . . left, right, right, left . . . mostly judging the gaps between the trees to perfection but sometimes cutting it too close and hearing the scrape of bark against metal.

Suddenly they were confronted by a wire fence, the boundary of the recreation area. Beyond the fence was private land, a nursery, its beds empty save for a straggle of deciduous saplings that hadn't been sold.

Drummond turned right, away from the picnic area and the van, ran along the fence for several hundred yards, then found a gravel track that would take them east again, towards the 299.

On solid ground, Drummond stopped.

Karen phewed with relief. "I think you enjoyed that. You've done it before."

"I've never been hunted before."

"It was them, wasn't it?"

"Had to be. Why otherwise would anyone drive a removal van down roads like that to a deserted rec area?"

"But why a removal van, Paul?"

"Well, let's think about it. When they almost demol-ished us in Shasta, where were they coming from and going to in such a hurry? Okay, let's revert to our expectation that they'll go for known haunts and associations in their search. For me, there are two sources up here – my parents' home and my father's offices. They're bound to cover both, meaning two vehicles. To answer your question, they'd use the van for its intended purpose, to remove – us. It's the perfect cover. Who takes any notice of a light removal van, except when it almost kills you?"

Karen nodded. "So the van could have been here, covering the house, waiting to abduct us when we arrived. But why did it suddenly leave here and go haring off to Shasta?"

"Maybe not to Shasta. How about Redding? The other vehicle, maybe another van, turns up at the Med Center. They find the XR3 there, think we're there, and call for back-up."

"That's good. So these guys go to assist . . ." she frowned, "but suddenly change their minds. There was no way they had time to get to Redding and back on our tails . . ."

"No." Drummond's tone was grave. "So something happened at the Med Center. Say the V's in Van One, let's call it, went looking for us in the Center. They'd find my father wasn't there."

"Would the office be closed?"

"I don't know. Evelyn Woods, my father's secretary, may have been there, she often works on after he leaves. But she couldn't tell them anything. Thank God we didn't go to the office before seeing Mike."

"So, what happened?" she asked deductively. "Van One does a search, finds your dad's office closed, or from Evelyn Woods that we haven't been there, and tells Van Two to get back to the house in a hurry."

"It sounds right, except . . ."

"I know. Except how did they know we were driving the Jeep? How did they get to track us down to the rec area?"

319

Drummond gnawed at his lip. "I can only think of one answer and I don't want to think of it – they're on to Mike. Finding the XR3 there and not us, they'd assume we drove off in another vehicle. Whose vehicle? Maybe they asked Evelyn if I had friends in the building, and she, innocently, told them about Mike. Or maybe seeing where the XR3 was parked, in a Hypnotherapy Center space, they went straight to Mike. Goddamn, that was a mistake. I should've got you to lose the car in a side street."

"Hey, don't be hard on yourself. It's easy to be smart with hindsight. In any case, Mike wouldn't tell them he lent us his Cherokee. He's written a book about these creeps, he's more paranoid about them than we are."

Drummond nodded. "True – so how in hell did they track us to the lake? Okay, let's skip the post mortem and get to the house. I'll call Mike from the Range Rover."

As the Jeep started forward, Karen asked, "Do we have to use the main road? Isn't there another way?"

Drummond winked at her, lifting her spirits. "There sure is. Hang on to your hat."

In Van Two, Blackbird pressed the Transmit button on his walkie-talkie to call up Seagull who had run down the tar-strip road to the picnic area with the two Tasers, knowing from the static beacon that the Cherokee was parked behind the building.

"Seagull come in, they're on the move!"

"I can hear the freakin' engine, can't I?"

"Then get back here."

"I gotta take a piss."

"Piss on the run."

Blackbird watched the scanner while Seagull came tottering back along the strip and threw himself into the van. "Fuckin' *Christ*, it's cold. We gotta get ourselves some proper gear, we'll die up here. Where're they heading?"

"Hell and gone, back along the lake. Drummond'll take a route we can't make in this thing. Call up Peregrine, they'll have to track. Tell them we're heading for the house."

"This thing's falling to pieces. Way it's going, we'll never get close enough to use these." He threw the Tasers into the shelf under the dash.

As Blackbird reversed the van into the strip road to turn around, he jerked a thumb at the rack behind his head. "Then we'll use these."

Clipped in the rack were two high-powered rifles equipped with silencers and telescopic, laser-beam night-sights.

Chapter Thirty

Mad Harry Drummond had done a few things right in his colorful, rollercoaster life. One of them was to provide his sons, at marriage, with real estate.

Motivated by his own precipitation from the ancestral home and hearth on the banks of Loch Linnhe, he determined they should begin married life endowed with these necessary comforts.

Robert, the canny one, newly wed to Sarah, had chosen the house on the lake, and renamed it Loch Linnhe in remembrance of his Scottish forebears.

It had been their dream to raise a substantial family in the five-bedroom, wood-clad house, their vision one of children boating and fishing on the lake, climbing trees, camping in the surrounding woods. But like most dreams, it fell short. After Paul, a benign tumor necessitated a hysterectomy, depriving Sarah of further children.

If the Drummonds loved their home, they cherished their privacy as much. Backed by ten acres of dense pine and deciduous trees, the house was completely hidden from the busy perimeter road above. A twisting gravel road, guarded at the top by an electronically-controlled steel gate, served the house. Visitors used an intercom positioned by the gate.

Paul Drummond approached Loch Linnhe with the greatest caution. The perimeter road was two-laned but twisting and narrow, barely adequate to cope with the summer traffic that had increased prodigiously in recent years, and busy enough even at this time of the year. If the van was ahead of them, perhaps lurking in wait around one of the bends, it could swing out and easily block the road.

Drummond was fully prepared for evasive action. He could brake and reverse, or throw the Jeep into a tight about-turn, traffic permitting. There was no way off the road. Dense woods crowded it on both sides. He felt as though he was driving into a box canyon.

Karen, seeing the possible danger and sensing his tension, asked, "How much further?"

"Two more bends, a quarter of a mile."

"What if they're waiting there?"

"Then we get out fast, the best way we can. But it's worth the try. We need the Range Rover, the phone, weapons. Most of all we need to lose this Jeep. We'll be in and out in fifteen minutes. Dad always keeps the Range Rover in good order."

"They'll be surprised you're here, shocked by what's happening."

He smiled. "It takes a lot to shock Rob Drummond. Remember, Mad Harry was *his* dad."

They cleared the next bend.

Drummond murmured, "One to go," his eyes constantly flicking to the rear-view mirror. There were several cars strung out behind them, but no sign of the van. He took a deep breath, tried to lose some of the tension that had taken possession of every muscle in his body. If they could get through the gate and down to the lake they'd still be vulnerable, but he'd feel whole lot better.

They reached the final bend. "Here we go . . . hold on tight for some fancy driving."

The gravelled turn-in that fronted the gate inched into view. It was unoccupied.

Drummond expelled a breath of relief.

He turned across the road, ran up to the gate, stretched through the window for the intercom button.

His father's voice grated from the speaker. "Who is it?"

"Dad, it's Paul . . ."

"Thank God."

The release mechanism clicked immediately and the gate began to swing in.

Drummond frowned at Karen. "He's expecting me!"

"Mike Fallon?"

"Must be."

He drove through, hurrying now, raising dust from the gray gravel, checking the mirror to make sure the gate was closing.

Karen asked, "Why would Mike call?" but it was more a thought than a question.

Drummond shook his head. He could think of several reasons: something about the tape, or about the V's being there, or simply to let his parents know they were on their way. But there was no point in speculating.

Nearing the bottom of the road, the trees to their left ended abruptly, and simultaneously the lake and, ahead, the house, came into view.

Karen murmured appreciation for the setting. "Oh, Paul, it's beautiful. What a place to grow up in."

He glanced out at the wind-riffed water, gray and cold as the low, scudding clouds it reflected. "You should see it in summer, with the sailboats and the skiers out there. It's really something."

They were running into a spacious pebbled yard. To the right were three brick-built double garages with pale green wooden up-and-over doors. Facing them, at the side of the house, French doors gave out onto a deep, raised terrace which continued around to the front of the house and broadened into a magnificent stepped patio, complete with shade trees, potted plants, and white wrought-iron furniture.

A hundred feet of lawn ran down from the patio steps

to the water's edge. There, a small sailing dinghy and an inflatable with an outboard motor rode the chop, secured to a wooden jetty reaching fifty feet into the lake.

Behind the house, as though keeping the encroaching trees at arms length, a flat, open space accommodated a sports complex of swimming pool, tennis court and miniature golf lawn.

The house itself, two-storied, with twin bays and porch and second-floor verandah, its woodwork painted pale green with cream trim, looked, to Karen's eye, quite splendid, elegant, regal. And quite what she had expected.

As their tires crunched across the pebbles in front of the garages, the French doors opened and a tall, gray-haired, angular man wearing an orange hunting parka hurried down the steps. In the gravity of his expression and his speed, they sensed trouble.

With the gesture of a wave to them, he strode straight to the middle garage and raised the door, beckoned them in. A two-tone brown Range Rover occupied the left-hand space, facing out. Paul drove the Cherokee alongside it and cut the engine.

He collected Karen's shoulder bag and the money bag from the rear seat, got out, placed the bags in the Range Rover, ready for immediate departure, then embraced his father.

Karen climbed down and joined them.

"Dad, I'd like you to meet Karen Beal. She's the *Times* journalist I've told you about . . . did that piece on Forensic Hypnosis."

"Yes, of course." Rob Drummond's smile was a replica of his son's. There was a great general likeness in build and style. "I'm delighted to meet you, though not in these circumstances." He frowned eloquently at his son. "What on earth have you two got yourselves into? Mike set my heart banging with the mention of political trouble."

325

"So it was Mike. We wondered about you expecting us."

"He phoned just after two. I've got the conversation on tape if you want to hear it."

Paul looked at Karen. "I think we'd better. I don't want to hang around long, Dad, but this may be very important."

Robert gestured to the Range Rover. "On Mike's suggestion, I've put some warm things in there, some food and two rifles. I dread to think why you should need those."

"I hope we don't." They started out of the garage. As Paul pulled the door down, he asked, "Is Mom in the house?"

"In the kitchen, she's making coffee for you."

"A quick drink while we're listening to the tape, then we're gone. I don't want to bring trouble down on you."

Robert slid Karen a pallid smile. "When didn't you?"

Karen had to skip-run to keep up with the men as they hurried across the firm pebbles and mounted the steps, entered a study-cum-library, passed through it, Robert leading the way, into a hallway, and across it into a huge modern kitchen, done in shades of gray.

Sarah Drummond, a handsome, slender, refined woman, with bobbed auburn hair, wearing an olive wool shirt and tan slacks, turned from the coffee percolator and held out her arms for Paul's hug. "Darling, what *is* all this about political trouble?" Her worried gaze embraced Karen, and she offered her hand. "Hello, my dear."

Paul introduced them. "Mom, we can only stay a minute. We've only come in to listen to Mike's conversation with Dad."

Robert, across the kitchen by the phone, said, "Got it right here." He brought a Sanyo recorder to the round table in the center of the room, saying to Karen by way of explanation, "I record all phone calls, have done for

326

ten years. Once had a patient who claimed she'd told me something vital over the phone and hadn't, but it caused no end of bother. If the conversation's innocuous, of course, I wipe it, but now and again it's useful."

Karen smiled. "I'm a tape recorder junky too. Never go anywhere without mine."

Robert said, "Sal, that coffee ready? Give these guys a cup. Here, sit down for two minutes."

As they sat, he pressed the Play button.

"Drummond."

"Rob – it's Mike. Has Paul been in touch with you in the last half hour?"

"Paul? No."

"He'll be there any minute. Look, I haven't got time to explain, Paul will fill you in, but he and the girl with him are in political trouble, in danger. Get the Range Rover warmed up, have some thermal clothing, food, and some weapons ready for them, and tell them to get away from the house fast. And hide my Cherokee."

"Mike, I . . ."

"Rob, I'm sorry to hit you like this, it sounds preposterous, I know, but it's for real. Tell Paul the *V's* were here and know about the Cherokee. Now, Rob, for their sakes, please don't ask questions, just do it."

"All right. I'm gone"

Robert clicked off the machine. "You want to hear it again?"

Paul shook his head. "No, Dad, that's fine." To Karen, he said, "So the V's went to his office. And knew about the Cherokee. But he didn't say *how* they knew about it. And he didn't sound as though they suspected he might have the tape. He didn't even mention the tape!"

Sarah, bringing a tray of coffee in china mugs to the table, sighed with concern and exasperation, "The vees,

327

Cherokees, tapes . . . Paul, for heavensakes, what's this all about?"

"Okay, Mom, Dad – in thirty seconds flat, here it is."

His parents sat stunned while he explained.

Sarah, wide-eyed, gasped, "Jack *Crane*?"

"Well, we're not a thousand percent sure, but it's a big possibility. If he is involved, you can see how potentially dangerous that tape is."

Robert frowned angrily. "You can't do this by yourselves, you need help. I know the local police . . ."

"Dad, thanks, but no. You know Dick Gage, and he told us to trust nobody. If these people can manipulate the Parker Center, they can sure jerk the local guys around."

"So what's your plan?"

"Simply to keep out of their clutches until midnight, pick up the tape and transcript from Mike, and get back to LA as fast as we can."

Robert got to his feet. "Then you'd better get going. The Range Rover's fully gassed up and the battery's charged. Get up to Shasta Lake, you can lose these people up there in the dark, then cut over to the Eighty-nine and work your way south through Tahoe."

"That's pretty much what I had in mind." Paul got up, said to Karen, "Let's go."

As they reached the door, the phone rang.

Robert muttered, "Damn," returned for the recorder and hooked it up, saying to them, "Go ahead, I'll catch up." He picked up the receiver. "Drummond."

Paul, Karen and Sarah had reached the library door when Robert's shout stopped them. "Paul . . . it's for you!"

Paul stared at Karen. "Mike."

He hurried back, took the receiver from his father. "Is it Mike?"

"No."

328

Paul frowned, brought the instrument to his ear. "Paul Drummond."

Peregrine chuckled. "Hi, Doc. Man, that was some chase you gave us. Now all you have to do is give us the tape."

Chapter Thirty-One

Karen and Sarah had returned to the kitchen. They and Robert stood motionless, watching Paul, knowing from his expression, from his silence, that crisis had overtaken them.

Covering the mouthpiece with his hand, he told Karen gruffly, "It's them. They want the tape."

His mind was racing, searching for a solution, yet seemed paralyzed, incapable of coherent thought. It was as though a buzzing vibrator had been switched on in his head.

Finally, when logic did break through the obfuscation of panic, it came in the form of Epictitus's erudite axiom about people being affected not by an event, but by their interpretation of it, and he found his mind slowing, clearing, steadying. Nothing had happened that he could not have expected to happen. It had been odds-on that the V's would catch up with them at any time after the LA shooting. Now that it had occurred, he had to find a solution to the problem, not surrender to the vapors like a Victorian heroine.

He decided that attack would be the best form of defense.

"Who are you?" he demanded. "What's your name? And who is 'us'?"

"Man, you're just *full* of questions. You can call me . . . well, you pick a name you think appropriate."

"Dick."

Peregrine hooted with laughter. "Doc, I like you, you got balls. Kinda gives us an affinity, doesn't it . . . Dick and Balls. As for the 'us', I can't tell you that, as well you know."

"In the interests of national security."

"Right on, you got it. I think we're gonna get along just fine. Now, about the tape, I *know* you're going to hand it over and save everybody a lot of grief."

"You're wrong there, Dick. But I might sell it to you, if the price is right."

There was an astounded silence, then a guffaw. "Man, you are not only full of questions, you're full of surprises, too. And what, pray, would the right price be?"

"Fifty thousand dollars. Cash. In used fifties."

"Whee heee."

Karen was staring at him.

He shook his head at her, said into the phone, "How about it, Dick?"

"Well, now, I'd have to pass the word down the line . . ."

"Do it."

Paul slammed the phone down.

Robert, Sarah and Karen stood transfixed.

Paul moved away from the instrument, telling his father, "Leave the recorder going, they'll be calling back."

Sarah said, "Paul, you don't really mean . . ."

"No, of course not, but I need time to think." He turned suddenly and strode back to the phone, picked up the receiver, held it to his ear. "Damn, they've cut the line. I was going to call Mike. We don't need that tape transcribed, just clarifed. If Mike could do that right now, cancel one of his appointments, and we could get away from here as soon as it's dark . . ."

Karen cut in, "But how? They'll be up there, covering the gate."

331

"I know. But there's another way out of here besides the road."

Robert said, "By water."

"Right. We could run the inflatable back towards Shasta, beach it, get up to the road, thumb a lift into Shasta and take a cab to Redding"

With a glance out of the window, Sarah protested, "But Paul, look at the water, it'll be dangerous out there in the dark. There's so much floating debris near the shore."

"Mom, I won't speed. I'll row out a way, start the outboard when we're past them. We could do it. It'll be pitch dark in an hour. If we can hold them off that long . . ." He paused, grimacing, continued pacing.

Robert asked, "What?"

"I'm thinking about ten things at once. I'm worried about you two . . . wondering about the phone in the Range Rover . . . wondering about how many of them there are up there – if they are *up* there. Maybe they're in the grounds, right outside. One thing puzzles me – why did they bother to phone? Why didn't they just burst in here and grab us and, as far as they know, the tape?"

His father provided a possible answer. "They could be under orders to try it the easy way – first. Perhaps you're standing too close to evaluate this. Step back and look at the whole picture. If Jack Crane is behind this, he's got to tread very carefully. First and foremost, he wants that tape. Once he's got it, you two don't matter. Even if you knew what was on it, what the Trice jingle meant, it wouldn't do you any good. You wouldn't have any tangible proof. *The Times* wouldn't publish hearsay from Karen."

She nodded. "That's right. As you said, Paul, even *with* the tape, they may decide not to."

"So," Robert continued, "right now the V's, as you call them, are happy that they've tracked you and cornered you . . . and the tape. They can afford a little time. This is a very small community. They'll suppose, rightly, that the Drummonds are very well known. I'm no Tom Keegan or anonymous messenger, neither are you. If they tried any rough stuff, there'd be an investigation, and that's the last thing Crane would want."

Paul nodded, partially satisfied. "Okay, that makes sense. But, Dad, you don't know these people, what they're capable of. If Karen and I managed to get away in the boat, they'd think nothing of grabbing you and Mom and holding you hostage for the tape. Believe me, you are both extremely vulnerable."

Robert looked at his wife. "Okay, so we get the heck out of here. We'll tog up and take a hike through the woods, over to the Bensons. We can phone Mike from there, tell him to get working on the tape, have it de-subliminalized by the time you get there."

Sarah was nodding agreement. "How many men d'you think they have up there?"

Paul said, "Possibly four. There were two in the van. The way they were throwing it around, I shouldn't think there were any in the back. We don't know how many turned up at the Med Center, but figure two, they seemed to hunt in pairs. The man I spoke to on the phone sounded Black. Neither of the men in the van was Black, so we'll assume the two at the Med Center joined the two in the van."

"Four," mused Sarah. "And a lot of acreage to cover. If I were them, I'd take up position pretty close to the house, make sure we didn't leave it."

Paul exchanged a glance with Karen, sparing a serious moment for a smile. "My mother's a military tactician. All these years, I never knew."

Karen shook her head. "I'm filled with admiration. Talk about a cool mind under fire."

Sarah waved it away. "It's simple math. Four men into

333

ten acres equals a lot of ground to cover. I'd use them to circle the house."

Paul said, "Dad, your binoculars?"

"In the study, on the bookcase."

"Let's take a look at these guys."

Jackdaw came on. "You got them?"

Hearing the anger, the desperation in the man's tone, Peregrine was glad he had something positive to report. A pissed Jackdaw was something you didn't need in your life. He'd worked for the guy before, three times in South America, and was familiar with the extent of his psychopathy when confronted with failure. Jackdaw was a crazy. But he paid so fucking well.

"Yes."

Jackdaw's radiation of relief came down the scrambled radiophone, as soothing as a lover's breath. "Good. And the tape?"

This was the bit Peregrine had been dreading. "Not yet."

He'd heard artillery fire quieter than the ensuing silence.

"Let me explain."

"Please."

"Seagull and Blackbird were tracking them in the van. Drummond must have got suspicious, did some fancy driving in the Jeep, took it into places the van couldn't follow. We were in Redding. We came over, picked up the beacon, tracked it to the lake, to Drummond's parents' house. That's where they are now, we've got them bottled up."

"How?"

"There's only one road down to the house, we've got it covered. I'm in the car, blocking the road. The other three are in the woods around the house."

"Who else is in the house?"

"We don't know. Albatross is at the bottom of the road. He says there are three garages, all closed, no sign of the Cherokee or other vehicles, so my guess is there are no visitors, just the parents and the runaways."

"You're sure they're in the house? Are you picking up anything on the bug?"

"Nothing. They haven't got it with them. But I've just spoken to Drummond by phone."

"You *what*?"

"I called the house, to let him know we're out here, to check he was there, and make sure he has the tape."

"And he told you he has?" Jackdaw asked incredulously.

"He offered to sell it to us – fifty thousand bucks, in used fifties."

"Jesus. And you believed him?"

"No. I told him I'd pass the offer along."

"And while you're doing it, he's phoning Christ knows who . . ."

"I cut the line."

"Yeah? There's hope for you yet."

"I'll splice it when I want to talk to him, but we need guidance here. Back at the Med Center, you told us to go easy with Drummond Senior. Same applies here. We go in there, somebody gets hurt, there could be a stink. Whoever you're working for ain't gonna like that."

"No." Jackdaw sounded hesitant. "Phone him back, offer him the money – tell him you want to hear some of the tape played over the phone. I want to be absolutely sure they've got it before taking further action."

"What kind of action?"

"I'll let you know."

Chapter Thirty-Two

They started in the study, Paul using a pair of Zeiss Jenoptem binoculars through the windows of the French doors to traverse an arc from the garages to the trees which descended thickly from the gravel road almost to the water's edge. He picked up the dark-suited, blond-haired figure of Albatross some twenty feet back in the trees.

Paul murmured, "There's one," and handed the binoculars to his father, pointing. "Big blond guy. He wasn't in the van, we'd have seen that hair."

Robert focused on the trees. "Hardly dressed for the terrain and weather, is he? He looks frozen . . . flapping his arms and stamping his feet. Not very smart to come into the mountains dressed for the office."

"We've drawn them out of the city. When they lost us in LA it must've caused a panic. Someone issued orders to check our known haunts and associations, and these guys headed straight up here. Probably never gave the terrain and weather a thought."

Robert lowered the binoculars. "Well, that could be very much to our advantage. Look at the stuff coming in over the lake. That's heavy rain. I reckon it'll be dark and throwing it down in half an hour."

Karen said, "May I take a look at him?"

Robert gave her the binoculars.

As she studied Albatross, she said, "He's speaking into a walkie-talkie. Probably complaining about the cold."

After a moment she said, "You were right about the rain, Doctor Drummond, it's starting now."

Paul said, "Good. Let's go upstairs and check around the house. Mom, can you find some warm clothing for Karen?"

"Of course."

"We'd better all get ready for the off. Dad and I'll do the checking around the house, you girls get kitted up."

They returned to the hallway and climbed a curved oak staircase, separating at the top, Sarah and Karen heading for the master bedroom at the front of the house, the men entering a rear bedroom which overlooked the pool and tennis court.

Paul picked up Blackbird, the muscular country boy with the lethal hands, immediately. He was sheltering in the doorway of one of the dressing rooms on the far side of the pool, squinting distractedly up at the leaden, fast-darkening sky, wiping the rain from his face.

Paul said with pleasure, "They sure don't like our Whiskeytown weather. I think this is one of the guys from the van. Hard-looking brute. Let's take a look on the north side."

From Paul's old bedroom, with its panoramic view of lake, woods and part of the tennis court, he spotted the diminutive Seagull in the trees, in the direct line of march Robert and Sarah would have to take to get to the Bensons' house.

Like the Drummonds, the Bensons, long-time residents of the lake, valued their privacy, and had allowed their woodland to run riot. In the dark and the increasing rain, a trek through the woods would be difficult, dangerous, even without the presence of the little man down there.

Paul voiced his fears. "You sure you and Mom can do this in the dark?"

"Of course. It'll be a stroll in the glen."

Paul gave his father a twisted grin. "I hear the echo

of our Highland forebears, the chilling warcry of the Drummonds." He returned his attention to Seagull. "We need a diversion, hm? Get this little twerp away from there. Draw them all away from the house while Karen and I get to the boat, and you and Mom slip into the woods. Any ideas?"

Robert shook his head, but was looking up at the sky, at the infinity of dense black cloud that was quickly turning the late afternoon gloom into darkest night, and beginnng to throw down its rain in earnest. "There's your diversion. In twenty minutes they'll be lucky to see the house."

"They'll move closer, even inside. Why haven't they come in for the tape, Pop?"

As if in answer, the extension phone on a table on the landing began to ring.

Paul made a move for the door. "That can only be them, they're controlling the line. Dad, would you get my oilskins out of the closet?"

He answered the phone.

Peregrine said, "You got a deal, Doc. But I want to hear some of that tape down the phone, just to make sure you've got it."

"And then?"

"Then we pay you the fifty grand."

"How? When?"

"Well, now, that's gonna take some time. This is Friday, the banks are closed till Monday . . ."

"Dick, don't bullshit me. We both know those used fifties never have and never will see the inside of a bank – right?"

Peregrine laughed collusively. "Okay, Doc. But let's hear the tape, then we'll talk delivery."

Paul sighed histrionically. "Well, now, this is getting a little tricky, Dick. You see, I'm having trouble believing that your lord and master, the guy you're taking orders from, has already outlined a plan for getting the money to us. So, why don't you call him, get some specifics, then call me again. It's going to take a while to find a tape recorder and set it up, so call me back in twenty minutes."

"Hey, Doc . . ."

Paul broke the connection, released the buttons immediately, got a dialling tone, began to stab out Mike Fallon's number, but heard the line die on him after three digits.

His father was standing beside him, a set of yellow oilskins over his arm. "What did they want?"

"They want me to play some of the tape we're supposed to have over the phone, to prove it's here."

"Oh."

"Yeah. I've bought us a few minutes." Paul was thinking. "Dad, do we have *any* weapons in the house?"

Robert shook his head. "The two rifles are in the Range Rover." Then a thought occurred to him. "There's your crossbow, but . . ."

Paul looked at him. "The crossbow? That's still around?"

He'd gone through an archery phase when he was sixteen, had target-practiced dedicatedly throughout one summer on the lawn, then tired of the bow and swapped it for a crossbow. By the end of the summer he'd wearied of shooting a straw target with it, and hadn't used it since. It wasn't a powerful weapon, and his father had forbidden hunting bolts, but the target bolts had metal tips and at close range could still be lethal.

Robert said, "It's on a beam in the root cellar. I hung it high, out of reach, caught Billy Benson fooling with it one time. But, Paul, you're not thinking of shooting our way out of here . . .?"

"Dad, right now, I don't know what the heck I'm thinking. I'm assembling facts, rummaging through possibilities. One undeniable fact is that there are four determined, ruthless thugs out there, on our property, who want something we haven't got, and are undoubtedly ready, willing and *aching* to break in here and kill us to take it. And by my reckoning, they're just waiting for the go-ahead to do it. Now, if I've got to shoot somebody to prevent that happening, I'm going to do it."

Robert's gaze shifted from Paul's face to a point across the landing. Paul turned to see the women standing there, dressed in thick woollen sweaters and pants, and listening.

Paul said, "Let's get down to the kitchen. We've got a tape recording to make."

In the Plymouth, Peregrine was taking the third irate radio call in as many minutes, this time from Albatross.

"What the fuck's goin' *on*, man? I'm soaked an' freezing to death down here!"

"I'm waiting on orders."

"Well, how 'bout *you* coming down here and *I'll* sit up there in a warm dry car and wait for orders."

"Won't be long. Any minute now, you get to shoot somebody."

Peregrine switched off, checked his watch. He'd give Drummond fifteen minutes. If the guy played the tape over the phone, *then* he, Peregrine, would contact Jackdaw, tell him it was here. In the meantime, he'd make up some bullshit scheme about the money.

The thing was, how would he know if the tape was genuine? He didn't even know what was supposed to be on the frigging tape, except it had something to do with the Trice article in the *Times*.

Peregrine stretched and yawned. He was tired and hungry. He thought about his woman in San Diego. There were times, lots of them lately, when he considered giving up contract work. He'd spent half his life chasing around the globe, setting up kills, bringing down regimes. It wasn't the work; he enjoyed that. You could take pride in the precision of a well-planned and executed

340

liquidation. It was the assholes he had to work for and take orders from.

It was the secrecy, the compartmentalization, that pissed him off. The Intelligence mob were obsessed with it. You never knew what was going on beyond your absolute need to know. Right now, he knew he was working for Jackdaw, but who was Jackdaw working for? Jackdaw wasn't Intelligence, he was a contract killer, like himself. But this whole scam reeked of Intelligence. And Jackdaw worked mostly for the community.

A couple of things he did know for sure. Whoever was handing down the orders from the top was big, big enough to scare the shit out of Jackdaw, and that took some doing. Big enough to put twenty men in the field after the LA fiasco.

The other thing he knew was that, big as Mister Big was, he was scared of what was on this tape.

Peregrine wished he knew more about the whole scene, what he was in to. Jackdaw had briefed them about the *Times* article, about the taped conversations between Drummond and the Ambrose character, and between Beal and the cop messenger at the time of the drop. But that was it, all he needed to know. He'd give a month's pay to know what the Trice thing was all about and who it was threatening.

The thought crossed his mind that he'd play the tape on the way back to LA, but Albatross would be with him, and he didn't trust that sonofabitch. If it ever got out that he'd listened to the tape, he was a dead man.

So, back to the tape Drummond was going to play. What would he hear? And how would he know it was genuine? Goddamn Jackdaw, he ought to be here, listening for himself. Well, screw him. All he, Peregrine, could do was listen and report what he heard. Then Jackdaw could make the decision for action.

His stomach rumbled and he peeled a stick of Juicy Fruit

341

to ward off the pangs. Fucking rain. Fucking place. He hated the cold, hated the north. He heaved a disconsolate sigh and thought about his woman in San Diego. But it made things worse.

They were seated around the kitchen table, Paul scribbling on a sheet of yellow legal pad. The Sanyo tape recorder was on the table, complete with microphone.

Robert asked, "You really think this can work?"

Paul said, "These guys can't know Ambrose's voice, can't know any more about Trice than we do. I'm just playing for time. I don't intend to give them more than thirty seconds, but it should be enough to convince them we've got the tape."

He finished writing, pushed the pad across to his father. "Take a look at that. When you're ready we'll record. Just read it straight, try and tone down your education a bit. You're supposed to be a sergeant technician in the army, or something like that."

While Robert scanned the page, the women exchanged wondering looks.

Sarah said, "My son, playwright and drama coach. Is there no end to his talents?"

Karen smiled. "I think all the Drummonds are quite remarkable."

Robert cleared his throat, said, "Okay, shoot."

Paul pressed the Record button, stayed his father with an upheld hand for a few seconds, then signalled him to begin.

In a slightly gruff, somewhat hesitant delivery, he said, "You want to know what the Trice jingle means. Well, I know what it means . . . because I was in Vietnam with Tom Keegan when the boys began to use it. First, I'll tell you who I am . . . because you'll want to check me out, make sure I'm not a hoaxer. My name is Arnold Breen . . . that's spelled B-R-E-E-N. From Nineteen Sixty-nine to 'Seventy-two I was a sergeant in the army. I served in Vietnam with Special Forces, but also spent time at the Army Chemical Center at Edgewood, Maryland, which is where I first met Tom Keegan. I was born in Crescent City, California, went to school there, won a science scholarship to UCLA, wanted to be a pharmacist . . . like Tom Keegan. But neither of us made it. As you know, Tom came out of the army without a memory, and the same thing should've happened to me . . . except I got lucky. Somebody screwed up at that clinic, left me with too much memory . . . and now that somebody is going to pay for what he did to Tom Keegan and to me."

The script finished, Robert looked up.

Paul punched the Stop button. "Dad, you were terrific. You had *me* convinced you were Arnold Breen."

The women mock-applauded.

Robert responded with a shrug. "We actors are only as good as our material."

Paul rewound the tape. "That's all they get, but it should convince them." He reached for the pad, ripped off several pages and tore them in pieces. "Okay, let's turn our minds to getting out of here. Don't let's kid ourselves, there's no way these people are going to pay fifty thousand dollars – or even one dollar – for the tape. I'm sure Dad was right, they've taken it easy on us so far because this is a sensitive situation. Things they could do to us in Palm Desert and LA without hesitation, they have to think twice about here. But that won't stop them the moment they know for sure that we have the tape. They'll come up with some cockamamie plan to get the money to us, or better still to get us away from here to pick up the money, but be assured that they'll end up with the tape and we'll be lucky to keep our lives."

He got up and went to the sink, dropped the bits of paper into the disposal unit and reduced the script to pulp.

He looked out of the window. It was raining heavily now, and so dark he could barely see the woods where the little man was sheltering. In another fifteen minutes it would be impossible to see the trees.

Drawing the curtains, Paul crossed to the door and switched on the lights. "Dad, talking about the root cellar has given me an idea. To leave the house, we have to do it in one of four directions. Our best bet is this way." He pointed to the window. "The trees on this side are closest to the house, and it's your direct route to the Bensons. So, we'll all make a break for the trees, then while you and Mom go on, Karen and I can get down to the lake and double back to the boat. But we won't leave by the kitchen door. We'll come out of the root cellar trap. We leave the kitchen lights on, so the little guy can see the door. Likewise, we'll draw the drapes and put lights on in the den, the study, and the living room. Back there where the trap is will be in darkness."

Robert frowned. "But the little man will still be in our way."

Paul looked at the women, saw their concern, returned to his father. "I know. And if necessary I intend to remove him from it."

Robert's frown became a grimace. "With the crossbow?"

"Whatever it takes."

Robert shook his head. "Paul, you're no killer. You're a healer. How can you even contemplate firing a bolt into a man?"

Paul put his hand on his father's shoulder. "You know I'll do everything I can to avoid it. Let's see what kind of play he makes. Maybe by the time we leave he'll be so wet and frozen he'll be off guard and we can get past him in the dark. Anyway, that's the plan. Do we go with it?"

Sarah nodded decisively. "Yes. It's better than sitting here waiting for them to burst in."

Karen said, "I'm ready."

"Dad?"

Robert braced his shoulders. "How my father would've loved this. Yes, we'll do it."

"Good. Let's get our oilskins on."

The phone rang.

Picking up the tape recorder, Paul answered it.

Peregrine said, "Okay, Doc, let's make you fifty kay richer."

Chapter Thirty-Three

Paul asked, "Are you ready?"

Peregrine said, "Let's hear it. I'm taking notes here, so if I say stop and replay, do it. Okay, shoot."

"Arnold Breen" began to speak.

When Paul switched off, Peregrine protested, "Hey, Doc, that was getting real interesting."

"Glad to hear it. But that's all you get. Now, about payment."

"You'll get it. Of course, it's going to take a little time. The money's in LA. I'm going to give the go-ahead right now, and they'll fly it up here to Redding. Say four hours. By eight o'clock we should be doing a trade."

"How?"

Peregrine chuckled. "Doc, you sound so sus-*picious*. Don't worry, we'll work something out. We only want the tape, not you guys. But tell me something . . ."

"What?"

"Why the sell-out? You don't seem like a guy who needs fifty thousand bucks."

"Dick, everybody needs fifty thousand bucks. But it's not for me. It's to compensate Miss Beal. This would've made one helluva newspaper story. It was probably a Pulitzer winner, would've made her name, and her fortune. She deserves some compensation, don't you agree?"

"Oh, all the way. Okay, just sit tight and I'll get back to you."

Peregrine disconnected the metal clips he was using to control the Drummonds' severed phone line, grinning as he visualized Paul trying for a call before it happened.

He ran an eye over his notes, checking he had the information Jackdaw would need. Sergeant Arnold Breen . . . Special Forces . . . '69 to '72 . . . Oh, yeah, Jackdaw would *love* this.

Maybe he'd make San Diego for the weekend after all.

"Right, let's go!" Paul pulled on his oilskins. "Mom, you take the living room – drapes and low lights. Karen, the study. Dad, the den. And, Dad, we need flashlights."

"Where they always are – in the drawer there."

They dispersed. Collecting two four-cell flashlights, a necessity at Loche Linnhe with its unlit acreage, Paul went into the hall and through a door under the stairs.

The cellars were huge, divided into three compartments. One housed the central heating furnace; another was a recreation room, complete with ping-pong table, dartboard, and keep-fit equipment. The third, in bye-gone days a root cellar, was now a junk room, a receptacle for Drummond detritus, sentimental stuff they rarely if ever used but hadn't the heart to throw away.

Using a flashlight sparingly, Paul located the crossbow, suspended with its quiver of six twelve-inch bolts from a nail in one of the crossbeams. He took it down, cocked it to test the condition of the cord, fired it empty. It worked perfectly.

Slinging the leather quiver around his neck, he withdrew a bolt and tested the sharpness of its metal nose with his thumb, experiencing a rush of apprehension as his father's words returned to him, "How can you even contemplate firing a bolt into a man?"

Could he really do it? Talk was fine, but when it came to it, could he pull the trigger?

347

"You down there, Paul?"

"Yes, Dad. Don't put the lights on!"

Paul returned to the foot of the stairs.

His father asked, "Shall we come down?"

"Yes. I guess we're as ready as we'll ever be."

Paul shone a flashlight on the stairs as they trouped down, gave the second flashlight to his father. Together, all wearing yellow oilskins, they resembled a lifeboat crew about to put out to sea.

Paul illuminated the way through to the root cellar. On the north wall, six stone steps led up to double trap doors, secured by a well-oiled bolt. The doors were opened at least twice a year, early summer and late fall, when canvas garden and patio furniture was moved from and to storage.

Climbing the steps, in utter darkness, Paul released the bolt and slowly raised the left-side door. Rain and wind struck him in the face. The night was now so dark that he could scarcely determine door from sky.

He rose one step, looked out in the direction of the trees. Less than fifty yards away across open lawn, he could not see them. To his right, the covered swimming pool was a faint, blurred patch of gray against the black ground. The tennis court was invisible. To the left, peering around the trap, he could see the merest lessening of darkness around the kitchen door and window, the haze too dim and distant to reach the cellar.

He returned his gaze to the trees. The little man was in there, straight ahead. Conscious of his rocking heartbeat, and the weight of the crossbow in his right hand, he tried to visualize the coming encounter, tried to empathize with this man, to get into his mind. He was wet and cold, miserably so. He was cursing the delay, calling up Dick, asking what the hell was going on, why couldn't they just go in there and get the tape?

He was undoubtedly armed. He was a killer. Maybe even the one who had shot the cop to death in LA.

Paul knew then what he, himself, had to do. In this moment of stark reality, his plan had to be revised. He could not, would not risk the lives of his parents and Karen by having them walk across the lawn and into the trees in their yellow slickers. Seeing all those phantom shapes coming at him out of the blackness, the man could easily open fire and slaughter them all.

What had to be done, he would do by himself.

Lowering the trap, he went back down the steps.

In a whisper, his father asked, "What did you see?"

Paul didn't answer.

Quickly, in the absolute blackness, he removed the quiver and shed his oilskins.

Robert asked, "What are you doing?"

"I'll be a couple of minutes. You all stay here."

"Paul . . ." His mother had read his intention. "Oh, no, I don't like this."

He slipped the quiver thong over his head, tucked the flashlight into his pants waistband, felt around for the crossbow, started back up the steps.

Karen reiterated Sarah's fears. "Paul, please . . ."

Raising the trap, he went up and out, closed the trap, and without hesitation started across the lawn.

What the mind can conceive, and believe, the mind can achieve.

He had programmed himself, had given himself permission, to immobilize a killer who threatened the lives of his family and friend, and dared not for one micro-second doubt his nerve and ability to do it.

Peregrine said into the car phone, "Okay, I got it. He's playing cute, didn't give me much, but what there is sounds pretty convincing."

Jackdaw grunted. "I'll be the judge. Let's hear it."

"You recording?"

"Do pigeons shit?"

Peregrine gave him the information.

When he had finished, Jackdaw let out an entirely uncharacteristic whoop. "Terrific! I'll get back."

In Sacramento, in the study of the Governor's mansion, Karl Hoffman took the call on the secure line.

"This is Jackdaw. Is he there?"

Hoffman covered the mouthpiece, said to Jack Crane, seated at the desk, "It's Jackdaw."

Crane held out his hand for the phone. "Yes?"

"I think we got it nailed."

For the next three minutes he reported the situation and played the recording of Peregrine.

Governor Crane's wink to his aide told Hoffman everything was going to be all right.

Crane said, "Good work. Now, track down Breen through our contact at Records. Make sure that's the only tape he's made, and he hasn't talked to anyone else, then lose him."

"And the people at the house?"

"Lift them out of there – then lose them. They can keep Keegan company."

"You got it."

Despite his warm clothing and parka, Drummond was shivering. The tremor had little to do with the wind and rain driving off the lake into the side of his face, and everything to do with what lay ahead of him, now only a few yards ahead, within the impenetrable blackness of the woods.

Half-way across the lawn he had stopped to arm the crossbow, his hands shaking so badly it took three attempts to get the bolt into the groove. Now he held the weapon awkwardly, dead-level, fearing the bolt would fall off at the crucial moment, his left hand gripping the flashlight and also supporting the weight of the bow, his plan being to blind the killer with the flashlight, to gain momentary advantage, and . . . and then to do whatever the situation called for.

Since leaving the root cellar, he had employed his capacity for mental discipline to keep at bay the host of negative possibilities, the what-ifs and maybes, that threatened to undermine his courage and determination, and have him scuttling back to the cellar for a re-think of the whole crazy plan. What if a sudden streak of lightning lit up the lawn like day? What if the darkness wasn't as dark as he thought, and the little man had him in his gun sights right now? Maybe he'd miss with the crossbow, he was shaking so much? Maybe the guy was wearing a bullet-proof vest and the bolt would bounce off it?

He drove the negatives out of his mind with a mantra, mentally repeating over and over, "Permission . . . permission . . . permission . . .", using it as a goad, twice to a step, to keep his concentration fixed and his feet moving, slowly, stealthily, towards the black maw of the woods.

And now he was there, at them, into them.

Almost immediately the wind dropped dramatically and the relative silence appalled him. He had assumed out there, in the wind, that his adversary could hear no more clearly than he, and was now relieved that he hadn't come over at a run, and that he'd come alone. The rustling of four sets of oilskins would've have sounded like ocean waves breaking on the shore.

Now, just into the trees, he abandoned all dependence on vision, and like a blind man gave his full concentration to sound, his own as much as any other.

He took a step, sensing the texture of the ground. The woods here were mostly of pine, the floor a carpet of needles, but littered with crackly cones and crackable twigs, and whippy saplings that rustled against the legs.

He strained to pick up human sound . . . a movement, a cough, a mutter . . . prayed the little man would use his radio. He wondered if the killer had a flashlight, and doubted it. It had been daylight when he entered the woods, and probably hadn't reckoned on such a wait.

Another step . . . another.

The killer had to be *here*, within feet of him. Positioned further back in the trees, he wouldn't be able to see the house.

Drummond stood rock still and concentrated totally on his his hearing, tried to sift out the rush of the wind and the spatter of rain through the topmost branches, begging for an alien sound . . . a scrape of foot, a curse, a sigh.

But heard nothing.

Until . . .

Peregrine picked up the phone. "Yeah?"

Jackdaw said, "It's a go. Get the tape. Use the Tasers, take them all out of there, nice 'n easy, bring them to Tahoe."

"Right *on*."

Peregrine slotted the phone, rubbed his hands together exuberantly. Action.

He reached for the walkie-talkie. "Peregrine to Seagull. You there, Seagull?"

"Where the fuck else would I be?"

Shock rushed scaldingly through Drummond's body. Dick's voice, then Seagull's, came out of the blackness almost immediately to his right, perhaps ten feet away. He stood paralyzed, listening, half-listening to the radio exchange, the actual words meaningful to him only as a pointer to the killer's position.

Dick's voice: "We've gotta green on this. I'm comin' down with the the van. Move in slowly. We'll meet up behind the house. It's a removal job . . . Tahoe."

352

"Everybody?"

"Whoever's in there. Start now."

The radio clicked off.

Drummond heard a branch snap and sapling swish as Seagull began to move.

The imperative need for decision battered him.

If he let Seagull go, would there be time to get back to the house, get his parents and Karen out of the cellar, and . . .

No.

He had to stop Seagull, cause some confusion, steal a few precious seconds . . .

He raised the crossbow and switched on the flashlight.

The powerful beam caught Seagull dead center.

The man froze, shocked, then reacted instinctively and fast. He turned, threw up his left hand, holding the radio, to shield his eyes, and simultaneously plunged his right hand inside his jacket.

Drummond found himself pleading, "Don't!" but knew there was no way the man would stop.

As the silenced revolver cleared the jacket and levelled at Drummond's body, he pulled the crossbow trigger.

The weapon bucked. The man dropped both hands slowly, stared, expressionlessly, into the blinding light, then buckled at the knees and fell face down in a clump of saplings.

Stunned, Drummond approached him, cautiously, had the presence of mind to pick up the radio and gun before getting close. He felt for a pulse, found one. From the position of the bolt tip protruding through Seagull's back, Drummond guessed he'd missed the heart but traumatized it with the blow. The man had literally suffered a heart attack.

Drummond came to his feet and started back through the trees, all caution abandoned now. The words he'd heard in the radio exchange came back him, making sense.

"I'm coming down in the van . . . it's a removal job . . . Tahoe. Everybody. Assemble behind the house."

He reckoned they had about three minutes. Peregrine, the man he'd called Dick, would already have contacted the other two men. One was already behind the house. The other would be moving in from the trees on the far side of the house. Peregrine would be pushing through the gate with the van and be at the garages in ninety seconds. Within two minutes they'd be assembled, wondering what was taking Seagull so long. They'd call him up, get no response, and come looking for him.

Drummond burst from the trees, into the rush of the wind and rain. Thank God for the Whiskeytown weather.

Racing across the lawn, he reached the cellar trap, pulled up one half, saw the blur of his father's face at the bottom of the steps.

He stage-whispered, "Okay, all clear. We've got one minute to make the trees! Come on, move! Bring my oilskins."

They scrambled up, Sarah first, then Karen. As Robert emerged, he whispered anxiously, "What happened? Did you . . .?"

"No. He's hurt, but alive."

Paul dropped the crossbow down the steps, disposed of the quiver, lowered the trap.

Karen hissed, "Listen!"

Faintly, over the wind, came the sound of a vehicle.

Paul said, "It's the van – it's coming for us. Move!"

They started across the lawn at a run, entered the trees at the same time as Albatross, wet and cold and armed with one of the silenced, night-scoped rifles, emerged from his trees on the far side of the house and linked up with Peregrine at the garages.

Farm-boy Blackbird was stamping his feet and flapping his arms in the open doorway of the dressing room. He scowled at Peregrine as he and Albatross approached. "Sure you weren't too uncomfortable sittin' up there in that stuffy car while we've been enjoyin' all this invigoratin' ozone?"

Peregrine grinned. "You boys got out of all that stressful communicating stuff nicely, didn't you? Where the fuck's Seagull?"

Albatross growled, "Prob'ly died of pneu-freakin'-monia."

Peregrine used his radio. "Peregrine to Seagull. Come in Seagull."

Silence.

"Shit. Now what?"

Albatross sniffed. "Like I said."

"Peregrine to Seagull. Answer me, asshole."

Silence.

Blackbird said, "Something's wrong. He wouldn't switch his radio off."

Peregrine started out of the door. "Find him."

The radio in Drummond's pocket squawked, "Peregrine to Seagull. Come in Seagull."

Leading them, deep into the woods now, using his flashlight, he came to a halt. Panting, he said, "Okay, this is where we separate. If all goes well, Karen and I'll be in Redding in a couple of hours. You stay at the Bensons, we'll call you from Mike's office."

Robert said, "You could come with us. The Bensons would lend you a car. I don't like you using the lake in this wind."

"No, Dad. We'd have to drive back past the house, and I want to keep as far away from these guys as possible. We'll get off the lake as fast as we can. Now, get going, you two." He embraced them both quickly. "And please be careful."

"You, too."

"Peregrine to Seagull. Answer me, asshole."

Paul said, "Now they'll come looking for him. Let them not find us."

Taking Karen's arm, he started down towards the lake.

Chapter Thirty-Four

Ten yards into the trees, using flashlights from the van, they found him.

They went into an immediate defensive posture, Albatross and Blackbird standing guard, sweeping the woods through the Starlite night-sights on their rifles, while Peregrine examined Seagull with a controlled flashlight.

"He's alive. But what the fuck's been goin' on here? Somebody shot him with a fucking arrow!" Gingerly he turned Seagull over. "It's not an arrow, it's a crossbow bolt. Now, who . . .?"

He looked in the direction of the house, purely a reflexive reaction in the darkness, his thoughts racing. Though there was no formal leader of the group – they worked equally under Jackdaw – Peregrine, with a keener intelligence and quickness of mind, seemed usually and naturally to assume that role.

"It had to be Drummond. No casual sucker in his right mind would be out here playing in the woods with a crossbow in this weather, and this ain't a hunting bolt." He did a quick search of Seagull's pockets, played his flashlight around the area. "His gun and radio's gone. It was Drummond, and they're out here somewhere now. They're making a break for it. And they're taking that fucking tape with them! Jesus Christ, you can't trust anybody."

He came to his feet. "Which way would they go? Okay, you guys, forget the scopes, they're gone. Use your flashlights, find some tracks. They can't be far ahead, Seagull used the radio just a few minutes ago."

"Footprints here," said Blackbird, and shone his flashlight ahead, into the trees in the direction the four had gone.

"Follow them."

"What about Seagull?"

"He'll keep. I want that tape – and them." They started off, sweeping the wet carpet of pine needles with their beams, picking up enough vague footmarks to make it easy tracking, Peregrine muttering more to himself than to them, "Can you *believe* that guy. Has me negotiatin' for fifty thousand bucks, an' all the time he's planning a break. Then he creeps out and shoots Seagull with a fucking crossbow! I told him he had balls. Well, he ain't gonna have 'em much longer."

Moving fast, they reached the place where the group had stopped, and separated.

Peregrine said, "What we got here?"

Blackbird shone his beam ahead. "Looks like there are four of them. Two went this way . . ." he swung his flashlight to the left, "two down here."

"Momma and Poppa," mused Peregrine. "But who went where?"

Albatross said, "This way heads down to the lake. There are two boats tied up at the jetty . . ."

Peregrine shot a look at him. "What kinda boats?"

"Sailing dinghy and an inflatable with an outboard . . ."

"Jesus, man, why didn't you say?"

"I just said!"

"They're going for the inflatable, bet your ass." Peregrine waved his flashlight at the other tracks, telling Blackbird, "Follow those. It'll be Mom and Pop Drummond. Just see where they lead, then come back to the house." He turned to Albatross. "We separate. I'll go down here, you go back, cut them off from the jetty. Careful how you handle it. Drummond'll have the tape, so don't shoot anything you don't have to. And don't use the radios, he'll be listening. Okay – go!"

Drummond and Karen broke from the trees at a point only twenty yards from the lake but three hundred yards from the jetty. Staying close to the tree-line, they picked their way carefully in the darkness, Drummond using the flashlight sparingly, lighting the ground a few yards ahead to ensure there was no obstructive debris, no fallen trees or holes where trees had been, then covering that ground in darkness.

The going was slower than he wanted. Along the edge of the woods, the grass grew in wiry clumps, the hummocks sometimes firm, sometimes spongey, and not to be trusted. A sprained ankle was one thing they didn't need.

Drummond had considered staying just inside the protection of the trees, out of the wind and rain, but the going there was no faster, and he felt better out in the open. The woods that offered them concealment also hid the V's, and he felt there was less likelihood of blindly running into them out there.

He was certain that by now they'd be looking for Seagull. Since the last radio message from Peregrine to Seagull, nothing had come over the walkie-talkie, so he assumed they were either grouped together, or had discovered Seagull's radio was missing and were maintaining silence.

Drummond felt its bulk and weight in his side pocket and considered getting rid of it, but decided to wait until they were in the boat. The weight of the revolver in another pocket was a paradoxically disturbing comfort. He hoped to God he wouldn't need to use it. What he'd done to Seagull was all the damage he wanted to inflict on another human being for the rest of his life.

Suddenly they had reached the end of the tree-line and faced the open lawn, the light from the kitchen a faint glow on its far side. He stopped so abruptly that Karen bumped into him.

He turned and took hold of her, whispered, "You okay?"

Her arms went around his waist. "Fine."

"You're terrific. Ready for a quick sprint?"

"Absolutely."

He grasped her hand, made one last sensory check of the darkness around them, and took off for the jetty.

Out there on the platform, the wind battered at them in squally gusts, the rain blinding them, as Drummond helped Karen down into the tossing inflatable. As her feet touched the solid plywood interior, the boat leapt up to meet her, buckling her knees, and she collapsed in a sprawl against the bulbous rubber bulwark.

Drummond waited for the boat to rise again, then jumped down and struggled to maintain a semblance of balance while he untied the fore and aft lines, secured to rings in the tire-fendered jetty.

Freed, the craft began to move away from the structure and towards the shore. Drummond knelt to the outboard, found the fuel switch. There was no point in rowing out. By now the V's would know they were running, and silence was of no consequence. The darkness would hide them.

Drummond pressed the electric starter button. The motor ground but didn't fire. He tried again. The third time it fired.

He turned, grinned at Karen's expression of agonized relief, held up his thumb, and opened the throttle.

Albatross came out of the trees at a run, dreading the prospect of Drummond and the girl having already got away in a boat. They'd screwed up, made a fundamental and unforgiveable error: they'd underestimated the enemy. And Jackdaw would be unforgiving.

Peregrine was right: who could believe this guy Drummond, what he'd done? He was a fucking doctor! Who'd have believed he could go out there in the dark and take on Seagull with a, f'crissake, crossbow?

Just showed you, never underestimate anybody when they were cornered. He wouldn't make the same mistake again.

Just out of the trees he stopped, brought the Starlite sight to his eye and picked up the jetty.

His heart leapt, with relief. There they were, in the freaking inflatable, Drummond working at the motor.

Albatross broke into a run.

On the wind, out of the darkness, he heard the motor fire. Clear of the house now, he angled to his left, cut across the front lawn, making a guess that Drummond would turn that way, towards Shasta and Redding, and would turn soon to offer a side-on target.

Half-way across the lawn, he dropped to one knee, brought the rifle to his shoulder. The incredible Starlite scope, a light-intensifier, banished the blackness of night and presented a sea-green image of the boat as though it was travelling under the water rather than on its surface.

Albatross smiled as he lined up the cross-hairs of the telescopic sight on Drummond's head, then traversed, longingly, to the girl's skull. His finger tightened on the trigger.

He murmured, "Gotcha."

And fired off ten silent rounds.

Clear of the jetty, Drummond accelerated gradually, turned the bouncing craft full into the wind, felt the propellor bite and the boat ease forward. He loved the inflatable. It was capable of miraculous acceleration and maneuverability, and could stop on a dime. But it didn't care for headwind.

Calculating he was about a hundred yards off shore and well -clear of debris, he swung left, parallel with the shore, and opened the throttle. The stern dipped and surged. The bow rose, throwing Karen forward, causing her to tighten her grip on the hand-ropes.

Then something weird happened. The bow, the entire boat seemed to collapse under them. They were no longer in an inflatable boat, but on a motor-driven plywood surfboard. The bulbous bulwark had become a ragged rubber skirt, and as the plywood decking struck the water, the force of the motor drove it under, up-ending the boat, pitching them out and forward in a nightmare cartwheel into twenty feet of black, freezing water.

Filled with air, their oilskins brought them quickly to the surface.

Drummond saw her thrashing arm and grabbed it. "Okay . . . okay . . . don't panic."

She spluttered and coughed. "I'm not . . . panicking. I'm . . . swimming."

"Are you all right? . . . are you hurt?"

"No. What in God's name happened?"

Peregrine's sardonic call came over the water. "Come in, Number One, your time is up!"

Drummond gasped. "They happened."

"They can see us! I can't see them, how can they see us?"

"Don't ask. Come on, we have to go in, they'll only come for us in the dinghy."

Helped by the following wind, they struggled into the shore.

Three men were waiting for them. Drummond saw that two of them held rifles equipped with silencers and large, distinctive telescopic sights, and knew at once both how the inflatable had been sunk and how the men could see them in the dark.

Drummond met the eyes of the grinning Black. "Peregrine, I presume."

Peregrine's snowy smile broadened. "Doctor Livingstone, *I* presume." He held out his left hand. "Let's have the tape, Doc."

"I don't have it."

Peregrine's smile vanished. "There are two ways to do this – hard an' easy. Which would you prefer?"

"Either way, I don't have the tape."

Peregrine sighed. "Okay." His right hand came up from his side, holding the Taser. "It's the hard way."

He shot Drummond in the face.

As the twin barbs embedded in Drummond's left cheek, the circuit closed, releasing a charge of twenty thousand volts, and climbing.

Drummond's nervous system went berserk.

When he came to, he was lying on the floor in the kitchen of Loch Linnhe, knowing he never wanted to experience such excruciating pain ever again.

Chapter Thirty-Five

They must have been watching him, because as soon as he opened his eyes they lifted him off the floor and sat him in a chair at right angles to the table. His entire body felt stiff and sore, as though from an excess of unaccustomed exercise. It took a second or two to realize Karen was sitting on the opposite side of the table. She was still wearing her oilskin, and shivering. Her expression was a grimace of gravest concern, as if she feared they'd done him deep, irreparable damage.

She asked, "Are you all right?"

He managed a smile. "Terrific. Are you?"

She nodded.

Peregrine and the weird-looking blond with the ice-blue eyes came from behind him. Peregrine leaned languidly against the counter top by the phone, arms folded, smiling. The blond stood guard by the door to the hall, his expression bland. Drummond couldn't decide who looked the more chilling.

He heard movement out in the hall. The muscular countryboy came in, carrying Karen's shoulder bag. He handed it to Peregrine, together with a slip of paper, and said, "The Cherokee's in the middle garage. That's the license number."

The Black moved to the table and emptied the contents of the bag onto it. Karen's tape recorder seemed to amuse him.

Placing it in clear view, separate from her other

belongings, he returned to his pose by the phone, his manner that of a patient, reasonable man who knew that, in Drummond, he was dealing with like kind.

He asked, "How're you really feeling, Doc?"

"Like I said – terrific."

"It hurt some, hm? And I only hit you with a half charge. 'Course, you were wet, and that made it worse. A full charge would've killed you."

Karen's anger flared. "It was totally uncalled for! He was just standing there, defenseless. You didn't have to do that."

Peregrine's smile was an acknowledgement of the loyalty. "I don't often do things that aren't necessary, Miz Beal. I wanted the Doc to know what a Taser shot felt like, so he'll know what *you* will suffer if he doesn't co-operate. You have a mighty pretty face. I'm a great admirer of female beauty. I'd hate like hell to have to shoot you in the face, but I will unless he tells me what I want to know."

He turned to Drummond. "Please believe that, Doc. Now, let's try that question again. Where's the Arnold Breen tape?"

Drummond knew that, as far as he and Karen were concerned, it was finished. He could not allow her to be subjected to that horrendous pain. If they used the Taser on her, he'd tell Peregrine everything he knew, so he had to do it now. In the long-run, what did it all matter? The Trice jingle would remain a secret. Two men would have died for nothing. And the Villains would have won again.

But rather all those things than to hear her scream in unendurable agony.

He said, "The tape I played you is in the recorder behind you."

Peregrine's grin twisted with genuine amusement. "Jesus, you're somethin' else."

"But it's not the one you want."

The grin froze. "Oh? How come?"

"Play it and see."

Peregrine reached for the Sanyo, flipped up the compartment lid, checked that the tape was wound for replay, and pressed the button.

Arnold Breen said his piece.

Drummond watched the look of expectation on Peregrine's face turn to puzzlement as the words ended abruptly, and all that came out of the recorder was the white noise hiss of a blank tape.

The black piercing eyes that turned on Drummond held no trace of humour. "Where's the rest of it?"

"There isn't any more."

Peregrine half-turned to Albatross and gave a nod. Albatross brought a Taser gun out of his jacket.

Drummond said, "I'm telling you the truth! That's not the tape we got from Ambrose. We made that tape here, at this table, to buy ourselves some time. There is no Arnold Breen. All that stuff was made up."

Peregrine moved with incredible speed, pushed himself away from the counter and back-handed Drummond across the cheek, knocking him out of the chair.

Karen screamed, "Leave him alone!" and came out of her chair.

Albatross caught her and shoved her back.

Peregrine, manic with anger, shouted, "If she moves again, shoot her!"

He hauled Drummond to his feet and threw him back into the chair. "You stupid sonofabitch . . . who the fuck d'you think you're messing with here?"

"It's the truth."

Peregrine turned away, paced to the sink and back again, trying to calm himself, wanting to kill this asshole who'd made a fool of him. At that moment Jackdaw would be trying to trace Sergeant Arnold Breen. The good news would be going down the line. Then Army Records would come back with the bad news . . . and the shit would fly. And goodbye San Diego.

He drew a breath. This had to be handled with reason and logic. He'd work off his anger on Drummond and the girl later.

"Okay – whose voice is that on the tape?"

"My father's."

"Where is your father?"

"I should think he and my mother are just about reaching the local sheriff's office about now."

"Doc, where is the Ambrose tape?"

"Why are you so sure there is a tape?"

Peregrine gave him a long, slow burn, as though deciding whether or not to smash him out of the chair again, then turned to look around the kitchen. Beside the sink was a glazed stone jar, designated Kitchen Things, containing cooking implements. He went to it and pulled out a metal-faced steak mallet.

He returned to stand in front of Drummond, hefting the mallet.

Karen gasped, "No!"

Peregrine raised the mallet as though intending to cave in Drummond's skull, but suddenly spun and brought it down with tremendous force on Karen's tape recorder.

The plastic shattered. He struck it again and again, reducing it to fragments, then stopped, sifted among the pieces and separated two items of electronic gadgetry, each no bigger than a thumb nail.

He pushed one piece towards Drummond. "Homing device. That's how we tracked you to the Medical Center . . . and picked you up in Shasta . . . and knew you were here."

Karen groaned. "My goddamned recorder, the only thing Joe Stills didn't sweep."

Peregrine flicked the second gadget to her with his

finger. "And a microphone. We heard your conversation with the phoney cop in LA."

He returned to lean against the counter top, picked up the piece of paper Blackbird had given him. "Okay, Doc, who owns the Cherokee? I can find out in about fifteen minutes, so you might as well save us a little time."

"It belongs to Mike Fallon. He runs the Hypnotherapy Center in Redding."

Peregrine scowled at Albatross. "The Hypnotherapy Center . . . where the XR3 was parked?" To Drummond: "Friend of yours?"

"Yes."

"And you left the tape with him." It was a statement. Drummond nodded.

"Why? Why didn't you bring it here, or mail it to yourself or someone else on the way up?"

"Because it's not a straightforward voice recording. All you can hear is Errol Garner. Ambrose's voice has been laid over the music subliminally. It needs special equipment to decode it."

"And this Mike Fallon has the equipment?"

"Yes."

"Does nobody else have this equipment, say in LA?"

"Yes, but we couldn't trust anybody else with the transcription."

"So you already know what Ambrose has to tell you?"

"No. But it's obviously extremely sensitive, probably political, and we didn't want anyone else hearing it before we did."

Peregrine glanced at Karen. "Sure, you didn't. The lady has . . . *had* one helluva scoop. Good. It's beginning to make sense. We've been kinda puzzled by your moves – why you headed for familiar territory we could pick up on, why you stopped at the Med Center when your father wasn't there. So, what is your arrangement with Mike Fallon about the tape?"

Drummond ran his tongue around the inside of his cheek. Peregrine's back-hander had split the flesh, and his lips were beginning to swell. "He couldn't get to the transcription right away. He had a full client schedule all afternoon. We were to call him later tonight, probably pick up the transcript around midnight, then head back to LA."

Peregrine checked his watch.

Drummond glanced at his own. It showed ten minutes to six and he brought it to his ear, thinking it had stopped, not believing so much could have happened in so short a time.

Peregrine asked, "What time will Fallon be finished with his clients?"

"About now, give or take."

"What's his phone number?"

Drummond told him, and he reached for the phone.

Kay Conners answered. "Shasta Hypnotherapy Center."

"Mike Fallon, please."

"Who is calling?"

"I'm calling for Paul Drummond."

"One moment."

Fallon came on. "Yes?"

Peregrine brought the phone to Drummond. "You know what to say. Say it right."

Drummond took the instrument, angled it from his ear so that Peregrine could hear Fallon. "Mike? You started on the tape yet?"

"Just about to. Geez, what an afternoon. They ought to rename Friday Neurotaday. Haven't even had time for a coffee."

"Mike, listen, forget the tape. Don't touch it. Someone will be calling for it in . . ." he looked at Peregrine, ". . . half an hour." Peregrine nodded. "Just give the cassette to whoever comes in, okay?"

Hesitation. "You all right, Paul? You sound funny."

"I'm fine, just bit the inside of my cheek."

Fallon chuckled. "Try food next time. Okay, buddy, will do. Kay's going home now, but I'll hang on. You staying with the folks for the weekend? Sure like to see something of you if you do."

"I'm not sure yet, Mike. I'll let you know."

"Fine. Call me at home."

Fallon rang off.

Peregrine returned the phone to the counter. "How much did you tell Fallon about the tape, about Ambrose, about you being tailed up here?"

"Practically nothing. I figured the less I told him the safer he'd be. When we arrived at the Center, I merely told him I had a sensitive job I needed doing, and asked to borrow his Jeep. Mike's a trained psychologist, he knows when to ask questions and when not to. You heard him – did he sound like a man who knows what's going on?"

Peregrine nodded thoughtfully. "Well, we'll see." He turned to Blackbird who had been leaning in the doorway all this time, manicuring his nails with a metal file. "Bring the Plymouth down to the house. Load Seagull into the van and take him to Tahoe. We'll take these two to Redding for the tape."

As the country boy departed, Drummond asked, "How is Seagull?"

Peregrine grinned. "Why, he's just dandy. He's only sorry he won't be around to kill you both himself."

370

Chapter Thirty-Six

They were allowed to change into dry clothes, sweaters and pants, Karen again borrowing from Sarah's wardrobe, and were then taken out to the car. Drummond sat in the rear of the Plymouth, with Peregrine on his right. Karen was put up front with Albatross. Peregrine held a silenced automatic in his right hand, and calmly threatened to shoot Karen if Drummond made the slightest move to escape. He said the same to her, promising to shoot Drummond if she should try anything. They were sure he would keep his word.

As they made their way up the gravel road and through the broken gate, Drummond reflected on the unreality and weirdness of being closeted in the confines of the car with two killers. Perhaps their business suits made it all the more weird. Despite everything, he found Peregrine an attractive personality. The psychologist in him compelled him to talk to the man, to probe his assassin's mind. It was also preferable to talk than to sit in silence, speculating on what would happen in Redding, on how much longer he and Karen had to live.

He said, "Mind if I ask you something?"

Peregrine smiled. He smiled a lot, seeming to enjoy his private world of amusement. "Hell, no, Doc, you ask away. You may not get an answer, but you can certainly ask."

"How much do you know about all this? . . . about

Ambrose and the Trice jingle and what could be behind it?"

"Practically nothing. Why?"

"I just wondered whether it would matter to you, whether you could be swayed into taking a sympathetic stance, if you knew more of the facts."

"Oh, I doubt that very much, Doc. I'm not really into judgement. I try not to involve myself in matters of right or wrong, fair or unfair. Those things are always subjective and just tend to make the job at hand very messy."

"You sleep well at night, having taken the life of a fellow human being?"

"Like a babe. I never concern myself with personalities. We've all got to die sometime, and I don't see that it matters too much when. Some die at birth, others live to be a hundred and ten. Who gives a shit? Maybe a couple of people in the immediate family. While we've been having this little tête-à-tête, probably a hundred people have kicked off in LA, maybe ten thousand in the entire country. Who cares?"

"What does matter to you, Peregrine?"

"Precision. Doing the job right. And the money. The pay's awful good, Doc. You know, I think you'd be terrific at this work. You're a psychologist, you understand people, how they think. That's part of the precision, reading the other guy's mind, out-thinking him, hunting him down. You gave us a good run on this. I've enjoyed the chase."

"You had an unfair advantage. If we'd known about the homing device and the microphone, you'd never have caught us."

Peregrine sighed. "There y'go with 'unfair'. We out-smarted you."

"Yes, you did. We'll know better next time."

Peregrine grinned. "Next time – yeah."

They lapsed into silence. Drummond could sense Karen's extreme anxiety, saw it in the rigid set of her

372

head and shoulders. He detested his feeling of helplessness, just sitting there being carted off towards God knew what fate. He felt angry that their perfectly good plan had been thwarted, not by superior human intelligence, but by a piece of high technology – a light-intensifier nightscope.

He wondered what Mike Fallon was doing right then. Mike's performance on the phone had been masterly. If his parents had reached the Bensons, and there was no reason to doubt that they had, and his father had phoned Mike, then Mike would deduce from Paul's call that he and Karen were in trouble, that the V's were in the house.

What action would he take?

One advantage they had was Mike's experience of the Intelligence mind. Mike knew through his research that nothing was too outlandish for contemplation or expectation when it concerned the Spooks, and he would not be taken by surprise. But what, in the short space of time available until their arrival, could Mike come up with to save the situation?

They were entering Shasta, the half-way stage, and Drummond sensed Peregrine becoming even more alert as the car slowed for traffic lights. The door handle, so close, offered an almost compulsive temptation, to Karen, he knew, as much as to himself; but neither would take the risk. Even before he had cleared the door, he would hear the deadly "phut" of Peregrine's silenced automatic, and the prospect of causing Karen's death wiped the temptation from his thoughts.

Through Shasta and out onto the road to Redding. Only ten minutes left. He had to try *some*thing.

He said to Peregrine, "Do you enjoy killing for the sake of it?"

Peregrine cleared his throat. "It doesn't work that way, Doc – not for me. I'm a technician, a mechanic. You ask the guy working in an abattoir the same thing, he'll probably give you the same answer."

Drummond nodded at the man driving. "How about him?"

"Can't speak for him. Maybe he gets off on it."

"You don't know your own partner?"

"He's not my partner. We're not cops."

"What are you, Peregrine – CIA?"

Peregrine laughed. "Shit, no."

"Freelance?"

"Something like that."

"What are your orders concerning us?"

"They vary, depending on the circumstances."

"As of this moment, what's your brief?"

"To pick up the Ambrose tape."

"How will you know if it's the genuine one?"

Peregrine nodded slowly. "Good question."

Drummond was silent for a moment or two, seemed preoccupied, then quietly began his attempt to save their lives. "Look . . . I told you the Ambrose information is subliminal, all you'll hear is Errol Garner playing some great classics. What I'm getting at is this – even *we* don't know if Ambrose is genuine, or if the subliminal message on the tape is valid. It might not have anything to do with the Trice jingle – the couplet that's causing all the furore. Let me fill you in on a couple of things you probably don't know . . ."

Drummond had slowed his speech, his pace of delivery, and lowered his voice to the deep, somnolent drone he used in hypnosis. To his listeners, it was not a noticeable ploy, merely the speech rhythm of a weary, reflective man, telling a story with which he hoped to appeal to his captors' sense of reason. What he in fact was doing was slowing their brain activity to Alpha rhythm, in which state the mind is most receptive to suggestion. The moderate speed of the car, the swish of its tires in the rain, and the metronomic sweep of the wipers were powerful additional hypnotics.

"It began quite simply." He paused, getting their attention, allowing the supplementary hypnotics to do their insidious work. "A man, a nobody, named Tom Keegan, was innocently involved in a bank robbery. He was abducted by the robbers, thrown through a plateglass window, and he lost his memory. I was called in by a friend, Lieutenant Dick Gage of West LA Homicide, to help Tom recover his memory. I used hypnosis . . . put him into a deep sleep . . . and in this deep sleep . . . he spoke the words: 'In a trice . . . it will be nice . . . Charlie will be put on ice'. It became apparent to me that the Trice jingle was very important to Tom, and therefore a possible key with which to unlock his amnesia. But out of the hypnotic trance he could remember nothing of the jingle. I believed that if we could find the meaning of the couplet, it would help Tom remember his past. So Karen wrote the article, asking if anyone else knew what Trice meant.

"We only had one response – Ambrose. He contacted us on her carphone, told us the situation was very dangerous, said he wanted five thousand dollars for his explanation on tape. And the following night, under circumstances with which I'm sure you're familiar, we got our hands on the tape. We played it immediately, in the car. At first, we heard only Errol Garner, but then, because I'm familiar with subliminal recordings, I picked up something in the background, a voice far too low for the words to be heard. I thought then of Mike Fallon, brought the tape to him, borrowed his Jeep, drove on to the house. The rest you know."

Throughout his doleful peroration, Drummond had been watching Peregrine surreptitiously, his gaze apparently fixed on the back of Albatross's blond head. Gradually, the Black had lost the edge of his alertness. He had blinked his eyes frequently, his posture had slackened, the hand holding the automatic had drooped and come to rest on his knee.

Karen had also succumbed to the hypnotic drone of his voice, and the click-click-click of the wipers. The tension had eased from her shoulders and her head had dropped a little.

Drummond could not gauge Albatross's response, but assumed he was equally affected.

It was not Drummond's intention to physically disarm Peregrine with force – the risk would have been far too great – but to psychologically disarm him with words, with suggestion.

He had about three minutes left to accomplish it.

Continuing in the same somber, mellifluous, tone, he added a slight edge of authority, and couched his views in positive terms, avoiding all negatives.

"The position is this, Peregrine . . . the Trice thing has got completely out of hand. It's a runaway. It's the kind of situation, exactly like Watergate, that started off as nothing, and, unless somebody puts a stop to it, unless *we* put a stop to it, *will* end up as great a national disaster as Watergate. Believe me, that's no exaggeration.

"Somebody . . . somebody big, somebody powerful, somebody prominent . . . has panicked. He's scared of Trice, afraid that it's meaning will be known publicly. So, indirectly, he's employing you and others to stop it becoming public. Tom Keegan was abducted and is probably dead. Ambrose, whoever he is, has emerged as another source of threat. His messenger, the cop, was killed in LA. There's obviously a contract out on Ambrose. Karen and I are under sentence. And how about Mike Fallon? And my parents? And the entire Metro staff at the *Times*? Where is it going to end? And for what? For a tape recording of *what*?

"Nobody but this Ambrose character knows what's on that tape – and it could easily be garbage. Behind Errol

Garner he might be telling dirty jokes, or reciting nursery rhymes. He might be a fruit cake. And it might be nothing but a five-thousand-dollar con. Think about it. How many more deaths is your boss prepared to sanction for a tape that *nobody, other than Ambrose, has heard?*"

Drummond, ultra-conscious of the passing time, of their closeness to the Medical Center, pushed on, "Another thing, and this I promise you, promise your boss. Neither my father, nor I, nor Miss Beal are without influence. Not only is Karen a respected member of the *Los Angeles Times* staff, but her father happens to be Sir Edward Beal, England's top policeman. If anything should happen to her, I can absolutely guarantee an investigation that will rock this country to its foundations. Similarly, if anything should happen to me, both my father and Lieutenant Gage will do the same."

"Now, come on, Peregrine . . . all this for a tape nobody but Ambrose has heard yet? It doesn't make sense. So, this is what I suggest. When we get to the Medical Center, you collect the tape from Mike Fallon and call your boss, tell him exactly what I've told you. Believe me, you'll be doing him – and yourselves – a great favor. A very . . . great . . . favor."

They were all strangely quiet as the car turned right at the furniture store, passed down the street of houses set back behind lawns, entered Trinity Street, pulled into the deserted Medical Center and parked in a slot next to Buttercup.

Albatross switched off the engine.

For twenty long seconds no one spoke, no one moved. The only sounds were the click and crack of cooling metal, and the patter of rain on the roof.

Drummond's work was done. He prayed it had been effective.

With a quavery indrawn breath, Peregrine roused himself, tapped Albatross on the shoulder. "Get in the back."

Peregrine got out, tucked the gun into his jacket, waited until Albatross, armed, was seated, then shut the door and walked off towards the rear entrance of the Medical Center.

Karen looked out at her car, murmured, "Nice to see Buttercup again." She sounded bone weary.

"Yes," said Drummond. He turned Albatross, and smiled. "You look very tired. Guess you haven't had much sleep."

Albatross yawned. "Doc . . . shut the fuck up, you talk too much."

Chapter Thirty-Seven

Hurrying across the lot through the slanting rain, Peregrine thought about what Drummond had said. His mind seemed to be filled with what Drummond had said. The guy made sense. The subliminal stuff on the tape might be garbage. Ambrose might be a conman. Or a fruit cake. And if nobody but Ambrose knew what the subliminals were about, what was the point in taking this thing any further?

What he needed to do was call Jackdaw, tell him exactly what Drummond had told him. He'd bet a year's wages Jackdaw didn't know that Karen Beal's father was Sir Edward Beal, England's top cop. Man, what a shit-stink he'd make if she disappeared. Same went for the *LA Times*. You didn't mess with one of their staff reporters and expect them not to notice.

What he'd do, he'd pick up the tape, then call Jackdaw from the car. He'd be doing Jackdaw, and themselves, a great favor. A very . . . great . . . favor.

He entered the building, found the door to the Hypnotherapy Center on his right, went in. The reception area was deserted. A door to his left was partly open. Through it he could hear the voices of two men.

He moved to the door and listened.

One voice, obviously a patient, was saying, ". . . wife has noticed a terrific difference. To be honest, up till now, she's been an unbeliever. She had a bad experience with a stage hypnotist one time, years ago, when she was a student. Like a fool, she volunteered to go up on the stage, and the guy had her crawling around on all-fours, barking like a dog. After that, the kids she was with gave her the nickname Woofy, and it affected her psychologically."

"It can happen. Excuse me, I think I heard somebody come into reception . . ."

"That's okay, Doc, I'll be on my way. So – I'll see you same time next week."

"Friday . . . six o'clock. Thanks, Mister Denny."

Peregrine backed up to the reception desk as the door was opened fully by Mike Fallon, wearing his white coat.

Mister Denny, in a fawn raincoat, offered Peregrine the merest glance, as fellow patients in a therapy situation do, and went past him to the outer door, settling a brown slouch hat on his head.

Mike Fallon regarded Peregrine pleasantly, quizzically. "I'm sorry, sir, I'm afraid the Center is closed now for the weekend."

"Paul Drummond sent me – for the tape?"

"Oh! Yes, of course. Please – come in."

The office was in a state of some disarray, the chairs askance, the desk littered with papers and files.

Mike Fallon fussed about, transferred the files to the top of a metal cabinet, shuffled papers together. "Boy, what a day. Friday's the worst, you know. People get anxious about the weekend. Have you just left Paul?"

"Yes, just now."

"Where is he – up at the house?"

"Yes. He called you from there. If I could have the tape, Doctor, I'm in kind of a hurry."

"Of course." Fallon pulled open a desk drawer. "I am so sorry I couldn't get around to doing it for him." He closed the drawer, opened another. "I did warn him I had a full case-load this afternoon . . ." With a frown of irritation, he shut that drawer, opened a third. "Now, where the devil did I put . . . ah!" He took out a cassette, peered at it, tutted, threw it back into the drawer, shut it, opened a fourth. "Sorry about this, it must seem terribly inefficient . . ."

Peregrine shifted impatiently. The guy was an asshole.

"But it'll give you an idea of how chaotic things have been around here this afternoon . . . ah, gotcha." With an apologetic grin, Fallon handed a cassette over.

Peregrine looked hard into Fallon's bespectacled eyes. "You're sure this is the right one?"

"Absolutely. It's unmarked. All the others here are labelled."

"Doc, make sure." He proferred the tape. "Play some of it for me."

Fallon frowned, surprised by Peregrine's assertiveness. "If you wish."

Opening a desk drawer, he brought out a Panasonic recorder, slipped in the cassette, pressed Play. Errol Garner's thumping intro to "Please Don't Talk About Me When I'm Gone" filled the room.

Peregrine listened to it intently for half a minute. "Where is the subliminal material?"

Fallon smiled. "You can't hear it. If you could, it wouldn't be subliminal."

"Then how does Paul know it's there?"

"Trained ear. Can you hear that whispery hiss in the background?"

"I can hear Garner grunting."

"Behind that."

Peregrine scowled with concentration. "Sort of."

"That's it. When it's put onto a hypnosis music tape, the subconscious picks up the message although the ear doesn't consciously perceive it."

Peregrine nodded. "Okay, Doc, give me the tape."

Fallon rewound it and handed it over.

"Thanks." Peregrine started for door. "Doc, what did Paul tell you about the tape?" He turned to face Fallon.

Fallon shrugged. "Nothing. He just said he wanted the subliminals lifting and transcribing. I was very busy, and he seemed in a hurry, and of course he knew I'd get to know what was on the tape when I did the work."

"Why did you lend him your Cherokee?"

Fallon stared at him. "Because he asked me. Let me ask you a question – why all the questions about Paul? Who are you? Is he in some kind of trouble?"

"Did he say why he needed the Cherokee?"

"Yes. Because he was going up to the lake and didn't want to risk the XR3 on those roads. *Is* Paul in trouble? What's going on, Mister . . .?"

Peregrine nodded. "Okay, Doc. Nice meetin' you."

He went out of the door.

When he emerged, it was raining even harder. Was it possible? He sprinted to the Plymouth and fell into the driver's seat, slamming the door. "Je-*sus*! How do people live up here in this weather? They've gotta be nuts. No wonder Fallon's doin' big business."

Albatross asked, "You got it?"

"Absolutely." He reached for the phone, punched a number. "This is Peregrine . . . give me Jackdaw."

While he waited, Albatross asked him, "Does Fallon know anything?"

"Fallon doesn't know where his ass is. Hey, Doc . . . no offense, but your buddy's a klutz. Took him five minutes to find the goddamn tape."

Drummond nodded. "He tries his best. Mike was never known for his organizing ability."

Jackdaw came on.

"Yeah," said Peregrine. "This is the situation – and you ain't gonna like it . . ."

Two things happened then, with stunning speed. The door Albatross was leaning against, as he sat angled to cover Drummond, opened, and Albatross hurtled

382

backwards, arms flailing, losing the automatic which was plucked from his hand an instant before his head smacked down onto the tarmac.

Simultaneously, a figure loomed up beside Peregrine, the door was jerked open, and a man in a fawn raincoat and a brown slouch hat rammed the muzzle of a .38 revolver into Peregrine's open mouth, and said, "Hang up – please."

Drummond gasped, "Jesus Christ."

Dick Gage grinned. "Not quite, Drum, it's only me. How're yuh doin', buddy?"

Gage told Peregrine, "Get out – ve-ry slowly. Karen, you get out, honey, and bring the keys. You okay over there, Mike?"

Fallon, wearing a khaki parka, covering the recumbent Albatross with the automatic, said, "Terrific."

"Paul, go frisk the punk, make sure he's not carrying in an ankle holster."

When Peregrine was out, Gage patted him down, took his weapon. "Okay, round the back of the car, face-down on the ground, hands behind your head."

Peregrine groaned, "In this rain? Hey, man, this is a thousand-dollar suit."

"You want holes in it?"

With Peregrine and Albatross stretched out, Gage handed Drummond the automatic, then used the keys to unlock the trunk.

"My, my, a reg'lar li'l arsenal." He pulled out the two Starlite rifles and two Uzi machine pistols. "You boys bin hunting something in the mountains? Sure hope you've got licenses for all these toys."

Karen said, "The bags are ours." She repossessed her shoulder bag and the five thousand dollars.

Gage said, "Okay, fellas, climb in here outa the rain."

Peregrine muttered, "Shit."

383

Gage slammed the trunk lid, then sat in the driver's seat, searched the car, found another automatic in a clip under the dash, spare ammunition and the two Tasers in the glove compartment, handed them out to Fallon and Drummond.

"Okay." He climbed out and locked the car. "Let's go to the office, drink hot coffee and think cool strategy." He put his arm around Karen's shoulder and gave her a hug. "Hi, kid. How'd you like Shasta so far?"

They sat around the desk in Fallon's office with steaming mugs of instant coffee, which Fallon had conjured up in the kitchenette behind reception.

Karen sat hunched, the mug cuddled in both hands, staring unfocused through the rising vapor at an unseen spot on the desk.

Gage leaned towards her. "You okay?"

With effort she dragged her eyes from the place and brought him into focus, smiling the lop-sided, spaced-out smile of a drunk. "I'm just absolutely beautiful. I'd be terribly grateful if someone would pinch me and wake me from this crazy dream – but then again, I'll be sorry to leave it. I know you're not really here. I know you couldn't possibly have just *popped* up like that and rescued us. I'd like to kiss you for doing that while I still think you're here."

Gage said, "You go right ahead," and puckered up. She keeled towards him, planted the kiss, and came to rest with her forehead against his.

Fallon cleared his throat. "I, er, don't mean to sound pushy, but I did pop up on the other side."

She smiled benignly. "You certainly did. I'll get to you later. But *how* . . .?" Her shrug begged explanation.

Fallon nodded. "Okay, me first. After you both left here, the full import of what you'd told me hit me. It takes a while for something as potentially big and dangerous as this to sink in. It's like telling somebody, 'Hey, there's going to be an earthquake tomorrow,' and they go 'Yeah? That sounds pretty scary,' and an hour later they go, 'An *earth*quake . . . holy shit!'

"It wasn't until Evelyn Woods came in and told me two guys – those two guys out there – had been into your Dad's office, asking about you and about the Cherokee, that it really got to me. That's when I decided two things: *I* needed to know what was on the tape pronto, not wait until I'd finished for the day, and *you* needed help. You'd told me Dick had warned you to trust nobody, so I couldn't call in the local cops – so I called Dick. Then I called all my Friday afternoon clients, rescheduled them for tomorrow, and got working on the tape."

Drummond stared at him. "You've done it?"

"Sure."

"And? Come *on*, Fallon, what's on it?"

The doctor rolled his eyes. "Oh, man. But let Dick say his piece first."

Gage said, "I was mighty relieved to get Mike's call. You guys were supposed to let me know where you were heading . . ."

Drummond said, "Dick, we couldn't use the car phone, we thought it might be bugged. As it turned out, we were almost right – except it wasn't the phone, it was Karen's tape recorder. When those guys bugged her apartment, they put a bug *and* a homing device in the recorder. That's how they . . ."

"Were able to track you here!" Fallon finished, gratefully enlightened. "And knew about the Cherokee."

"And tracked us up to the lake," said Drummond. "And wait till we tell you what happened up at the lake. But you first, Dick. How did you get up here so fast?"

"By chopper."

"Police chopper?"

"No, private."

Drummond frowned. "I think we owe you."

Gage nodded, winked at Karen, "You can pay me out of the Pulitzer money."

She came alive, all weariness wiped away. "You think?"

"Baby, I *know*. Between what's on the tape, and what I've got to tell you . . ."

"So, tell me, dammit."

"Okay, chronologically. Nine o'clock, Wednesday night. The cop was shot, you get the hell out of there. The traffic was locked tight for fifteen minutes. By the time I reached the scene, it hadn't happened. There was nothing there. My guess is – especially now I know about the homing device – the guys in the van picked up the cop and his motorcycle, and thereby gave you and Drum a chance to get out of range.

"After that, I went home, listened all night to the police frequencies. Nothing. Yesterday, the same. Not a word about a shooting on the coast highway or about a dead or missing cop. Total clampdown. Last night, around six, I dropped into Duke's. I get a phone call. It's Bill Ryman on the Metro desk, worried sick about you, wondering where you are."

Karen smiled. "He's such a dear."

"I told him you were okay – praying you and this big lug *were* okay – that you were following a lead and would be getting in touch with me any time. So he said would I give you a message." Gage's eyes twinkled. "Would I tell you that Ambrose had called and wanted to meet with you urgently."

She flashed a look at Drummond. "*Meet*?"

Gage nodded. "Ryman said Ambrose was going to keep on calling the *Times* until he reached you. So I gave Ryman my home number, and asked him to ask Ambrose to call me, and I'd give him some information about you."

"Did he call?"

"Yep – midnight. The guy was very cagey, used a call box, sounded dreadful."

"Dreadful how?"

"Depressed. Very depressed. We waltzed around for a while, me trying to convince him I was a personal friend and privy to everything that's happened. I told him I knew about the tape and that things had gone wrong at the delivery – and that's when he broke down. I mean, cried. And then he said, 'Those bastards murdered my son. You tell Miss Beal I want to meet with her, to tell her everything, and she can use my real identity when she writes the story. Now I want to nail that evil sonofabitch!'"

She gaped at him, waiting for him to finish. "Which evil sonofabitch?"

Gage's eyes flicked across to Mike Fallon. "You tell her."

Fallon picked up a sheaf of papers and handed them to her. "The transcript. Pulitzer on a platter."

She seized the pages, speed-read through them, frowning, uttering tiny gasps, finally looked up at the men in turn, then settled on Drummond who was waiting with an expression of such contrived patience, she laughed aloud, hysterically.

"It's all here! Just like you said!"

As she handed the pages to him, she became suddenly very sober.

"My God, how frightening. We've got Watergate Two."

Chapter Thirty-Eight

Strategy.

As Drummond dropped the transcript onto the desk, reacting to its revelation with an astounded whistle, Karen asked with an equally astounded laugh, with shock, uncertainty, exhileration, "What are we going to *do*?"

She clutched her forehead. Her eyes were huge and fever-bright. "You know . . . about every month or so at home, somebody wins a fortune on the football pools. The equivalent of three million dollars. And they're usually working class people who've had to struggle all their lives to pay the rent. Suddenly they have all the money in the world . . . and the first question they must ask is: 'What are we going to *do*?' I feel like that right now."

She reached for the transcript. "This is a career fortune. It is *dynamite*. Especially now that Ambrose has agreed to reveal his identity and testify. The *Times* will run this, for sure . . . but, my God, what will it do to the nation? It'll devastate the political scene. Karen Beal, an inconsequential English hack, a guest in this wonderful country, has the power right here in her hands to pitch the presidential election into a state of utter chaos . . . to virtually alter the course of American political history!"

She looked at them, appalled. "I mean, come *on*, fellas. Help me out here. What am I going to *do*?"

Absorbing the impact of her words, attempting also to embrace the awesome potential of a news break, the men

388

exchanged looks and pondered the problem for a long silent moment.

Karen returned to her coffee, murmured into the mug as she sipped from it, "Woodward and Bernstein, where are you when I need you? At least Watergate crept up on you, developed piecemeal. What would you have done if the whole thing had been handed to you in a ten-page synopsis?"

Drummond said, "I think you've hit it on the head there, Karen. They probably wouldn't have been allowed to handle it in that form. They might have got credit, but it would've been taken over by the top brass – and I think that's what you've got to do with this."

Gage said, "I agree. I think what we have to do is set up a meeting with Ambrose, your senior editor, and ourselves, get Ambrose to tell the full story, and let the paper make the decisions from there. They have the clout, the political connections. I don't doubt they'll want to run the story – my God, it's going to sell an awful lot of papers – but things might be arranged behind the scenes to ease the national trauma."

Karen nodded thoughtfully. "Set up a meeting where?"

Drummond answered, "Somewhere safe. We've got to be very careful. Jack Crane probably knows by now that the walls are closing in on him, and the cornered rat fights dirtiest."

Gage frowned. "How d'you figure that – about Crane?"

"Things we haven't told you yet, Dick, that happened up at the lake. Peregrine, the Black in the trunk, wanted proof over the phone that we had the Ambrose tape. I got my Dad to record thirty seconds of bullshit, purporting to be Ambrose, giving an identity of a Sergeant . . . what was his name?"

Karen laughed. "Arnold Breen – served in the Special Forces in Vietnam. It was brilliant."

Gage said, "Incredible. And they bought it?"

389

Drummond nodded. "Apparently – until they caught us and we had to tell them the real tape was here. The point is – Peregrine would undoubtedly have passed the Breen name on to his superiors. They want Ambrose very badly. With their connections, my guess is the V's would go straight to Army Records for Breen's address . . ."

"And find there was no Sergeant Arnold Breen in Special Forces," mused Gage.

"Right. And if they don't know it at this moment, they soon will. Then Jack Crane will know. But there's also something else that's happened that'll tell Crane the boom's being lowered."

"What's that?"

"Peregrine was making a call to someone code-named Jackdaw when you opened the car door and rudely stuck your gun in his mouth. He'd managed to say something like: 'This is the situation and you ain't going to like it'." Drummond turned to Fallon. "He'd just been in here. What was it Peregrine had discovered here that Jackdaw wouldn't like?"

"In view of what you've just told us about the phoney recording and the Sergeant Breen business, I'd say Peregrine was about to tell Jackdaw that the information on Ambrose's tape was subliminal . . . and there was no way you could know Ambrose's real identity."

"Right. So, there's Jackdaw, whoever and wherever he is, listening to Peregrine telling him he ain't going to like the situation, then hears your voice telling Peregrine to hang up, and the line goes dead. Bingo. Jackdaw's killers are in trouble. Jackdaw doesn't even know where his boys are – they made no phone calls to him from the time we left the house. Since we came in here, he may have tried to contact them on the car phone or at the house, but zilch. Ergo, Jackdaw, and therefore Crane, already know things are coming apart. When they learn that Arnold Breen doesn't exist, the doody will really hit the fan."

Dick Gage was nodding, pulling ruminatively at his nose. "Good – Jack Crane is already on the run. And bad – he's going to be more desperate than ever to silence you and Ambrose and recover the tape."

"If he can find us," said Drummond. "He doesn't have the homing device working for him now."

"How did you find out about that?" Gage heaved a sigh. "Look, you'd better fill me in about what happened up at the lake, so's I have a full picture to work on. I'm going to have to plan this carefully, make calls, pull strings, and I need all the facts."

Drummond said, "You sound like Jack Webb. Okay, you won't believe this, but here goes."

The lieutenant and Mike Fallon remained silent, dumbstruck, exchanging looks of blank astonishment as Drummond concisely reprised the action.

Gage stared at him, at Karen. "It's a screenplay for a B-movie. A fucking *crossbow* – excuse me, sweetheart. You actually shot a killer with a crossbow?"

Drummond shrugged. "It was all I had."

Karen laughed. "Oh, boy. Such cool. Dick, he was bloody marvellous."

Drummond said, "Guys, I was scared witless. I went on pure adrenalin. Even thinking about it now makes me quake."

"Well, I think you're both incredible – and your folks," said Gage. "Drum, phone them now at the Bensons, tell them to stay there, not to go back to the house under any circumstances. When Jackdaw comes looking for his goons, the house is one place they'll look."

Drummond got up to use the phone.

While he dialled and talked, Karen asked the lieutenant, "What are we going to do with the twosome in the trunk?"

Gage grunted. "Drive them into the nearest lake." He rubbed at his forehead. "I've been giving them some thought. They could be very useful to us as a lever, maybe with information about Jackdaw and his connections. I'm going to fly them back to LA, book them as material witnesses to the shooting on the coast highway, tuck them away for a few days in Hollywood or Pacific divisions, keep them incommunicado."

"Dick, that shooting – when Ambrose said they'd murdered his son, did he mean the cop, the messenger?"

"That's how I took it. But the man wasn't a cop, I'm certain. Even Crane couldn't have covered up the murder of a police officer. Anyway, we'll find out for sure when we speak to Ambrose. And we'll find out for sure what those bastards did with the body."

Drummond rang off. "Everything's cool. Dad says his practice is going to be extremely boring after this. He's getting more like Mad Harry every year."

Gage got to his feet. "My turn to make phone calls. We'll hire a chopper, fly back to LA, get the punks locked away, you'll sleep tonight at my place. Then we'll contact Ambrose and your editor, arrange a meet for sometime tomorrow."

Drummond said, "Mike, I wish you were coming with us. They might come around here looking for these two guys."

Fallon shook his head. "I'll be okay. From what you said, Peregrine didn't get a chance to tell Jackdaw about me. If they come to the Center, I don't know a damn thing. But, hey," he grinned, "I'd have loved to come with you. Your Dad's right, it's going to be mighty dull around here after this."

"Well," said Drummond, "it ain't over yet. And I reckon there's going to be plenty of excitement for everybody before it is."

"Yes," said Karen, swept again by the enormity of what they were about to set loose. "For everybody."

392

Chapter Thirty-Nine

In the Operations Room of his cliff-top home, situated on the perimeter of Fort Ord Military Reservation to the north of the Monterey Peninsula, Frank Elgin, code-named Jackdaw for this operation, put down the phone on a call that had turned his guts to prune juice.

Seldom afraid, even less seldom panicked, the information he'd just received from his contact at Army Records momentarily paralyzed him.

A tall, rangey, iron-muscled man of fifty-five, with close-cropped, salt-and-pepper hair, and the bony, deeply-lined, wolverine physiognomy of an ageing warrior, he sat in his leather executive chair and stared at his own reflection in the huge plate-glass window, transformed into mirror by the blackness of the stormy California night.

A veteran of countless official and unofficial operations, overt and covert, in thirty-two countries, he was no stranger to failure, to aborted missions, to unbelievable fuck-ups due to erroneous information, human error and acts of God, but none had assumed the importance or had carried the dire consequences of the failure he now sensed was rushing towards him – as unavoidable and lethal as a heat-seeking missile.

The operation had seemed so simple.

Tom Keegan – in one of those acts of God – had suddenly surfaced in a bank robbery caper. LAPD got interested, called in Drummond, and out came the Trice jingle.

Silence Keegan.

Simple.

Then that cunt on the *LA Times* had gotten interested, and up had come Ambrose. And the tape.

Get the tape. Silence Ambrose.

Simple.

He'd put twenty men into the field to find Drummond, Beal and the tape.

Peregrine, one of the best, had phoned from Whiskeytown that he had them cornered, had heard a piece of the tape, and had given him Arnold Breen.

Simple.

Then the last call . . . weird. "This is the situation and you ain't going to like it." And the other voice: "Hang up – please."

Who the fuck was that?

What the fuck had happened?

Where the fuck had Peregrine called from?

Jackdaw had called the Drummond house, called the car.

Nothing.

And just now – the call from Records.

There never had been a Sergeant Arnold Breen in Special Forces, serving in Vietnam '69 to '72.

Was the tape Peregrine had heard genuine?

Had Ambrose given Beal a false identity to protect his ass?

But why bother to give any identity? Why not just his explanation about Trice?

Most of all – where were Peregrine and those other three morons?

WHAT THE FUCK WAS GOING ON?

Jackdaw came out of the chair, strode across the huge, pine-panelled room, entered a corridor and pulled open the door of his Communications Room.

His son, Brad, a physical clone, was sprawled in a

394

chair at the console, surrounded by an array of highly sophisticated radio, telecommunication and electronic equipment.

"Anything?" Jackdaw knew there was nothing, that Brad would have punched through any incoming calls, but Jackdaw needed the movement, needed to talk.

Brad shook his head.

Jackdaw dropped onto a leather couch. "Something's wrong. I can go with the Arnold Breen crap, that could be Ambrose playing games. But that last call from Peregrine scares the shit outa me."

"How about we try Seagull and Blackbird in the van?"

"Yeah, do it."

Brad roused himself, punched buttons.

A voice came over the intercom. "Yo?"

"Blackbird?"

"Yeah."

Jackdaw took over. "This is Jackdaw, where are you?"

"Paradise."

Jackdaw stared at his son. "The asshole's on something. Blackbird, you answer me! Where the fuck are you?"

"I'm in Paradise! On State Seventy. Heading for Tahoe."

Jackdaw experienced a rush of relief. "You got them."

"Got who?"

The relief turned to a mush of renewed dread. "Well, who'd you think – Drummond and the girl . . ."

"Hell, no. Didn't Peregrine call you?"

"About what?"

"What went down at the house. Drummond shot Seagull with a freakin' crossbow! He's hurt bad. I'm taking him to Tahoe for treatment."

Jackdaw clutched his head, tried to calm the ocean roar of panic that inundated his mind. "Okay . . . nice 'n easy . . . tell me exactly what happened at the house."

When Blackbird had finished, Jackdaw said with ominous restraint, "Okay, take Seagull in."

Brad severed the connection.

Jackdaw said, "Try the car again."

A stranger's voice answered, "Peregrine."

Jackdaw's blood sang in his ears. "You're not Peregrine."

"Is that Jackdaw?"

"Who the hell are you?"

Driving the Plymouth out of the Medical Center, Dick Gage grinned at Drummond, seated beside him, said into the phone, "I asked first. Are you Jackdaw?"

"Yes."

"Well, I'm a police officer, Jackdaw. I want you to know the game is over, finished, kaput. I've arrested your two goons, Peregrine and Albatross. Doctor Drummond and Miss Beal are in safe custody, somewhere where you'll never find them. So, if I were you, I'd forget all about the Trice affair and everybody on the good guys' side connected with it. Look out for your own ass, my friend . . . Jack Crane is going to be a mite peeved with you."

Jackdaw said to his son, "Get me Polo."

When the voice answered, Jackdaw said, "I have to tell you our mutual friend is in deep trouble. The Trice thing has got away from him. It is my sincere opinion that he's about to become a very real embarrassment."

There was a protracted pause. "Thank you for letting us know. Should house-cleaning be required, do you wish to handle it?"

"It would be my pleasure."

"I'll get back to you."

Chapter Forty

Saturday.
   Eight pm.
   Venice, Los Angeles.

It took a dozen phone calls throughout the day to bring it together. Ambrose was being extremely cautious, made many stipulations, including physical sight of Karen and her identification, before he was sufficiently convinced that the people he was about to meet were who they claimed to be. Even then, to her dismay, he appeared beside her rented car, at the place in Santa Monica he himself had stipulated for the identification, armed with a .357 magnum.

Finally they were assembled in the Marina Del Rey apartment of George Serl, editor of the Metro section of the Los Angeles Times.

Present were Ambrose, Serl, Karen, Drummond and Dick Gage.

Serl, a tanned, balding, genial widower of forty-five, who lived to edit and to sail, had offered his apartment for the meeting when Karen had outlined the situation to him early that morning. Though cautious, Serl was nevertheless very excited about the potential of the story, and without reservation had agreed to give Karen full credit at publication, regardless of eventual authorship.

Serl, Drummond and Gage were already at the apartment when Ambrose and Karen arrived.

Ambrose was Black, and huge, six feet five, two-eighty, all of it bone and muscle. He wore blue denim, shirt and pants, with a battered suede jacket barely concealing his shoulder holster.

Drummond studied him closely as he entered the living room, his bulk dominating it. In his mid-fifties, Ambrose appeared extremely fit, Army fit. He radiated a physical threat that reached out immediately to the other men. From the corner of his eye, Drummond saw Dick Gage take a defensive step back, his right hand making a reflexive twitch in the direction of his own hidden shoulder holster. And yet, behind the giant's facade of grim toughness, behind the scanning, watchful eyes, Drummond detected a center of gentleness and sadness that somewhat calmed his apprehension about the man.

Drummond made the first move. He offered his hand. "Hello, I'm Paul Drummond. I was in the car with Karen . . ."

"Sure. Glad to meet you, Doctor."

"This is George Serl, Karen's editor on Metro. And Lieutenant Dick Gage, LAPD, West LA Homicide. You've spoken to him, of course. Dick's not here as a cop, he's an old and trusted friend who tried to help Tom Keegan.

Ambrose shook hands with both men.

When Serl invited everyone to be seated, Ambrose seemed to choose a chair with instinctive care, away from the curtained window, and one from which he could see the door.

Serl offered drinks or coffee. Everyone chose coffee, and he dispensed it from a Cona flask.

Drummond said to Ambrose, "Before we start, I'd like to ask you what you meant when you told Dick 'they'd' murdered your son. Was he the messenger who delivered the tape? Was he really a police officer?"

Ambrose looked down at his interlocked fingers. A

great heaviness bowed his massive shoulders, and he drew a sigh. When he spoke, his voice rumbled deeply like an angry animal's growl. "He was my son. He was a cop, one time, in Seattle, but he got hurt and retired. He has . . . had a small radio and electronics shop in Inglewood I help out in. It was his idea to dress up like a cop, as the best means of stopping you on the highway. He was wired, for my benefit, so's I could hear what was going down. I was in a car a mile behind him."

"You heard the shooting?"

Ambrose nodded. "How did those bastards know he was delivering the tape?"

Karen said, "We were wired, too, though we didn't know it. I think, maybe, we'd better tell you the how, what and why of everything that's happened since we last spoke to you on Wednesday night, to help you get things into perspective. It might also help towards recovering your son's body. We assume it hasn't been recovered?"

Ambrose shook his head. "That's one of the things that've been tearing me apart. I'd like to hear what you have to say."

Between them, Karen, Drummond and Gage covered the events of the two days.

Before they had properly finished, Ambrose's face was contorted with deep anger, and tears glistened in his eyes. "Those sonsabitches. Look . . . let's forget what I put on the tape. That was the bare bones of it." He looked directly at George Serl, then at Karen. "I want to give you the whole story. I am just so *sick* at what's going on in this country, at what these . . . men are doing to the people, and have been doing for a helluva long time. If only your paper could let the public know what's going on . . ."

George Serl said, "That's what our paper does, Ambrose – that's it's reason for being."

"Yeah, I know, but you guys have got to be careful.

399

You need corroboration, records, proof . . . and these people are masters of the cover-up. They make records, and people, disappear. They're above the law. They can do anything they damn-well want."

Serl was nodding. "I know. But trust me to do everything we possibly can. On your tape you made some incredible allegations. A presidential candidate is involved. You give us the full story and we'll check everything that it's possible to check, and, believe me, if we can find a way, we'll go with the story."

Ambrose sighed deeply, gathered himself. "You'll want to record this."

Serl got up, went to a bookshelf, brought back and set up two Sony recorders.

"When you're ready."

Ambrose began.

"My real name is Wendell Curry. That's the name the Army knows me by, but I've been using false ID since I left it. I'll get to why in a minute. I was born in Asheville, North Carolina, in 'Thirty five. My father worked on the railroad, my mother was a cleaner in a hospital. She wanted to be a nurse but didn't have the education. But through her I got interested in mind/body subjects, dreamed of being a doctor or a psychologist, which for a Black kid in those days was as likely as being president.

"My dad joined the Army in 'Forty-three, got killed in Italy. I was eight, had a sister, six, and a brother, four. Mom was crazy about education, way ahead of her time. She borrowed books from the hospital, taught us kids far more than any school. I'm giving you this personal stuff because it's checkable, and may help you to believe the unbelievable when I get to it."

George Serl said, "We welcome it, Wendell – may we call you Wendell? It gives the story substance. You tell it as you want."

"As a family, we got lucky. Mom transferred to the VA hospital and met an Army doctor, a real enlightened guy, who supported her ambition for us kids, lent her all kinds of books, even paid for some private tuition for us. I made it to college in Winston-Salem, played a lot of football, won a scholarship to NC State in Raleigh, majored in Chemistry, and by the time I graduated had developed a real interest in biological warfare. I joined the Army in 'Fifty-nine."

Curry paused to drink some coffee. His big hands were steady as he raised the mug. Drummond sensed that he was beginning to relax with the people in the room, to concentrate on the story he was telling, to embrace fully the opportunity to tell it. Drummond saw abreaction at work here, the out pouring of bad memories, a cleansing of the soul. Curry was about to rid his psyche of a lot of dark, long-held secrets, the burden of ancient, crippling guilt.

Curry continued. "After basic training, I took a long, intensive course in CBR – chemical, biological and radiological warfare – at the Army Chemical School, Edgewood, Maryland."

Drummond and Karen exchanged looks.

Curry said, "They really got to us there. Brainwashed us. Frightened the shit out of us – about what the enemy was about to do to us. About his capability and intention. This whole thing has to be seen in the light of those times. This country was *paranoid* about Communism. The Cold War was raging. In 'Fifty-nine we sent military advisers to Vietnam. Early in 'Sixty, MAAG – the US Military Assistance Advisory Group – began strengthening our numbers out there. What I'm saying is, Vietnam really began that early, even though we didn't send actual troops there until 'Sixty-two. And believe me, the spooks – the Intelligence people, were in there long before that. Those guys were *always* there, from right after World War Two.

401

"Okay, so there we were at Edgewood." He paused, brow-furrowed, searching for the words. "I guess it just creeps up on you . . . this unconcern for human misery, for human life. You're a soldier, a professional. You take an oath to uphold this and defend that, to protect your country against its enemies. You learn to obey orders without question. Lines of morality get blurred . . . very blurred. Then they disappear altogether."

Curry looked up at them, each in turn. "In the cause of national security, I became party to things which, in retrospect, I'm deeply ashamed of. And I'm not talking about things done to the enemy – real or imagined – I'm talking about things done to Americans. To our own servicemen, our own people.

"Believe this – this country is controlled by the military, allied with the multinationals. Maybe two or three dozen guys have got the US of A right here." He balled his right hand into an iron fist. "What the Pentagon says, goes. And what it was saying in the 'Fifties through to the 'Seventies was – *mind control.*

"What with all the rumors about Communist brain-washing of military and political prisoners, they really believed the Commies were light-years ahead of us in the field of Mind Control, and the paranoid Pentagon launched a massive counter-offensive with research into drugs, hypnosis, radionics, ultrasonics, you name it. Nobody will ever know how much tax-payers' money was allocated for the program, handed out in research grants to hospitals, psychiatric hospitals, universities, military and civil scientific departments, what have you. If there ever were records of expenditure, you can bet they no longer exist. But by today's value, it has to be billions."

Drummond asked, "And you walked right into this paranoia when you arrived at Edgewood?"

Curry gave a mirthless laugh. "Oh, man. You could cut

402

it with a knife. You'd have thought the Commies were lined up a hundred deep around the perimeter, armed with syringes and ultrasonic death-ray machines, about to boil our brains. The irony of it was, we were as good as, if not better than, the Communists at Mind Control right then, and Edgewood hit us with everything it had. Within a couple of weeks we were all seeing Reds under every bed, behind every bush, even among ourselves. We were mind-raped, no doubt about it. That's when the morality lines began to blur. No experiment, no test, no treatment was too extreme if it furthered the cause of national security. Even a human life, an American human life, was a fair price to pay for the cause."

George Serl asked, "Did you personally witness the death of any innocent person during these experiments?"

"Not at Edgewood. We were in training. If anything went wrong, a guy took a bad drug trip or came out of hypnosis or ultrasonic treatment looking weird, he disappeared. But later on, in the field, in this country and abroad, I saw a lot of deaths."

"Did you cause any?"

Curry nodded. "Of course. I was a soldier. I obeyed orders."

Drummond said, "Wendell, can you give us some examples of the kind of experiments you did at Edgewood?"

"The lab boys were coming up with new drugs all the time. I guess over the years I must have participated in the testing of two hundred or more. Psychopharmacology was really coming into its own by the 'Sixties. We had drugs to distort, accelerate, or depress the mental state and behavioral characteristics of a person, with a highly selective action on particular parts of the nervous system. So we tested for control of aggression, pacification, suggestibility, memory, all kinds of things.

"Then we used drugs combined with various techniques

of hypnosis – live voice, taped voice, post-hypnotic suggestion, multi-level activation."

Drummond asked, "For what purposes?"

Curry shrugged. "For the training of assassins . . . spies. If someone wanted a secret message carried outside the chain of command, we could hypno-program a guy, improve his memory so that he could carry a whole book of code, then give him amnesia and seal off the message with a post-hypnotic code word. If he was captured, he could be tortured to death but he wouldn't remember anything about the message. Even if the enemy used hypnosis, the message would be buried under several layers of hypnotic command. The right words had to be used to trigger his memory, and the enemy might take years to find those."

"And the assassins?" asked Dick Gage.

"There are certain areas of the brain that control our inhibitions. When those are controlled, the subject will carry out his assignment, whatever it is. We conditioned men to do it in such a way that they experienced no guilt. They had no guilt because, after the job, they had no memory of doing it." Curry's mouth twisted in a tight smile. "Kinda makes you wonder about those political assassinations in the 'Sixties, doesn't it?"

Drummond said, "You also mentioned radionics . . . ultrasonics."

"Yes. The Pentagon was manic about that field. I believe they had visions of a cyborg army, a million guys with electrodes implanted in their mastoid sinuses, transformable from ordinary Joes into kamikaze killers at the flick of a switch. Quite feasible, of course. Emotions can be produced by artificial radio signals.

"Another use for radionics was EDOM – electronic dissolution of memory. There's a chemical in the brain called acetylcholine. It carries electrical impulses from the eyes, ears, nose, and the nerve endings to the part of the brain where the memory is located. Memory is a recording of these electrical impulses. By electronically jamming the brain, acetylcholine creates static which blocks out sights and sounds. A guy would then have no memory of what he'd seen or heard. His mind would be blank."

Again, Drummond and Karen exchanged looks.

She said, "Tom Keegan."

Curry said, "Yeah, Tom, but we'll get to him later. I'm giving you this background so's you'll understand what happened to him. Let's get to Vietnam."

He rubbed a hand over his gray-flecked, curly hair. "Y'know, it beats the hell outa me how Jack Crane could've got as far as he has without being exposed for the goddamned phoney he is. I'll tell you, that guy is as near as you can get to being a Pentagon cyborg without the implantation of an electrode – and I wouldn't bet they *haven't* stuck one in his head.

"Crane is a Pentagon creation, through and through. For twenty-five years he's been molded by the military for the White House. You think they don't want a President who's totally in rapport with their aims and ambitions, who'll give them everything they want? They've built that guy into a super-hero. Take a look at his military record – the one available for public inspection, that is – and what d'you see? You see a regular soldier who's served his country with distinction, and whose swan-song just before retirement was a Medal-of-Honor rescue of his men from behind enemy lines. Well . . . bullshit.

"Jack Crane was in Military Intelligence all along. He was in and out of Vietnam more times than the Viet Cong. He changed uniforms more times than a Marine grunt in a wet Delta operation. He could be anything he wanted to be. You remember our declared aim in Vietnam: 'To win the hearts and minds of the people'? Well, Jack Crane was after their minds, all right – by any means at our disposal . . . drugs, hypnosis, radionics, whatever. The guy wasn't a soldier, he was a spook. And that glorious rescue operation just didn't happen. It was a total Pentagon fabrication."

Karen said, "You sound so positive. How d'you know all this?"

He looked at her with eyes that conveyed gentleness and deep sadness. "Because for much of the time I was with him."

Curry reached for his coffee and drank some, his gaze centering on the table, perhaps seeing a vision of those by-gone days.

"I first met Crane at Edgewood in 'Sixty-one. He'd brought in a batch of fifty volunteers from units all round the country."

"Volunteers?" queried Serl.

"Army personnel. They'd be offered two, three weeks easy living to undergo certain tests. There were always plenty of volunteers, usually no more than one or two from a unit in case anything went wrong. They were hardly ever told, truthfully, what the tests would involve."

Karen frowned. "They were deliberately lied to?"

Curry smiled. "Hell, yes. This was, after all, a national security matter. You don't go giving out information about secret drugs."

"What about their Army records . . . laboratory records?"

"Their Army records could be falsified, left blank, or destroyed later in a computerization up-date, any damn thing. Lab records? You tell me."

Drummond asked, "On this first occasion when you met Crane, what tests was he interested in making?"

"The effects of the drug Bulpocapnine. It's an alkaloid, affects the central nervous system and cerebral cortex, causes catatonia or stupor. Crane wanted the men tested for loss of speech, memory, will power, sensitivity to pain. It was very effective."

Karen grimaced in protest. "And these were American

406

soldiers? Volunteers who didn't know what they were getting into?"

"Right. I got to know Crane pretty well during that visit. Man, that was one hard sonofabitch. Jesus, when I think about the total bullshit the media has spewed out about how much he loved his men and how they'd follow him into Hell itself, I want to throw up. He had no 'men'. What he had was a license to be anything he wanted to be, go anywhere he wanted to go, do anything he damn-well pleased. He was a spook, with a free pass from God. Or a couple of dozen Gods."

Serl asked, "Where did you work besides Edgewood?"

"All over – the country and the world. I went to Vietnam the first time in 'Sixty-three, part of a small technical group headed by Crane. The place was in turmoil, Buddhist riots all over the country, guys burning themselves to death in the street. Crane seemed right at home."

"What was the purpose of the visit?"

"To test a drug called Anectine in field conditions – meaning on the Viet Cong. The ARVN – the South Vietnam Army – had a bunch of prisoners they felt had information about the Cong's plans for a push from Cambodia. Our local spooks asked Crane for help."

"And he gave it."

"Damn right. Anectine is an evil little mother. It's a powerful muscle relaxant, leaves the victim totally without involuntary muscle control. The body lets loose its waste, breathing stops, and unless the drug is counteracted, the guy dies. The trick is to keep him just alive. He experiences sensations of suffocation and drowning, deep horror, terror, as though he was slipping over the brink into death. Bring him back from that and he's liable to tell you everything you want to know."

Karen groaned in disgust. "I feel ill just thinking about it. And Anectine was used in this country . . . on volunteers?"

"Not only on volunteers. It was tested on guys who didn't know they were getting it. Prisoners in jails, that kind of thing, for behavior modification, to make them better citizens."

George Serl asked, "What other field experiences did you have with Jack Crane?"

"Mostly they were concerned with behavior modification and control. The government was scared of numbers – the hordes that the Commies could put into the field, not only in Vietnam but all over. They figured what we needed to counteract the problem was an incapacitating agent that we could put into the enemy's water supply or spray from the air, knock them out in large numbers, win a bloodless war. It sounded great in theory. We did a lot of research on this at Edgewood, came up with a drug known as 'BZ', a hallucinogenic, ten times more powerful than LSD. We tried it out on more than two thousand volunteers at Edgewood, then took it into Vietnam."

"With what result?" asked Drummond.

"It was inconclusive. Too many logistical problems connected with population distribution, weather, water supply. The stuff worked okay, the problem was application."

"What was the effect of BZ on the victim?"

"Chaotic. They lost all normal competency. Most of the volunteers, trained soldiers, couldn't follow the simplest instructions. They fell down laughing, giggled helplessly for hours on end. This was followed by long periods of amnesia."

Yet again, Drummond conferred with Karen. "Tom Keegan's dream and hypnosis recall – men in green uniforms falling down laughing." To Curry, he said, "To your knowledge, did Keegan witness a scene like that – either at Edgewood or in Vietnam?"

"Okay, let's get to Tom. But first . . ." Curry stood, "I have to use your bathroom."

Serl got up. "Of course. Down the corridor, first on the right."

Serl stopped the recorders, turned the tapes. As he refilled the coffee mugs, he said, "Can you *believe* this stuff?"

Drummond nodded. "Personally, yes."

"He sounds thoroughly genuine," said Karen. "It's too horrifying to be made up."

Gage said, "We'll check the tape with the Psychological Stress Evaluator, but I'd say he's telling the truth – at least as he knows it."

Karen said, "My God, George, what a story. And Jack Crane is virtually our . . . your next President."

They heard the toilet flush and went silent.

Curry emerged, smiling at them ruefully as he sat down. "I know, you're trying to decide if this is the truth or I've been BZ-ed. Well, that's another story, but let's get to Tom Keegan.

"I first met Tom early 'Sixty-nine. He'd done his basic at Bragg and came straight to Edgewood. He was a brilliant chemist. First off, he was really keen. We had the best lab facilities in the world up there, and Tom was like a kid in a toyshop. He did some important research on defoliants, herbicides, and biological agents. But then he was brought into the mind control area, and the human experiments we were doing shocked him. He said he didn't want any part of them, that he'd rather be the box pusher that his army record said he was."

Drummond said, "That agrees with what Keegan's aunt told Karen and me. She said Tom was dismayed that he'd joined up for science and technology and been made a supply clerk. She also said that when he came home for his father's funeral, he seemed strange, that he'd grown spiritually older, as though he'd seen things no man should ever see. Her words. She's still very Irish."

Curry nodded. "Yeah, well, Irish or not, she was right.

Tom wasn't cut out for that kind of crap. But they got to him, hammered home loyalty, duty, and the terrors of Communism, and gradually he became just de-sensitized enough to carry on."

"Doing what?" asked George Serl.

"All kinds of shit. The Pentagon was heavily into what they called 'harassing agents' – chemicals that cause incredible headaches, vomiting, and severe pain. Tom hated it all, he was a really nice guy, wouldn't hurt a fly, yet here he was inflicting this mayhem on other nice guys in the name of national security. Hey, tell me we're not all brainwashed by our own government."

Karen said, "His Aunt Cissie said she didn't see him for two years after his father's funeral, and that she received his first letter from Vietnam at Christmas, 'Sixty-nine."

Curry rubbed his brow, recalling. "That'd be right. He'd put in almost a year at Edgewood before we took him into the field. He was in and out of 'Nam a lot during the next two years."

"Always as part of a Jack Crane team?" asked Serl.

"Always. Crane insisted on the best available talent, and Tom was the best."

Drummond said, "But what would he, you all, actually do out there?"

"All kinds of experiments, mostly covert on our own men, overt on captured Viet Cong. Most of the drugs we experimented with were odorless, colorless, tasteless, totally undetectable. They could be administered in food or drink, inhaled by spray or applied on the skin. We would experiment with personnel in situations of varying degrees of danger, observe their reactions, their response to orders, test the duration of the drug."

"But how did you manage to get close enough to the men to do it? You surely didn't arrive with Army Chemical Center Human Guinea Pig Research Team stencilled on your jackets?"

410

Curry grinned. "No, Doc. We usually took volunteers in, went in as Army psychologists. Those guys were always dropping in and out of units."

"Were there many drug misfires, Wendell?"

"A few."

"Deaths?"

"Other than Trice? A couple."

George Serl said, "Okay, let's get to Trice. I'd like to hear it live, right from the top, as detailed as you can."

Curry drew a sigh, settled himself mentally. "Late 'Seventy-one, things were going from worse to disastrous in Vietnam, and the Pentagon was adding a lot of panic to its paranoia. America was about to lose its first war – to a bunch of peasants in black pajamas, the way most people saw it.

"Tom Keegan had been working on an approach to mind control by inducing molecular changes in the biologically active substances in the brain. RNA – ribosenucleic acid – was the one he was targeting because a change in it would mean a change in the proteins being formed, and would provoke enzyme changes in units of the central nervous system.

"Tom and the team came up with a substance called Tricyanoprope, and began to test it in the lab. Immediately there were indications that the stuff increased suggestibility, and Jack Crane ordered it out to Vietnam for field tests. Tom objected, said he didn't like certain negative aspects that preceded the suggestibility phase."

"Such as what?" asked Drummond.

"Such as a type of mania, hysteria. The volunteers got wildly happy, tried to climb walls, swing on lamps. They wrestled with one another, I mean threw each other around the room. A couple of guys got hurt. But Crane wouldn't listen. He was obviously under pressure to win something in 'Nam that wasn't winnable. So we went out.

411

"The Highlands in Vietnam were a bad place, I mean real spooky. Mountains covered in mist and dense jungle. There could be ten thousand Cong half a mile away and you wouldn't see them. The guys hated the Highlands, they were terrified of them. So Crane figured it was a good place to try the Tricyanoprope. We took out a company of one hundred and twenty volunteers, most of them with some jungle experience. It was all top secret. None of the regular Army or Marine guys knew we were there, or if they did, they asked no questions. National security ruled. The power he had, I reckon Crane was acting on orders from the very top.

"We set up camp under canvas. The weather was atrocious, raining and cold. Crane had told the men they were there on a special endurance trial, to try out new revolutionary C-rations that would make them less pervious to the elements and to fear."

Drummond frowned. "And they all believed that?"

"Listen, Doc . . . when Jack Crane tells you something, you believe it. That's the danger of the guy. Look what he's telling the entire nation right now – JACK CRANE AIN'T ABOUT TO LET IT HAPPEN – and they're lapping it up. And two, four, six years down the line when he's telling us – WE GOTTA NUKE THE BASTARDS FIRST! – we'll still be lapping it up."

Drummond nodded. "Go on, Wendell."

"So – he gave them a few days to get good an' wet and cold and scared, sent them out on long patrols, got them bitching real good, and then brought them all together and presented them with the 'special C's'."

Curry shook his head. "Man, I can see it now. It was early evening, just getting dark. The rain had stopped. One hundred and twenty guys sitting there, wearing green fatigues, helmets, no flak jackets because there'd been no contact with the Cong since we arrived, but all armed with automatic weapons and grenades. Crane giving them

412

the spiel as he hands out the rations. And they started eating.

"It began with one guy who called out, 'What's in the C's, sir?' And Crane said, 'The name's a bigger mouthful than the rations. We call it Trice.' And the guy cracks, 'Hey, Trice is nice!' There were a lot of jokes about Trice Crispies and Tricicles, and then another guy called out, 'It will be nice when Charlie's on ice,' meaning when the Cong were all dead. And then the jokes really started flying, 'That'll just take a trice,' and 'It'll be real nice in a trice when Charlie's on ice,' and they kicked it around, breaking up with every new version, until somebody came up with a rhythm, snapping his fingers, 'In a Trice, it will be nice . . . Charlie will be put on ice!'

"That really got to them – as the Tricyanoprope was doing. Can you hear it? A hundred and twenty guys all snapping their fingers and chanting, 'In a Trice, it will be nice . . . Charlie will be put on ice,' and laughing, killing themselves laughing, falling over, standing up and jiving around, standing up and falling down, crawling around on all fours, helpless with laughter, hysterical with it, one guy starting to climb a tree, a guy named Marty who Tom said was from his home town, climbing this tall tree like a monkey, going up like he was on strings. And the other guys going crazy, really spaced out, starting to kibbitz with one another, pushing, boxing, wrestling, like they were celebrating a big football win; real, real happy."

He drew a deep, shuddery breath, and for a moment there was silence in the room. "Then suddenly they weren't so happy any more. The mood changed just like that." He snapped his fingers. "They were angry. They were really goddamned mad. A fight started. Others joined in. And in maybe five seconds they were all into it. I saw Tom yell something at Jack Crane but he was standing there wide-eyed, loving it, thinking he'd got lucky, that Tricyanoprope had turned out to be some

413

fucking secret weapon that transformed nice happy guys into stone aggressors.

"But he lost that look when the first shot was fired and Marty came hurtling down out of the tree. After that . . . oh, man . . . it was a nightmare. What in hell got into those guys' minds can only be guessed at. Maybe they hallucinated, thought the Cong had shot Marty, thought all the other guys were VC's, there in the near-dark, I don't know. But they slaughtered each other. They just stood there, yelling and screaming and totally unafraid and emptied clips into each other.

"Tom Keegan was standing paralyzed, watching it, so I grabbed him and hauled him off into the jungle and kept him quiet until all the shooting was done. It didn't take long. In maybe two, three minutes it was all over, and then there was silence like you've never heard, up there on the mountain. I left Tom hidden and crept back. Jack Crane was standing there, on the edge of jungle, looking at that bloody mess with, I swear to God, no more than disappointment on his face. He looked at me with those diamond-cutter eyes and said, 'In war, men die. This was a Cong ambush. Trice never happened.'"

George Serl murmured, "Jesus Christ. Our next President."

"Yessir."

Drummond said, "And Tom Keegan?"

"Was in a real bad way. When we got back to Edgewood, he disappeared. I was told he'd had a nervous breakdown and was hospitalized. I never saw him again. I can guess what happened. They microwaved his brain, scrubbed his memory."

"Only not quite.

Curry nodded. "Yeah, not quite."

"And you?"

Curry smiled. "They tried. But I'm the guy that invented

the game. I got out, took a new ID, scrubbed my own memory."

"Until they killed your son."

A terrible sadness wiped away the smile. "Yes." He gestured to the recorders. "Well, there it is. It's the truth. And it's yours. Do with it what you think is best."

Karen said, "We owe you five thousand dollars."

Curry looked at her and shook his head. "I'll settle for a whole lot more. Just find a way to stop Jack Crane."

Chapter Forty-One

Sunday.
Six pm.
Los Angeles.

From the morning room in Leo Krantz's twenty-million dollar Bel Air mansion, Jack Crane stared out of the French doors at the lavish Romanesque swimming pool, not seeing its overblown ornateness and pretentious statuary, the target of much good-natured ribbing by Leo's equally wealthy and powerful friends, but listening to his aide, Karl Hoffman, on the secure phone behind him, trying yet again to raise Jackdaw.

Something was wrong.

Trained in political sensitivity to the rightness of things, to the tone of a voice, to the response from both enemies and friends, he could feel an awryness in the air as surely as he could sense the atmospheric stillness and heaviness of an approaching storm.

The last contact with Jackdaw had been Friday night. His men had Drummond and Beal trapped in the house at the lake. Drummond had given them the name Arnold Breen. Crane didn't remember any Breen, but Edgewood was vast and Tricyanoprope in itself had been known by at least a hundred people. Only the Trice episode was an absolute secret, for the eyes of top brass only. Apart from Crane, Tom Keegan and Wendell Curry had been the only witnesses to what had happened, and they were both out of it, Curry long-dead in a boat explosion.

So who in hell was Arnold Breen?

Did Breen really know anything about Trice? . . . really know Tom Keegan? Or was it some kind of scam?

Why was it taking Jackdaw so long to get back to him? By now he should have located Breen, should've had the tape, should've reported that Drummond and Beal were tucked away in Tahoe. What in hell was going on?

Maybe their contact at Records was off duty at the weekend?

Maybe Jackdaw was waiting until it was all neatly tied up before reporting in? Yeah, maybe that was it.

But why couldn't they raise Jackdaw by phone?

Crane was pervaded by an overwhelming weariness. The long, long campaign had been gruelling; three years of party dinners, forums, caucuses, primaries, national conventions, and then months of nonstop jet travel on the stump. In the previous twenty-four hours alone he'd flown six thousand miles and made four major speeches. Landing at LAX at midnight, he'd come straight to Bel Air, to the house his industrialist friend Leo Krantz had loaned him, to prepare for the TV debate, scheduled for eight o'clock, in two hours time. After only four hours sleep, he'd plunged into a final mock debate rehearsal. His team had grilled him intensely until three o'clock that afternoon, then he'd spent an hour at the Pauley Pavilion, a mile away at UCLA, doing light and sound checks. Only in the past hour had been able to clear the house of people and grab some time for himself, to think about Trice and Breen and . . . and where the fuck was *Jackdaw*?

"Nothing," Hoffman said, putting down the phone.

Crane turned from the door. He was in shirtsleeves, looked rumpled, sweat-stained, exhausted. There was a wildness in his eyes, an amalgam of anger and fear.

He checked his watch, ran a hand through his close-cropped hair.

"Something's wrong. I can feel it here." He slapped the back of his neck. "Jackdaw's never been out of reach – never."

Hoffman said, "Jack, take it easy. You're tired. Go lie down for an hour . . ."

Crane dismissed the suggestion irritably. "Call Tahoe. Find out if Drummond and the girl have arrived."

Hoffman punched the number, listened for ten rings, shook his head.

Crane exploded. "What?"

"Nobody's picking up."

"That's crazy! Where the fuck is everybody – in church?" Crane paced to the door, enfuriated, trembling.

Hoffman said brusquely, "Christ, Jack, look at yourself. Relax. If you won't lie down, go take a shower. You're facing Byrne and a tough panel in less than two hours, going out live. D'you want to look like shit to seventy million voters? Forget Trice for tonight."

Crane wheeled on him, fire-eyed, thrust out an admonitory finger. "Something's wrong. I'm walking into something here, I can smell it."

"What're you talking about? There's nothing wrong. You're riding high, Jack, fifteen points ahead and untouchable. What you are is tired. It's been a killer campaign. Things get distorted. I'll keep trying Jackdaw and Tahoe while you get ready."

Crane wasn't listening. He was pacing, finger-combing his hair, talking more to himself than to his aide. "You're never safe from the past. Things can come out of it when you least expect it. We should've taken Keegan out at the clinic. Fucking experts. Who in hell is this Ambrose? Maybe we should try Records ourselves?"

"No, Jack, we keep our distance. It's what you pay Jackdaw for. He's never let you down."

"Then where is he now? Why hasn't he called? And why is nobody answering at Tahoe?"

"There'll be perfectly good reasons. Jack, what are you afraid of?"

Crane stopped pacing, stared at him, flung out an arm in the direction of UCLA. "I'm afraid of those media assholes! They know this is their last chance to pick through my shit before November. Let's talk what if's, Karl. What if Jackdaw has screwed up in Whiskeytown? What if Drummond and Beal are on the loose with the tape? What if right now the *LA Times* knows all about Trice? What if one of the panel says, 'Governor, you've ridden to political prominence on the Vietnam war hero ticket. Would you like to tell the nation about Tricyanoprope and how one hundred and twenty drugged American soldiers under your command shot each other to death?'"

Hoffman shook his head. "It won't happen."

Crane bellowed, "Why the fuck not? Where's Jackdaw? Where are Drummond and Beal? Where's the tape?"

"If it happens, you deny everything . . ."

"But the question itself will destroy me! Don't you see that? There are a lot of people out there who hate Jack Crane. They'll *want* to believe Trice happened. The question alone could wipe out my lead. Then, d'you think those media vultures are going to be satisfied with my denial, and leave it at that? If they've got the tape, they're going to dig. Byrne's people are going to dig. And Byrne will hammer me with it for the next three weeks. It's what I'd do in his place."

"They'll dig, but they won't find anything."

"Karl, shit sticks! I'll be thrown on the defensive! Everywhere I go, Trice will be *the* issue. Jesus . . ."

Crane slumped onto a stool at the wet bar, clutching his head. "How could things get so out of control?"

"You want my honest opinion? It's you who's out of control. You've pushed yourself too hard. Presidential campaigns are inhuman, and you're exhausted. You're allowing panic to get to you, seeing disaster before it happens." Hoffman moved closer, lowered and injected supportive fervor into his voice. "Hang tough, Mister President Elect. There're only three weeks to go and you're home free. *If* they hit you with Trice, hit 'em right back. Deny, deny, deny. It's a Byrne conspiracy, a desperate move by a desperate man. The tape is the raving of a Vet psycho, a lie. The question is an attempt by the liberal, self-seeking media to sensationalize a one-horse presidential race, to smear the name of a winner, a revered war hero, to prevent the implementation of his dream: the restoration to American society of the old-time values of respect, discipline and self-reliance. But, by God – JACK CRANE AIN'T ABOUT TO LET IT HAPPEN!"

Slowly Jack Crane turned his head, still held captive in his hands, and smiled at his long-time friend and aide. "Karl, what would I do without you? How shall we reward you? Chief of White House staff? Head of CIA . . . SA?"

Hoffman returned the smile. "Whatever serves you best, Mister President."

Crane got off the stool, drew a deep breath, braced his shoulders, patted Hoffman on the arm. "I'm going to shower, shave, and dress. Have a bite to eat. Then we're going to the Pauley Pavilion and kick the shit outa old Milt Byrne and those liberal, self-seeking pricks." He crossed the den, and as he entered the corridor leading to his bathroom, called back, "Rustle up a steak, Karl. Rare! I'm in the mood to sink my teeth into raw . . . bloody . . . flesh."

420

At the time Jack Crane was entering his shower, Karen Beal and George Serl were emerging from the Times Mirror building in downtown Los Angeles. They had attended an extraordinary meeting, convened with difficulty by Serl, of senior managing, editorial and legal staff. Interrupted in their Sunday leisure pursuits, they had listened, stunned, while Karen recounted the events resulting from her Trice article, and Serl played the recording of the Wendell Curry interview. An hour of bemused, exhilarated, cautionary discussion had followed. Out of it had come praise and congratulations for Karen, tainted by the legal admonition that the paper required additional, hard evidence of Crane's involvement in the Trice massacre, or at least a second, independent source to support Curry's testimony.

On the sidewalk, disappointed, frustrated and angry, she pleaded with her editor, "George, hell, I know the rules, but in this case there *isn't* a second source. Apart from Crane, Curry is the sole survivor of the massacre. And as for proof, what are we going to do – fly to Edgewood and ask if we can photocopy their records? In Curry's words – what records? Do they believe that Crane wrote up a report on Trice when he got home?"

Serl nodded, commiserating. "Well, I did warn you this would happen. As they said in there, Curry sounds genuine but might be a kook. If we went to print without hard evidence, Crane would slap us with a lawsuit bigger than the trade deficit. And there are the political and economic considerations. This *is* the leading presidential candidate we'd be bringing down. Imagine the GOP's and Crane's supporters' reaction to the *Times* if we published without proof – or even with it? His gun-totin', neo-fascist followers would probably torch the building."

She sighed despondently. "So what do we do – just leave it? Forget Trice? Forget Tom Keegan? Forget all the other poor slobs who've had their minds bent out of shape by Crane and his merry band of mad lab chemists?"

"Forget? Hell, no. We dig. Karen, listen, don't worry about it. I know the board, you don't. This is too big for you to handle by yourself, and, with respect, you're a Brit. They'll put a lot of people on this, tap sources you don't know and could never imagine, but you'll get the byline, for sure."

He touched her face affectionately, paternalistically. "You've done an incredible job." His glance went beyond her to a car drawing up to the curb. "Here's the Lieutenant and Paul Drummond now."

She'd called Dick Gage before leaving the office. She and Drummond were staying with the Gages, and Dick had insisted on collecting her.

Serl checked his watch as he walked her to the car. "Will you be watching the TV debate? It starts at eight."

"I wouldn't miss it for anything." She opened a rear door. "I'd sell my soul to be on that panel tonight . . . to be able to ask Jack Crane just one question."

George Serl smiled. "Oh, really? I wonder what that could be?"

She climbed into the car but lowered her window for a final word. "Is it possible he can get away with this? We've only got three weeks. Once he's elected, he'll be virtually fireproof."

Serl said, "Three weeks is a long time in politics. Nixon blew his chances in ninety minutes in the Kennedy debate. Maybe Milton Byrne will see Crane off tonight."

"And if he doesn't?"

"Well, let's see what happens."

Serl waved them off and headed for his car, pondering the chances of bringing to print the biggest story to hit America in fifteen years.

Something had to happen, his reporter's instinct told

him. A thing this big, you just couldn't keep a lid on. Somehow, in some way, it would get out.

His job was to see it got out first in the *Times*.

Karl Hoffman waited a full minute after Crane had entered the bathroom, then went down the corridor to listen at the door.

Satisfied that the governor was in the shower, where he invariably remained for at least fifteen minutes, Hoffman returned to the morning room, collected a wireless phone, and walked out of the French doors to the pool area. Hidden from the house behind shrubbery, he punched a number, a different number from the one he'd been trying in the house.

Jackdaw answered guardedly, "Yes?"

"Raven. What's the update?"

"Polo just called. It's agreed that our friend has become a serious liability. The paper has it and they won't let it go. It's only a matter of time."

Hoffman said, "A pity. So many years, so much effort."

"There are others. That, too, is only a matter of time. Polo congratulates you. You will, of course, handle the successor."

"My pleasure."

"Where is our friend now?"

"In the shower. He wants a rare steak before the event."

"Good. It fits nicely. This is how Polo wants it handled."

Hoffman listened, said, "No problem," switched off the phone and returned to the house.

Chapter Forty-Two

At eight o'clock they were sitting in the Gage den, Karen and Drummond on a brown slub two-seater settee, Dick and Anne in armchairs on either side.

On the giant color TV screen, a CBS political correspondent was discoursing on the presidential candidate debate, and on previous debates, while the cameras roamed the huge Pauley Pavilion, transmitting long shots and close-ups of the thousands of invited guests, and of the panel of three journalists, Cheryl Conran of ABC News, Nancy Harding of NBC News, Dorothy Brice of *Newsweek*, and the moderator, John Dell of Cable News Network, who had just taken their seats at a table on stage.

Several feet in front of them, set twenty feet apart at a slight angle to the table, but essentially facing the audience, were two panelled lecterns. Behind the stage-right lectern, concealed from the audience, but just visible to the occasional camera eye, was the wooden ramp upon which the shorter candidate, Jack Crane, would stand.

On each lectern was a glass carafe of water, response-time warning lights, and two secured but adjustable microphones.

The political correspondent, Bill Rolph, was telling the estimated viewing audience of over seventy million, "As we await the arrival of the two candidates on stage, the atmosphere in the hall is tense. In recent years, in these less leisured times, television debating between presidential candidates has become immensely important to the American voter, an occasion of great interest and excitement. Whenever two presidential candidates meet face-to-face, the confrontation invariably generates an electric excitement. And because presidential campaigns for so many Americans have come to be compressed into these highly charged ninety-minute contests, the stakes for the antagonists are immense.

"And it is not so much that we expect one candidate to out-perform the other with style, wit and profundity of knowledge, as that one will commit a gaffe so glaring that it will doom his chances of the White House. That is what makes these presidential debates such fascinating, electrifying theater. At any moment, something can be said or done that will make or – more dramatically – break, a candidate's bid for the office of President of the United States."

Karen remarked, "Yes, and we know just the question to ask to bring that off. Oh, *boy*, would I love to be on that panel."

Bill Rolph continued, "Such, indeed, must be the hope of Milton Byrne's strategists. A renowned debater and a man of encyclopedic knowledge of domestic and foreign affairs, Byrne has allowed himself to be driven back onto the defensive throughout the latter stages of this contest by Jack Crane's brutally negative campaign, which has vilified Byrne's liberalism, and questioned his stance on defense and his toughness against crime. Properly handled, this debate could be Milton Byrne's golden opportunity to negate the force of that unremitting attack, to present a true perspective of his beliefs and intentions, and substantially reduce Crane's lead, which, according to the latest polls, now stands at fifteen points."

Behind him the audience erupted into applause as the two candidates appeared on stage and walked to their lecterns.

Visually, the contrast between the men could hardly have been more extreme. Milton Byrne was tall, patrician, slightly stooped with thick-framed glasses and slightly unkempt gray hair contributing to his professorial persona, wearing a gray wool suit that draped rather than fitted his angular frame. He looked as though he had just walked across campus from his last political science class of the day.

Jack Crane, dressed in a beautifully cut dark blue suit, a power color, strategically chosen for the occasion, looked braced, militaristic, extremely sharp. In the strong television lighting, he looked tanned, vital, ready for battle, the pit bull terrier fully primed to savage the lumbering Saint Bernard.

As the cameras went to close-up, filling the nation's screens with Jack Crane's face, with the triumphant light of steely fervor that radiated from those eyes, Drummond found himself nodding with an understanding of how so many men could have offered themselves for drug experimentation, could have allowed Crane to subject them to absolute terror, and not have protested.

Wendell Curry's words returned to him: "Crane is a Pentagon creation, through and through . . . as near to being a Pentagon cyborg without the implantation of an electrode – and I wouldn't bet they *haven't* stuck one in his head . . . when Jack Crane tells you something, you believe it. That's the danger of the guy."

There was no denying that Jack Crane radiated charisma, no denying that he would be a strong, forceful leader. But down which road would he lead the country? Towards Peace and Plenty, or, as a Pentagon cyborg, towards an erosion of personal liberty, Mind Control, war?

As though picking up the question by mental telepathy, Dick Gage, nursing his third ice-cold Bud, said, "Thing is – would you buy a used M-Four tank from this guy? Caveat emptor, USA. What you buy tonight, you're stuck with for four years."

Anne observed, "Hobson's choice, isn't it? Look at them both. Byrne seems cocooned in cobweb."

"He might surprise us."

"Pigs might fly."

As the applause, whistling, yipping subsided, the moderator, John Dell, a forty-year-old with a grave mien, introduced himself, the candidates, the panel, and explained the rules of debate.

He then asked his own first question of Milton Byrne. "Senator, throughout this campaign we seem to have heard a great deal of criticism regarding your position on crime, with very little positive response from yourself. Would you care to clarify your position for us?"

Anne Gage said, "Good question. Come on, Milt, here's your chance, sock it to 'em. Let's see some passion."

Milton Byrne cleared his throat, and in controlled, melifluous, senatorial tones responded, "Yes, John, I would. But first I would like to say this. There has been a growing danger in previous elections of televized debates trivializing presidential politics. Indeed the necessary encapsulation of reporting on television throughout a campaign embodies the danger of trivialization. Let me ask our viewing audience a couple of questions for their earnest consideration. Is a candidate's position for or against, say, capital punishment the acid test for the presidency?" In extreme close-up, the wise, avuncular, pedagogic face asked, "Can any one of you believe that a man who has become his party's presidential nominee can truly be 'in league with the criminals' or be 'soft on crime', even assuming that dealing with crime is a prime function of the White House?"

Dick Gage groaned, "Christ, he's giving us a lecture."

Karen said, "He's absolutely right, but I'm sure it's not what seventy million viewers want to hear."

Anne murmured, "Pigs ain't gonna fly tonight."

As the cameras cut briefly to Crane, picking up his reaction to Byrne's response, Drummond said, "Look at that crocodile smile. If Byrne keeps this up, he'll bury himself. Crane won't even have to try."

Byrne was going on, "It is an indisputable fact that guns kill and maim. It is their function. And it follows that the more guns there are in public possession, the more killings and woundings there are going to be. Throughout my opponent's extremely negative campaign, he has spent a great deal of effort and money focusing the public's attention on my apparent shortcomings, attempting to equate my fear of guns and hatred of what they do to people with a softness towards crime and criminals. My question to you and to him is – is it right that such an issue should, throughout a campaign, transcend, in the contest for public scrutiny, such vital issues as the stability of the economy, homelessness, drug abuse, abortion, the global trade imbalance, and our relations with the Communist world?"

Over responsive, though contained, applause, Byrne went on, "In short, John, my position on crime is that I loathe it, and will do all in my power to support and encourage the law enforcement agencies whose job it is to prevent it. More than that I cannot say at this time."

John Dell said, "Thank you, Senator. Governor Crane, would you care to give us your position on crime?"

Crane smiled broadly, braced his shoulders. "Can't wait."

Laughter and applause from the audience.

"But firstly, I'd like to say this . . ." Mocking Byrne.

More laughter and applause.

"On behalf of our seventy million viewers, I'd like to

428

thank Senator Byrne for his mini-lecture on 'Presidential Politics In Our Time'."

Over audience laughter, Dick Gage said, "Crafty bastard, never misses a trick."

"Yes, indeed, Senator, it *is* the age of television. And to offset its many advantages, there may be several drawbacks, one of which is time. Whether you like encapsulation or not, it's here to stay, and like everyone else, politicians have to go with the flow, learn to adapt, step into the Twentieth Century. I can understand your yearning for the old days, for the slower days when men had time to sit around a pot-bellied stove and jaw about political issues in fine detail. I can understand your longing for the more innocent days when a liquor store hold-up was a rare event, when house-breaking was virtually unknown, when drugs were something that Orientals did in opium dens, and when it was safe for a woman to walk to the store without fear of being robbed or raped or mutilated or murdered.

"But, Senator, wake up to reality. Those days are long gone. In the classic phrase: it's a jungle out there! And if you think you can change that by taking away the people's right to defend themselves, by taking away their right to bear arms given them by the Constitution, then, I'm sorry, but you're as out of date as one of those pot-bellied stoves!"

Thunderous applause.

Crane, shouting over it, "And if he's elected president, JACK CRANE AIN'T ABOUT TO LET IT HAPPEN!"

Anne Gage sighed, "There y'go, Milt, that's how you do it. Crane hasn't said a damn thing. He hasn't answered the question. But he's got them all wetting themselves with desperation to vote him in."

Gloating, soaking up the limelight and the applause, Crane used the time to pour a half glass of water and sip from it, sending a mock toast to his opponent across the stage.

He took a second sip. He was thirsty. His mouth felt suddenly dry, his tongue cloying and tacky. It was more than the familiar stage dry-mouth which invariably afflicted him at the beginning of a public appearance. It was that goddamned steak. Karl must've gone a little overboard with the salt and pepper.

As the applause died, he took a third sip and put down the glass. Too much drinking would be picked up by the cameras and interpreted as nervousness. But, damn, he was thirsty.

The moderator turned over the questioning to Cheryl Conran of ABC News, an attractive red-head with an immaculate fringed bob, wearing a dark green silk suit.

She smiled becomingly, for seventy million viewers as much as at Jack Crane. "Governor, you are a soldier . . ."

"Correction, Miss Conran – 'was' a soldier. Now I'm a politician."

Conran lost her smile. "I don't believe there is such a thing as a 'was' soldier. The training is too ingrained. Your instincts have to be militaristic, your natural reaction must be to fight."

Crane smiled, far more for seventy million viewers than at her. "I admit that I'm a fighter. That's why I'm here. What was the question?"

To his dismay, he felt sweat – the politician's nightmare – break out all over his body. A scalding flush flooded his face. Perspiration oozed from the pores of his forehead and rolled down the sides of his cheeks. The fucking water. He shouldn't have drunk so much.

He made a half-turn from the audience, as though to face his questioner, plucked a white linen handkerchief from his breast pocket, and, under the guise of genteelly blowing his nose, wiped at the burgeoning sweat.

He suddenly felt terrible . . . feverish, weak, nauseous.

430

Every nerve in his body seemed to be twitching. His heart was pounding and his lungs felt starved of oxygen.

What in Christ's name was happening?

Drummond spotted his dilemma first. "There's something wrong with Crane. He's sweating badly."

Karen, seeing it now, said, "He's afraid of what could be coming – the army thing. She going to hit him with her fears of him warmongering."

Drummond shook his head. "No, he looks . . . strange. Ill. Look at his hands, they're trembling."

In a holding room off the main hall, Crane's team of ten advisers and strategists, including aide Karl Hoffman, viewing the debate on TV monitors, were also aware of their candidate's condition.

The room became charged with expletives and the dynamism of their dismay.

"What the fuck's he doing with that handkerchief? He looks like fucking Satchmo!"

"He looks nervous."

"He *is* nervous! He's shaking!"

"He's sweating like a bastard, it's rolling off him."

"Jesus, if we can see it, so can America."

"He looks ill. He's lost his tan. He looks freakin' green!"

"Karl, was he okay before you came over here?"

"He was fine, terrific."

"Did he eat anything?"

"Yeah, he had a steak and salad."

"Food poisoning!"

"No way. I prepared it myself. The meat was fresh, and I washed the salad."

"Okay, get the doc to stand by. If he gets any worse, we're pulling him out. Right now, he's losing us the election."

"My question," Cheryl Conran said with a slight edge on her voice, "is prefaced with an observation. You are

431

a hero of the Vietnam war, one of the few recognized heroes to emerge from it. America is still suffering from the ignominy of that conflict. It might well be that you, as a military . . . an *ex*-military man, if you insist, would seek to use the power of the presidency to eradicate that ignominy at the first opportunity. In other words, to take us into war as a means of restoring our hurt military pride, and, perhaps not incidentally, attracting a great deal of personal glory. My question is: How innately prepared are you to commit this country to another foreign war?"

Jack Crane knew he could no longer delay facing the audience and the cameras. He also knew he was seriously ill. Half way through the long question he had begun experiencing an appalling physical weakness. Starting in his feet, it was drifting up his legs, sucking the energy and strength from his muscles, forcing him to lean against the lectern for support.

With a desperate effort to continue, he turned a sickly grin to the cameras, managing, "Not so much a question as a . . . as a speech . . ." when to his absolute dismay his sphincter control collapsed and waste gushed from his body.

With a cry of disgust and disbelief and terror he pitched forward across the lectern, throwing it off-balance, reached out for an invisible support, for unattainable help, as the lectern teetered and tipped and finally crashed down onto the stage, Crane on top of it, gasping for breath, now rolling to one side, eyes and mouth gaping, hands clawing at his chest, ripping away suit jacket and shirt, nails brutalizing flesh, tearing at the skin to open up the lungs for breath, for air, for life.

Pandemonium swept the audience. Shocked, astounded, they came to their feet, surged towards the stage. A minicam operator ran out of the wings and filled the nation's screens with a brutal close-up of Jack Crane's face, contorted in a silent scream of terror, then zoomed back to include the bloody, naked chest.

At first stunned to immobility, Senator Milton Byrne and the panel now made a move towards Crane, looking around, calling for medical help, not knowing what to do but urged simply to move.

From the holding room, the advisory team fought their way into the auditorium, pushed their way through the milling crowd and onto the stage, Crane's personal doctor among them. Shoving panel members and camera people aside, they ringed Crane protectively while the doctor did his work.

In the melée, no one noticed a uniformed usher gather together the broken pieces of carafe and drinking glass and remove them from the stage. If anyone had, they would have dismissed the action as a safety measure, and approved.

In the Gage den, the four shared shock with the nation.

"A heart attack?" speculated Dick Gage.

"He seemed to display all the symptoms," said Drummond.

Karen, staring at the furor in the hall, shook her head. "My God, can you believe it."

"Not hardly," murmured Drummond.

On the screen, for a brief moment as a cameraman managed to elude gathering security officers and push his lens between bodies, Jack Crane's face came into view. The eyes were open, staring, the lips peeled back in a rictus of terror, but there seemed a rigidity to the musculature than denied the presence of life.

"He's dead," stated Dick Gage. "The guy's dead! Jesus wept, what now?"

The phone purred. Anne Gage answered it. With her hand over the mouthpiece, she told her husband, "It's Wendell Curry. He's asking for Paul."

As Paul got up, Dick said to her, "That's okay. I told him to contact them here."

Drummond took the phone. "Yes, Wendell."

"Did you see it?"

"We're sitting here stunned. It looked like a heart attack."

Curry chuckled. "Yeah, didn't it. But it wasn't. It was Anectine. Evil little mother. Crane died of suffocation. I saw the Cong tear at their chests like that in 'Nam."

Drummond gasped. "Somebody killed him? Who? How?"

"Could've been in the water he was drinking. Colorless, tasteless, odorless, remember? As to who? My guess is his own guys. When you got the secret of Trice, he got expendable."

"My God, what people. And to do it like this, in full view of the nation."

"How better? He lived a hero, died a hero, victim of his war . . . leastwise until the story gets out. If Miss Beal needs any more help, call me."

"Thanks, Wendell."

As Drummond relayed Curry's opinion, Bill Rolph was announcing on screen, "Governor Jack Crane is dead. Although no official statement has yet been issued, Doctor Morris Standfield, the governor's personal physician in attendance here at the hall, was overheard to diagnose the cause of death as 'heart failure'. At the moment, as you can plainly see behind me, the scene at the Pauley Pavilion is chaotic . . ."

The phone buzzed again. Again Anne answered it.

She said, "Karen, it's George Serl."

Karen sprang up from the settee, took the phone. "George?"

"This alters everything."

"More than you know," she said breathlessly. "Wendell Curry just called, spoke to Paul. He swears Crane was

434

assassinated – with Anectine, that awful drug. And if we want any further help, he's available."

"Oh, brother. Okay – get to the office as fast as you can. You've got work to do!"

Thirty minutes later, as Dick Gage watched Karen enter the Times Mirror building, he said to Drummond, "Drum, I've been thinking . . . how about I have a little talk with our friends Albatross and Peregrine? With Crane dead, maybe we can do some horse trading, find out what happened to Tom Keegan, and what's so interesting at Lake Tahoe, and who the hell Jackdaw is, that kind of thing, in exchange for their freedom?"

"Worth a try, old fruit."

As he pulled away from the curb, Gage said, "I guess you and Karen are out of danger now. You want I should drop you at the beach house?"

"That'll be fine, Dick, thanks."

Gage grinned. "You sound kinda numb."

"That's the word. Did it all really happen?"

"I'm not sure. We'd better check out the *LA Times* tomorrow. They might just mention it."

"Yeah. Hey, Dick . . ."

"What?"

"How about we stop at a liquor store, pick up a couple of packs of ice-cold Buds?"

Gage went rigid, half-closed his eyes as though in a trance. "You command, Doctor . . . I must obey."

"Good. Make that four packs. And you're paying."

Chapter Forty-Three

Wednesday.
Nine pm.
Palm Desert.

Drummond turned the Daimler off the I-11 and started the gradual ascent to his foothills home. Beside him, Karen was asleep in the reclined seat, and had been for most of the two-hour journey.

Near exhaustion himself, Drummond had driven slowly, keeping his mind alert by listening to the muted radio, to the almost continuous reporting of the ramifications of Jack Crane's death, each new development and revelation sending a shock-wave through the nation.

By midnight Sunday, an official announcement after post mortem examination declared that Governor Crane had died from Anectine poisoning. Anectine pills had been found loose in Crane's suit pocket, mixed with, and almost identical to, the breath-refresher tablets Crane invariably carried.

Cause of death: Accidental ingestion of a lethal drug.

So went the official cover-up.

But the mention of Anectine gave the *Los Angeles Times* the opening it was looking for. Within hours Wendell Curry's story, under Karen's by-line, was on the street, and the nation's press was up and running.

For the past seventy-two hours, Karen had virtually lived at the Times Mirror building, writing, attending further in-depth interviews with Wendell Curry, being interviewed by press, police, and government officials. And for most of the time Drummond had been with her, recounting over and over his own experience since the first Tom Keegan consultation.

This evening, seeing her almost too exhausted to talk, Drummond had insisted on a forty-eight hour respite, and had whisked her away from the fury, with little hope of being left alone in the Valley, but certain at least of one good night's sleep.

Approaching the house, the newscaster was announcing that Congress had begun an investigation into the Trice affair, and that the White House was commissioning a special report on the testing of drugs by the Intelligence community, with a demand for access to even the most sensitive files in the Military Intelligence Classified Index.

Drummond wondered how far they'd get. He had a sudden vision of multitudinous shredding machines bursting into flames through overwork. But because of Tom Keegan and Wendell Curry and Karen, Pandora's Box was now wide open, black secrets were pouring out, and things could never be the same again.

Drawing up at the house, he cut the engine, left the headlights on, and got out.

As he walked up the side of the house to the kitchen door, the guest room behind the garage reached out to him, a dark and morbid presence. Unlocking the kitchen door, he could see the pools of blood around the sink, and feel Tom Keegan's hand about to touch his shoulder.

Inside, he switched on lights, moved through into the living room, switching on more lights, all of them, needing to dispel shadows, darkness. The house was tainted, polluted by violence and death. A place to leave. Now, he doubted the wisdom of returning here, even for two days.

Crossing the room, he drew back the drapes and opened

437

the sliding glass doors wide, relishing the flow of cool mountain air, the escape from discomfort that the open doors offered.

The house had been electronically swept. Through Dick, he'd arranged for Joe Stiles to clean this house, as well as the beach house and Karen's apartment. Yet still he felt their presence.

A pity. He'd liked the house. Maybe he and Karen could spend the forty-eight hours looking for another. It would be therapeutic, fun. They could both use some fun . . .

A shuffling sound behind him sent his heart rocketing. He whirled.

Karen, holding their cases, droop-eyed and tousled, the crumpled jacket of her beige business suit tossed over one shoulder, leaned in the doorway, her head resting against a post. "Gotta room for the night, mister?"

Drummond laughed. "You scared the hell outa me."

He went to her, took the cases. "Princess Suite this way, madam."

"Second thoughts . . . I'll just sleep here."

The phone rang.

Karen groaned. "Please don't let it be for me."

Drummond put down the cases and went to it, prepared to pick it up or leave it to the answer machine.

Dick Gage's voice, sounding energized and excited, said, "You there yet, Drum? If you're not, get back to me. This is too good to leave on the machine."

Drummond picked up. "Yo, buddy. We just got in. Karen's sleeping standing up in the doorway."

"She won't be after this. I've just taken a call from the Tahoe City police. An hour ago a guy walked into their office. He's on some kind of drug, can't remember where he's been or how he got to the office, but was carrying a piece of paper with two names and phone numbers on it – yours and mine. Oh, yeah, there is one thing he remembers."

438

"What's that?"

"His name. He says it's Tom Keegan."

"I'm so glad you're not going to sell," said Karen. "It's so beautiful up here."

In bikini and swim trunks they were sitting on the terrace where Tom Keegan had sat, the San Jacinto Mountains close behind them, and out there the Living Desert and the country clubs and the grand vistal sweep across the valley to the shimmering San Bernadinos.

It was ten o'clock and the sun was right for sitting. They'd slept well and breakfasted well and were feeling very relaxed and good in each other's company.

After the fear and fury of recent days, the serenity of the Valley was incredible.

"What will you do about the Malibu house?" she asked. "Will you continue your LA practice?"

Eyes closed, face to the sun, Drummond smiled. Lazily he answered, "Right now, I'm just so damned happy about Tom Keegan that my world is very beautiful, and I'm disinclined to change a thing in it."

"I'm glad. I'd hate to lose you entirely to the Valley."

He peered at her through one slitted eye. "Would you, now? Well, I guess that clinches it." He closed his eye. "Tell me, do Brits swim?"

"Only in water."

"Hm. Maybe I ought to put in a pool."

"That," she said, "would be lovely."

In Ventura, Aunt Cissie's world was also very beautiful. Caring for Tom would give new meaning to her life.

In San Diego, Peregrine was happily telling a lady of his decision to change both his name and his employment, and inviting her to live with him in Mexico.

In Los Angeles, an ecstatic vice-presidential candidate was in secret conference with two men who were assuring him that, with the support of the people they represented, the presidency was only a matter of time.

One of the men was Karl Hoffman.

The other sometimes used the code-name Polo.